ACROSS
the
NARROW
SEA

A Romance

Sam Hanna Bell

THE
BLACKSTAFF
PRESS
BELFAST AND WOLFEBORO, NEW HAMPSHIRE

First published in 1987
by The Blackstaff Press Limited
3 Galway Park, Dundonald, Belfast BT16 0AN, Northern Ireland
and
27 South Main Street, Wolfeboro, New Hampshire 03894 USA
with the assistance of
The Arts Council of Northern Ireland

Printed in Northern Ireland
by The Universities Press Limited

British Library Cataloguing in Publication Data
Bell, Sam Hanna
Across the narrow sea.
I. Title
823'.914[F]   PR6052.E447

Library of Congress Cataloging-in-Publication Data
Bell, Sam Hanna.
Across the narrow sea.
1. Scots — Northern Ireland — Down — History — 17th
century — Fiction. 2. Down (Northern Ireland) — History —
Fiction. I. Title.
PR6052.E447A67   1987   823'.914   87-10289

ISBN 0 85640 377 6 (hardback)
        0 85640 378 4 (paperback)

for Fergus and Angélique

I

'Now, I bid ye once again, Neil, rise off your arse and haud your brither's stirrup!'

Under his father's furious gaze Neil rose from the bench. Brogues dragging on the cobbles, he crossed the courtyard to where his brother stood at the horse's head.

'Lift your feet!' Violently the old man struck the jamb of the doorway that framed him.

Neil Skene Gilchrist was aware of the half-moon faces peering from the windows of the manor house, from entrances to stables and byres. He steadied the stirrup and turned to his brother with a sardonic gesture. 'Mount, Gilmor.'

'Off with your bonnet, sirrah!'

The youth dropped the stirrup and turned slowly. 'For why, Father?'

The old man took a step forward. 'Because when I'm laid in the kirkyard, you'll give your fealty and submission to your elder brither as sixth laird o' Balwhanny.' With a dry smirk he continued, 'Never too early to start what we mean to pursue. So off wi' your bonnet when ye help Gilmor tae his saddle.'

Neil pulled his broad bonnet lower on his brow. 'Let Gilmor start as *he* means to pursue. Let him call a horseboy.'

'Dare ye give me lip, my birkie?' The old man started forward. 'You'll do as you're bid, or spend *your* days around Balwhanny as a horseboy!'

Neil released Gilmor's fingers not ungently from the reins and mounted the horse himself. He touched his bonnet to his father. 'To hell with you, Balwhanny,' he said. The title included both the old man and his own birthplace. He rode out through the crumbling gateway.

To the east the sun was shepherding the mist from the Glenkens.

A furlong or so along the rutted track he knew that the hills folded over his last glimpse of Balwhanny. Reining in, he looked back. He had half-feared, half-hoped, that someone would ride after him. But who was fit to do that – his doitert brother, his father, that shambling sodden old man? His ancestral home lay on a slope. A sunken gable had set the windows askew and the crazed panes flung back the light jagged as thistle-spikes. The roofs of house and offices were bonneted in houseleek and lichen, and the uncared-for walls of the courtyard mouldered softly under their flinty parapet. Over the whole lay a gloom of decay that no morning light could dispel. On the slope rising behind the manor he could see the signs of his handiwork. Since his return from the law school at St Andrew's College he had laboured to bring some order in the neglected woodlands of Balwhanny. Amid the straggle of timber and undergrowth he could see the clearances where he and Davie Hunter had planted saplings of pine and ash.

But where should he ride now and how was he to live? The Prodigal Son had had the wit to secure his portion from his father before he left home. He fingered the few coins sewn into the skirt of his coat. No doubt there were friends in Edinburgh who would give him lodgings until he found work. But behind this thought another more exciting idea was mounting, the outcome of which he couldn't quite discern.

A short distance along the road and he would pass the cottage of Hunter Murray, his tutor. Neil half-hoped that he would not yet be astir. But as he approached, the dominie came round the gable of his dwelling with a lipping bucket drawn from the well. Master Murray rested the bucket on the ground and flexed his aching fingers.

'You're early on the road this morn, Neil.'

'Aye, I'm. . . I'm leaving Balwhanny.'

'Leaving Balwhanny?'

'For good. . .'

'So? And what garr'd ye do that? Light down and tell me.'

'Oh. . .' It seemed a foolish thing to relate and he felt a certain disloyalty at the thought of doing so. But it had been to the man before him, not to his father, that he had turned in his boyhood. Obediently he dismounted. 'The laird would make a groom of me, to hold Gilmor's horse and doff the bonnet. And every serving-bodie gaping at us.'

'And you're no for returning?'

'No, Master.'

'Ye parted in anger?'

'I can't say Balwhanny gave me his blessing.'

The dominie nodded. 'So ye left them – a crabbit auld man and a poor simpleton –' He held up his hand as if to still a rejoinder. 'Ye never had much thought for other folk, Neil. Aye, aye. . . But you're your own man now. Eighteen, aren't ye? And where are ye bound for, my braw blade?'

Neil's rancour was dispelled. Now was the time to put into words the aspiration that had been budding as he rode from Balwhanny. 'I'm for London, Master. To follow King Jamie.'

The dominie stared at the youth. 'The King left us in 1603, Neil – five years ago. The scent ye follow across the Tweed is cold –'

'The word is that he still loves a Scot.'

Murray smiled sardonically. 'In a grey bonnet and woollen hose? Have ye any money?'

'A little gold.' He fingered the hem of his coat. 'In Balwhanny ye keep tight hold of your wealth.'

Murray frowned at the sneering tone. 'Ye should have had other riches. Ye may yet rue the days ye scattered in the three years I won for ye at St Andrew's College –'

The youth broke in impatiently. 'That's water lang run under the brig. I confess I had no great love for the law books.' He mounted. 'Ye taught me more than to read and cipher, Master.'

The dominie bowed briefly and reached for Neil's outstretched hand. 'Ye have a lang road ahead of ye, Neil. I wish ye God speed.'

3

Neil plucked off his bonnet. 'I'll send ye word of my fortune – or lack of it. Goodbye, Master.'

Murray watched until rider and horse disappeared on the westward track. Then he carried the pail of spring water into the cottage.

Twelve hours later and twenty miles to the south-east, Alexander MacIlveen finished a day's ploughing. He unyoked the horse while his son scraped clay from the plough-coulter. Alexander looked back on the day's labour. The darkling air was descending on the farthest corner of the field. The new-turned soil lay umber and expectant. It looked well, he thought, the furrows as straight as any osier wand.

'We should hae the oats and barley sown before the week's out,' said his son.

'Aye. Fetch the spade, Sorley.'

A flying-beetle hummed above him in the dusk. As the sound of its flight died, they heard the beat of horse's hooves approaching. The soft dash and jingle of harness bespoke a gentleman's mount. The two peasants drew back to the shadows.

'He's riding from the laird's house,' said Sorley.

His father was staring into the dusk. 'It's Ogilvy.' Pulling at his bonnet, Alexander stepped forward. 'Goode'en tae ye, Mr Ogilvy.'

The mounted factor reined in, looking down on the two cottars. 'I didn't think to come on ye still abroad, MacIlveen.'

'We wanted tae finish the ploughing. Sorley was saying we might get the seed in by next week.'

'Aye, you're doing well, both of ye. That's the brunt of my errand. The laird and his lady returned from Edinburgh yesterday and he took me out with him to survey his tenants' holdings. He's well pleased with the look of your place, Alexander.' The factor tightened a rein to still his horse. 'So he has bade me raise your rent by three pounds. That means he wants to see ten pounds from ye on next gale day.'

Father and son gaped upward at the figure on horseback. In the earthlight his face wore a mirthless smile.

'If it's any comfort to ye, Alexander, you're no alone among your neighbours –'

Alexander clapped his hand to his head like a man who had received a sword-stroke. 'Ten – *ten* pounds! I couldnae raise another bodle, Mr Ogilvy! We scrape and scringe tae find the seven pound!'

'Aye, but then you've made the farm all the more valuable to yourself –'

'And tae the laird,' Sorley broke in abruptly.

The factor stared coldly down at the youth. 'Your better is speaking, callan. Keep your neb out o' this.'

Sorley stepped closer. 'If our farm's in guid heart, it's nothing that you, or your master the laird, did for it.'

'I warn ye, boy, keep your tongue ahint your teeth!'

Sorley pushed his way between his father and the factor. 'We improved the place with our sweat! *For that ye would raise our rents!*' As he strained forward, shouting, the factor's horse sidled nervously.

Alexander laid a restraining hand on his son's shoulder. 'Sorley,' he said, 'Sorley. . .'

The factor shifted in his saddle. 'I warn ye for the last time, ye insolent cur –'

Sorley twisted from his father's grasp. 'Dinnae be tossing that whip from hand to hand, Mr Ogilvy. Daur ye raise it to me and I'll hae ye off that cuddy's back quicker than I would swat a fly off my porridge!'

The factor let a squeal out of him that had as much triumph as rage. 'Did ye hear that, MacIlveen? Your whelp threatened me with violence!'

'Ah, Mr Ogilvy, the bairn's a bit headstrong –'

'"Bairn", is it?' The factor drew up his reins like a man

5

pressed for time. 'He's a bairn grown too big for his breeks. I'll see to it that he's fitted with an ampler pair!'

The darkling air added menace to this seeming jest. Alexander, uncomprehending, stared at him.

'A pair of trooper's trews for him, MacIlveen. If it's fighting he wants he can get a bellyful serving his king.' Over his shoulder the factor cried, 'I'll get the laird to sign the papers and we'll have your bold bairn lifted afore the sun sets again!'

Father and son stood motionless until the hoofbeats died.

Then Alexander glanced at the black stretch they had turned and delved. It was a task the completion of which never failed to move him with a quiet joy and thanksgiving. But his son to be taken from him. . . *Thou shalt carry much seed to the field, and shalt gather but little in; for the locust shalt consume it. . .* 'I don't understand,' he muttered, shaking his head, 'I don't understand.'

'Father,' cried his son urgently, 'Ogilvy was galloping to the laird's house!'

'Aye, come. Let us hear what your mother thinks. I'll take the horse.'

Meg MacIlveen was familiar with the trodden pads through the peat moss, and where, on either side, the water-filled turf cuttings gaped. It was a modest acquirement but of the same nature as the instinct that guided her day-to-day existence. It was a life of much hardship and few landmarks: the Presbyterian kirk, the family and its well-being, a circle of neighbours. Hers were a laborious, stiff-necked people, fearing God as they knew Him. They were taught that little in this world had any permanency, although their anonymous generations would outlast those of their lords and masters. In the past their faith had been harshly dealt with; for the present they stood on vigil. As tenants-at-will they hoped for the best, ever aware that the whim of the laird or his lady could put them on the roadside. But to Meg the story she now listened to was no less a catastrophe for all that.

6

'But Mr Ogilvy can't do this to us, Alex man,' said Meg at last. 'It's out of a' sense!'

'He can and he will,' said Alexander, accompanied by his son's sharp nods. 'What's best to be done, Meg?'

For Meg MacIlveen and her like there was only one human intercessor, one person willing to listen. 'When you and Sorley finish your supper, take yoursel' and the rent money up to the manse. Mr Chisholm may dine at the laird's table but he'll listen tae an elder o' his kirk.'

The meal finished, father and son hastened to the manse. The Reverend Robert Chisholm, elbows resting on his study table, hands lightly clasped, listened to their story until they stumbled to silence.

'Alexander, you've been an elder of my kirk for years and an auld neighbour.' The minister raised his head with an encouraging smile. 'In what way can I help ye?'

Sorley MacIlveen felt a chill enter him. Although he and his father stood close to the table's leaf it was as if the Reverend Chisholm had pressed them back with his fingertips.

Alexander fumbled in the breast of his shirt. 'I brought the rent with me. I thought if ye were to gie it to Mr Ogilvy, with my promise that I'll strive tae raise the other three pound.'

'Alexander!' The minister leaned forward to emphasise the gravity of his words. 'This has gone far beyond any question of rent. The factor is threatening your son's liberty!'

'I ken that but I can't believe it. I thought it no more than the clishmaclaver o' an angry man. . .'

'I think it no idle threat, Alexander. And your son's behaviour has done nothing to lessen it.' The minister studied the grain of the wood between his elbows. 'I understand – I've heard it said – that the factor has been instructed to clear the holdings that lie within sight o' the manor windows. It's the wish o' the laird's lady –'

'I knew it!' cried Sorley. 'I heard it in Ogilvy's voice!'

The minister addressed himself to Alexander. 'When the laird hears that your son had the boldness to raise a stour over the rent he'll be 'feard that some of your neighbours might do the same. He'll be the more determined, therefore, to have the lad taken up and carried into the army.' He eyed the youth speculatively. 'Some carles among us have to fight for king and freedom, ye ken,' he added with a dry smirk.

Alexander ignored this. 'Then what's best for us, minister?'

Mr Chisholm was suddenly all briskness. 'You'll have to bundle and go, Alexander.'

The cottar stared at the minister unbelievingly. 'Ye mean. . . but ye can't. . . give up our bit o' land and the dwelling?'

'Aye. Get your family far from the grip o' the laird.'

'But there's a life's work there! And a life's work for Sorley! Only this e'en we ploughed the moss field.'

'It'll lie fallow. For a certainty your son will never sow it.' The minister tapped the table. 'Alexander, even now the factor's servant is riding for the barracks at Cumnock with a letter from the laird.'

Stubbornly the cottar clung to what seemed slipping fast from him. 'But where can poor folk go, Mr Chisholm?'

'Ireland.'

Dumb-struck, father and son gaped at him.

'Ireland!' cried Alexander at last. 'What in God's name would we be doing in Ireland, minister!'

The blow delivered, the Reverend Mr Chisholm advanced smoothly and eloquently. 'Fulfilling the behest o' your king, Alexander. From his court in London, King James, out o' his love and tender affection for his ain people, has announced that there is good fertile land in the north of Ireland to be planted by Scottish and Protestant men, leal, industrious and of good repute.' He paused. 'Aye. . .' he breathed as if to dissemble an oration too well-kenned.

'Are there lairds there?' queried Sorley.

The minister looked up with the expression of one asked about a territory where the rising and setting of the sun had been suspended. 'Aye, there are lairds there, callan.' He drew his inkhorn forward and took paper from a drawer. 'I have in mind Mr Kenneth Echlin, a gentle from Renfrew who has settled a score of God-fearing families on his lands at Ravara, a place in the county of Down. Ye would have guid Scots neighbours, Alexander.'

The cottar, numb under this catastrophe, could only pull at his beard, pointed by nature rather than the shears.

It was Sorley who asked, 'Will this laird Echlin give us protection?'

'No one is likely to follow ye that far. Your concern is to get away from here before daybreak. I'll give ye a letter to the Reverend Mungo Turnooth, a minister of the Gospel taken to Ireland by Mr Echlin.' Under the eyes of Alexander and Sorley, the minister's quill flowed fluently across the paper. He dried the letter at the lamp, sealed it and gave it to Alexander. 'Deliver that into the hands of Mr Echlin or Mr Turnooth. Until then be canny where and when ye show it, for it is by nature a passport.'

'The rent, Mr Chisholm.'

'Aye.' The minister lowered his eyes, sorely tempted to push Alexander's hand away. 'Leave it, I'll see the factor gets it –'

Sorley's fingers came down on the coins. He stared into the minister's face. 'Not a doit o' our money for Ogilvy!'

'We're near a quarter in debt, Sorley,' said his father.

'Let them get their rent out o' our leavings – the twa cows, the plough, the pots and pans –'

'Before that happens I'll have Sam Gowan sell them for what they're worth,' cried Mr Chisholm eagerly.

'They're worth more than the rent, minister.'

'Then I'll send the roughage o' money after ye.'

'How will ye ken where to send it, reverend sir?'

Mr Chisholm considered the shrewd young face under its tangle of red hair. Perhaps, all in all, it wasn't a bad thing this bold birkie should be going from among them. He gave a dry

9

smile. 'Have ye forgotten, boy, that it's I who am furnishing ye with an address?'

Alexander glanced round the chamber where he and his fellow-elders over the years had communed with their pastor on the affairs of the congregation. The firelight touched the solid furniture, the leather-bound divines in the bookcase. He turned towards the minister. 'Thank ye. . . for a', Mr Chisholm.' His bonnet pressed to his mouth the cottar stumbled from the lamplight to the outside darkness. The cleric made to step after Alexander, hand outstretched, but halted as Sorley scooped the money from the table. It was an excuse not to follow his elder. 'You're ready to go, Sorley?'

Sorley pocketed the coins and pulled on his bonnet. 'Aye, minister.'

'Let you and your family be on the road for Portpatrick before dawn.'

'Aye, minister.'

Mr Chisholm stood in the manse doorway watching the youth speed surefooted across the peat moss until father and son vanished in the night. He closed the door, filled with bitterness against the woman in the Big House.

Meg MacIlveen stared at her husband, then her son. 'Leave everything and go. . . flee. . . to Ireland. . . but why?'

'Well may ye ask, Mother,' said her son sharply, 'but that's the minister's cure for it. And Ogilvy's man's on the road for Cumnock barracks!'

As if bereft of her wits the cottar's wife began slowly and clumsily to empty shelf and cupboard. Then, pricked by the haste of the two men, her good sense asserted itself. With her daughter Ellen's help she bundled up crockery, cooking pots and linen. Alexander and Sorley brought spades and sickles and forks and the long-handled wood axe from the outhouse. With few words the family sped back and forth between cottage and wagon.

Once Ellen paused: 'What o' the beasts?'

'The minister is to send Sam Gowan for them,' replied her brother.

All they could take was carried out. The cart was laden so heavily that the body and the lower ends of the shafts were hidden. Meg was the last to leave the cottage. She gazed around the earth-floored room, the hearth-light flickering on the bare shelves, the stools drawn up to the mute table. Her husband came looking for her.

'Meg, it's time we were on the road.'

'Give me a last look, Alex man. We didn't ken how blessed we were when we sat down thegither.'

'We said grace for what we got, wife.'

A sob broke from her. 'My ain bit table and stools. They're mournin' at our going!'

'Clavers, Meg! They're dead wood. Sicca things have no thoughts.' As he drew her away, a turf with a spark of life in it crumbled in the hearth.

'Should we no smoor the fire, Alex?'

'Come away, woman. We'll kindle a fresh one in another land.'

2

Although they had had little rest since a long day's ploughing, men and horse breasted the hills of Ayr at a steady pace. Father and son walked at the horse's head while the women settled themselves as best they could in the wagon. None of them welcomed the dawn fingering across the sky. How far did the laird's edict run? Could he have a bodie taken up beyond his demesne walls? Meg and Ellen were told to keep an eye on the road they had travelled.

Like most of their neighbours, the MacIlveens rarely had need to venture far. On a few occasions Alexander had journeyed to the market at Pinwherry. Towards that village he now pressed with as much speed as horse and load would allow. Then, towards noon, Ellen spied a rider cresting a distant fold of the hills.

'A long way back, Father. . . a mile, twa miles,' she hazarded to Alexander's anxious query.

'That's no far, lass. He'll be up with us afore long.'

Sorley leapt up on the roadside bank, the better to see. 'There's but one. We could make a stand against him.'

'Bold words, bold words,' muttered Alexander. 'On, lad, on.'

But as the afternoon passed the horseman made no great effort to come up with the family. They were within two or three miles of their destination when they heard the growing clip-clop of horse's hooves. It did not escape his mother's eye when Sorley drew out a pitchfork from among the voluminous bundles.

'Sorley,' she cried warningly, 'Sorley, leave all to your father!'

Without speaking Sorley laid the fork where it would be free and put his shoulder to the tailboard of the wagon.

Leisurely, the rider closed with them. He was, Ellen observed, a braw young man in a broad bonnet and striped hose. As he rode past he gave a cool beck of the head to the four watchful peasants.

Alexander drew the horse up and leaned his brow on its sweating flank. 'Thank ye for this deliverance, O Lord,' he said.

'Amen,' echoed the other three.

An hour later they rumbled into the main street of Pinwherry. Alexander brought horse and cart to a halt before the village inn. In the doorway a stout red-faced man in an apron was taking the air. The cottar approached him.

'Can we bide here and have a sup and a bite to eat?'

The innkeeper ran his eye over the four people and their conveyance. 'Maybe aye, maybe no. Where are ye fleeing to – Ireland?'

'Maybe aye, maybe no,' retorted Alexander. He turned to his family, pointing into the dusk. 'We'll travel on and stop by the roadside.'

The man in the doorway unfolded his arms. 'Don't be in sicca pucker o' haste, guidman. Have ye a letter or any papers?'

Alexander involuntarily put his hand to the breast of his coat.

It was enough for the innkeeper. 'Come in,' he said. 'I'll see what I can do for ye.'

Alexander followed him into a large shadowy chamber, odorous of food and peat smoke.

The innkeeper pointed. 'Ye can have that table in the corner. Brose and bannocks. No beds. Can ye settle the score for that?'

'Aye. It'll serve us well. Thank ye.'

'Bring the women in. The callan can drive the wagon into the yard and shake out a handful o' fodder.'

Alexander saw that they were not alone. Seated in the hearth corner, a plate of collops and a wine cup before him, was the

13

horseman who had overtaken them on the road.

'Archie!' The voice was peremptory, that of authority.

As he slipped away, Alexander saw the young man hand up his cup to be refilled.

Soon the innkeeper returned with the brimming cup and a bottle. 'I trust, Master Neil, that ye don't mind me bringing a cottar family in for a bite and a rest?'

The young man shrugged. 'It's a public house and you're its keeper. I'll want an early start in the morn, Archie.'

'I'll see to it, sir. May I make so bold as tae spier after your road?'

'I'm for Dumfries, Archie. On the way to London.'

'My certes, London! That's a lang and awesome traik. I thought the laird would hae sent a couple o' buirdly carles wi' ye, Master Neil.'

Young Neil Gilchrist smiled. 'Buirdly carles aren't thrang at Balwhanny these days. Send in candles, like a good fellow.'

Alexander and his family came in, stepping as lightly as they might, stealing cautious glances at the young man beside the hearth. A serving-girl bustled in and rattled down bowls, platters and horn spoons on the table. The family gazed intently at the food set before them, blind to the grim inquisitive face peering in at the window or the babble of voices from the taproom. Alexander raised a hand and gave thanks prayerfully over the bread and the mess of peasemeal. 'Amen' signalled the rattle of platters and clack of spoons. At last, hunger eased, they sat back eyeing each other contentedly. When they talked their words were few and their voices muted. Neil Gilchrist drained his cup. He was about to take up his light when the figure of a man filled the doorway.

As he teetered on the threshold the newcomer scanned the room, eyes glittering in his bruised drunken face. His monstrous stature was made broader still by the plaid that looped his shoulder and trailed to the heels of his mud-crusted boots. A tankard dangled from his hand, dribbling ale. Attracted for a moment by the candlelight, the man's peering eyes flickered over Gilchrist and the laird's son stiffened as if an affront had been offered. But the stranger's quarry was the MacIlveens. He trod heavily across the floor and set his tankard down with a clatter among their dishes. Thrusting Sorley away, he made room for himself, arms sprawled on the table. His mouth, dark as a peat-hole, opened in a grin. 'G'even, frien's,' he said.

Bewildered, the family stared at the intruder. Perhaps it was the custom of the tavern that a frequenter should seat himself where he pleased. But there were empty benches in the room.

'G'even, guidman,' said Alexander. 'Is there aught we can do for ye?'

The interloper leaned closer to the family and his garb stank in their nostrils. 'I hear tell', and his voice was low, 'that you're for Ireland, neebors.'

'You've heard mair than we have said,' returned Alexander.

'Na, na, guidman,' said the other with a grin as if indulging the cottar. 'For what else would ye hae a load o' chattels on the road to Portpatrick? You're for Ireland. And you're taking me wi' ye.' He raised the tankard to drain it and over the rim his red eyes watched the cottar's face.

'We canna do that!' burst from Sorley.

The brutish stranger turned on him. 'Open your gab again,' he whispered rocking the empty tankard, 'and I'll leave a reft in your skull that'll no be easy tae solder thegither.' His face, dark with malevolence, loured down on the youth. Involuntarily, Meg stretched forward. 'Not a mouse-squeak from ye, auld wife, or I'll scatter him. Look ye,' he continued to Alexander, 'ye have a letter in your pouch. It'll get ye across the sea and into Ireland. I'm going wi' ye, as your ploughman.'

The muted voices conveyed little to Neil Gilchrist. He overheard some talk of Ireland, of a letter, of a ploughman. He was half-aware of contention among the group in the corner, a squabble among peasants. It angered him that the innkeeper

15

should have admitted this unsavoury brute to the room in which he was dining. He could not lightly forget those drunken pig eyes flickering over his person. . .

Alexander shook his head. 'Ye don't travel wi' us – and that's an end to it.'

The bully stretched out to take the cottar's arm in a merciless grasp. 'Don't say that, guidman. Don't say that. You and your family have a lang and lonely road afore ye reach Portpatrick.' He dragged Alexander closer. 'Ye ken me as Lachie Dubh, your ploughman. When we're in Ireland we go our ain ways. I'll trouble ye no mair – think o't, guidman.' He released Alexander with a last cruel crushing of his arm.

At the spasm of pain on her father's face, Ellen gave a squeal of fury.

Neil Gilchrist leapt from his chair and strode into the hallway. 'Archie!' he bellowed. 'Archie!'

The innkeeper, wiping his hands on his apron, came from the taproom.

'Archie, that ill-favoured loon within –'

The innkeeper was peering over the young man's shoulder. 'Aye, Lachie Dubh.'

'A gruesome brute. I want redd o' him. And,' as an after-thought, 'it's likely he's pestering the travelling family.'

The innkeeper took another glance. 'Ach, they're a' labouring folk cracking thegither, Master Neil,' he said lightly.

'He offends *me*. Get him out.'

For a moment Archie's face betrayed his opinion that there could be limits to the deference accorded a younger son of an impoverished lairdie. He stepped into the chamber. 'Lachie,' he called, crooking a finger, 'you're wanted in the taproom.'

The ruffian sprachled to his feet. He pointed his tankard at Alexander. 'Give heed to my words, frien',' he said. Crossing the room he made as if to pause before the young man but Archie urged him through the doorway and out.

'There ye are, Master Neil,' said the innkeeper with a tight little smile.

'I didn't think to find birds o' prey here, Archie.'

The innkeeper shrugged. 'I can't get rid o' him, Master Neil.'

'Put the dogs on him,' suggested the other with relish.

'To what end? If he's no here spending his money, he'll be lying up with some drab in the village. He came here two-three days ago on his way to Ireland.'

'A good riddance.'

'No sailing-captain will take such an ill-faured brute lacking a testimonial. And time and siller's running out on him –'

'Time? What's he fleeing from?'

The innkeeper shuffled. ''Tis said he's wanted for murther in Roxburgh or some sic place –'

Gilchrist stared at him. 'Harbouring a murderer, Archie? Certes, if it becomes known that ye had cognisance o' his crime, it'll go hard with ye!'

The innkeeper was shaken. 'Aye, true, Master Neil, true. I'll get rid o' him for good and a'. I will – I'll cast him on the road –'

'Dinnae make such a clatter o' your good resolution, Archie,' he interrupted drily. 'The law might see little difference in harbouring a murderer and letting him loose on honest folk.'

Neil returned to the public chamber leaving the innkeeper puzzled as well as perturbed. Archie had never known Balwhanny's younger son give a straw for any concern other than his own. Neil picked up his candlestick, hesitated, then approached the family seated at the table.

Alexander half-rose from his place. 'Thank ye, sir, for reddin' us o' that. . .'

The laird's son gestured. ''Twas nothing, guidman. We're a' the better o' his absence. Tell me,' he continued 'for I could not help but overhear, you're for Ireland?'

There was a pause. Alexander nodded. 'Aye.' None of the faces looking up seemed willing to expand on this.

One drunken evening at dinner-table the laird of Balwhanny

had talked much of the king's plans for the north of Ireland. His younger son now had a desire to have his curiosity satisfied.

'Why are ye for Ireland? Have ye kin there?'

Silent and apprehensive, the family sought each other's glances. As Neil Gilchrist turned on his heel the mother spoke.

'We'll make a fresh start there, sir, gin it's God's will.'

He looked back as he left the chamber. The father sat with head drooped and eyes half-closed. The lad was stretched forward on the table, head pillowed on his arms. Mother and daughter had settled against the wall, the girl's fair hair spread on her mother's shoulder.

Gilchrist paused at the taproom door. 'Archie,' said he, 'could ye no find somewhere for those two women to lay their heads?'

Archie watched the young man mount the stairs. All this fidge about a cottar family! It couldn't be over the lass, for she was little more than a bairn. He shrugged and called for a pallet to be thrown down for mother and daughter.

Neil stripped before a comforting fire. That family were in luck that a gentleman had been at hand... the foulsome dog... catching himself in the chipped mirror he paused, recalling the fell stare of the brutish creature. On the long road to London a pistol or something of that nature wouldn't come amiss. He would ask Archie in the morning. 'We'll make a fresh start,' the guidwife had said. He smiled as he settled his pillows. There was a comic similarity in their lot. It was as if, for an instant, a comet and a lamp were moving on the same path.

Early afoot as Neil was in the morning, the MacIlveen family had already breakfasted. He heard father and son yoking horse and wagon in the tavern yard. Archie brought him his meal and the information that Lachie Dubh had disappeared.

'No loss, Archie, no loss,' said Neil eyeing the rib of beef with relish.

'Feth, aye. I hope he's not on the Portpatrick road waiting for

18

that cottar family –'

The laird's son thumped the table in anger. 'And what in God's name has that to do wi' me, Archie?'

The innkeeper gaped. 'Why, nothing. . . nothing. . . I'll fetch your ale, Master Neil.'

His breakfast had been spoiled for him. He cursed Archie's loquacious tongue. Instead of being free to go about his own business. . . to have to concern himself about that glackit auld delver and his family journeying on in faith and ignorance. . .

As Archie sat down the tankard the young man scanned him morosely. 'It's a lang road to London, Archie. I'll buy or borrow a firearm from ye.'

'We've only an auld flintlock and that's no fit for a man on horseback. Ye might fare better in Dumfries – but wait,' the innkeeper smote his forehead, 'there's a sword upstairs that your uncle Nicol left –'

'My uncle's been in the clay these ten years –'

'He left it in settlement o' a bill, but what use is it to the likes o' me? I'll fetch it.'

He returned with a rapier and belt. Neil examined the weapon dubiously.

'It looks a bit asklent.'

'No wonder. It's been kicked around for ten years. And I'll thank ye, young sir, no to draw under this roof. It's ill-luck.'

Neil had recovered his good humour. 'As ye say, Archie. How much?'

'What your uncle owed has lang gone out o' mind. The sword is yours.' He examined the laird's son anxiously as the young man buckled on the weapon. 'If it's Lachie Dubh ye hae in mind, take tent. He's a bloody-handed carle. I wouldn't have Balwhanny learn that I –'

Neil gestured impatiently. 'I'll follow no farther than where the road parts for Dumfries and the south.'

He had ridden barely a mile when he glimpsed the MacIlveen family on the road. He stopped to look at the rapier. What he saw was disappointing. The scabbard which seemed handsomely chased was tarnished, the hilt dented. The most strenuous tugging revealed no more than six inches of blade, although what he saw shone bravely. 'A whetstone and a drop of tallow wouldn't be amiss,' he murmured, draping the weapon behind him.

He could not avoid overhauling the wagon. Mother and daughter were perched like fowl on the swaying load. Father and son trudged on either side of the nag's head. Meg greeted him with rather more warmth than was shown by her menfolk. It was enough to make Neil rein up. Impelled by a curiosity he could not explain he dismounted to walk beside Alexander.

'Can ye tell me now, guidman, why ye are for Ireland?'

The father kept silent, the son eyed Neil with a look that was far from cordial.

'Why are ye aye spierin' us on that?' Sorley's tone was brusque and nettled the laird's son but he kept mute for he sought an answer.

'You'd gang a better gait, sir,' said Alexander at last, 'if ye spiered after what's ahead o' us, rather than what's ahint.'

'Ye are right. What then, do ye expect?'

'A place where we can go about our day's work in peace.' The cottar thought it behoved him to add, ''Twas our minister, Mr Chisholm, told us o' guid land going in this place – where is it, Sorley?'

'The county o' Down. A laird, Echlin o' Renfrew, has farms for them willing tae work them.'

Brief as the callan's words were, they left Neil with a sore heart. He had heard of such a scheme at the dinner-table in Balwhanny. His father had returned from Edinburgh flushed with liquor and self-esteem. Certain influential nobles and gentles, he told his sons, had revealed to him a royal project to plant lands in the north of Ireland, once held by Irish rebels who had now fled the country. A commission would sit in Edinburgh to consider applications from persons of quality and substance to undertake the settlement and cultivation of estates up to three thousand acres. '. . . They pressed me to put my name forr'd for consideration,' his father had continued. 'A thousand acres for the outlay o' one thousand five hunner pounds Scots –'

'And what was your answer, Father?'

'Eh?' Pulled up by the curt query, the laird glowered at his younger son. It was not he who should have asked the question. He leant back in his chair, a smirk on his dribbling lips. 'I told them I would discuss the matter wi' my son and heir.' Suddenly the old man had flung himself forward, hands outstretched beseechingly to the poor chuff across the table.

Neil watched with mingled revulsion and pity.

'Wouldn't it be a grand thing to hold an Irish estate, Gilmor? Certes, ye could look your Skene cousins fair in the een, then!'

Summoned from his shadowy world, the simpleton glanced anxiously from father to brother.

The drunken man rambled on. '. . . The Crown would grant the land in fee-farm. . . the first two years' rent would be waived. . . a stout castle wi' a bawn to be built in that time. . . a challenge for a man, Gilmor, for a spunkie laird. . .'

Neil listened with mounting passion, angry and shamed that the well-born should have made game of a threadbare country laird, doited in drink, who had strayed into their company. He had scorn for the aged man with his delusion of family grandeur; pity and a painful affection for the crazed brother entrusted to bring lustre to the house of Gilchrist of Balwhanny. He faced his father, his voice harsh. 'Did ye tell your grand acquaintances that ye would be hard put to gather fifteen hunner bawbees in a meal sack, let alone pounds!'

The laird started in his chair as if he had been stung. The face he turned on his younger son was dark with fury. 'How dare ye speak to me like that, ye whelp,' he screamed. He brought his fist down till the pewter jangled. 'Leave the table, sirrah, leave the table!' As Neil mounted the dusty creaking stairs his

21

father's voice, shrill and fleering had followed him. 'Your dead mother thought to see ye an advocate striding the law courts o' Edinburgh, ha! Awa wi' ye, ingrate, awa wi' ye!'

Well, he had gone from Balwhanny, farther, doubtless, than his father had wished. But at least he was heading towards freedom. As he listened to the scant knowledge his fellow-travellers had of what lay ahead of them the thought came that, like the hare, they were circling back to what they hoped to flee.

'I'm leaving ye,' he told them, 'where the road runs to Dumfries.'

The mother's housewifely instinct was immediately astir. 'If that's the way o't you'll have a bite and sup afore we part.'

The horse was let graze, and the family and the laird's son sat down to the provision that Meg and her daughter drew from a cranny in the load. That all were journeying towards new beginnings engendered a mutual feeling of goodwill and kindliness. For the MacIlveens the fear of pursuit had lulled. The young man forgot, for a time, the difference of degree between himself and the peasant family, and the unknown road that lay before him.

They travelled together until they came to a track that forked to the south-east.

'This is where our ways part,' said Neil.

Alexander helped him mount. 'The Lord go with ye, young sir,' he said.

The MacIlveens settled to the long traik ahead. Alexander took Ellen's place on the wagon and the girl walked at the horse's head with her brother. They travelled, trusting in the God of Moses and Abraham that the hoof-pocked road, slipping among the Wigtown hills, would lead them to the coast.

3

Neil Gilchrist reproached himself. The road before him was a long and arduous one, and carrying his sword – well, it had been in the family – to his Grace, King Jamie, no mean errand. To have squandered the morning, sprawled on a dyke, munching a cottar family's bread and cheese! For the future he would keep an open eye and a closed mouth and let other folk gang their ain gait. He paused to let the horse drink at a wayside pool. The ripples died and his reflection stared back at him. What he saw there made him slowly clamber down from his horse: a flopping grey bonnet, a dusty suit, striped woollen hose, a rusty weapon on his buttock. Were these the furnishings of an ambitious young man at the court of Whitehall? Would they suffice the meanest scrivener seeking passage to Virginia? If by chance he were to meet any of the gentry who had made game of his father. . . names stick in minds. . . he could hear the old man braying it. . . *Gilchrist of Balwhanny*. His cheek darkened at the thought. . .

Meg, aloft on the load, was the first to see the figure hunkered on the roadside ditch. 'Alex,' she called, 'ahead o' us – a man skulking in the dyke.' The hump of the plaid was only too familiar, 'It's thon fearsome bodie from the tavern!'

As Lachie Dubh came down from the ditch, Ellen dragged the horse to a standstill. The ruffian, cudgel in hand, planted himself in the middle of the road.

'I'm here for your answer, frien'. D'ye take me to Ireland wi' ye?'

Neither of the MacIlveen men spoke. Sorley backed away and, blessing his memory, fumbled and found the axe. As Alexander slid down from the load he drew out the pitchfork with him. They edged forward on either side of the horse. Alexander elbowed his daughter back. Their tormentor's lickerish gaze followed the girl.

'Gin ye deny me again, guidman, I'll tummle that lass in the dyke —' A squeal of fury from Meg made the bully glance upward. 'And you too, auld hen, when I hae trod the pullet.'

If Lachie Dubh thought father or son would break, he was wrong. Together they shuffled forward until they were level with the horse's head.

'You're no going with us, man,' said Alexander. 'I'd as lief have the Deil for company.'

'Awa wi' ye, ye gangrel, and let honest folk by,' added his son.

The horse shied as Lachie swung the club at the youth's head. Sorley, grabbing at the bridle was pulled aside. Before Lachie could strike again Alexander lunged forward heavily. The tines of the fork were deadened in the thick plaid but the thrust of the cottar's muscular arms sent their opponent reeling, giving Sorley time to recover the axe. He went for Lachie, swinging the axe sledgewise. As the ruffian wheeled Alexander stuck the two prongs into his arse. Cursing in pain and rage Lachie sought the ditch bank. Malevolently he glowered at the MacIlveens.

'Ye think ye hae Lachie Dubh betwixt ye?'

'Betwixt us we'll split ye like a herring,' responded Sorley, swinging his axe.

But to the distracted women looking down from the wagon it seemed that none of the three was free to make a move. Their assailant feared that if he tried for the top of the ditch he would leave head and shoulders too long unprotected. He was in no doubt now that the callan would indeed use the axe. The MacIlveens feared that the brutish creature, in a rush, would overbear them.

'Over the sheugh and away wi' ye, man,' said Alexander, waving towards a coppice of rough undergrowth that ran into the hills.

'Come fo'rrard ye pease-bogles,' invited Lachie, fondling the cudgel.

None dared give a step. Bloodshed seemed inevitable. Then, from a distance, they heard the beat of horse's hooves. Meg saw the rider top the brae behind them. She waved frenziedly. As if taken aback, the horseman did no more than touch his broad grey bonnet in response. As he cantered forward there was a prim severity on Neil's face, that of a man who could not be expected to offer an explanation of his behaviour. His look changed abruptly when he rounded the wagon and saw what had brought the family to a halt.

'Lachie Dubh, ye dog!' The laird's son drew his mount in so close that the bully had to skip back smartly from the dancing hooves.

'Haud off your cuddy,' Lachie roared, 'or I'll break its back!' and, circumscribed as he was, he flourished the cudgel.

Neil swung the rapier forward and drew. Six inches of steel were exposed, then the blade stuck. With commendable presence of mind he rested his fingers on the hilt and leaned from the saddle. 'Take tent o' this, ye gillravager. Foot the road ye came and ne'er look back. Away wi' ye, or as God's my judge, I'll sned the head from your shoulders!'

Lachie eyed the ring of hostile faces. A mounted swordsman was a more dangerous adversary than a couple of peasants. His pig eyes ever watchful, he began to sidle along the dyke. When he had cleared the rear of the wagon he half-leapt, half-tumbled over the bank. Clutching his backside he waddled across the meadow. At the edge of the scrub he turned to shout and shake his club. The wind blew his words away. Only the malevolence of his voice came to the people on the track.

'Whatever it was, it wasn't a blessing,' said Sorley, turning to put the axe back in the wagon.

Meg was scrambling down from the load. 'For a' that, we hae been granted a blessing. Alexander man, say a word o' thanks tae the Lord.'

Alexander and his son pulled off their bonnets. Neil felt obliged to follow them. For the five bowed heads on the road to

Portpatrick the cottar offered up thanks for their safe deliverance.

Sorley regarded Neil with rather more favour. 'Would ye have cut off the blaggard's head?' he inquired.

Neil gave it as his opinion that separating a head from its trunk required exceptional strength and skill. In a burst of confidence that surprised him, he revealed he couldn't even draw the weapon from its sheath. Meg read this as a further manifestation of heavenly favour. She also chided him gently for misusing God's name, a reproach which he bore in good enough spirit.

Courteously the older MacIlveens forbore to question Neil on his change of direction. It was Sorley who asked if he had forsaken the road to Dumfries and London.

'I'm for Ireland,' replied Neil coolly. 'I'm my own master.'

'True, young sir,' said Alexander with a glance of reproof at his son. 'And I hope ye have been guided to a wise choice. But Mr Chisholm, our minister, put only our names on the letter I bear. I haven't read it – I canna read – but Sorley and Ellen can read and scrive. As I understand it, ye need a letter for Ireland –'

'Dinna fash yourself, guidman,' interrupted Neil abruptly. 'I think I can call on enough suasion to get me across the sea.'

'I hope that to be so,' cried Alexander cordially. 'How we all fare is in the hands o' our Maker.'

Neil found it irksome to keep to the laborious progress of the wagon and he was not disposed to walk with the cottar family. But with the sun in the evening quarter they entered Portpatrick more or less together. At a notary's signboard he left the MacIlveens to find their way to the harbour. A large coble, its flat bottom rising on the incoming tide, was moored at the quay. Two or three seamen, at the direction of a man in a blue knitted cap, were stowing cargo amidships, and Alexander's heart quickened to see ploughs and harness go aboard. He leaned over the jetty.

'We want to cross to Ireland,' he called.

Blue Cap looked up, scrutinising father and son. 'Hold there – I'll be with ye.' Further orders to the crewmen and he clambered up to join the MacIlveens. Established on the quay, he gave a hitch to his breeks, understandable in the circumstances, for his belt was weighed down by a short sword, a pistol and sundry dirks.

The cottar lifted his eyes from this armoury to gaze apprehensively over the grey shifting waters that stretched westward. He gestured. 'Ireland?'

'Aye.' Blue Cap continued to study father and son until Alexander grew restive.

'Well, guidsir, ye ken our errand. D'ye take folk across the water?'

'Aye, but no everybody that wants, gets. Captain Hannah doesna carry ill-favoured rogues.'

'Where is he?'

'Standing afore ye.' The mariner gave a hitch to his belt. 'What's your name and where are ye from?'

'Alexander MacIlveen and this is my son. Where we're from is of no import. It's where we're going –'

Captain Hannah, aware that he had his crew as audience, shook his head with a forbearing grin. 'Aye, but I dinna know ye, Master MacIlveen. Ye could be fleeing from the law. Hae ye any paper or writing on ye?'

Alexander fumbled in his coat and pulled out the letter. 'Mr Chisholm, our minister, set this out for us. It's for. . .' at a loss he looked at the writing on the missive.

Sorley took it from him. 'It's to be put into the hands o' the Reverend Mungo Turnooth at Ravara in the county Down. D'ye want tae break the seal?'

The captain frowned. 'Don't be so pert in the tongue, callan. If ye hadn't a passport none o' ye would set foot on my deck.' He turned to Alexander. 'Are those your weeminfolk, by the wagon?'

'My wife and daughter.'

'Four of ye. Ye know ye can't take your wagon and horse?'

Father and son gaped at each other.

'Then what's to do wi' them?' said Sorley at last.

'In the marketplace you'll find a cattle vendor, Charlie Gaw. Offer him your nag and cart. He'll deal fairly wi' ye. If ye take my advice you'll put most o' your siller into three-four sheep or siccan livestock. You'll be all the more welcome at Ravara. Ye can pay your passage out o' the rest. If you and your family bring your chattels fo'rrard we'll get them stowed. Now, hasten, guidman, for I want to leave on this tide.'

Spurred by all this brisk advice the MacIlveens lowered their bundles and tools to the coble deck. Alexander and Sorley took the empty wagon to the head of the town. They found the dealer Gaw, sold – or rather bartered – horse and wagon for four ewes and a tup, the balance in cash.

Alexander laid a hand on the flank of the beast with which he had opened so many furrows. 'You'll see he gets a guid master?'

'Masters, like nags, come in a' hues, frien',' said the dealer, leading his purchase away.

Saddened, Alexander watched until man and horse disappeared. He joined Sorley in herding their small flock towards the harbour. 'Have we been wisely guided, son?' he said at last.

'What reck? We had no other road.'

'Aye. We've put our hand tae it now.' The cottar looked around. 'I wonder what became o' Master Gilchrist?'

'Likely taken his ain way. A laird's son has no hands for plough or sickle, Father.'

But Neil Gilchrist was at the quay when they arrived. He had shown Captain Hannah a letter from the notary attesting that he was a person of good repute; from the same personage an agreement to sell the horse that he couldn't take with him.

'And did ye buy stock wi' the money?' asked Sorley smugly.

Neil thought this no one's business but his own. But after a moment he explained that he had charged the notary to send the value of the horse to his brother, an answer that impressed everyone favourably except Sorley, who thought to himself that the laird's son was a bit of a coof to part so readily with money when he was leaving the country.

The MacIlveens had never grazed sheep. Meg had kept a goat at times, but never more than one and not too long at a time. The laird's factor had had a sharp eye for the signs of prosperity on four legs. Now Alexander watched anxiously as the crew tossed *his* sheep, their forelegs langled, into the beam of the vessel. It was all done so adroitly that he comforted himself that this was the skill of long usage.

'Aboard with ye now,' said the captain. 'The weemin to the stern.'

Neil and the family clambered awkwardly into the boat, groping for nooks in which to settle. Captain Hannah thrust away from the jetty. According to their nature the five voyagers watched the band of dark water widen. Meg gave herself into the hands of God in Heaven. Her son and daughter turned to stare out to sea in mingled excitement and apprehension. To Alexander, watching the shoreline slip away, realisation came, in a deeper thrust of pain, that now indeed he and his were cast on the floods. The laird's son had settled himself between the gunnel and a bale of cornstraw. He was as ignorant as the cottar as to what lay ahead but, unlike Alexander, knew that the channel could be crossed in a handful of hours. And re-crossed in as brief a time, if need be. To cast the dice twice was not granted to those who had sailed for Virginia. . .

Under its lug-sail the coble leaned away westward. A ponderous object under a tarpaulin shifted slightly and righted again as the vessel came up. Neil spied the shape and brassy gleam of a cannon. The captain removed his burdened belt and leaving it nearhand, settled at the tiller. Neil was about to comment on this show of weapons, then thought better of it.

'Ye have carried many persons to Ireland, Captain Hannah?'

'A brave wheen in the past twa-three years, Mr Gilchrist.'

'How do they fare?'

29

The captain, leaning on the tiller, shrugged. 'That a' depends on their mettle.'

'And in their trust in the Lord, sir,' came Meg's voice from the shadows.

'True, true, guidwife, gin they don't sit with their hands aye in prayer. There's fruitful land for them that's no afeard o' work.' He shifted the tiller, adjusting his course. 'There was a plentiful harvest last year. They raised enough for their own needs and had a roughage over to ship across and sell in Portpatrick and Campbeltown.'

Sorley, nursing the arm still painful from the cudgel blow, sat up and took notice. For the first time they had heard the word of one who knew, firsthand, what this unknown place had to offer a hard working youth.

A rhythmic throb grew in the darkness ahead. Compared to the coble's laborious progress the sound sped towards them with an eerie swiftness. Over the wave tips came a file of long-necked birds, deflecting, with a melancholy cry, to sweep past the lurching vessel. Ellen sought for her mother's hand.

'Nothing mair, lass, than auks seeking their breakfast,' declared Captain Hannah.

But his words did not dispel the feeling among the voyagers that the doleful passing of the birds was a foretelling of the unknown land ahead.

The vessel was now plunging across the grey sliding shoulders of the mid-channel flow. To Neil it was incomparably more menacing than the leaden dance of the inshore waters. He turned his mind firmly away from the depths under the shallow hull. Captain Hannah lay at his ease, arm hooked on the tiller. The heads and shoulders of the crewmen were a denser black against the darkness of the night. Suddenly one stirred, pointing:

'Cap'n, to starboard – I don't like the look o' her.'

Neil saw only a splurge of spray, luminous in the dark water, running on the same course as the coble. Then the bulk of a two-masted vessel hove into sight against the dim starlight.

'What is she? Who is she, Captain?' Neil asked.

The captain jerked away the tarpaulin, revealing a small brass cannon. 'Make ready, Hamish,' he said to the watch-out. Then he answered Neil over his shoulder, 'Bluidy reivers frae Kintyre, Mr Gilchrist. Nicol, take the tiller.' As the second crewman obediently scrambled aft, the master cupped his mouth and bellowed into the darkness. A hail, a warning? 'Any o' you men handle a firearm?' Captain Hannah then asked his passengers.

Neil reached out a hand.

'Give me one,' said Sorley brushing his mother aside.

The third crewman drew a couple of weapons from beside the cannon and handed them up. Hamish was bent busily over the cannon.

Again Captain Hannah shouted into the darkness. Neil caught only a fragment of the words '. . . nothing but a cottar family. . . a wheen o' sheep. . .' The strange vessel deviated not a span but drew rapidly on them. She was no larger than the coble, but even to Neil's eye her lines were not those of a craft employed in wallowing across the channel on lawful business. The white blob of a face appeared above the prow. As Neil braced himself to ready his musket he was interrupted by Sorley MacIlveen holding out his half-loaded weapon. Brusquely he elbowed him aside and lifted his musket to his shoulder. The intruder was now running so close that spume boiled up between the hulls. The face was that of a man stationed in the shrouds to spy who and what were in the coble. Neil caught the glint of a dagger in the fellow's mouth and took aim. The captain flourished his pistol in a signal. Hamish put a light to the touch-hole, Neil drew on the musket trigger.

The discharge of the cannon rattled the coble from stem to stern. If it had been the gunner's intent to hole the adversary he was sorely out. The ball struck the prow, throwing up only a scatter of splinters. Neil's marksmanship was more accurate.

He saw the dirk drop from the agonised mouth of the man in the shrouds. Then its owner curled like an eddy of smoke to follow it down to the waves.

The master of the pirate boat put the tiller hard over. The stretch of water between the vessels widened. From the free-booter came a splutter of musket-fire.

'Load, Hamish!' cried Captain Hannah. He turned on Neil. 'I didn't order *you* to let fly,' but he stretched out to thump Neil's shoulder in approval.

The laird's son might have resented this well-meant buffet but allowed that he was under command. Neil turned to Sorley MacIlveen. But the youth, his firearm now primed and ready, shrugged him away.

The moon, riding through threadbare cloud, entered the sky. The other vessel showed no readiness to close again. To the watchers in the coble she seemed in the cold light to float misshapen like a maimed seabird.

The captain let out a grunt of approval. 'Ye did better than ye thought, Hamish. Ye brought down her fore-sail. Let's get clear o' her –'

Frustrated, Sorley emptied his weapon into the night.

'Nicol,' said the captain coldly, 'take the musket from that callan afore he does himsel' or us a mischief.'

The blunt prow of the boat plunged and crashed westward, leaving a gleaming wake of phosphorescence.

Captain Hannah took over again at the tiller. 'Ye didn't think, Mr Gilchrist,' said he, 'to run across sea-reivers in this sowp o' water.'

Neil thought the channel wide and deep enough for his liking. 'Fortunately you did, Captain.'

'True, sir. There's a plague o' gillravagers skulking in the lochs and isles that come down on any bit boat on its lawful way betwixt the ports. They're maistly abroad at night.'

'It puzzles me that those marauders didn't open fire when they first came up with us.'

'It's no everybody will pay ransom on a corpse.'

'Ah. . . ransom.' Neil glanced around the shadowy deck. 'I'm afraid we wouldn't count for much, Captain.'

'Blessed are the poor, Mr Gilchrist.'

'And yet ye warned them there was little aboard –'

'I did. But there's them fleeing Scotland with a price on their head that are worth pursuing. As far as I'm able they don't sail with me.'

'I know of one such brutish creature – he pestered the guidman MacIlveen to take him as his ploughman.'

'There's gommerils that have crossed into Ireland whose only ploughing has been a furrow across some guid Christian thrapple.'

'Such is this creature, Lachie Dubh by name. He's wanted for murder. He was on the road to Portpatrick.'

'I'll keep a watch for the said Lachie, Mr Gilchrist.'

As the darkness thinned, a piercing chill entered the limbs of the huddled passengers. Grey light touched the waters astern. It brought little comfort to Ellen MacIlveen: the waves, now bright, now sullen, were so many faces grimacing and muttering at the vessel's onward passage. Silver seeped into the eastern sky. From afar came a cockcrow.

The captain pointed. 'That's Ireland,' he said.

Achingly, they scrambled to their feet. To cottar family and laird's son ignorance of what that mute coast held for their future disposed them to silence. Captain Hannah, on the other hand, was all practised and persuasive advice.

'I'll land ye on the beach at Donaghadee. From there you'll take the road to Ravara through the village o' Newtownards at the head o' Strangford Lough.'

Alexander gestured towards his heap of chattels.

'There's nags for hire to carry the weemin and your bundles. The callan and you'll have to herd the sheep. And you, young sir, you're with the guidman and his family?'

The laird's son drew back a step. 'The letter in my possession

33

takes me to Mr Echlin of Ravara.'

The captain, aware that such authority was unlikely to come from a Portpatrick notary, nevertheless acknowledged his infelicity with a beck of the head and turned to give directions to his crewmen.

As they drew nearer to the coast of rolling drumlins, in the early light they saw men and women stirring around a clachan of fishermen's cabins. The captain had the sail down and his flat-bottomed boat drifted into shallow water. There was still a depth of three or four feet when he dropped anchor, signifying that this was the place of debarkation.

'Help your weemin to the beach and come back for your chattels and the sheep.'

Sorley plunged overboard. They heard him gasp as he soused into the water. He coaxed the hesitant Ellen onto his shoulders and stumbled and foamed ashore to set her dryshod on the sand. Alexander, taking Meg in his arms, followed his son. When the MacIlveen men returned the laird's son was helping the crewmen pile the family's possessions on the gunnel-lip. Piece by piece the household goods were carried to dry land.

Two men and, a little behind them, a middle-aged woman came down from the clachan.

The woman, watchful, called, 'You're from Portpatrick, guidwoman?'

Meg and Ellen looked up from sorting their chattels.

'Aye.' Meg glanced at the cluster of cabins. 'Where's this?'

'Donaghadee.' The woman moved a little closer. 'You're bound for. . .?'

Meg, lost, looked at her daughter.

'Mr Echlin's of Ravara,' said the girl.

'Come away up,' said the woman, 'and get something warm in ye.'

All went well with unloading the sheep until one of the ewes, still hobbled, scrambled out of Sorley's grasp and went overboard on the seaward side. The youth was about to spring after it when the captain caught him by the arm.

'Don't chance it, lad, unless ye can swim. The next wave'll bring her in.'

But when Alexander and Sorley dragged the sodden animal from the surf it was dead. They stared disconsolately at it.

'It's an ill start, son,' said Alexander.

'That man,' said Sorley, glowering at the captain's busy figure, 'shouldn't have meddled. I could have saved it.'

'Your mother'll see the Deil's hand in it.'

They were joined on the strand by Neil and men from the clachan who had herded together the rest of the flock.

'If we had a spade,' said Alexander, 'we could bury it.'

A man laughed. 'For why would ye bury it, frien'? You've mutton and a sheepskin there. Clod it over a nag's back and take it wi' ye.'

Sorley nodded as one taking a lesson to heart. 'Where will we get horses?'

The villagers consulted. 'We could hire ye a couple,' said one, 'if ye have the siller.'

'We have little o' that commodity,' replied Alexander cautiously. 'But we'll hire one if we cannot hire baith.'

The two horses were brought down from the clachan. 'We'll need them as soon as you're fit tae ride back. We've ploughing tae finish.'

'We had ours. . .' began Alexander and fell silent.

On a sudden impulse Neil unpicked a seam of his coat and produced a broad gold piece. He gestured to the horses. 'I'll buy if you'll sell,' said he.

While the men from the clachan swithered over the offer the MacIlveens viewed the laird's son in doubt.

'Don't put us in your debt, Mr Gilchrist,' said Alexander in a low voice.

'Debt? You have your sheep – I have my horses –'

One of the men turned to Neil. 'It's no light matter, sir. Horses are hard to come by. But we'll get two mair across from

35

Galloway. We'll sell.' He weighed the gold coin in his hand.

Neil shook his head. 'I can't break it. Make up the rest to us in food and drink.'

Meg and Ellen joined their menfolk. Meg shook her head over the drowned ewe. It was a bad beginning.

The neighbourly woman laughed. 'Heth, we have seen a herd o' fair cattle lost on this strand when wind and tide's in the wrong airt. The Lord was with ye, guidwife.'

Neil grinned as he helped secure the family's bundles. It was the first time he had heard Mistress MacIlveen over-reached in comprehending the ways of providence.

Mother and daughter were mounted on the other horse. Alexander and Sorley rounded up the sheep. Neil asked the way to the Echlin estate. One of the men traced their route in the sand. They were to hold west to the village of Newtownards. That road was well-trodden.

'And beyond that?' asked Neil.

The man shrugged. Beyond that they would journey southwest. That was all the fisherman knew.

4

Wheels, hooves and brogues had beaten a clear narrow track
rising and falling across the drumlin countryside. First went
Neil, his horse humping the baggage and the carcase of the ewe,
followed by the MacIlveen women on the other horse. Then the
sheep, with Alexander and his son on the trot to keep them
from heading into the brushwood. The men were glad to
stretch their legs as the seawater dried on their breeches and
hose.

At times they had to halt to let wayfarers with laden pack-
horses pass. Their greetings were received with a silent watchful nod, an acknowledgment and no more.

'They don't deeve ye with their talk,' said Ellen aggrieved, as
she watched a traveller disappear.

'We're birds in flight, lass,' said her father. 'Gin we find a
bough to settle on, we'll have a' the crack we need.'

Here and there in patches by the roadside the scrub had been
driven back. As the travellers drew close to the village of
Newtownards the husbanded stretches merged into a pattern
of ploughland and pasture. Set among the worked land were
cabins of wattle and rush thatch. In the village itself the dwellings, clustered round a roughly roofed castle, were of much the
same structure.

Leaving Sorley and Ellen with the animals the others separated to make purchases in the two or three huckster stores.
Meg replenished her stock; Alexander, now that he had the
promise of two plough-horses, bought a double swingle-tree.
Neil added a linen shirt to his scanty wardrobe. Seeing him eye
a musket, the shopkeeper brought it out for his inspection. Neil
weighed, tried the lock, sighted down the barrel. With a little
haggling he bought the weapon, powder and shot, and returned to join the others. Alexander asked a passer-by the road

to Mr Echlin's of Ravara. The man pointed the way out of the village.

'Hold round by the head o' the lough. Your road runs with the sun. That's all I know o't.'

'We can always spier the way from some other traveller,' Sorley suggested.

The man looked at them in a strange manner. 'Aye, if ye were to meet such a bodie. A safe journey to ye.'

Plodding beside the packhorse's head, the laird's son scanned the countryside. As the drumlins unfolded there crept over him an uneasy feeling. Something was amiss. The land was full of sound and movement. He observed with an appreciative eye the springing hares in the glades, the bobbing scuts of rabbits by the wayside. A burn that ran for a time beside the path was pinpricked by rising fish. At the plod of hooves wildfowl rose from the waterways of a bog. The calls and alarms of pigeon and blackbird sounded through the tangled woodland. Neil had picked up enough husbandry at Balwhanny to recognise the maturity and value of the timber that flowed in drifts between the hills.

But over this wild fertility hung an air of desolation. Strips of land that had been worked were now invaded by hazel, alder and bramble. There was no sign of humankind or habitation. He called on his memory for stories he had heard; he could remember fragments only, for what had they held for him? Reports of the late queen's servitors harrying to their death the evil-disposed and treasonable Irish, man, woman and babe. Then the assiduous labours of lawyers in his present Grace's reign to render guilty of trespass those who had clung on in thicket and swamp.

He recalled an evening in a Kircaldy public house when a wool-merchant, who had somehow got into the company, said that Ireland had been more ravished by the English than America had suffered at the hands of the Spanish. They had listened because he carried more drinking money than the assembled students together. It was, as far as Neil could recall, the only time he had heard so much of this distant country a good sixteen miles off the coast of Kintyre. But now he could interpret the deserted clearings on the drumlin flanks as the exuvial remnants of a dispossessed people. He waited for the others. 'You've come to a fruitful land, Mr MacIlveen,' said he.

Alexander, holding the ram's horn, stroked his beard and looked around him. Where were the ploughlands, the grazing, the dykes and sheughs marking off one man's land from that of his neighbour's? 'Aye, maybe so,' he said cautiously, 'maybe so.'

They ate by the roadside. Again the handing around and sharing of food and drink fostered a mutual warmth, the deeper this time because of the alien surroundings.

The meal finished, Sorley and Neil set off to gather in the sheep. From the brow of a hill they looked down on a roof of branches and tendrils, broken only by the sombre foliage of scattered holly, yew and juniper. On the distant rising ground to the west stood a massive darkness of forestry which Neil guessed to be oak.

It was the first time they had undertaken a joint task away from the others. Neil was of the opinion that the cottar's son was an unlikeable youth, disrespectful to his betters. As for Sorley, he squinted under his eave of red hair at Neil. What mischief could have set a laird's son on the road with little more than a dusty suit to his back?

Sorley looked around him. 'No sight o' cot or cattle.'

'None.' Fretfully, Neil dug his heel in the turf. 'Yet this damned desolation can't be totally uninhabited –'

They heard the distant clap of a musket shot. A wisp of smoke drifted up through the trees ahead of them.

'There are folk in this wilderness!' cried Neil.

Together they plunged down the hill to join the others.

The party had travelled a furlong or two when Neil, in the lead, saw two men and a young boy drawn back a little from

39

the path. The elder and taller of the men wore a fringed russet mantle that fell to below his knees. Neil had seen such a garment on Highland lords in the streets of Edinburgh. As he approached he pulled off his bonnet. A silent stare was the response to his salute. He replaced his bonnet slowly. When he spoke the tone of his query was no more than cool civility.

'Can ye tell me, sirs, if we are on the right road for Mr Echlin's of Ravara?'

There was a silence. Then the older man, looking beyond Neil, spoke: '*Níl aithne agam ar fear ar bith a bhfuil a leithéid d'ainm air.*'

Neil turned to the second hunter, a man in his early thirties. Of middle-stature, his muscular body was clad in a padded hunting jacket of leather, over a saffron shirt. Neil glimpsed the handsome silver-chased fowling-piece on which he leaned. The stare he turned on the young Scot was as inimical as that of the older man. His mouth twitched in a mirthless grin.

'*Is strainséirí anseo muid,*' he said and turned away.

The attitude of the two Irishmen was plain enough to the laird's son. He did not have to call on his small stock of Gaelic to interpret a rebuff. He removed his bonnet. '*Tapadh libh, a dhaoine uaisle,*' said he, '*air son ar modhalachd,*' and had the small satisfaction of seeing the younger man's eyes widen momentarily in surprise. Smarting, he overtook the cottar family and would have pushed past had not Alexander questioned him.

'What news, Mr Gilchrist?'

'None. The old man said he knew nothing of Mr Echlin. The other claims that they themselves are strangers here.'

'He's a liar,' said the cottar's son. 'There were dead birds and hares at the bairn's feet. They wouldn't have killed so much game if they didn't live close by.'

Sharp eyes, sharp lugs, thought Neil looking at the red-haired youth with some disfavour. 'Well. . . they could be of the people who once owned this land.'

'For why did they give it up?' inquired Alexander.

'They held enmity towards his Grace, the King. So it was taken from them.'

Sorley shrugged and looked uncomprehendingly at his father.

Alexander gathered up his herding stick. 'If the land's fit for working we're fit to work it. Bring up the sheep, Ellen.'

The travellers became aware that they were not alone. On either side, keeping pace with them, the undergrowth stirred and rustled. Neil thought he glimpsed a hostile stare from a face quickly averted, now a shoulder, now a body thrusting beside him through the foliage. He shouldered his musket high, then thought better of it. He saw the MacIlveens peering fearfully from side to side at the glimpses of this barely visible and disconcerting escort.

The track climbed, briefly freeing itself from the hemming undergrowth. Looking down they saw they were on the border of another territory. Here the woodland had broken into thickets clinging to the hillsides. Alexander leaned forward as if he would penetrate the creel of branches.

'There's ploughland 'twixt them clumps o' bushes, Mr Gilchrist!'

The movement and rustling around them had ceased. Those who had dogged their steps had turned away and melted into the woodlands.

'Look!' cried Meg, pointing.

A tendril of smoke drifted above the treetops. Not the brief hostile puff from a musket shot, but the unhurried spiral that every heart recognised as rising from a family hearth.

They hurried down the slope, Neil not the last, seeking tracks among the tree-boles, tearing themselves free of briery snares, splashing across a burn, driving their animals through the last tangle of undergrowth.

They were on the edge of a wide clearing. On the other side sat a cluster of cabins, women and children at the doorsteps. A ploughman was opening a patch of land, the oxen led by a young girl. On the opposing hillside a man swung a billhook. Seconds after each stroke the note came echoing to the travellers like a welcoming bell. Alexander paused to watch the plough-work. He crumbled a fragment of the dark soil in his fingers and, for the first time since he fled his holding, he smiled.

'Can ye tell me, guidman, where I'll find the Reverend Mungo Turnooth?'

The girl halted the oxen and the ploughman examined the newcomers.

'Are ye for settling?'

'Aye.'

'Then it's Mr Daniel Drummond you'll have to see.'

Alexander drew out Mr Chisholm's letter. 'We were bade see the minister –'

'And rightly so. Mr Turnooth has the care o' our immortal souls. But if it's land you're spiering after, ye see Dan Drummond the factor.'

The word 'factor' had an ill sound to father and son, and it showed in their faces.

'Where's he to be found?' demanded Sorley.

'He's in his office doon there by the clump o' birches. Chap on that door.' He grasped the plough shaft. 'Fo'rrard lass,' and the girl, with her goad, set the oxen in motion.

The nearby countryside had been cleared to the hills and the brow of oakwood observed by Neil. Where fragments of the primeval forest still stood in the ploughland, their end was tokened in the scatter of bleached root stumps grubbed out by man and horse. An avenue, wide and firm, edged with rowan trees, led to what Neil guessed was Echlin's dwelling. What he could see of the house through the foliage was a strange mixture of old and new.

As Alexander knocked on the door of Mr Drummond's office, Neil instinctively drew aside from the cottar family. The door opened, and the factor, quill in hand, stood on the threshold.

Alexander pulled off his bonnet. 'Mr Drummond?'

'Aye.' The soberly-garbed little man took in the wan faces, the burdened horses, the cluster of sheep. His scrutiny paused for a moment on the young man, standing apart, bonneted, sword at belt.

'Landed from Portpatrick, eh?'

Alexander nodded and drew out the letter. 'For the Reverend Mr Turnooth. . .'

Reaching forward, Mr Drummond waggled his fingers in a peremptory manner. The cottar made to return the letter to his pocket.

'Ye want a cot and land, guidman?'

'That's our intent, sir.'

'Then let me have the missive.' The factor opened the letter and read it, lips moving. 'Alexander MacIlveen,' he raised his pen as if to enumerate them, 'and your family.' He turned to Neil. 'And you. . .?'

'I'm not named in the letter. I took passage with these guidfolk. My name is Neil Gilchrist,' he hesitated, 'of Balwhanny.'

'Aye,' said Mr Drummond. He turned to the cottar and pointed along the track ahead. 'Take your family to that lodging in the hollow. There or thereabouts you'll find Rushin Coatie. She'll give ye a meal and beds and show ye the stabling.'

Alexander was confused between the identity of the female he was to seek and the awareness that Mr Chisholm's piece of writing was out of his possession. He reached out but Mr Drummond waved the letter dismissively. 'Mr Turnooth's awa. He'll con this on his return.'

Alexander took the horse from Neil Gilchrist and with a grave shake of the head led his family and his animals away.

Drummond turned to the laird's son. 'And you, Mr Gilchrist of Balwhanny, have you any letter, passport, paper?'

The ironic stress nettled the young man. But he smiled. 'I have a letter from a notary. I trust that will satisfy ye.'

'– And Mr Echlin. Come in and seat yourself.'

The lodging was a long structure of sod and wattle, a loop of smoke rising from a hole in its rush-thatched roof. As the MacIlveens and their animals slithered to a weary halt a woman appeared in the doorway. She was not a sight to revive the flagging spirits of the family. The skin of her face, what they could see of it, was the colour of bran. From under a bonnet grey lichens of hair hung down, veiling her eyes and dangling either side of her pinched nose. Beneath the hem of a long garment of woven rushes peeped a pair of horseman's boots.

She clawed back a lock of hair. 'Ye have seen Dan Drummond, guidfolk?'

'Aye. . .'

'Tether your nags and come awa in with ye.'

The main room of the lodging held a table and two long benches. The lower portion was partitioned into sleeping quarters for men and for women.

Meg collapsed on a bench. 'I'm fair wabbit out.' But as she saw the others about to follow her she rose sternly. 'Down on your knees, Alex man, give thanks.'

And Alexander, pulling off his bonnet, slid to his knees to offer thanks for their safe-coming to this place. The lodge-keeper perfunctorily bent her head while she continued to heap glowing turf against a capacious black pot.

His thanksgiving completed, Alexander asked her if she knew of an empty dwelling on the estate.

With a grunt Rushin Coatie lifted the pot from the hearth and set it on the table. 'That's Dan Drummond's concern, my man,' she replied.

Meg peered into the pot. A thick brew bubbled round a fowl. 'Nothing like a sup o' broth, guidwife,' said the lodge-keeper with a grin.

'We have mutton,' said Sorley, 'if we but knew how to get the wool off it.'

'There's plenty here to learn ye that, callan,' said Rushin Coatie. 'I'll fetch ye barley bread.'

The odour of new timber hung in Mr Drummond's office. Scattered across a table were estate charts, papers, inkhorns and quills. The factor pointed Neil to a chair. He perched himself on a corner of the table.

'Ye understand that I must lay some knowledge afore Mr Echlin?'

'I do. I've told ye how I came to this place, and of my readiness to satisfy anyone with a right to such information as to my chara – as to my situation and family.'

'Ah,' said the factor, sitting down to dip his pen. 'And that – your name again?'

'Neil Skene Gilchrist of the house of Balwhanny in Ayrshire.' It was evident that the lairds of Ayrshire, great or small, meant little to Mr Drummond. But he dutifully noted down the title in full.

'Had it been your intention to undertake a proportion of land, Mr Gilchrist, ye would have submitted the proposal to the council in Edinburgh,' said Mr Drummond and left it to his hearer to choose between statement and query.

Neil chose the former. 'I understand that to be the way o't.'

This time the factor took the matter head-on. 'Do ye see yourself working the land?'

'Mr Drummond, if ye are spiering whether I have the money to rent a farm, the answer is – no.'

The factor, now about his master's business, laid down his quill. 'Aye, that's all verra fine and well, young sir. But what do ye see as your employment, where the burthen o' folk are cottars, and those who are not, masons, carpenters, smiths and the like? And where there's no town as yet, within a day's ride?'

'I can only hope that the society you describe will find a fitting

45

occupation for one gentle born,' said Neil coolly.

Mr Drummond thought such an eventuality unlikely but he held his tongue and busied himself lighting a lamp against the gloaming. As Neil watched the flame catch he realised that for the best part of two days he hadn't laid his head on a pillow. He made to rise.

But the factor had still his duty to pursue. 'Ye didn't spend all your days around your father's house?'

'No, for two years I read law at St Andrew's.'

Mr Drummond's attention was hooked. 'Ah. . . St Andrew's.' There was a hint of deference in the next question. 'But two years, young sir: ye didn't finish your schooling. . .?'

Neil stood up. 'Mr Drummond, I'm weary. I'll be in better frame to answer your questions after a night's sleep. . . if I knew where that might be.'

Suddenly, in the dark outside, there broke a hubbub of voices and the whimpering of dogs. The door was thrust open and a man entered, dragging by their scruffs the carcases of two doglike beasts. Behind him a younger man entered, cradling a pair of muskets in his arms. Neil hurriedly drew back his feet as the man dropped his burden on the floor.

'Claim the bounty on these vermin, Drummond.'

'I will, Mr Echlin,' said the factor, a discreet finger to his nostrils.

The laird of Ravara straightened. He was of middle stature, muscular and compact. A scar puckered his right cheek. A man in his early fifties, Neil guessed. Echlin, in his turn, surveyed the stranger.

'And who is this?'

Drummond gestured. 'Mr Neil Gilchrist of. . .'

Neil declined to help him out. 'Your servant, sir,' he said with a bow.

Echlin took the seat relinquished by his factor. His young companion had leant the weapons in the corner and now stood quietly by.

46

'Very well, Mr Gilchrist, *why* are ye here?' The questioner's eyes were wary.

'It's a long tale, Mr Echlin, and I'm not at all sure I know the answer.'

'Are ye on an errand for the government?'

Neil stared. 'Why no, sir.'

Echlin grimaced briefly as if at some blunder of his own making. Then he turned to the young man at his elbow. 'Come forward, Angus. Mr Angus Ross, dominie of my school.'

With outstretched hand the schoolmaster acknowledged Neil in the most open and friendly manner he had yet encountered.

The laird seemed to think that confidence in the newcomer had advanced far enough. He rose abruptly. 'Ye won't be riding farther tonight, young man. Mr Drummond, can ye give him a bed?'

The factor was confident that Mistress Drummond could supply a night's bed and board for the traveller.

'Breakfast with me at Rathard House, Gilchrist. We'll learn your mind then. I'm an early riser.' Neil bowed. The laird touched one of the wolves with his toe. 'Have Ronane save the pelts, Dan.'

'Aye, Mr Echlin.' As his master put his hand to the door the factor continued, 'A cottar family arrived, seeking land.'

'Will it not keep till the morn, Dan?' said the laird impatiently. 'Where are they now?'

'At the lodging-house. There's the Barclay place, Mr Echlin,' and there was a canny note to the factor's voice.

'Aye.' Echlin plucked his lip. 'Would they be fit to hold it?'

'There's a father and son. They seem hardy enough carles.'

'Well, if it's the Barclay holding keep the news from the auld kimmer Rushin Coatie, till ye have them settled. I bid ye goodnight.' Echlin, ushering the young dominie before him, left the office.

The factor wrinkled his nose at the lupine stench. 'The laird

47

had no call tae drag these in here. But whiles he likes to sign with a flourish. I'd be obliged if ye would help tae shift them from my office.'

Neil had to employ both hands to move the dead animal and wondered at the strength of the laird's wrists. With Mr Drummond leading in the gloom, the two dragged the carcases to a bothy among the trees. The factor pushed back the leather curtain and entered.

'Leave it here,' he said dropping his burden on the earth floor.

In a corner, embers smoored over, a fire glowed dully.

Neil smelled the unmistakeable odour of a cooling trough. 'Ronane is the blacksmith?'

There was silence as the factor dropped the curtain. Then, 'Aye, the smith. . .' Brief as they were, the words carried a burden of enmity. He stooped in the darkness. 'Give your hands a rummle through the grass, young sir. Mistress Drummond will no thank us if we bring this stink into the house.'

Neil did as he was bade, dragging his fingers through the frost rime on the grass.

Satisfied, the factor took a path leading to a substantial cottage. Neil followed him, stumbling as much through fatigue as the unevenness of the track.

5

Mrs Drummond, if surprised at Neil's arrival on a doorstep where strangers were few, welcomed him cordially enough. The daughter, a pretty girl of about seventeen years, set another place. During supper he did his best to entertain mother and daughter with an account of what he had last seen and heard in the streets and parlours of Edinburgh, the wisps of rumour and hearsay that had drifted to Balwhanny from the court of King James.

In turn, the factor's wife repaid the guest with her version of the small hierarchic world into which he had stumbled. Occasionally her husband's hand fluttered as if in warning. While this served to keep Neil awake, it did little, as far as he could hazard, to curb the good lady's tongue.

According to her the laird was the finest of men, of gentle birth, courteous, brave. Rhetorically, to her husband, she said, 'Where did he see service, Mr Drummond?'

'In a Scottish regiment under the Prince of Orange,' replied Mr Drummond briefly.

She drew a finger down her sonsy cheek. 'That's when he got the sair wound.'

'And Mr Ross, the schoolmaster?' asked Neil.

'Ye met Angus Ross? Una,' and the good woman beamed on her daughter, 'assists him at the school.'

'Ah,' responded Neil, turning a felicitous smile in the same direction.

'A most civil learned young man, Dominie Ross,' continued Mrs Drummond, 'as one would expect gin he was chosen by the laird to accompany him to Ireland. Furthermore,' and the factor's wife tittered slightly, 'he pleases my lady Echlin, and that's the assay mark here, Mr Gilchrist.'

Mr Drummond's finger flittered agitatedly, but his wife,

leaning forward, ignored him.

'I don't use the title lightly, Mr Gilchrist. The lady is the sixth daughter o' some Scots lord. Night and day she prays that the King will lift her husband up with the kiss o' the royal sword on his shoulder. . . ye ken my meaning?' Mrs Drummond's smile did nothing to sweeten the malice.

The factor pushed his chair back. 'Mr Gilchrist's wearied. Let us kneel.'

Neil went down awkwardly. Since his mother's death it was an acknowledgment that had fallen into disuse at Balwhanny. The factor gave thanks for the departed day, invoked divine protection on his household and the stranger under his roof. Neil's thoughts fled from the droning voice like sparks from a knife-grinder's wheel. There was to be no return for him. He had closed the door on the dusty churlishness of his home, on his brother's harrowing idiocy, his father's crazed fantasy that grew as his inheritance fell apart. As to London, he was, two days later, miles farther from the court of King Jamie. Very well. He would stay in this place. Surely, amid all this planning and building and tilling there must be something for a young and literate man? Perhaps, he peeped through his fingers at the bowed shoulders of his host, something in those plans and ledgers that cluttered the factor's desk? He looked forward to the morrow with anticipation.

'Amen,' he echoed eventually and rose stiffly from his knees.

In the morning the factor came to him with hot water, a razor, a towel and a plea that he should ready himself as quickly as possible. Echlin breakfasted early. As they stepped out a raw mist was lifting sluggishly from the woodlands and Neil shivered in his thin clothes.

'Has Mr Echlin a family?'

'Three. There's Hamilton, a captain in his Grace's army. He bides in London, ye ken, but he's at Rathard House this past week. Sent on an errand to Dublin, he came north to see her Ladyship. He's well acquainted with the royal household, Mr Gilchrist.'

'To his father's satisfaction, I'm sure,' said Neil with a twinge of envy.

'And even more to her Ladyship's. Her ewe lamb,' responded the factor with a wink, displeasing to Neil. 'Anne, the daughter is here too, on a visit from Scotland. She'll go back when the laird hears o' fitting company crossing for Portpatrick. Captain Hamilton says he had no time tae convoy her, but must be off to London – and *that* didn't please the laird.'

'And the third?'

'The younger son, Francis, is at college in England. I've seen him but once.'

There was nothing untoward, thought Neil, in such a disposal of a landowner's family. Yet it seemed to him that the laird and his wife had left themselves oddly bereft; as if their own sojourn in this place was transitory. 'I can understand the two gentlemen being absent, each about his concern. But would not Lady Echlin prefer to have her daughter live with her at Rathard House?'

'Heth!' Mr Drummond shook his head at the young man's naivety. 'Miss Anne's still at the beck of her tutors. Where would a well-born young lass find the like here? No, sir, Miss Echlin is in the protection o' her grandad, the Earl of Finnart.'

Although he sensed that the factor would be happy to oblige, Neil decided that further questioning on his part would sound like impertinent curiosity. In silence he followed the other. A rabbit started from under their feet. The laird of Ravara could do with a rabbit-warren, Neil decided. But he kept his lips closed on that too.

'What do ye ken of the MacIlveen family, Mr Gilchrist?'

'Nothing. It was a chance meeting on the road.' Another meeting came to mind and he told of the encounter with the two Irishmen and the child.

'By what ye say, the auld one was Fiach MacCartan, and the younger man his nephew, Turlough and Turlough's brat, Turlough Óg, as he's called. What were they about?'

51

'Hunting. Young MacIlveen saw game they had shot.'

'No!' For all his haste the factor stopped. 'On Mr Echlin's land?'

Neil shrugged. 'How can I tell? It was all a wilderness to me.'

They had arrived at the rowan-treed avenue that led to Rathard House.

'Thank ye, Mr Drummond,' said Neil. 'I can find my own way now.'

The factor hesitated as if he would like to have accompanied the young man. 'Aye,' he said turning on his heel, 'no doubt but we'll meet later.'

The avenue rose gently to a pair of gates, large and solid, flanked by a postern. This massive wooden contrivance had been set into a circular earthwork of much earlier construction. Invading trees and brushwood had been torn from its flanks and the gaps sealed with stone and clay. Neil's encounter with Echlin had been brief, but this employment of the new and the ancient pointed to the man: resourceful at turning to advantage whatever lay to hand.

Rathard House was itself a feat of compromise. The stump of an earlier castle had been added to by recently built wings, each two windows wide. Neil mounted the whinstone steps to where a leaf of the main entrance stood open. A doorkeeper came forward to relieve him of bonnet and rapier.

'Step in,' said the man, 'I'll tell the laird you're come.'

The chamber in which Neil stood, the great hall of the original structure, was illuminated by high slits like gashes of light in the thick walls and the glow of the fire in the capacious hearth. As his sight adjusted to the shadows he saw in the far distance of the chamber, two figures, motionless, staring at him. One was a podgy lass in her teens, her tawny locks in the grip of a young elegantly dressed fellow. The sullen face she turned on Neil was streaked with tears. With a cry of rage and pain she freed herself and fled into the shadows. The young man came striding across the hall, kicking the dry rushes from under his feet. One of the hounds rose at the hearth as if to follow him, circled and settled again. His face pale, his mouth drawn down in a pucker of ill-humour, he swept past Neil without word or look. If that was a game, thought Neil, it was rough sport.

Left to himself Neil crossed to the hearth and the two hounds shifted obligingly to allow him a share of the warmth. Staircases, against the east and west walls led to a gallery running halfway around the main hall. Three or four doors opened from this gallery towards the rear of the house. As in the factor's office, the odour of new wood hung in the air. He stepped softly across and ran his fingers appreciatively over a new-turned handrail. There were also several pieces of fine furniture similar to what was left of the elegance of Balwhanny; there they were masked in grime and colly, here they glowed. He had barely regained his place when a door in the shadow of one of the staircases opened and Echlin appeared. He came forward briskly and pleasantly enough.

'Hunger didn't drive ye, young man.'

'I regret if I'm late, sir,' replied Neil, wondering in what manner his attendance could have been more prompt.

The laird waved him toward a small table set in the inglenook. 'We're early astir here, Mr Gilchrist. I don't suffer slug-a-beds.'

As if the words were a bidding, a serving-girl brought breakfast for the two. Echlin started on his food more intent, it seemed, in satisfying his hunger than his curiosity. At last he paused and took a swig from his cup. 'Well, young man, what's your mind this morning?'

'If I can be of use I would as lief stay.'

'You're not in any sense a fugitive?'

'No.'

Echlin examined his companion across the table. 'Too many young Scotsmen o' your kind cock their bonnets for London, or loiter at home, like drones destroying their own honey.'

There was little of that sweetmeat at Balwhanny, thought Neil. 'I must tell ye, sir, I have no capital or any craft that would be readily useful here.'

Echlin nodded as much as to say that such frankness might or might not weigh in the speaker's favour.

'For two years I read law at St Andrew's. I gave that up to help my father. It was a mistake. . .'

Echlin resumed his meal. His guest related how he had indeed set off for London, his meeting with the cottar family at the inn, how on a sudden impulse that he could not explain, he had decided to try his fortune in Ireland. There was no response from his listener and Neil picked up his knife again. Above him a door opened in the gallery. Looking up he saw a woman leaning on the handrail. She was, the young man guessed, about forty. He would have thought her handsome if he had not been immediately repelled by the arrogant air in which she scanned the hall. Her gaze ran over him with a chill indifference. Then she gathered her dark robe around her and was gone. Guiltily he lowered his eyes.

The laird had never turned his head. 'The Lady Echlin, Gilchrist,' he said, calmly mopping his plate with a fragment of bread.

To Neil there was a family likeness in the cold insolence of Lady Echlin and the fellow he had disturbed tormenting the girl. 'I fear, sir,' he said, 'that I may have intruded on two members of your household when I arrived.'

Echlin drained his cup. 'Likely my elder son, Hamilton, and his sister. They leave tomorrow if God grants us guid weather. Anne for Scotland, he to take up his duties in his Grace's army.'

There was a sudden irruption at the main door. Three or four tradesmen, laden with tools came bustling in.

Echlin rose abruptly. 'Come, Mr Gilchrist, we're holding back the work.' They had barely risen when the serving-lass began to clear the table. 'Your mistress was seeking ye, girl,' said the laird.

Before Echlin and Neil had gained the open the hubbub of hammer, chisel and saw sounded through the house. On the ancient rath men were busy raising and strengthening the earthwork.

'I understand, sir, that one of the conditions of your undertaking is that you should raise a defence around your house?'

'That's so.'

'A defence against. . .?'

'The Irish, Gilchrist,' Echlin did not seem prepared to enlarge on this.

'Ye were fortunate to find so much left by earlier hands.'

'I would be a fool not to turn their labours to my advantage.'

Neil had some small difficulty in steering himself and his sword through the narrow postern.

The laird grinned sardonically. 'Ye came well accoutred against your stroll from Drummond's house, young man.'

'I was reluctant to leave my sword there. It would have looked as if I had come to roost.'

The other stopped. 'Ye mean you're standing in all ye own?'

'I had to borrow a nightshirt from the factor.'

Echlin resumed his steady pace. 'Why did ye not complete your studies?'

'I had barely funds enough to live at college and none at all to fund a practice even if I had finished. Then I was needed at home. . . at Balwhanny.'

'How did ye employ yourself there?'

'Since my mother's death the house had fallen sadly into disrepair.' He glanced at the man striding beside him. 'My father has neither the means or the will to put matters right. My brother who inherits. . . my brother is an ill man. . .'

Echlin apparently felt no call to express sympathy. 'Ye haven't answered my question.'

'In my grandfather's day Balwhanny was well wooded. It had fallen away since his time. When I returned home I tried my hand at clearing and planting.'

'With what result?'

'On limited means with success,' said Neil firmly.

After a few paces the laird asked: 'The MacIlveens, were they tenants of Balwhanny?

'No. As I said I met them by chance on the road.' Neil felt that the question had little to do with what was going on in Echlin's mind. But what those thoughts were he could not surmise.

6

The clatter of cooking-pots wakened Meg. Never having known what it was to rise second in the morning, she hastened to excuse herself to the lodge-keeper.

'Haud your tongue, decent woman,' cried Rushin Coatie, 'the cock has barely closed his neb!'

Grace said and breakfast over, the family gathered outside. They examined the unfamiliar landscape with curiosity and apprehension. Sorley, between the horses' heads, sniffed the keen air and watched life stir among the cabins. Housewives let out their fowl, feeding them in arcs of grain cast from their aprons; men came to the doors to scratch, eye the sky, gather spades, billhooks, tethers, for the day's labour.

The youth eyed the plump busy fowl appreciatively. 'They feed corn to their chuckies here?' he asked Rushin Coatie.

'The guid Lord blessed us with full sacks last year.'

Meg also was scrutinising the poultry. 'What class o' fowl was that in the broth, last night?'

'You'll no find its like in that flock. It was an auk. In time, your menfolk will fetch ye one from the lough. They come cheap.'

'An auk?'

'Aye, one o' them black lang-neckit birds ye see skelpin o'er the water.'

Ellen gave a cry and vanished behind a bush. She reappeared wiping her chin with her hand.

'Lord help ye, daughter,' said Rushin Coatie, grinning, 'have ye boked up your breakfast? Hut tut, I'm 'feard you'll need a strong wame to bide here.'

'What o' the ewe?' asked Sorley, impatient to be about the business of the day.

'Leave it. I'll have Dugal, the caddy from the forge, skin it for ye.'

'Take of it what will serve ye, guidwife,' said Meg magnanimously.

'That was my intent, guidwife,' returned the lodge-keeper. 'Now, off with ye to Dan Drummond.'

Mr Drummond half-rose from his chair to watch the family assemble themselves, their animals and chattels outside his office. He opened the door and summoned Alexander in. The others pressed around the doorway.

Mr Drummond seated himself. 'Mr Echlin says ye may take over Barclay's place, MacIlveen. There's about two-three acres and a bit o' a cottage.'

'What o' the rent, Mr Drummond?'

'Willing labour, guidman,' a voice said.

Meg and her children fell back to allow Echlin and Neil enter the office. Outside, Sorley again edged forward to overhear the talk.

Echlin seated himself. 'Alexander MacIlveen?'

'Aye, sir.'

'Well, MacIlveen, you and your family will diligently work the land you're given. Do that to my satisfaction and you'll be free of rent for two years.'

Alexander was about to speak when the factor plucked his sleeve to keep silent.

'When called on you and your family will give me three days labour each quarter.'

'Aye, willingly. . .'

'What ye need in tools, seed and plants, you'll seek from Mr Drummond, to be paid out of your first crop. Timber you'll find aplenty, but you'll first seek permission to fell. Anyway, all this you'll see plainly when Mr Drummond takes ye to the holding.'

The cottar, bonnet clasped to breast, tried to express his understanding of the offer. Then he turned to Neil. 'What of the horses, Mr Gilchrist?'

'Ye may be the first to need them, Alexander. We'll come to

some way that's convenient to both.'

'And the gun?'

'Aye, for the time being.'

Drummond, like a man whose memory had been pricked by this mention of arms, rummaged in a corner. He brought forth two long-handled pikes, their slender wicked heads looking new-forged. As he left with the cottar and his son, he thrust these into their hands, with the news that they would be charged as tools.

'Tools?' Neil looked at Echlin.

'Here – as tools, Gilchrist.' The laird studied the young man. 'For someone unsure of his destination, ye came well-furnished.'

'The horses? There was no other way I – they could have travelled from the coast. I was the only one with money in his pocket.'

'Livestock's aye welcome.' The laird settled himself more comfortably. 'I'll accept your word,' he said, 'that you're not fleeing from the law.'

'Ye have it, sir.' Neil began to rummage in his jacket. 'I have a letter from a notary acquainted –'

'Enough. I have your word young man. I've been listening to your story –'

The door was thrust open and Dan Drummond came in. He glanced sharply from Neil to the laird. Good God, thought Neil, he thinks I'm after his damned ledgers and quills.

Echlin sat up. 'Barclay's holding must be nearer than I remembered,' he said displeased.

'I thought to send Dugal of the smiddy wi' the family –' began the factor.

'It would have been more in my interest to see to it yourself,' said the laird curtly. Neil shifted in discomfort and wished himself elsewhere. As Drummond turned to go his master added, 'But now that you're here I need your counsel as to how we can best make use o' this young man.'

The factor had no ready advice. Echlin addressed himself to Neil. 'I've much woodland here. It needs tending. If you're willing I'll appoint ye my – my arborist, eh?' The look that the laird turned on Neil conveyed his satisfaction with the idea and the coinage.

'Yes, I'm willing – if ye think I'm fit for the task.'

'That's for you to prove. Don't we need such an overseer, Dan?'

Scenting an encroachment on his office, he nodded glumly.

The response in no way pleased the laird. He took a turn round the office. 'Lady Echlin,' he began, 'wishes a watermill built to take advantage of a grain harvest like last year's. You, Gilchrist,' and he nodded at Neil, 'will see to a supply of proper timber. You, Dan, will set a fair spread o' duty-days among those fit to help with the construction. Now, what more is needed?' His listeners kept a discreet silence. 'A running stream – not standing water.' Echlin's voice was harsh, the heavy ring on his finger clacked on the table as he emphasised each word. 'No still water – and no still men. I'm accountable to our liege lord, and to my family, to make Ravara thrive. And it will, for my fortune lies wholly in it.' Now he directed his words to the factor. 'The duties I delegate to my servants are no auld wife's barley cake to be broken into crumbs and squabbled over. What we lack here, Dan, is not labour but labourers. And the chiel, gentle or simple, who has no stomach for the task, would be better out o't.' The laird paused to view the two men. 'I trust I dinna hae tae boil my kale twice, gentlemen?' The homely saw was given teeth by the manner of its delivery.

The other two nodded. They understood. What Neil had feared, an admonition of the factor, embarrassing to witness, had turned out to be as much a caveat as to his own future performance in this community.

'Now,' the laird turned his attention to Neil, 'at times you'll need men. The factor will see to that. And a beast under ye. Take one of your horses back from the cottar. And unless ye want to break a limb in the woods get rid of that damned sword. Get yourself a shorter blade – a guid dirk. And a petronel when you're on horseback.'

Neil unbuckled the rapier. 'It's of little use, for I can't take it from its sheath.'

'Let me have it.'

Clamping the weapon between his knees, Echlin grasped the hilt with one hand and the sheath with the other. With a scream the blade came free. He feathered it in the air. 'A bonny rapier. Why did ye allow it to rust?'

'I borrowed it from an innkeeper on the road.'

The laird paused to read something close to the hilt. 'Then it has come home. See: "Nicol Gilchrist *Per angusta ad augusta*".' He handed the weapon back.

The young man eyed it, smiling. 'My uncle Nicol. . .'

'He travelled the same road?'

'Aye, on a day long past. He's dead these ten years and more. No doubt he meant to return for it.'

The discovery had worked a subtle change in the other two. Echlin scrutinised the young man with a livelier, if guarded interest. The factor saw the social gap widen between the newcomer and himself.

The laird handed over the scabbard. 'It's a good blade. It deserves a better edge. Leave it with Ronane the smith. Now, Daniel, go this time to see if the cottar family have reached Barclay's. And take Gilchrist so that he may recover his nag.'

The laird's astute employment of their names put the factor in better humour. He bounced to his feet, beckoned Neil, and led the way down the glade path along which they had dragged the dead wolves. A sturdy lad, in the fritters of breeches and shirt, was carrying a pail of water into the smithy. From within came the strokes of a hammer on metal, now belling, now flat and jarring.

The hammering ceased. They heard the clink as the tool was laid on the anvil. Neil did not expect a man of mean physique,

61

but he was surprised at the stature and demeanour of the figure that bowed under the smithy lintel to step into the morning light.

'Ronane, this is Mr Neil Gilchrist. The laird has appointed him as arb. . .' Drummond turned to Neil.

His appeal went unheeded. 'Ronane,' Neil said pleasantly enough, 'Mr Echlin requires ye to clean and put an edge on this blade.'

The smith took the sword and, with even less effort than that of the laird, drew it. As he examined the blade Neil examined him. There was something disconcerting about the carle. One could be tempted to deal him more advertence than his occupation warranted. The leather apron that fell from his shoulders to his knees was mottled and scorched, holed in places. He wears it like a coat of mail, the young man thought.

The smith fingered the weapon delicately. He surveyed Neil with a cool appraising gaze. 'It's a good blade.' The tone was that of one addressing no more than an equal.

'That's my understanding.'

'I'll tend to it.' As Neil watched the smith retreat into the gloom his eye caught a graceful outline half-shadowed, half-illumined by the glow of the fire, a shape that was no part of a smithy's furnishings.

Fretfully Mr Drummond turned on the boy. 'Have ye a nag tethered at the back?'

'Aye.'

'Fetch it. Mr Gilchrist and me are for Barclay's.'

Neil had no wish to ride pillion with the factor. 'It's a fine morning, Mr Drummond. If ye don't think it too far, I'll prefer to walk. On the way ye can point out those places ye think should have my attention.'

The factor glanced at him suspiciously. 'They wouldn't be on this road. But if you've a mind to walk, let us walk,' and off he set at a pace.

He was in bad humour, the factor. Neil, a pace or two in the rear, was puzzled and amused to see his head jerk as he emitted a string of sounds which the young man eventually recognised as aye – aye – aye. He overtook his companion. 'Mr Drummond. . .'

'Eh, that scarecrow! The insolence o' the Deil's buckie wi' his "aye" and "aye" to his betters! Heth, Gilchrist, I tell ye that the factor has a hard row to hoe where tenants and servants are gathered from all the airts, leaving Heavens kens what infamy ahint o' them!'

'Why,' said Neil chaffingly, 'is the callan an evil-doer?'

'No,' cried Mr Drummond. 'But like master, like man! He's Ronane's shadow. And that reminds me, Gilchrist,' continued the factor pettishly, 'ye didn't back me when I tried tae describe to Ronane the office the laird put on ye –'

'I have no call to explain my presence to a blacksmith, Mr Drummond.'

A moment's thought and the factor accepted this with approval. 'You're right, young sir, we have *our* place and the carle and his like have theirs.' But a short distance and Mr Drummond's sanguine assurance had faded. 'Och,' he groaned, 'the man's mair than a smith.'

'A farrier, then?' queried Neil lightly. 'Did I see a curved wand in the smithy? It looked like wood to me.'

'Ye saw a bow – a war bow.'

Neil glanced quizzically at the other. 'Left, no doubt, to be restrung.'

'It's no plaything, Gilchrist. Ronane could pin a man's bonnet tae his head at a hundred paces and more.'

'Come, factor, ye didn't see him kill a man with that thing?'

'No, but to amuse the laird I've seen him split a herd's staff at that distance. And I've seen him nail a running stag as neat as Mistress Drummond skewers a leg of mutton.'

'Where did he pick up the weapon – and the skill to use it?'

'From the savages in Virginia.'

Neil stopped to stare at the factor.

Drummond smirked, pleased with the effect of his words. 'What I'm trying to insense in ye, Gilchrist, is that ye shouldn't take Ronane on the strength of a leather apron —'

'He has been in Virginia?'

'He went there in the late Queen's time, found himself ajee once too often wi' authority — blood was spilt — and came back. He served for a time as an officer under the laird.'

'And Mr Echlin brought him here?'

'He had to. The law in Scotland would hae taken Ronane up.'

'It must have been a heinous deed that drives such a man to hide in a smithy's cot.' The words were barely out of his mouth before the young man recognised them as injudicious. He stepped hastily forward to distance himself from the matter.

If the factor had anything to add it was cut short by a man stumbling out of the scrub on to the path a few yards ahead of the two. The newcomer, trailing an odour of liquor, passed Neil and placed himself squarely before Mr Drummond.

'I'm on my road to see ye, factor.'

'Not now, McBratney,' said Mr Drummond testily. 'I've business.' The factor made a dab to the left on the narrow path, then to the right, only to find himself effectively blocked by the appellant.

Neil, unable to proceed without Drummond's guidance stepped aside, out of sight but within earshot.

'One o' my beasts has fallen sick —'

'Ech, man, what o't?'

'A guid milking cow. We couldn't rise her in the byre this morn.'

'Why come to me? I canna cure her. Tell your tale to Calum Wishart —'

'This is no for Wishart, factor. It's that auld witch, Rushin Coatie —'

'Watch your words, McBratney!' There was sharp alarm in Drummond's voice.

'My woman saw her go by our place, yestere'en. She's put the evil eye on my beast.'

'I'm warning ye, McBratney. Her Ladyship will no take kindly to such wild talk. You'll be well-advised to heed my advice and see Calum Wishart.'

There was no response. Mr Drummond, his face creased in exasperation, joined Neil.

'I could not but overhear that, factor. An irksome start to the day.'

Mr Drummond perked up at the note of sympathy. 'Tam McBratney? An honest enough loon but very querimonious and much given to liquor. He has a poor house, too many bairns to feed and a wife that's aye girning. If he doesn't act with sense he's likely to lose a good animal. Come, this is our road.'

They began the ascent of a long and gentle incline.

Neil thought that what had passed in the encounter with the cottar was as safe a topic as any to pursue. 'As ye said, it's wild talk to accuse the old woman –'

Mr Drummond rounded on him. 'No, Gilchrist, that was *not* what I said. I warned McBratney against accusing the auld carlin in or out of her Ladyship's hearing. It was Lady Echlin that employed Rushin Coatie as keeper of the lodging-house. She doesn't take kindly to folk crossing her in her decisions. If the Deil himsel' came for that sooty beldame he'd get short shrift, I warrant ye!'

'Auld women,' began Neil sententiously, 'don't make alliance with demons. It's coofs like McBratney start such talk.'

Mr Drummond gave him a cool look. 'Saving your presence, young man, but there's mightier mortals than you or me differ on that. I have looked into King James's *Demonology in the Form of a Dialogue* and his *News from Scotland*. The laird has them among his books. I doubt not but he'll let ye read them if you're so inclined.'

Uncertain as to how Echlin viewed such works from the

royal pen, Neil thanked the factor for the information and Mr Drummond, having again established his authority, was content to trudge onward in silence. They had almost reached the brow of the hill when Neil asked:

'This Calum Wishart – a man skilled in the treatment of livestock?'

Mr Drummond let a tee-hee of a laugh escape. 'A physician, Gilchrist, a physician that doctors all here from man to mouse. But he's mair than that –' then realising that the words had a familiar ring, he checked. 'But you'll meet him. . . you'll meet him in due course of time.'

7

The two men paused on the lip of a broad sweep of ploughland and pasture, that dipped to a waterlogged hollow then rose again to a farther and distant brow of tangled woodland. Two-thirds of the way up this arable stretch, between two cabins stood a cluster of men and women.

'The MacIlveens' new neighbours, factor?'

'Aye, some of the Purdie family.'

As he advanced again at Drummond's leisurely pace Neil saw that the peasants stood in a semi-circle before a stubby, sombrely-dressed figure who appeared to be haranguing his audience. He was a person of consequence for the men had removed their headgear, Alexander, as usual, clutching his bonnet to his breast. A flat wide-brimmed hat shadowed the orator's face, his cloak hung down to his boots. Neil was irresistibly reminded of a wether-bell.

'The Reverend Mr Turnooth?'

'Aye.'

The young man, curious as to how the cottar family fared, would have approached closer but Mr Drummond halted him.

'I'm all for the Good Word, but no over-greedy. We'll bide here.'

Neil glanced at him. The minister and the factor, another snag under the surface of Ravara?

The cleric removed his hat, the tenants bowed their heads. The prayer, rising and falling in vehement entreaty, came faintly to the two onlookers. There was a strangeness about this gathering in the limpid morning air. All around was activity in the small world cleared in the brooding woodlands. But there was a rightness about it satisfying to the hearts of its partakers. Neil had learned that Alexander would not yoke a horse or Meg claim a strange roof over her head without the warranty of Jehovah.

There was a closing 'amen', bonnets were pulled on, the cottagers drifted away, a briskness noticeable in Sorley Mac-Ilveen's movements, as one impatient to be at a task waiting too long.

The Reverend Mr Turnooth was descending the gentle slope. A short man approaching you is always at a disadvantage, thought Neil. But the minister achieved some dignity by stepping slowly, setting down his square-toed boots firmly from under his long skirts. There was no more than a cool cordiality on the face under the shallow clerical hat.

'Good morn tae ye, reverend sir.'

'And to you, Mr Drummond,' rejoined the minister, his eyes on Neil.

'This is Mr Neil Gilchrist, taken into the laird's employment. The Reverend Mr Turnooth. . .'

Mr Turnooth brushed aside any formality of an introduction. 'I understand that ye succoured the MacIlveen family in their journey here.'

'Nothing more, Mr Turnooth, than one traveller would offer another.'

'You didn't present a letter from your minister in Scotland.'

'If you're speiring after my bona fides, reverend sir,' replied Neil distantly, 'they are with Mr Echlin. Ye may inquire there.' He turned to the factor. 'I would like a word with the MacIlveens.'

'Why not?' said Mr Drummond, who seemed to have derived some quiet pleasure from the exchange.

'By your leave, gentlemen,' said Neil, aware that the minister swivelled on his square-toed boots to watch him go.

As he approached, the women who had stood with the MacIlveens in prayer hurried away to the cabin on the left. It was then that Neil saw that the upper end of the other dwelling was derelict, the thatch tumbled and the walls blackened as if by smoke.

The cause of young MacIlveen's impatience was now evident. His father and he, with the help of the neighbouring man, were already raising a gable of wattle and rushes between the ruin and the two rooms still habitable. Neil glimpsed Meg and her daughter redding out the larger compartment. Neither looked up at his approach.

'There's a lot o' daylight showing, Alexander.'

'It could be worse. This neighbour-man, Tam Purdie, is helping us bigg the gable-end again. This is Mr Gilchrist, Tam.'

A drooping lid partly concealed Purdie's left eye, but the stare of the good eye was sharp and disconcerting. The man's stooping height and his long muscular arms reminded Neil of a wind-torn thorn on a braeside. He drew himself up to match the cottar.

'What happened here, Purdie?'

'The Irish put fire to the place. Andra Barclay and his woman they kilt. The three bairns were burnt in the dwelling.' The speaker jerked his head. 'They're lying over there.' Over Purdie's shoulder Neil saw the soft undulations in the sward. 'That was afore the minister opened the graveyard down at the kirk.'

The young man's gaze rose to the tangle of wildwood above the cottages. He understood now why Echlin had instructed that the lodge-keeper should be kept in ignorance until the family had been shifted. 'How did you escape?'

'I have three sons —' Purdie snickered. 'We're a' buirdly fighting-men. We gave the wood-kernes a hot sup when they came at us.'

'And the Barclays. . .'

'The Irish fired their thatch. We couldn't get the puir souls out in time.'

The gentle breasts of the drumlins, some already banded by plough-work, stretched to the frown of the distant forest. Already half-a-day's labour lay behind the men and women busy in meadow, cowshed and coppice. After what he had been told there seemed to Neil an urgency in the strokes of axe and

69

billhook as if death as well as wildlife must be deprived of its lurking-place. Below him, close to the clustered heart of the settlement, he spotted a solid building. Although patched with newly-quarried stone it bore an earlier symmetry of style.

He pointed. 'The kirk?'

'Aye. The bishop's church afore that,' said Purdie.

The young man turned to Alexander. 'Can this house be made habitable?'

'With the Lord's help, sir, we'll make a home o't.' There was a resoluteness in the cottar's voice that stirred respect in Neil.

'The season's no too far gone,' said Purdie, 'for this guidman and his son to open a bit o' land. We'll lend him a plough.'

'And take which horse ye want, Alexander,' said Neil. 'Send Sorley down to me with the other.' He turned and almost trod on Mr Turnooth's toes.

Drummond was close behind. Plainly the factor and the minister had found little to converse about.

'Now that you've seen what the laird has given your acquaintances, Mr Gilchrist –'

'What the Lord has given, factor,' put in Mr Turnooth.

Drummond sighed. 'Aye, just so, minister. Are ye for back, young man?'

As the three turned to descend the slope, Neil said: 'Would it not be fitting to change the name of that holding, Mr Drummond?'

'There's no such name on the estate map,' answered the factor. 'Let Alexander MacIlveen prosper and the name'll change briskly enough.'

'He has gained himself doughty neighbours.'

'Aye, buirdly carles, Tam Purdie and his sons,' said Mr Turnooth. 'And well placed for any foray o' the Irish from that airt. I hope the MacIlveens are fit to stand with them.' Neil offered no opinion on this and the minister continued: 'I understand from the factor that ye have been given some authority in Ravara.'

'That's not how I see it, Mr Turnooth. I've been given a task.'

'Aye, as arborist, heh!'

'The word is Mr Echlin's choosing. It means simply –'

'I'm well-acquainted with what it means! A whimsy-whamsy title, but I'm pleased that ye see it as a task –'

'There are tasks of greater import ahead of us,' the factor cried impatiently. 'Her Ladyship is looking a cornmill.'

'A timely project,' said the minister, smoothing down the front of his cloak. 'As Pharoah took Jacob's counsel, let laird Echlin store food against the coming of the lean kine.'

'And where are we to get the storehouses, reverend sir?' queried the factor in a voice close to a sneer. 'And what of the guidfolk whose excess grain earns them an honest penny in Scotland?'

'Let us take your second puzzlement first, Daniel,' said Mr Turnooth with an air of forbearance. 'This coming Sabbath I'll ding some sense into the heads of my congregation. As to your first query let laird Echlin find use for the Gibeonites he allows to infest his lands against the laws of God and King.'

Neil could see that the biblical allusions meant something to the factor. Himself they escaped completely. 'Gibeonites, minister?'

'I mean the papist Irish, young man. The hewers of wood and drawers of water, if the factor here and his master obeyed the dictates of Providence.' He brought them to a halt where a path led away. 'Have ye a Bible, Mr Gilchrist?'

Neil confessed that a copy of the sacred work was not in his possession.

'I'll see one's put in your hands. Consult it, and you'll no be puzzled by the discourse of the literate folk in Ravara.'

'I have looked into the scriptures before today, sir,' retorted Neil.

'Then refresh your memory and revive your soul with a closer perusal. Even in the first psalm you'll find counsel on men – and trees, heh! Good day to ye, gentlemen.'

With mingled irritation and amusement Neil watched the stumpy figure of the minister disappear in the thickets that bordered the path. 'Does the manse lie that way?'

'It does. It's tended for him by his spinster sister, Mistress Tabitha, and at times a serving-lass.' Mr Drummond had found little to help him in his encounter with the minister. 'I wish,' he groaned, 'Almighty God would tether that guidman to his own concerns and duties.'

As yet Neil had seen few of Echlin's tenants, and there was not one, in speech or dress, that he could not have met on the roads of Lanark or Ayr. 'The Irish the minister spoke of – where are they?'

'Come,' said the factor, 'I'll show ye.' As they crossed the field Neil saw where a rock outcrop had been quarried. 'For the needs of the manor and the kirk?'

'Aye,' said the factor, 'but the needs o' the kirk came first.' Before them lay a tract studded with underwood that stretched to the distant glint of the lough. 'You'll find them in that airt,' said Mr Drummond.

'I see no ploughland.'

'The Irish *bodach*s are no much given tae the plough beyond their immediate needs. They make little use o' the soil the Lord God gave them. As to their cattle, they drive the herds across the country, in the summer grazing them in the hills, and down here to the loughside in the winter. They call it creaghting and the laird dislikes the practice –'

'Mr Echlin is their landlord?' asked Neil in surprise.

'Let me insense ye how matters are on that head, for it's better coming from the factor than any clishmaclaver you'll hear in other quarters. When the laird undertook to plant Ravara he found the Irish in this airt and he let them bide –'

'Against the conditions of the patent given him in Edinburgh?'

The factor hesitated. 'Maybe so, maybe so, but we don't delve and sow here with law books, young sir. Mr Echlin is a landlord as much as a soldier and he sees no sense in his tenants dropping their plough-stilts for their pikes at every alarm.'

'I can understand that. But what gain is in it for Mr Echlin?'

'Nothing other than what I've told ye – peace on his borders. To the Irish that'll accept it, he's given seed and plough-coulters, and some o' them raise as good crops as any in Ravara. But they're an ungrateful tribe. Come market day and not one grain of corn or one stirk's bellow goes through this estate.'

'But they must sell them in some manner –'

'Ech aye, man, they sell them – at Newry or Newtownards cattle fairs. And with them on that day goes Fiach or Turlough MacCartan as convoy.'

'With Mr Echlin's knowledge?'

'A gentleman's agreement, Gilchrist. Compromise is a rare and valuable commodity in this land.' The factor pointed again. 'Beyond that clump of woodland, the scope still held by the MacCartans marches with Ravara. The Irish drift back and fo'rrard across the boundary as suits them. And those are the buckies that Mungo Turnooth would hae me put to the building o' her Ladyship's mill! I might as well try tae yoke the mist.'

They turned to go. 'Did Mr Echlin and his company settle alone in this wilderness?'

'Heth, no. The laird and his lady have neighbours. Mr James Lowry took land at Ballymacashon some two years ago. And of late a Mr Luke Cordwaine has undertaken two thousand acres at Edenmore, just beyond us here. You'll no see much of Cordwaine's household. He's a Sassenach and her Ladyship is no over eager for his acquaintance.'

'Why,' asked Neil laughing, 'because he's an Englishman?'

'No, that's not the way o't. It's because his father was no more than a Birmingham brass-turner – although the story is that he's as rich as Croesus and on that account not unknown to King Jamie. Now, put an inch tae your stride, if ye please,' said the factor, himself stepping out vigorously. 'My belly's bose.'

Neil followed but halted suddenly. 'The wood-kernes that slew the Barclays were of the same tribe as. . .' and he gestured towards the scene they had left.

The factor nodded. 'Aye, ye could say that.'

'Dispossessed and those in possession, tenant and gill-ravager,' Neil muttered. 'Neighbours and bluidy enemies living cheek by jowl. There's no sense in it, Mr Drummond!'

But Mr Drummond's empty stomach was urging him homeward.

Neil too, was ready for his meal. Seated at the factor's table, coping as adroitly as he could with Mrs Drummond's chatter, he watched Una lift and lay the dishes. He wondered where this girl, neither peasant nor gentle, found her place in the sober world of Ravara. Mrs Drummond hinted that she had aspirations beyond it for her daughter. . . but her husband had informed Neil that the dominie had the laird's goodwill in all he undertook. There and then Neil resolved, if he ever gained a private existence in this place, to keep it out of the hands of the man and woman in Rathard House.

The factor reached for his hat. 'If you're ready, Mr Gilchrist,' he said.

Echlin and Angus Ross were waiting at the office. The laird listened to Drummond's report of the settling of the new tenants and approved that the Purdies showed willingness to be neighbourly. He turned to Neil. 'You've seen something of Ravara?'

'Only the worked parts, as yet. It occurred to me that ye might consider the making of a coney-warren.' As he spoke he felt the factor's gaze on him.

'What profit would be in that?'

'It would give ye meat and fells, sir. And lessen the damage to saplings.'

'What would it cost me?'

'It would take up about two acres of dry soil, a ditch thrown up to keep the rabbits in, trees planted and a hutch in the middle for the buck –'

'Ye seem to have the mechanics clear in your mind.'

'– I constructed one at Balwhanny, laird.'

Echlin considered the young man for a moment. 'Very well,' he said at last, 'recommend a site and draw me up a statement of materials and what labour would be required.'

Neil acknowledged the charge, wishing, now that it was too late, that he (or the laird) had drawn Drummond into the business. He was aware that the factor's gaze was still upon him. The laird then addressed Ross. 'Can ye find room for Gilchrist at the schoolhouse, Angus?'

'Readily. There's a bed in the other room.'

'Wishart can spend mair nights in his own bothie.'

The dominie smiled in response. 'He can, sir.'

'The auld wife, Chrissy Maclennan can tend ye both.' The laird turned to Neil. 'It'll serve ye till ye find a place for yourself, Gilchrist.'

'As ye say, sir.' Neil moved to the door. 'I bid ye goodnight, gentlemen. Mr Ross, I'm at your pleasure.'

The schoolhouse door was ajar. As Ross pushed it open a figure outlined in the hearthlight gave a final stir to a porridge pot and rose to meet them. Ross closed the door firmly.

'Calum – Calum Wishart, this is Neil Gilchrist.' said Angus Ross.

The two men acknowledged each other.

'Until he finds a place the laird has lodged him here.' The dominie turned to Neil in the friendliest manner. 'And he's welcome. Seat yourself, Neil.'

Stretching, Calum Wishart took a book from the mantelshelf and placed it in Neil's lap. 'A Bible from Mr Turnooth, sir.'

Neil sat up. 'The reverend gentleman has a good memory.'

'On some matters, infallible,' replied Wishart. 'I've delivered the volume, Mr Gilchrist. Be so good as to handle it with care.'

'I'm as aware of its material as of its inherent value, Mr Wishart,' responded Neil. He turned it over. 'It's been well-thumbed.'

'Read the name in it,' said Wishart.

Neil turned the cover and read out *'Tabitha Robertson Turnooth.'*

'The minister's sister – a guid lady,' said Ross.

'But not one of the Elect – which is why the book has been so thoroughly perused,' added Wishart.

It was a matter that Neil could happily have left for another time, if ever. But with the sacred work on his knee he felt that a polite interest was called for. He turned to the dominie.

Ross also looked as if the subject need never have been raised. He frowned reproachfully at Wishart but that worthy was busying himself with the potstick.

'The story is that Mistress Tabitha's father, himself a man of the cloth,' began the dominie, 'came to her when she was little more than a lass and said to her: "I have travelled lang in prayer wi' the Lord, daughter, but I have no surety that ye are o' the Elect."'

'Ah,' said Neil as one punctuating a tale.

'Ye came on the Doctrine of Predestination when ye were at college, Mr Gilchrist?' Wishart inquired.

His face was grave but Neil sensed a squeak of sardonic amusement in the voice. 'Very likely. But I can't say that it had us tossing and turning on our pillows.' He yawned. 'There's more to the story, Angus?'

''Twas her name in the Bible started me, Neil. I wouldn't want ye to misunderstand the guid lady's nature when ye meet. Fearful of damnation, from that day out she behaved as one of God's Elect to convince herself that she was indeed one. Here, among the people of Ravara, from the meanest cottar to the folk at Rathard House, she's known for her willing help, her goodness of nature, her wise counsel –'

'Gentlemen,' said Neil reaching forward, 'if ever the need arises I'll avail myself of the guid Tabitha's help. Wishart, ye did wrong to bring me her Bible. Take it back. No, I insist!' and he thrust the book forcibly into the other man's hands. 'I see I

76

should have bought a Bible in your village instead o' a musket.'

'For why, Mr Gilchrist, should Mungo Turnooth wish to bestow the volume on ye?' asked Wishart.

'I can't recall. . . I was with the factor at the time. . . for the health of my soul, I suppose. No,' he was sufficiently amused to stir upright in his chair. 'No, as a pass to the literate society of Ravara.' He sank back '. . . Or words to that effect.'

'Words spoken to you, but aimed at the good factor. Dan hath never fed of the dainties that are bred in a book. He hath not eaten paper, as it were. He hath not drunk ink.'

Neil blinked at the frayed figure. I could debate that, he thought. Dan Drummond has no equal here as a consumer of ink. 'On the matter of the factor looking into books, I think you're somewhat agley, Wishart. He tells me he's read the King's discourses on demonology –'

Wishart gave a dismissive gesture. 'No more than primers for his occupation. As the factor he carries a periapt in his pouch to reassure some gawk who swears his beasts have been blinked.'

'When he was faced by one such this morning he put more faith in your physic.'

'What was the cottar's name?'

Resenting the tone of the query and having forgotten the man's name anyway, Neil drew deeper into the chair. Through half-closed eyes he surveyed the figure on the other side of the hearth. The locks and beard that framed his face were wispy, bleached like wheat straw. His clothing and footwear told of rough tracks and briery snares. But there was no air of the simple-minded cully about him; the expression was alert, quizzical, that of a man secure in a store of knowledge, hard-gleaned. I don't much care for this fellow, thought Neil. If the schoolhouse is a roost for nightbirds, the sooner I find a place of my own the better.

8

To the MacIlveens, the weather, bright or dour, streamed from the hand of God. It was for man to labour without stint under the glancing sunlight and drying winds of spring. On their knees after supper the family asked for clement weather on the morrow and the Lord granted their prayer. Within a fortnight the holding was ploughed and harrowed and as ready as any in Ravara to receive seed.

'My certes,' said Tam Purdie rubbing his leathery palms together in approbation, 'but you're hardy folk, Alexander.'

'God was wi' us, neebor.'

To save candle they went to bed in the gloaming. Meg and Ellen cooked kale runts rejected by the beasts. The oatmeal was spooned like sacred provender from the meal-ark to the cooking-pot. To leave food uneaten was sinful. With their needles the woman and the girl held together the tatters of clothes that hung on their menfolk. Stones and morning frost wounded the feet of Alexander and his son. Their least broken shoes were kept for walking to the kirk twice on the Sabbath. The oats sown, Ellen took her turn in dragging the harrow to hide the seed from the birds.

Their existence thawed with the season. Step by step Meg and Ellen entered into the system of barter that held in Ravara. They had little to offer, but their bearing and reputation won them credit. Ellen's skill as a needlewoman became known. She returned home from households in the plantation carrying food and occasionally a little money.

One morning Sorley went out to find a delicate green braird shining across the cornfield. He called his father. Carefully the two studied the ground. There was no thick drift of rising blades in one place and sparseness in another. Alexander had sown with a cunning hand. 'Give thanks, son,' he said and

Sorley bent his neck in veneration of the soil.

Dan Drummond, on his rounds, looked across the family's corn, scratched his chin and rode off without a word. Next morning he was back, summoning Alexander and Sorley indoors. He laid a pouch of money on the table. 'The laird is willing tae buy your corn crop.'

Alexander hesitated, at a loss. 'The growth's no far fo'rrard, Mr Drummond.'

'Far enough for me to judge.'

'Aye. . . well. . .' the cottar looked at the faces of his family.

'Take it, father!' cried Sorley eagerly.

'We don't want to get into debt, factor,' said Alexander troubled.

'What debt, man? Don't ye see Mr Echlin is offering this out o' guidwill towards you and your family?'

'Lairds of guidwill are no o'er thrang in our acquaintance,' said Meg drily.

'You're living in a different place now, guidwife. Mr Echlin is pleased with your endeavours.'

'We wanted to harvest our first crop, Mr Drummond.'

'And so ye will, man, so ye will. You'll keep the thrissles down, mow the crop and stook it for carting. Mr Echlin would buy it from ye in the end, anyway. In the meantime ye have the siller in your hand.'

The money wrought much the same effect on the family as the spring weather on their fields. Carefully doling it from the drawstring purse, they mended in body and spirit. The hunger hollows in their cheeks filled out. Father and son were still astir at scraich of cockcrow, but now they handled themselves like men assured of their standing among their neighbours. Meg and Ellen found their way to Newtownards and brought back ends of frieze and crewel. Busying herself, Ellen had her family clad again in some decency. A full-uddered goat appeared, tethered in the outfield and a scatter of poultry at the doorstep. Contemplating these signs with prayerful humility, Meg was assured that the Lord Jehovah looked favourably on the strenuous labour of her family. An elder tree that she asked from Neil Gilchrist she planted beyond the dwelling to ward off evil spirits.

Echlin gave Neil money, but not through the factor. The payment was made the day after the laird had inspected the beginnings of the coney-warren. Having heard that the cottar family had been given a purse on the promise of their crop, Neil concluded that Echlin paid on results of labour he could see and said as much to Angus Ross.

'No, I don't think that's the way o't. I think Mr Echlin will pay you as he pays me, on set dates, and,' the dominie grinned, 'Dan Drummond will enter it in one of his muckle ledger-books. Are ye satisfied with your wage?'

'I can't tell. I've no landmark to go by. Anyway, where can I spend it?'

'In the summer ye could visit Scotland –'

'That's not my intent,' said Neil curtly.

Ross looked at him for a moment, then briskly said, 'This is market day in the village. We'll ride in this afternoon and you can buy yourself decent footwear and the making of a suit.'

With school closed for the day, the two horsemen set off, a temperate breeze nudging them on their way. Ross had purchases to make: paper, ink and sundries for the school, drugs, salves and the like listed by Wishart.

'Heth, and ye surprise me,' said Neil. 'I thought he concocted his nostrums from the meadows and the ditches.'

'Calum isn't a hedge-doctor, Neil. Or rather, he can use simples when no more is called for. But when the need arises he draws on *materia medica* of a more subtle nature.'

'And where did he learn his trade?' asked Neil sceptically.

'From his professors in Glasgow. But, like many another, he didn't stick to his books.'

Neil kept silent.

'Ye don't warm to Calum?'

'I would more readily if I knew what he was at,' answered Neil. 'There are times when I think he is talking over the heads of the company. That irks me. Out of him comes some flether o' words like – like a worked stone set in a dry-stone wall –'

Ross laughed, delighted. 'As well it might! They come from orations, essays, play-books –'

'I hope he has his cures as glib.'

'Years back he earned a living with other men's words. He was a playactor in London. More precisely, a physician to a travelling company, pressed at times to carrying a halberd or speaking a line.'

'London. . .?' Neil felt a stab of resentment. Everyone he met here seemed to have lived for a time in the greater world. . . to have come into possession of more than one skill. The track narrowed so that for a time the two young men rode in single file. When Neil drew abreast again he asked: 'Did the laird bring Wishart here?'

'He walked in among us one day and Mr Echlin, learning what he was, give him shelter.'

Neil, in a jaundiced mood, wondered if 'shelter' meant that Echlin had taken Wishart, on his arrival, into Rathard House. He didn't ask. At that moment the amiable nature of his companion was not to his taste. A flow of colour caught his eye. A pretty young woman, dressed in green, came forward from a cottage door. Her hand resting on the gate, she smiled on the passing horsemen. Neil plucked at his bonnet and she bowed. He would have drawn rein but Ross was proceeding on his sober way. It was impossible for the schoolmaster to have missed the woman in her frilled and verdant gown. Swearing mildly, Neil overtook him.

'A handsome lass.'

'Aye – handsome,' Ross agreed readily enough. Pride kept Neil from saying more.

As they rode into the village Neil remarked on its growth.

'Aye, there's folk arriving daily, Scots, mostly.'

'But not seeking land?'

'Serving the needs of them who do. A profitable occupation forbye being virtuous, as Mungo Turnooth puts it,' added Ross with a grin.

There was a considerable coming and going of men, women and children across the wide marketplace. Neil's attention was drawn to a group at the north corner. Echlin was there and facing him Neil recognised the younger of the MacCartan men. Ronane stood a few paces withdrawn from the laird and behind MacCartan stood a heavily-built fellow that Neil guessed was of the Irishman's household. Ross and he dismounted, handing the reins into the keeping of a penny-earning urchin. Echlin raised his hand in summons. As the two approached across the wide square Neil was struck by the likeness of the Irishman and the laird. They stood aloof effortlessly from the bustling market-folk. If there was animosity between the two it was concealed in a polite deference to what was being said. There was a difference in age and MacCartan wore the finer clothes, but their bearing was mirrored. They could have passed as kin, possibly brothers.

Tack tent, said Neil to himself, for this man will not allow that we have met before. And on Echlin's introduction it was as he had foreseen. MacCartan and he exchanged the briefest of salutes.

'Ye employ a keeper of trees, Mr Echlin?' said MacCartan lifting his gaze from Neil. 'Never in a hundred years, to my knowledge, has such a reeve been known in the oak-groves of the Dufferin.'

'Ye have an enviable memory, MacCartan.'

'It is a family memory, Echlin,' said the Irishman with a thin smile. 'And I shall add my scroll to it and my son, Turlough Óg, after me. For you and I are like the sun and moon. You govern by day, I by night.'

Echlin stared at him. 'That would be an unholy alliance – and not to be tolerated!' A moment and he had recovered his composure. 'Doubtless ye have business in hand. I bid ye good day, sir.'

Stiffly the two men parted and the laird led away Neil, Angus and Ronane.

'You, Gilchrist, find Crawfurd the tailor, tell him her Ladyship needs him and that he's expected at Rathard with his patterns, goose, needles and thread in a week's time.' It tickled the laird to recite the catalogue of the tailor's craft. He continued amiably: 'You, Ross, be spry in your purchases for I want ye both at John Bell's tavern within the hour. Come, Ronane.'

Neil watched them go. 'Ronane's a man with little to say for himself.'

'What call has he to talk and his master present? I'll direct ye to the tailor's and then go about my business.' As the two set off across the square Ross asked: 'What think ye of Turlough MacCartan?'

'That he's mastered the English tongue gey nimbly since I first met him on the road to Ravara. I thought for a moment there would be a set-to between him and Mr Echlin.'

'That's unlikely. Believe it or not, Neil, but each holds the other in esteem. They're much alike in nature.'

'"As the sun and the moon" as the Irishman put it. But true, I thought as much as I looked at them.'

'Yet governance forbids friendship,' said Ross. 'What's more, there could be bloodshed, whether those two will it or no. And your cottar family could bear the brunt o't.'

Neil had long given up explaining to the people of Ravara that he had no proprietory interest in the MacIlveens. Yet he felt his hackles rise at this threat of injury to Alexander and his family. 'For why?' he demanded brusquely.

'To the Irish there's something orra about that scope o' land the MacIlveens hold. At the top o' the brae a great flat stone o'erhangs it. I've been up there. It could have been a druidical altar – or a place of enthronement –'

'*Druids!*' exclaimed Neil.

'It's only surmise on my part,' said Ross defensively. 'But ye heard of the end the Barclays suffered.'

'Aye. . . but the Purdies were in that tulzie, too. I'll allow that you're better acquainted with these matters, Angus. I promise ye I'll have a word with Alexander MacIlveen.'

Tailor Crawfurd, scrambling down from a table where he and an assistant sat crosslegged, busily stitching, declared his pleasure at the visit of the two young men to his establishment; all the more so when he learned where they had come from. 'Feggs, from Mr Echlin's household, eh?'

Ross went about his errands, leaving Neil with the tailor. Measurements were taken, lengths of cloth adroitly displayed in the lane's daylight, textures fingered, a sober solid material, that won Mr Crawfurd's approval, chosen.

'Call in a week's time, Mr Gilchrist, and I'll hae a fit-on ready.'

'It's Mr Echlin's wish that ye come to Ravara.'

The tailor was taken aback. 'Ech, no,' he said fingering his mouth. 'I do that no longer. I'm a master tailor, not a journeyman.'

'I know nothing o' the niceties o' your craft, Mr Crawfurd. I only repeat Mr Echlin's words – and wait, that Lady Echlin would wish to see ye when you're at Rathard House.'

'Ech. . . well. . . it's not that I wouldn't oblige her Ladyship. But ye live at sicca distance. Your tracks are as crookit as a ram's horn, forbye the black woods full of wolves and wood-kernes. . . I tell ye, young sir, Mistress Crawfurd wouldn't close an eye. . .'

Neil plucked up his bonnet. 'The choice is yours, master tailor.' But he hesitated in the doorway. Was it right to leave the man in such a quandary? And what if he didn't turn up at Ravara? 'I tell ye what, Mr Crawfurd,' he said over his shoulder, 'I'll see to it that ye travel by daylight and that you're accompanied coming and going.'

'Ech. . . well now. . .' the tailor came forward but Neil was away, hurrying down the busy lane. A word to Echlin that perhaps Ronane could look to Crawfurd's safety. There was a mischievous pleasure in thinking of that taciturn individual riding escort to the tailor. He said nothing of this to Ross when they met at the pothecary's on their way to Bell's tavern.

Although the dining-room was crowded, Echlin had secured the personal attention of Bell the owner of the tavern. When food and drink were on the table and the tavern-keeper gone, the laird gave his reason for summoning the two young men. 'I require,' said he, 'that you two should set out my family tree on a presentable parchment.'

Neil and Ross glanced at each other.

'I've no knowledge of such matters,' said Ross.

Neil kept silent. Once upon a time his father had set him to trace a tincture of the noble house of Skene in the blood of the Gilchrists. Thankfully term time had called him away and when he returned to Balwhanny his father was pursuing other hares.

'It should be within the competence of college men,' said the laird impatiently. 'I'll let ye see what material I have. If ye need more, then one of ye may set out for Edinburgh or wherever such records are kept.' At these words a small cloud appeared on the horizon of Neil's mind. Echlin looked from one to the other. 'Well, what say ye? Are ye willing to undertake the task?'

The two protested they would undertake the task happily, the schoolmaster declaring that the long summer evenings should greatly facilitate the work.

In the market square dealers and hucksters were bringing down their stalls, wagons were setting off on homeward roads, villagers were drifting away in twos and threes.

'I wonder,' said Neil as the two young men rode out, 'what fancy the laird has to climb the family tree?'

'That I can't answer.'

'Could it be MacCartan's jibe on *his* lineage?'

'Ye may find in Edinburgh that Mr Echlin's line is of as high esteem as that o' the Irishman.'

Neil pulled sharply on his rein. 'Angus, it's not my intent to go to Scotland.'

'Why not?'

'Because I couldn't be in that airt without visiting my kin. And I couldn't slink past them. That would be craven. You may go.'

'I will not be away from my duties for that length of time. Of the two of us *you* could be easier spared at Ravara.' The dominie urged his horse on as if he would leave his companion.

Faith, thought Neil, here's a great pother about little. So put out was he by the schoolmaster's uncommon petulance that before he knew he found himself riding by the cottage where he had seen the girl in the green dress. She was again at the gate, drawn there, no doubt, by the sound of the approaching horsemen. Behind her a second young female bent negligently to a flowerbed in which there was as yet no life. The girl at the gate smiled, offering sweet invitation to idle. Neil pulled off his bonnet, frantically aware of the receding dominie. His nerve broke. He heeled his mount and rode on, bearing with him a flash of stoney-faced outrage. Drawing alongside Ross's horse he leaned into his companion's face.

'Did ye not see the lass smiling on ye!'

'Aye.'

'Then why ride on?'

'To deliver thee from that strange woman which flattereth with her words –'

'Damn it, Ross, ye never heard her voice. She did no more than smile on a passing stranger!'

'– as a jewel of gold in a swine's snout,' intoned Ross, 'so is a

86

fair woman which is without discretion.'

Neil drew away. 'I think you're out o' your wits, man,' he said at a loss for anything else to say. Muttering something about biblical cant he dropped to the rear.

The two were now travelling at a sharper lick than their early comradely outgoing.

I should have let him ride on, thought Neil, even if the laird has ruled that nobody from Ravara travels alone from the village. But he knew he wouldn't have done so. The ties were now too strong that bound him to Ross, to the schoolhouse, to the life at Ravara. The realisation filled him with gloom. Morosely he eyed the dominie. His abrupt rebuff of the damsels at the cottage encouraged speculation. On the other hand, as good as betrothed to the factor's daughter, nobody expected him to indulge in dalliance. He could have had a thought for me. He's no coof. He knows well that I dare not toy with a tenant's lass and there's not a woman of my station in the length and breadth of Ravara. Faith, I'll seek to make amends to that girl in the green gown. . . In more cheerful mood he spurred his mount to keep up with the smart pace set by the dominie.

They were dropping down the incline to the demesne entrance when they heard the hubbub of voices and the scurry of running feet. Men, women and children were streaming from fields and cottages to disappear in the dip beyond the factor's office.

The two young men stared at each other. 'What Deil's work is this?'

The clamour growing ever louder in their ears, they rode across the clearing in front of the dwellings, over the schoolhouse road, past Drummond's office until they were forced to draw rein on the verge of the throng clustered before Rushin Coatie's lodging-house. With his back to the door, swinging a musket, stood the cottar who had accused the old woman of witchcraft.

Neil sprang from his horse. He took a man by the elbow. 'What's the meaning of this splore?'

The cottar waved towards the demented figure with the gun. 'Tam McBratney has nailed auld Rushin Coatie in –'

'– and put sods on top o' her lum so the smoke canna get oot –' volunteered a boy.

'She'll choke in the reek, sir,' added a woman.

'Then why are ye standing here? Release her!'

The man freed himself from Neil's grasp. 'McBratney's full. He'll blow the heid off the first man that tries.'

'Where's Mr Drummond?'

The first woman had been carried away in the swirl of the crowd. Another answered. 'Him and the minister rode off at noon to the Donach slate quarry.'

Neil glanced around him. His eye fell on the schoolmaster. After a moment's hesitation he was about to call on his aid when a voice sounded in his ear:

'I'll take on McBratney wi' ye, Mr Gilchrist.'

He turned to meet the steady gaze of Dugal, the forge-boy. The tattered caddy had become a man overnight, he thought, an apprentice who had served his time to no ordinary master.

'As ye will,' said Neil. 'That gun may or may not be loaded – so step canny.'

One on either flank they threaded their way through the crowd. For all their caution their purposeful progress caught the eye of the crazed man in the doorway. He waved his musket threateningly.

'Tam,' the young blacksmith called, 'let the auld woman out.'

McBratney lifted the weapon on his forearm. 'Stand off, Dugal, or I'll blow ye baith to hell.'

Behind him Neil heard men and women stumble over each other to get out of range. He felt called upon to make some mark in this preposterous tulzie. 'McBratney, put down the musket and let us talk –'

88

The weapon came waveringly up to cover him. Both heard the click of the lock drawn back.

'Tam,' said Dugal, 'ye canna hope to kill us baith in the one loading.'

Neil shot an angry glance at him. The observation carried logic into the region of lunacy.

Dugal nodded in response. Great God, thought Neil, he expects us both to rush this madman. Sweat prickled on him as he measured the distance between himself and McBratney, seven, maybe nine paces. . .

Then, as he tensed to spring, behind him, with alarming rapidity, grew the beat of hooves. Horse and rider came hurtling down the incline, the people throwing themselves off the track to avoid being trampled. The horse was pulled up in a sprachle of stones and dust. Flinging aside a heavy cloak the rider dropped nimbly to the ground. It was Lady Echlin, in her hand a heavy whip, the lash curled round her knuckles. A pace or two and she was on McBratney, cutting the weapon from his hands, belabouring head and shoulders until he broke and ran under the chastisement.

Panting, Lady Echlin lowered the whip. 'Ye let matters get sorely out of hand, Mr Gilchrist,' she observed as she watched them tear open the door of the lodging-house.

'My lady, Mr Ross and I have but ridden in!' Neil protested, and wondered at being thus saddled with authority.

Two or three women, making soothering noises, were leading Rushin Coatie out. She leant heavily on her helpers, she reeled a little in her step, but Neil could have sworn that through the tangle of locks a sharp eye was fixed on her Ladyship.

'The auld beldam is playacting,' said her Ladyship crisply. Then in a high clear voice: 'Tend to her and redd up the lodging-house.' She sought until she found Tam McBratney, skulking in the crowd. She pointed her whip at him. 'You! That loon – how is he named?'

Those nearest the culprit quickly edged away. 'McBratney, m'lady. . . Tam McBratney. . .'

'McBratney? You'll answer for this, carle. Mr Gilchrist, help me mount.' In the saddle she looked down on Neil. 'If you have no urgent business, I'll have your attendance to Rathard.'

Neil dutifully hooked a finger in the bridle. That temerarious entrance into the thick of the crowd was still with him. 'Permit me to say, my lady, you are a bold horsewoman.'

His comment was received with approbation. 'My father, the earl of Finnart, aye kept an excellent stable and so did his forebears. Which brings me to what I have in mind. I want ye to set out, to good effect, my husband's family line.'

Surprised, Neil would have halted in his stride, but the horse, smelling its oats bucket, plucked him forward into an ungainly stumble.

'I learn that the King has knighted a William Herrick for cutting a hole in a great diamond worn by his Grace. It seems to me,' continued her Ladyship, 'that and more should kiss the shoulder of one who has cut a hole in this wilderness.'

Neil murmured agreement. 'The laird has voiced such a wish to us – I mean the dominie and me. We have undertaken to go through the relevant papers at Rathard –'

'That will not suffice,' said Lady Echlin. 'As a soldier my husband had to divest himself of much baggage at times. But ye will be given a letter to his kin at Dalkeith. There, and in Edinburgh if ye are so directed, ye will find ample information for the task –'

Neil brought the horse and himself to a halt. 'M'lady, I cannot go to Scotland.'

The lady looked down at him, disbelief turning swiftly to anger. '*Cannot*, Mr Gilchrist?'

'Yes, madam.'

'Cannot or will not?'

Neil barely checked a shrug. In his strait who could distinguish one from the other?

'What hinders ye – no, I'll not spier after that.' With a tug of the rein she freed the horse's head from his grasp. She leant forward, her handsome face pale. 'As I understand it, Gilchrist, Mr Echlin took ye in when ye had little on your back and less in your pouch. I've set my heart on this for the laird. If it slips away through your obduracy, ne'er count on me for aught in the future.'

Neil watched as she rode through the long reaches of the evening light until she vanished on the rowan-fringed avenue. Trudging back he was overcome by a great weariness with Ravara and all it held: with the schoolhouse, with Ross in or out of humour, with the sententious Wishart sprawled at the fireside. His evenings were empty. At the manse he suffered the dry sarcasms of Mungo Turnooth. To sit at the factor's table was to subject himself to Mrs Drummond's incessant prattle. There had been few invitations to take supper at Rathard House; after this encounter with her Ladyship they would be fewer.

He promised himself that Bell's tavern and the village streets would see him more often. There were good-looking lasses in Ravara. He had observed them in kirk and passed the time o' day as he rode about his business. But they were not for the likes of him. Any trifling or wantoness and the iron strictures of the kirk, its wakeful supervision of morals and conduct among his neighbours, would see to his chastening. He didn't need to have that spelt out. It was bred into his blood and bone. He grinned mirthlessly as he recalled her Ladyship's valuation of him on his arrival at Ravara. His only solace now was the money, laboriously translated into gold pieces, in the pouch at his bedhead.

9

Astride the roof-ridge of the cottage, Sorley MacIlveen viewed the limits of the family holding. To the north-east it marched with that of the Purdies. No outlet there. To the south the arable sweep of the hillside was abruptly broken by rocky knowes, a barrier to plough or spade. He didn't have to turn to see what lay at the bottom of the holding, a rushy hollow beyond the power of father and son to drain. Ahead, the dark forbidding boscage running over the brow of the hill.

'I need mair land, and by the Guid Man, I'll have mair land!' he said aloud, punching a handful of reeds into a rift in the thatch and clamping it with an osier scobe.

Three days later as Dan Drummond rode past the cottage, Sorley hailed him. The factor came to a halt.

'Mr Drummond, I want mair land to work.'

The factor looked down with a sardonic smile. 'Do ye, MacIlveen? And you with only a wheen of sheep on the whole outfield? I think your eye's bigger than your belly.'

'There's no money in sheep, ava. I want land for cattle.'

'And where are *they* to be found?'

'They'll be found when I have the grazing of them.'

From his saddle the factor studied the red-haired youth. He did not like him. He did not like the peremptory way in which he addressed his betters. But he knew it was not in his master's interest to discourage a cottar determined to prosper. 'More beasts on the holdings, more bairns in the crib, Dan. That's our orders,' the laird had said.

The factor turned to look up the slope of the land. 'Mr Echlin expects every tenant to make full use of what he's given.' He pointed to the growth topping the hill. 'Give them braes a shave up to the muckle great stone, MacIlveen. You'll have land in plenty then.'

The youth looked up morosely at the mounted man, 'Is that the best ye have to offer, Mr Drummond?'

'That's *all* I have to offer ye, callan,' said the factor. On his road back it dawned on him that young MacIlveen had never mentioned his father.

Sorley partly absolved himself by telling Alexander that it was the laird's will that they should clear all the upper hillside. The labour was not new to them for earlier in the year they had cut back some of the undergrowth that flourished like a beard around that strange protruding lip of rock. Fortunately, there was no heavy timber to fell and grub out. Father and son, with saw, billhook and sickle, hewed their way into the thicket, while Nicol, youngest of the Purdies, dragged the cuttings away for wood-ash.

One noon Sorley was disturbed in his labour by a stirring and rustling in a clump of hazel. A man was watching him from the depth of the thicket. The expression of the watcher was of such glowering malevolence that he stumbled back in fright. For a moment the two stared into each other's eyes. Then the intruder slithered backwards out of the bushes. Fear and rising anger rooted Sorley where he stood. Cautiously he parted the leaves to see the stranger go. Three or four men rose, it seemed, from the ground. Together they disappeared over the crest of the brae.

The encounter left young MacIlveen little stomach for any more hacking and hewing. He shouldered the billhook, summoned the boy Nicol, and started for home. Tam Purdie, his wife and daughter, were with his parents and Ellen. He told them of the interloper skulking in the hazel clump '. . . There was murther in his look.'

'There was more than one of them,' put in young Purdie.

'Have ye seen their likes afore?' asked Tam Purdie.

'No, they weren't *bodach*s,' replied the boy. 'They were better clad, like fighting men.'

'Ha, wood-kernes!' exclaimed Purdie.

The MacIlveens had heard the word often enough from Purdie. Confident that he had been led to this tillage by a providential hand, Alexander received his neighbour's warnings with a muted scepticism. To Meg wood-kernes came from an infernal world, kin to the bogles and kelpies of the oak forests. But Sorley was ready to believe in malefic flesh and blood.

'Nicol,' said Purdie to the boy, 'you and Doug take the nags and warn the Orrs and Crockarts and all them with land running up to the woods –'

Meg glanced apprehensively in her daughter's direction. 'On no more than a glimpse o' some wanderer in the bushes, Tam?'

Purdie turned his good eye on her. 'No mair's needed, guidwife. Better lost sleep than a bleezing thatch down on ye.'

Bewildered, Alexander turned to his neighbour. 'What's all the skirl about, Tam? We've harmed nobody.'

Sorley spoke in the weary voice of one answering by rote. 'Father, I've told ye. The Irish say it's their land.'

'Enough, man!' cried Purdie impatiently. 'We've had all this afore. Sorley, away and tell Dan Drummond what ye seen.'

It was Sorley's turn to look discomfited. 'The factor'll think I'm easily scared at some bogle girning at me out of a bush, Tam. . .'

Purdie shook his head. 'It may sound like great cry and little wool, as the Deil said when he pluckit the sow. But I don't think Drummond will be of that opinion. At the very least that chiel was trespassing on your holding. Let us hope it's no worse. But it'll be enough to send Dan off for the laird. Now away with ye, m'birkie.'

Sorley gone, Alexander turned to his neighbour. 'Ye think it's more than trespass?'

'Feggs, aye. It was wood-kernes he seen. The breed that finished the Barclays. They'll be on us afore cockcrow. Ye have a musket –'

'Aye.'

'– and pikes. I'll send our Rab over to ye. That'll be three of us to a dwelling. As for the weemin,' Purdie looked at Meg and Ellen, 'they can shelter in the kirk with Sarah and Elspet here,' and Purdie indicated his wife and daughter.

Meg rose abruptly. 'D'ye think I'm leaving my family at this time? No, Tam Purdie, that's no our gait of going, and let ye mark that!'

'Neighbour,' cried Purdie's wife, 'the women aye go to the kirk to pray with Mistress Tabitha.' As an afterthought she added, 'Some o' them sing psalms.'

'They couldn't be better employed,' said Meg approvingly. 'Ellen and me will do our praying here.' She waved away Alexander's protest. 'That's the end o' it.'

Sorley MacIlveen was not far out in his surmise. Mr Drummond listened to his warning with peevish scepticism.

'And this gomeril roosting in the bushes never spoke to ye?'

'Not a word. Tam Purdie says he was a wood-kerne –'

'But Purdie wasn't there!'

'No, 'twas only me. And now that I've told ye –'

'Now that you've told me,' cut in the factor sharply, 'your errand's finished. Off with ye!'

In pettish ill-humour Drummond watched the youth depart. The impudent callan had come close to telling him his duty. He could scarce believe that the MacIlveens would try to make a chuff out of their landlord's factor. And the mention of Tam Purdie bothered him. Young MacIlveen wouldn't dare call on the name of that sagacious hard-bitten neighbour lightly. All through supper and into the evening the warning stuck in his mind like a burr. When his head was on the pillow it was still with him. At last, with an oath, he deserted the startled Mistress Drummond's warm flank, sprang on to the icy floor, huddled into his clothes and set off for Rathard House.

The Purdies had left when Sorley returned home. Meg and Ellen had set platters and spoons. Alexander, until called to supper, sat at the hearth with the air of a man prepared to be resolute if he but knew what to be resolute on. There was little talk among the four. They had finished the meal when the door opened and Rab Purdie came in. The young man was burdened with two muskets and a pike, and hung around with powder and shot horns. Meg stared at the weapons.

'You've brought a gruesome load, Rab.'

'The Lord grant we don't need them.' His eyes lingered for a moment on the girl. 'Will you and Ellen no go down to Mistress Tabitha at the kirk?'

'No,' said Meg.

'Then fetch out what will carry water from the well.' As Sorley made to move with the others Purdie waved him back. 'You keep a watch on the brae.'

The youth obeyed without demur. His neighbour had been under siege before.

In the falling darkness Alexander and the two women carried up the brimming receptacles. Rab Purdie stretched his long frame to cast the water high across the roof. As it fell drenching the thatch the liquid arcs caught the last glint of daylight.

A hoarse cry from Sorley brought all to a halt.

'In with ye – in with ye!' cried Rab, hustling father, mother and daughter before him and shooting the wooden bar in the door. Over Sorley's shoulder he watched activity stir on the crest above the cottage, the comings and goings of men silhouetted against ever-growing torchlight. 'They're on the move.' Purdie looked around him. 'Ye were lavish with windows when ye built this new gable to the house,' he said, indicating the two apertures.

'It was for daylight, Rab,' said Alexander.

'Aye. Here,' the young man put a musket in Alexander's hands. 'You take the left-hand window, Alexander.'

The heavy weapon drooped in the father's grasp. 'I don't have it in me to shoot a fella-man –'

'Teach yoursel',' said Rab curtly. Then he stooped, eyeing through the aperture into the darkness. 'If ye see anybody coming down the slope all ye need do is pull the trigger.' He patted the musket. 'The blarge of that thing in the mirk will frighten the shit out of them.'

Willing to believe that his task was little more than that of a callan scaring rooks from corn, Alexander settled to his watch.

The rest of the family were as ready to follow young Purdie's bidding. Meg wedged the table against the door.

'Pull that musket in, Sorley, or it'll be torn out o' your hands. . . Ellen, to the back wall. Two guns aye ready for firing, two loading.'

Powder, shot and wads before her, the girl hunkered down at the end of the chamber ready to employ her dexterous fingers.

A thud on the roof brought all to a halt. They watched the trickle of sparks, between lintel and doortop, as the brand slid from the wet thatch. From his spy-hole Sorley watched the parabolas of a dozen flung torches spin through the dark air to splinter in a cascade of fire against the houses. Then the ridge broke into a mass of charging men, flaming brands, the glint of weapons, white shouting faces. 'Fire, Father!' Sorley screamed and the discharge of their firearms merged with the fusillade from the Purdies. Alexander was never to know if his ball struck anyone, if there was a cry of pain amid the fury of hatred streaming down the flame-pitted hillside.

For an eerie moment the uproar stilled, the only sound a soft slithering as if men crept close along the walls of the dwelling. 'Your pikes, men. . .' said Rab, his voice low. As father and son reached for the weapons the door shuddered under a great dundering blow. Rab snatched a firearm from Ellen. He was bringing it to his shoulder when a musket was fired from the other side, blowing away a corner of the door in splinters and sending Ellen and him to the floor. From beyond the door came the sound of a man whimpering.

Rab raised himself to his knees. 'God's curse on that loon, Doug,' he snarled, 'he could'a kilt us all!' Then he saw Ellen down, blood streaming from her head. He reached her before

97

her mother did, raising her up, gently easing her fingers from the wound.

Meg took her from his arms. She parted the heavy hair. 'You'll live lass,' she said, ''twas only a skelf o' wood hit ye. I'll put a bit clout on it —'

But the girl freed herself and crept back to her task.

Alexander stretched himself painfully. 'There's nothing to be seen out there, Rab, and yet. . .'

'Aye, and yet. . .' The young man cocked his head, his eyes on the shadowy rafters. 'Listen.'

They heard a fissling sound above, then the impact as a heavy stake was plunged into the thatch. It was the signal for a general assault on the upper end of the house. The walls shook to the impact of bodies. Alexander, for a moment confused, had the musket twisted from his grasp. Rab Purdie, uncertain as to his target, fired into the rafters. He had the meagre satisfaction of blowing a hole open to the stars now paling in the sky.

'Why aren't they giving us cover frae the other house!' he cried angrily. 'Here, lass,' he thrust the empty weapon to Ellen.

A probing torch came through Sorley's window. It fell to the floor, scorching his legs. He thrust savagely in response and heard a grunt of pain as the pikeblade went home. As he trod down the burning embers he saw the torch-thrower dragged away. And with the wounded man, across the face of the hill, their assailants were retreating.

'They're away, they're away!' the red-haired youth cried. He flung down the pike and reached for his musket.

His father grasped his arm. 'If they are, let them go, in God's name.' Hopefully the older man turned to Purdie. 'Is this the end of them, Rab?'

Perplexed, the young neighbour shook his head. 'That I can't say. There's no reason why they should draw off like this —'

Then from down the hill came a distant hallooing and a peppering of musket shots.

98

Meg was at the ragged hole in the door. 'It's neighbouring men!' she cried exultant. 'Neighbours – thanks be to the Good Man – Sam Gill and Ross Campbell – the laird and Mr Gilchrist – and others with them –'

' 'Twas them the Irish saw coming,' said Rab Purdie.

But to Meg and Alexander the mightier Presence that had been with them that night took precedence. When the laird and his followers gained the cottage they stood at the back of the chamber, bonnets off, until Alexander had thanked the Lord God Almighty for a safe deliverance from their enemies.

No word of the foray had reached the families to the north and west of the estate so that only a handful of women and children came to the kirk. To most of the cottars the distant fires seemed no more than the Irish setting a scatter of bushes ablaze. On his way to the meeting-house the minister culled from memory a portion suitable to the occasion. He strode into the building and leant his musket against the pulpit.

'Our foes have turned back,' he informed his sister and the other women. 'Let us give thanks.' Raising voice and hands he chanted:

> The mighty men were gathered around me,
> not for my offence, nor for my sin, O Lord.
> Behold they brag in their talk, and swords
> are in their lips; for who, they say, doth hear?
> But thou, O Lord, shall laugh them in
> derision, thou shalt laugh at all the heathen.
> I will sing of the power and will praise
> thy mercy in the morning: for thou
> hast been my defence and refuge in
> the day of my trouble. . .

He stood for a moment, lips moving. Then he opened his eyes. 'Now,' said he, 'go to your homes. In the morn, when your milking's done, return here with your menfolk so that we may indeed praise the Lord for his mercy. . .'

After the service the factor asked Neil to ride out with him to the MacIlveens. They found the damage to the two dwellings slight. Sorley, his scorched leg bandaged, was busying himself at the rift in the thatch. Alexander and Tam Purdie were measuring boards to repair the broken door.

Drummond dismounted beside the cottars. 'D'ye need aught, MacIlveen? There's seasoned wood below and new hasps in the smiddy.'

'We've timber enough, factor, and the hasps are still sound,' responded Alexander. He turned to look up the hill. 'It's by God's grace we're not fashioning a coffin this morn.' The elderly man viewed the now silent ridge with a look of enmity that Neil had never seen before.

'It wasn't MacCartan's people that came at us last night,' said Tam Purdie.

'Why do ye say that, Tam?' The factor's query was grudging. Neither he nor the cottar had any wish to absolve the Irish that lipped the border of Ravara. But the laird would expect a faithful report.

'They weren't MacCartan's *bodach*s. They were better clad. Mair steel and leather in their garb. And they had the glib of hair hanging from their brows,' and Purdie drew a finger down his forehead.

'You've seen their like afore?'

''Twas the same breed murthered the Barclays.'

'D'ye think they'll return?'

'No. That's not their gait. But for all that, factor, we ran out of powder and shot. And Alex MacIlveen lost a musket.'

'I'll see to it, Tam.' Drummond looked across to where Neil was listening to Meg's narrative of the assault. 'If you're ready, Mr Gilchrist.'

At midday Echlin summoned them to attend him at the factor's office: the minister, Calum Wishart, Neil and Angus Ross. The laird arrived, to Dan Drummond's discomfit, attended by Ronane. Mr Turnooth, suspecting a dilution of authority in Ronane's presence, gave that individual a hard stare. It did not go unobserved by Echlin. Seated, he looked around the others.

'Afore we settle to the main business, let me tell ye that I've brought Ronane to Rathard House. The work inside and around the house goes too slow for my liking. That and the outside servants, the stables and the like, take me away from my care of the estate. All these will now be in Ronane's hands. He'll be my. . .' The laird sought for a word.

'Seneschal?' suggested Wishart, grave-faced.

The laird nodded. 'That'll serve. Now, to yestere'en's intrusion on my property. It seems we suffered little –'

'By the mercy of God,' interjected Mr Turnooth.

'By the mercy of God, reverend sir,' echoed the laird. 'One man is dead. A brother of the Mackechnies was found on the road to the village. It could have been Irish kernes. I think it more likely to have been the work of reivers lying in wait for he was stripped of all he had. But the two families at Barclays place seemed to have suffered little more than dunts and scrapes?' and the laird looked from Dan Drummond to Neil.

As the factor sat glum, Neil answered. 'The assault on them was determined enough. The raiders tried to fire the MacIlveens' thatch and force the door. The exchange was hot enough for the Purdies to have come to the end of their powder and ball. Indeed, laird,' said Neil boldly, 'Tam Purdie should be here. He kens more of this affray than the rest of us thegither!'

'You're right, Gilchrist. I'll make it my concern to speak to him.'

Drummond, reminded that he had a message, said: 'Purdie's of the opinion that the MacCartans, father and son, had little to do with last night's work.'

'On that too, I'll sound him,' responded Echlin, turning away as if he had no wish to pursue that scent.

The factor spread his fingers on the table in the gesture of a man who considered business completed. 'It could have been worse, sir.'

101

'It *should* have been worse,' said Ronane suddenly.

Echlin considered the figure that stood, arms folded, in the corner. 'True, Ronane. They could have worked more ruination. Yet they didn't. . .'

Ross glanced at the others before he spoke. 'It's the families at Barclay's place that have twice taken the brunt. . .'

'What o't, Angus? My lands run closer there to MacCartan's border.'

'It's that flat rock above the MacIlveens. It means much to the Irish. A crowning-place for their chiefs, maybe. . .'

Mr Turnooth let out a derisive exclamation.

'Go on, Angus,' said Echlin.

'I've been up there. I'm not saying the surface has been worked with chisel and hammer, but that great stone didn't come there by chance. There's still a track leading away from it as if it was often frequented –'

'As a vantage for spying,' said Mr Turnooth grimly.

The laird leant back in his chair. 'This is a newance to me. What d'ye make of it, Dan?'

The factor conveyed that to him the matter was one of deepest mystification.

'Have the MacIlveens worked the land close to this boulder – this rock, the dominie talks about?'

'Not as yet, laird, for it's too steep for horse and plough – forbye, there's a tangle of brushwood.' The factor recollected that he had urged young MacIlveen to clear the brae. 'But they'll be up there with spade and mattock afore long.'

'Then bid them draw their headrig back from that place. Ten scotch ells or whatever ye think fit –'

'No!' The Reverend Mr Turnooth struck the table, his outraged stare on the laird. 'Give up our land to the Irish for some papist cantrip! Not an inch – not a crumb of the soil that has been entrusted to ye, Kenneth Echlin!'

'*Our* land –!' the scar on the laird's cheek darkened. Amid the numb silence of the others he struggled with his fury. 'Mr

Turnooth,' he said at last, 'as ye well ken I spent much of my life under arms. The safe-keeping of *my* property is the task closest to my heart and well within my competence.' He continued in a calmer voice: 'If there's aught to Ross's idea it will be put to the test. Better that,' his voice rising again, 'than to see my tenants taken from their holdings to stand guard night and day. That I will not have!'

The minister, his demeanour as aggressive as ever, arose and drew his cloak around him. 'We've heard no word of bringing the Irish to boot,' said he.

'Nor will ye,' responded Echlin curtly. 'That's a matter for the government. For the Lord Deputy, if need be.'

Mr Turnooth stumped out. At a sign of dismissal the others followed, leaving the laird and Drummond at the table. Echlin sat silent as if his mention of the Lord Deputy had started speculation that was not entirely agreeable.

Dan cleared his throat. 'What'll I tell the MacIlveens, sir?'

'Eh, the MacIlveens? Gloze 'em, damn it, gloze 'em!' Then recovering himself: 'Tell 'em you've decided that brae's not fit to work. You need no other reason.'

'What if they complain they're losing land? What if that red-haired son –'

'Dan, haven't ye land down at the Langstane Burn waiting to be grubbed and broken?'

'Aye, true. . .'

'Then offer 'em a patch there. Now, put by what you're doing. I want ye to come up to Rathard with me. . .'

Their daily concerns keeping them apart, Neil, Wishart and the dominie did not meet again until supper-time. All three seated at the schoolhouse hearth, Ross proceeded to spoon out the meal from the pot.

'How long,' asked Wishart accepting his platter, 'before word of last night's foray reaches the ears of the world?'

'There were folk from the other side of the estate on the road early this morning for Newtownards,' said Ross.

103

'The world begins at Newtownards, Angus. I had in mind Dublin or Carrickfergus or wherever Chichester pursues his viceregal course.'

Neil looked up. 'Of what interest would a local skirmish be to the Lord Deputy?'

'An Irishman need only raise his hand –'

'Or his voice,' added the dominie.

'– and he's a named man. Echlin, being a prudent carle, will see to it that this break in the peace gets to the viceregal lug. At the same time he and the MacCartans will cry truce.'

'But if they should meet?' said Neil. 'They're both men of dry tinder –'

'Oh, they'll meet, Neil,' said the dominie. 'The courtesies will be cool. But both wish to steer clear of a rift that would be hard to mend. The circumspect word will pass between them in the market or some such place.'

'Auld Tam Purdie has the right of it,' continued Wishart. 'Last night's ding wasn't the work of MacCartan's people. No doubt the marauders were *sib* to Turlough. Like our own Hielan' gentry they're as mixed throughother as sheep's wool on a whinbush –'

'Who were they then?'

'To put English on it, they consider themselves "dispossessed gentry" – men driven from their ancestral places.'

'But the MacCartans *must* have kenned what was afoot!'

Wishart set down his empty platter. 'I don't doubt that they had Fiach's tacit approval. But no more than that. He and his son hold what they have by agreement with Echlin. Ye heard the laird say as much. And Echlin, who wasn't behind the door when the Lord God made foxes, kens how far MacCartan would have to go to save face.' Wishart stood up, yawned and stretched his long frame. 'The Crockarts have a sick woman. I promised to drop by.'

As he crossed to the door a pile of manuscript on the windowledge caught his eye. He frittered the leaves through his fingers. 'Still scaling the laird's family tree?'

'Mr Echlin has declared himself pleased with what he's seen,' replied Ross. 'He thinks it fit to take with him to London.'

Wishart paused, his hand on the door hasp. 'Angus, who in London ever heard of Kenneth Echlin? He'll spend his time kicking his heels in ante-rooms and his treasure greasing the palms of pert nobodies. In return he'll be offered fingers to kiss and arses to lick –'

'You're putting Mr Echlin down against your better sense,' said Neil sharply. 'To military men near the king he's known as an able commander.'

'There's much else here,' said Ross rescuing the papers from Wishart, 'that's outside your knowledge, Calum.'

Wishart shrugged. 'Great lords with pedigrees as high as Jacob's ladder have come away empty-handed from the same pursuit of honour or station. . .

> What Hell it is in suing long to bide;
> to lose good days that might be better spent. . .

Ah well,' he lifted the hasp, 'I bid ye guid e'en, young sirs.'

On the day Watty Mackechnie's body was found his kinsmen set out in search of the murderers. Hardy men, thirsting for revenge, they pushed far into the hills. They found only cold embers in a glade that could have been left by any wanderer. Then there had been petty raids, seemingly for food, on cottages in Mr Luke Cordwaine's territory. A housewife disturbed an intruder in her dairy. A second man, an ugly rogue she described him, stood outside on watch. The fellow in the house drew a knife on her. But her cries being answered by a serving-man, the miscreants made off across the meadows to be joined by two others of the gang, one bearing away a lamb.

Porson, Cordwaine's steward, immediately mounted a pursuit. By hard riding he and his men closed on the fleeing robbers until their horses could advance no farther in the thickets. The English, not being nimble in such conditions, had to watch their quarry draw away into the deep forest. Porson was certain that there were four or five in the band, their leader a hulking creature with a blanket looped over one shoulder. He was of the opinion that they were not Irish.

Dan Drummond was returning from the MacIlveens when he was given news of the incursions. 'Our thanks to Mr Porson,' he said to the messenger. 'I'll tell Mr Echlin.'

Dan, therefore, was doubly laden with news as he approached Rathard House. All in all, he considered that he had brought off the MacIlveen business gey neatly. Other than a muted grumble from Sorley, father and son had agreed to draw back the upper boundary of their holding to where it could be 'worked by man and horse'. Not one of the three whispered of retreat.

Shifting nimbly from restitution for lost furrows to reward for diligent husbandry, the factor told the two that the laird had given favourable consideration to the request for more tillage; half-an-acre and more was to be had at the Langstane Burn. Alexander, if a bit hazy about the asking, expressed thanks for the granting. The factor caught the telling grin on the son's face. The prick-eared birkie musn't get away with the thought that his plea had any weight in the matter.

'You'll not be allowed to work the Langstane field for a wheen of weeks – maybe a month or mair. Because,' some thrawn instinct prompted the factor to add, 'her Ladyship wants to have a cornmill built. You'll have to do your stint at the work.'

'What mill?' Sorley didn't trouble to hid his derision.

Aye, 'deed, thought Drummond. Her Ladyship's mill hung like a shadow in the factor's mind. 'The mill will have to be turning in time for the next harvest,' he said coldly. 'You and your father will give a shoulder to the work like all the rest of the folk.'

But Sorley's mind was farther up the Langstane Burn, on the land that he and his father were to enter. 'Will the two years' remission of rent hold for the new plot, factor?'

Dan Drummond stroked his chin thoughtfully. 'Only a gowk would see it any other way.'

At Rathard House Drummond reported the raids on their neighbour's tenants and repeated the English steward's opinion that the intruders were not Irish.

'They're Scots,' said Echlin, 'and well Alfred Porson knows it. Porson's a shrewd chiel. Scots vermin, Dan, and they must be got rid of. I'll see Ronane about mounting a pursuit.'

It was an undertaking that the factor was happy to see delegated. 'I've told the MacIlveens of your granting them the bit of land at the burn –'

'Did they make any ding about drawing back from the brae?'

'They did not. On the contrar, sir, I'm to convey their dutiful respects and thanks. I told them,' continued the factor, determined to make hay while the sun shone, 'that they couldn't start on the new letting until they had worked their stint at the building of the mill – her Ladyship –'

'Aye, the mill,' said Echlin brusquely. 'Have you and Gilchrist supplied the timber?'

'It's been cut and drying this six-month. And Dugal had the iron lying at the smiddy for the making o' the plates and pins and nails. Herron, the mason, can lay his hand on the mill-stones –'

'Aye, aye,' interrupted the laird. 'Why hasn't the work gone forward?'

'Gilfillan the carpenter is of the opinion that we've nobody fit to start on the waterway. . . following an interview with her Ladyship –'

'We need a mill-wright?'

'Aye.'

'Have you or Gilchrist looked for one? God's name, Dan, have I to ride the countryside myself?'

Hastily declaring his readiness to repair the omission, the factor picked up his bonnet. He turned at the door. 'Her Ladyship's spiering as to why Tam McBratney hasn't been examined for attempting Rushin Coatie's life –'

Echlin stared hard at his factor, 'Dan,' he said. 'Dan, don't anger me. Give your mind to pressing business – get off your hurdies and find a mill-wright.'

Away from the laird Dan Drummond blew out his cheeks in relief. He had managed to get in the shot about Rushin Coatie. That would please Lady Echlin. In the business of the mill-wright things had gone a bit agley. But young Gilchrist had the broader shoulders to carry the laird's displeasure. He found Neil in the schoolhouse.

'Mr Echlin's raising a stoor about a mill-wright. Have ye found one yet?'

'No,' said Neil from where he sat. 'I'll have a word with the laird –'

'It's no words he's seeking,' declared the factor in a manner

108

he considered a fair imitation of the laird's present mood. 'Talk grinds no flour. Ye would be well-advised to ride into the village tomorrow morn. Ye could start at John Bell's tavern. When you're there,' continued Dan Drummond staring with distaste at the remains of the young man's meal, 'ye could treat yourself to a decent dinner.'

A market-day crowd thronged the square and spilled into the village alleys. The main room of the tavern was rapidly filling with those who had travelled a distance that morning. Neil stood hesitant amid the rising surge of voices. A few heads turned and turned away again reassured by his appearance. Each man present knew his fellow, his accustomed place at the tables. A deal of business was transacted here on market day among these solid God-fearing men, merchants, shopkeepers, farmers, who had sloughed the hodden of the cottars they once were. Diligent in their duties, they were now enjoying the privileges of which they were the authors. They were men who made little distinction between the Irish and wolves running in the virgin forest. Outside the labourers, hucksters and travelling folk drifted past to the shebeens.

Fortunately for Neil's comfort, Bell recognised him as one of the young men who had supped there with Echlin. The tavern-keeper made a place for him adjacent to a couple of substantial patrons and summoned a servant-girl to take his order.

The meal finished, Neil sat back replete. As the plate was whisked away, one of his neighbours leant forward and tapped the empty tankard.

'Something of the same, sir – or a glass this time?'

Neil turned to his interrogator and met a pleasant ruddy expression that seemed to extend to the fringe of white hair on the scalp. But peering out from the folds of flesh the eyes were shrewd, inquisitive.

'Thank ye. A glass would be welcome.'

'Robert Bothwell of Bothwell and Leslie, grain chandlers.' Mr Bothwell jerked his thumb over his shoulder. 'Mr Charles Leslie.'

Neil acknowledged both. 'Neil Gilchrist. . . of Ravara.'

'Ha!' Mr Bothwell drew his shiny visage back in cordial enlightenment. 'Ravara! We have done business wi' Mr Kenneth Echlin – a braw gentleman, sir!'

Neil murmured assent. The brimming glasses arrived and were raised in mutual goodwill.

Mr Bothwell moved closer. 'Would ye know if Mr Echlin or any of his folk are in need of corn seed? We have a fine hard grain to hand. . .'

'Winnowed as clean as a whustle,' interjected Mr Leslie round the bulk of his partner's broadcloth.

Neil was about to disclaim any such knowledge. Then he realised that it would ill-become him not to be versed on such an important matter. 'There was seed saved from last year –'

'Certes, aye!' cried the grain chandler.

'– then again,' continued Neil, 'there's been new settlers come in and new land opened.' Gazing at the chandler he nodded thoughtfully. 'Thank ye, Mr Bothwell I'll carry your word to the laird. You could be of service to me.'

'How, Mr Gilchrist?' responded the chandler, with indulgent smile and watchful eyes.

'We're in need of a mill-wright in Ravara.'

'Ha!' Mr Bothwell slewed round to take in the room. 'D'ye see those three? One's Alfred Porson, steward to Mr Cordwaine of Edenmore –'

'I know Mr Porson. The other is the master mason that worked at Rathard House.'

'Aye, but it's the third you're after, the dark-avised one. Mr Glyn Williams, a most skilled mill-wright.'

'Is he working for Porson?'

'He's finished at the Cordwaine place. He's ready packed but waiting for a sail from Donaghadee to take him down the coast to Dundalk –'

'Mr Bothwell, I would be greatly obliged if you could have Williams brought here –'

110

Mr Bothwell raised his hand for the serving-girl and winked at Neil. 'A word in the lassie's lug.'

Neil watched the girl thread her way across the room, saw Williams rise at her message to follow her to their table.

The newcomer looked questioningly from one to the other. 'Mr Bothwell. . . gentlemen. . .'

The chandler hooked a seat forward with his square-toed boot. 'Sit yourself down, Mr Williams, and meet Mr Gilchrist of Ravara.'

'Thank you for joining us, Mr Williams. We need a mill-wright at Ravara.'

'And I'm on my way to Dundalk.'

'Not until you get a passage, I understand,' said Neil.

The young man smiled. 'As well-informed as ever, Mr Bothwell,' he said glancing at the chandler. 'Yes, that's true. But there's work waiting for me there.' He studied Neil for a moment. 'If it's to your place I go, can you assure me of work?'

'That I can,' answered Neil fervently.

'Good. Let us leave.'

Neil was taken aback. 'Now?'

'Now. I had my few belongings bundled and ready for the voyage.'

Neil thought he was called on to order another bottle but Williams went off to collect his baggage and Mr Bothwell, administering a hearty slap to his forehead, declared that he and Mr Leslie had to retain clear heads for the afternoon's business. Could the bottle wait for some future occasion? The young man thought it could, took a cordial farewell of the chandlers, and left the tavern with the mill-wright.

As they rode away from the village Neil studied his fellow-traveller circumspectly. He seemed over-young to be, in Bothwell's words, 'a most skilled mill-wright'. It troubled Neil. He was in no mind to arrive back at Ravara with a goose rather than a swan and suffer Drummond's sly amusement and the laird's vexation. On the other hand the young man looked

111

well-accoutred in dress and mount, one who could sit at table with shrewd chiels like Porson and Bothwell. . .

'You've travelled far, Mr Williams?'

'And long,' replied the other with a smile. 'My father, brother and I set off from Llangollen in Wales over two years ago. We are a family of mill-wrights.'

'Ah,' said Neil '. . . Wales.' Without being too clear from whence Williams came, he guessed it would be as far away as London, a journey he had shied away from.

'And how did you come here?'

'My father stayed to work in England,' answered Williams, who seemed ready enough to be quizzed. 'My brother and I travelled from mill to mill until we arrived in Scotland. Hearing there was work in Ireland I came over.'

'You heard aright,' said Neil half-convinced. 'How many mills have you built in the past two years?'

The Welshman shrugged. 'There were three of us together for most of that time. Not all building has to be started from the ground. Over here I've found sound mill-houses but the machinery was from another day with the waterwheel running horizontally in the stream.' Williams looped the rein over his arm to demonstrate. 'Now I do away with that and have an upright wheel built, as is the English way, carrying the drive to the grinding stones by a trundle wheel, a lantern pinion and spindle –'

'Mr Williams,' cried Neil cheerily, 'at Ravara all will be new, built from the ground!'

As they rode Neil swithered how best to introduce Williams at Ravara. It could be to his own advantage to present him at Rathard House. But everyone knew it was Lady Echlin who had clamoured for a mill-wright. To appear hotfoot with one might seem truckling, even obsequious. And the laird employed a factor for the business of hiring workmen. He would deliver Williams to Drummond and let him deal with terms of employment, board and lodgings.

112

Early as Neil was astir on the following morning, Dan Drummond was before him. He met the elated factor coming back from the Big House. 'Her Ladyship sent one of her lasses down to me with her thanks.'

'I cannot think,' said Neil heavily, 'of anyone more deserving of it. Is Williams to stay with ye?'

'Feggs, no! Her Ladyship has found him quarters at Rathard.'

It soon became apparent to everybody with an interest in the matter that the Welshman knew what he was about. A stroll along the stream in the company of Lady Echlin on that first morning and he marked where cutting should begin. He told those cottars summoned by her Ladyship that with willing labour they could expect to mill the grain from the next harvest. A small eyot to bear the mill-house divided the strongly running waters. Echlin and Dan Drummond viewed the site approvingly.

'Where I would have started myself!' declared the factor.

'If your neb had been pointed to it, Dan. See that Williams has aye sufficient stones of the right girth to lay the course.'

The terms in which the piece of land at the Langstane Burn had been offered rankled with the MacIlveen men. To balance their loss of the strip on the brae with a grant that made demands on their time and strength seemed unjust.

'We're beholden tae give the laird three days labour,' Alexander reminded his son.

'When our own ploughing's finished. That's the custom,' replied the youth stubbornly.

The work round the homestead was completed to the last turn of a spade. A week and more was frittered away in sullen idleness. They knew that the work on the mill had started. They watched Tam Purdie and his sons come and go as they served out their duty to the laird.

At last Meg tired of idle men at her hearth; she had watched with growing unease her son over-riding his father's good intentions.

113

'This'll no do, Alex man. Mr Gilfillan has sent for ye twice. Ye could have worked your days at the mill lang syne.'

'No afore we open the new patch –' began Sorley.

She turned on him. 'Hauld your tongue, ye whelp, when I'm talking to your father!' In face of her flaring anger the youth fell back. 'Take a bucket in your fist and away to the well for a go of water!'

The bucket when he went to lift it was full; for all that he went outside.

Meg now faced her husband. 'Alex, whatever honest work has to be done, do it. You're an elder of the kirk and it behoves ye to show an example. I'll say no mair.'

Alexander, glancing at the distraught face of the good woman, vowed to himself that he would not be party to further strife in his family.

But being a man aye pricked by a sense of what was fair, he understood Sorley's bitterness even if he could not follow him in his over-riding hunger for land. That evening he said to his son: 'Your mother's right. We owe the laird the days and we maun pay them. But if we can't work the patch 'til then, we can go and look at it.'

They slipped away from the cottage, stepping briskly down the rig of their ploughland, across the seeping hollow at the bottom, through the brushwood that separated carse from burn. They crossed the burn by the fallen long stone that bridged it and gave it its name. From far down the stream's course they could hear the voices and hammers of those working on the mill. They stood for a time contemplating the ground allotted to them.

'It's cleaner than I thought,' said Sorley.

'Aye.'

Mist was gathering in the bordering trees but in the field itself the timber had been felled and the boulders were few and to Sorley's eye not too deeply bedded. His father was moving slowly up the field, stooping now and then to touch the soil.

114

Sorley crossed to a boulder close to the boundary and gave it a tentative shake. His heart leapt in his bosom as a voice sounded over his head.

'Ye shouldn't be here.'

Sorley looked up. A girl sat in the crook of a tree. Her elfin, not over-clean face looked down on him with a stern expression.

'Losh, ye scairt me!' He laughed in his relief. 'Ye could be one of the Guid Folk if I didn't know ye were Elphie Miskimmin!'

The girl brushed back strands of dark hair from her brow and cheek. 'My father and brothers'll no want you here.'

Sorley looked up sharply. 'Why for no? Were they after the piece?'

She broke off a twig and chewed it, considering her reply. Sorley could see that she wanted to answer in the affirmative but was unsure where that might lead her.

'Maybe aye, maybe no,' she said.

'We were granted it by Dan Drummond. If your family doesn't like that, they can see him. Me and my father,' he turned to the approaching figure, 'are going to work it.' When he looked again the girl had gone, only the swaying bough indicated that she had ever been there.

Alexander was crumbling a handful of soil. 'It's guid – it's heavier than ours.'

'It would be, close to the burn.'

They recrossed the water and took to the path winding through the boscage. It was evident that Alexander was pleased with what he had found but Sorley's replies were brief and both trudged on in silence.

The youth was chewing on the girl's hostile prediction. The Miskimmins were not a family one would choose as neighbours. They concocted strong liquor to their own detriment and that of their neighbour-cronies. They returned from Newtownards with empty purses and broken heads. They sang, they danced in the most shameless manner, the scraich of their

115

fiddles broke the Sabbath stillness. Only unavoidable business took the factor near their doorstep. The Reverend Turnooth, of harder mettle, threatened to have Gilfillan the carpenter knock up a higher stool of repentance for the exclusive use of Sawney Miskimmin or any one of his three sons on their too-frequent penitential appearances in kirk.

'Whose farm marches with that piece of land?' asked Sorley jerking his thumb backwards.

'Jack Stewart's.'

'And beyond Stewart's?'

His father thought. 'It would be them Miskimmins.'

So the impudent young quean had crossed two or three fields to perch in that tree and spy on him. There was a sudden thump of hooves and rounding a corner the two were brought up short under the nostrils of Lady Echlin's horse. The rider pointed her whip at Sorley.

'You, where are you coming from?'

'The Langstane Burn.'

She leaned from the saddle. '*My lady*. . . were you at work at the cornmill?'

'No, we were looking at a patch o' land.' The youth saw the quiver of the whip-hand '. . . m'lady.' The two words fell from his lips like goat droppings.

She turned on Alexander. 'What's your name?'

Alexander clawed at his bonnet. 'Alexander MacIlveen, m'lady. This is my son. We were –'

'Have you given your three days labour to the building?'

'Not as yet –'

'Let the both of you report to Gilfillan at six o'clock o' the morn. I won't forget your name, MacIlveen.'

When they were alone Alexander faced his son. 'Deil take ye. This shame wouldn't be on us if you had done what was right.' He strode away separating himself in his anger from the youth.

Next morning, bearing oaten bannocks and a flask of butter-milk, the two set out for the work site. Alexander had recovered

116

his spirits. A common task, if only for a day or two, held out the offer of alliance and solidarity with men of his own tongue and mind. Since the attack on his house he had felt a great if inarticulate need of that. Threading their way through the busyness they presented themselves to Gilfillan.

'We have no skill in carpentry, Mr Gilfillan,' said Sorley hopefully.

The craftsman looked him up and down. 'Carpentry?' he repeated with a snort of laughter. 'You're here for lifting and laying, m'birkie.'

Alexander was given a spade to help dig the tail-race of the mill, Sorley, horse and tackle to bring forward field stones for channel and walls. As every stone came free he thought morosely of those still embedded in the soil further up the burn.

11

Echlin made no mention of Neil's part in bringing the mill-wright to Ravara. The young man was further piqued that Williams should have found quarters in Rathard House. He, a laird's son, on his arrival had been directed to a bed and platter in the schoolhouse.

But as the days passed he changed his mind. If Dan Drummond had it aright, Rathard only saw Williams when he tumbled in for a few hours sleep. From early morning until last light he was at the Langstane Burn. He was peremptory in his demands on both craftsmen and labourers, irritated when a cottar, blessed with a good pair of hands, disappeared to his own place, his stint of labour served.

The thatched mill-house rose rapidly on the islet, the grinding-stones were dragged to the site and mounted, the walls and beds laid for the channels. On the day Williams declared the work completed Echlin rode out to join Dan Drummond, Neil and Calum Wishart on the slope above the mill. Below them, around the dam, stood the tradesmen and labourers, in their midst the squat figure of the Reverend Turnooth, Bible in hand. Angus Ross had broken school early so that the scholars might witness the memorable event. With Una Drummond he stood close to the edge of the mill-race, wary that some bold spirit might take a header into the channel. But the children were content to cling to their elders' legs and stare in fearful expectancy at the great motionless wheel.

Neil looked around. 'Where's Williams?'

'At the levers,' said Wishart, 'assuring that minister and mill start in unison.'

Echlin turned as if in reproof. Then the minister's voice rose in blessing.

'Doff,' said the laird.

Obediently those with him removed their bonnets.

Prudently Mr Turnooth kept his benediction brief. Williams opened the sluice. The water gushed down the channel, filling the buckets of the mill-wheel, turning it ponderously on its axle. There was a ragged shout and a tossing of bonnets from the men. The children crept forward to stare at the monster slowly revolving in a fretted nimbus of spray.

'He has Gilfillan with him – Williams,' said Dan Drummond, thumbs hooked in pockets, nodding blithely to the mill-house. 'Giving him final instructions. . .'

The factor had good reason to feel canty. The mill was up at last. Other than the stour about McBratney's attempt on the auld woman's life, Lady Echlin was off his back. He had observed, neatly enough, her latest bidding: that the tenants must have their grain ground at the new mill and that a sixteenth of the meal be left at the Big House granary after each milling. The first part had been easy enough; the likes of such a fine mill was not to be found within easy distance. As to the second he had left that to the kirk elders and was relieved that such a weighty body of opinion thought the multure fair and just.

The sluice was closed, the water shrank to a tiny rivulet, the wheel fell motionless.

Williams came from the mill-house across the causeway and climbed the slope. He turned and gestured to the mill. 'I wish you good harvests, Mr Echlin.'

'Thank ye, Mr Williams. Gilfillan has knowledge of the machinery?'

'Yes. He's a craftsman. He can instruct whoever you appoint as miller.' The mill-wright turned to Neil. 'Mr Gilchrist, I've seen little of you. Ours was a fortunate meeting.'

Neil was unable to suppress a smirk as he took the other's hand. 'And a timely one, Mr Williams. . .'

The laird mounted. 'I expect ye at Rathard House for a glass of wine. Bring Gilfillan with ye, Dan, and Mr Turnooth if he'll join us.'

Echlin paused to look down on the scene. It was a sight to please any landowner's heart. His tenants were returning in peace to their fields and homes, each man already a wiseacre on meal and mill-stones. As he rode through the dappled woods the laird felt a peculiar satisfaction in the building of the mill. He had erected a solid house and raised a bawn as laid out in his undertaking. But they were no more than any man would furnish, shelter and protection in an alien territory. The corn-mill went beyond that, into a climate of stability and peace. For all his soldiering abroad, Echlin had never rid himself of a childhood lived among elders who read much into omens and portents. In the turning of that great wheel he felt that he had made a propitiatory gesture to the soil and its bounty.

As he entered the house his wife paused on the stairway. 'It went well?'

He took off his riding coat and handed it to a serving-man before he answered her. 'Ye should have been there.' The hounds stirred from his path as he crossed to the fire. 'It went well. I've to settle with Williams. He'll be here with the others. No doubt you'll wish to commend him. Pray see that there are refreshments.' Hands to the blaze he stood with his back to her. At times she angered him, voicing her demands, keeping aloof from their execution.

But next morning she was early astir, riding down to the cornmill with her husband. Gilfillan, alert to such a visit, was there with a boy to tend the horses. Her Ladyship followed his explanation of the machinery and the process of milling with lively attention and, at times, praise for the workmanship. Finally she gave approval of Archie Gill as miller.

'I know the carle. An intelligent honest fellow, well fitted to running my mill. Thank ye, Gilfillan.'

'You'll permit Dan Drummond to inform Gill of his new duties?' her husband asked drily as he helped her mount.

'Why not? Isn't the ordering of estate servants in a factor's care, Mr Echlin?' said she, giving rein to her horse.

120

Echlin found Drummond in his office. 'Dan,' he said, 'I've decided on Archie Gill as miller.'

'A guid choice, sir.'

'Gilfillan will school him in the work. He can mill what's left of last year's grain. How did ye fare with Robert Bothwell?'

'It looks guid clean seed. He says he can deliver on time.'

The laird picked up his whip. 'I may meet him in New-townards –'

'One thing afore ye go, sir. The MacIlveens are working the bit of land at the Langstane.'

'Good. What o't?'

'Alexander MacIlveen complains that the Miskimmins are trespassing on it.'

'For God's sake, Dan,' cried Echlin impatiently, 'tell Miskimmin –'

'I'll send –'

'You'll ride out yourself and tell Miskimmin I won't have hilt nor hair of him or any of his brood go near that field. And add, Dan,' said the laird, 'that if I have to send word a second time, Ronane will be the bearer o't. Now, what else?'

Dan Drummond steadied himself, lowered his voice and his brows and said: 'Her Ladyship blames me for not proceeding with the business of Tam McBratney and Rushin Coatie –'

To his surprise and much to his relief the laird waved his whip in a gesture of capitulation. 'Dan, we can't go on with this nonsense aye biting at us. Her Ladyship maintains that one of his Majesty's subjects, no matter how mean, has been put in jeopardy and I've a duty as a magistrate. I think she grossly over-colours, but I'll look into it. And now,' continued Echlin in his customary brisk manner, 'send Archie Gill to Gilfillan. In the meantime pay him a keeping wage till we learn what's the likely output of meal,' and off went the laird, leaving behind a blithe factor grabbing for his bonnet to go in search of Archie Gill.

Drummond had ridden little beyond the Crockart place

when he overtook Neil and Gill. They drew up at his hail.

'Where are ye for?' asked the factor.

'The woodland beyond Lough Reagh.'

'Aye, well, Archie Gill can't go with ye.'

'But I need him to keep tally,' protested Neil.

'I'm 'feard I have to take him from ye. I want him to start at the mill theday.'

'And what am I to do?'

'Take Dan Crockart. He can cypher. Away with ye, Archie, Mr Gilfillan is waiting.'

Waiting till Gill was out of earshot, the factor leaned forward in his saddle, confidentially. 'Her Ladyship wants the laird to prosecute Tam McBratney for trying to murther Rushin Coatie.' Dan nodded sagely, the carrier of confidences.

'Dammit,' said Neil turning away. 'I've more. . . Faith, I thought everyone had forgotten that.'

'Not her Ladyship.'

'How does she propose to set about it?'

'As I tell ye. She's set the whole matter on the laird's shoulders.'

'He'll not thank her for that.'

'It's his bounden duty,' replied Dan Drummond severely. 'Don't ye understand that the life of one of King Jamie's subjects, no matter how mean, was put in jeopardy? It's an orra affair, young man.'

Neil glanced at the factor. The emphasis with which the words had been delivered, as much as the words themselves, seemed a mimic of something not fully apprehended by the speaker.

'Aye, true enough,' said Neil. 'Well, I hope I find Dan Crockart at home now that I've lost Gill.'

Echlin had barely left the factor's office before he regretted his acquiescence. Turnooth, aye ready to meddle in other matters, should have dealt with the drunken loon, McBratney. Now, had he, a magistrate as set out in his undertaking, laid hold on the murderers of puir Watty Mackechnie, he would have hanged them out of hand. But was this frivolous inquisition fit work for one who had been a distinguished soldier in the field? Yet the stubborn harping of his wife stuck like a burr in the mind. The building of the mill had distracted her for a time. . .

'Gill,' he informed her after supper that evening, 'took up his duties as miller today.'

'I hope he acquits himself. The mill adds much to our property, husband.'

'It does. And much of the credit must go to you, my dear.' He studied his wineglass. 'I don't think you've been away from Ravara for more than a day or two since we settled. Would this not be a fitting time to take a holiday? Visit your brother at Finnart, take Anne to Edinburgh? She has seen perhaps too little of her mother.'

'And what of you, husband?'

With a laugh the laird scouted any idea that his burden could be lightened. 'Ah no, my dear Seraphina, I can't be absent at this season.'

'No more can I, my love.'

The laird set down his glass sharply. 'In God's name, why not, madam?'

'Because there is still much that does not please me. Remember, Kenneth, that *my* treasure also went into the purchase of this place.'

'I hadn't forgotten. . .' began Echlin. Then, 'List me what is so pressing if ye please.'

'Willingly.' She marked them off on her elegant fingers. 'Gilfillan hasn't completed the furniture in all the bedchambers. The state of the garden and orchard is much as it was a year ago. We may have missed planting the flowerbeds for another year.'

'Aye, the flowerbeds. . .'

'These are serious matters, Kenneth. As it is now,' and she

123

swept her hand to encompass the establishment, 'surely it must remind ye of an army billet? Carles tramping through the house day in, day out, the endless clatter of hammer and saw. Outside, heaps of mud where there should be sward.'

'I've brought Ronane up to oversee the work –'

'And no doubt he'll see some task hurried forward, provided he keeps his neb clean with Gilfillan. But for house and gardens only I know what's lacking. I long for the day when our sons and their friends can sleep under this roof. And for the day our daughter Anne can wed from here. But not until it's what it should be, a seemly property, a gentlefolk's residence!'

'My dearest Seraphina,' declared Echlin rising from his chair, 'you've breached me completely! Ronane. . . I'll have a word with Gilfillan too. . .'

She motioned him down again. 'Finally,' and she bent back a long finger in emphasis, 'you must punish the cottar who assaulted the lodge-keeper.'

The laird felt like one who had walked into an ambush. 'Attempted murder, ye said?'

'And witchcraft.'

'Witchcraft!' cried Echlin.

'Was not that the counter-accusation?'

'I heard as much,' agreed Echlin.

'I don't want the old beldame harmed. I gave her my protection and that must not be set aside in the public eye.'

In spite of himself the laird grinned. 'You would sit as judge and jury. . . but *witchcraft,* madam –'

'– is a bane that greatly exercises the King as you well know. It will do you no hurt,' said Lady Echlin, 'if his Grace hears of a subject, far-removed from Whitehall, who shares his abhorrence of sorcery and is not idle in his investigation.'

'Aye, but would it ever reach him?' asked the laird in misdoubt. 'Even word sent to London under seal is laggard.'

'Then miss no chance, husband,' said Lady Echlin crisply. 'Great oaks from little acorns grow. You could,' she glanced at him, 'tell the factor to set the inquiry afoot.'

'Faith no!' cried Echlin. 'It'll have my attention tomorrow morn.' He drained his glass and set it down firmly on the table top.

His determination remained with him when he left Rathard House after breakfast. The reflective task of shaving can reveal paths hitherto unsuspected. At times he had been more puzzled than angry with his wife's pursuit of this vagary. True, the life of the auld carline, her creature, had been threatened. But now it seemed that his wife's stubborn insistence on an inquisition was as likely to have arisen from her desire to have his name heard in the King's ear. And of that coming to pass the laird was very sceptical. But he had put his hand to it and was determined to finish off the business as briskly as possible. The problem was how to bring that about in a manner that would satisfy his wife, and the local gossips, yet see justice done to the coof McBratney and the lodge-keeper. In the end the laird spoke to Calum Wishart.

'Calum, I've decided to bring Tam McBratney before me for his damage to the lodge-keeper's house.'

'And what o' the old woman?'

'Well, what of her?'

'The accusation was of laying a spell on the man's beasts. That can't be brushed aside.'

'Aye, so.'

'You'll need the minister sitting with you –'

'Mungo Turnooth!' burst out the laird angrily. 'What has he to do with it?'

'On two counts, laird,' answered Wishart, 'Ye may visit grave punishment on Tam McBratney if ye find him guilty of attempting Rushin Coatie's life. But the inquiry may be satisfied to rule that he's displayed as penitent in the kirk. The minister would have to be consulted on that. Further, I can't see how the ecclesiastical arm can be ignored in a charge of witchcraft.'

125

The laird assented grumpily enough.

'We could have the schoolhouse when the day's work is done. Your good self and Mr Turnooth weighing the evidence. The dominie could preside.' Taking Echlin's silence as agreement, Wishart continued: 'I'll speak for McBratney but someone has to speak for the old dame. Gilchrist is as good as any. Lend him your books.'

'My books. . .?' said the laird.

'Aye, the two volumes on demonology by King Jamie.'

'Ye think they would serve him?'

'They would be to Gilchrist as a brief,' declared Wishart.

'He can have them. Tell him not to bend back the covers.'

'He'll be so advised.'

'The examination is called for the evening after next – Thursday. I'll tell the factor. You carry that word to Mr Turnooth with my respects. And to Gilchrist and Ross.'

That evening, when Wishart hoped to find Neil and the dominie in their lodgings, he called at the schoolhouse. 'Gentles all,' he announced, 'Tam McBratney is to answer for his assault on Rushin Coatie.'

'So I've heard,' said Neil.

'Feth,' said Ross, 'but I thought that had gone cold.'

'I would hazard that her Ladyship has blown on the embers. These learned works are for you,' continued Wishart handing the laird's two volumes to Neil.

Neil turned them over. 'What would I want with these?'

'They constitute your brief. You've been retained to defend the old woman on a charge o' witchcraft –'

'What are ye talking about, man!'

'On my suggestion you appear before the laird and Mungo Turnooth here in the schoolhouse, on the evening after next –'

'I'm damned if I do. You're playacting, Wishart. And I'll take it very sore if ye did mention my name –'

'Softly, softly,' said the other. 'You're not alone in this. Angus here is to preside –'

126

'What's expected of me?' cried the dominie in alarm.

'To sit in a posture of dignified watchfulness throughout. If ye can throw in a word you've earned your keep. I'm speaking for McBratney, for neither side is competent to speak for itself. The laird and the minister will deliver the verdicts. I see,' Wishart closed his eyes, 'her ladyship seated to the one side, Dan Drummond to the other –'

'What of a muster of trumpets and drums?' demanded Neil. 'Ye see this as no more than a bit o' theatre! Tell me,' he continued, rising from his seat, 'what if I don't know enough to save the auld kimmer? Do I trim a stake and gather kindling? There are enough dark gomerils here like McBratney who would see her burn –'

'Lady Echlin doesn't want Rushin Coatie harmed.'

Neil could not repress a snort of laughter. 'A burlesque, no less.' He shrugged. 'I'll look into the books.'

'The minister has to be told. I would welcome your company to the manse.'

Neil seized his bonnet. 'I wouldn't want to be absent when you tell *him*, Calum man.'

On the way to the manse Wishart gave as his opinion that when news of the wood-kernes' attack on Ravara had made its slow progress through Newry to Dublin and across the sea to London, it would bring a government agent to Rathard House. Important therefore, continued Wishart, that the people of Ravara and their laird act in a manner responsible and law-abiding '. . . wherefore, friends, the weight of this investigation, or whatever you're pleased to dub it.'

'Sagacious Wishart,' said Neil, persuaded for all that.

A cur stretched on the manse threshold gathered itself, barked, and crept into the shrubbery to watch them chap on the door. It was opened to them by Mistress Tabitha with a flour-daubed hand. Her brother stood at the desk in his study. He surveyed the visitors with a sardonic smile.

'Guid e'en, to ye, gentlemen,' he said.

127

'We've come on the business of –' began Wishart.

Mr Turnooth raised his hand. 'I ken why you're here. You're here for guidance. I trust you've committed yoursel' to nothing foolish?'

'Nothing, so far as I'm aware of, minister.'

'Guid.' Before closing the volume on the desk Mr Turnooth slipped in a goose quill as a marker. He selected a staff from a dark corner. 'It's time for my breath of air,' and he led them from the house. Outside he called on the dog. It sidled forward with vigorously wagging tail.

Ross bent to pat the animal's head. 'He ran off when he saw us coming.'

'Like yoursel', Angus, he's of a mansuete nature. It's welcome in dominies but not much use in a watchdog. But my sister's fond of him.' He quickened his pace, drawing the others after him. 'Lady Echlin sent me word of what's afoot. Ye understand that in matters such as this I'm sole arbiter.'

Neil prickled at the cleric's overweening words to Ross. 'Have ye informed Mr Echlin of that, minister?'

'With respect, Mr Turnooth,' interjected Wishart, 'the laird considers it his duty to act as magistrate as well as landowner. It is laid down so in the undertaking, framed, I understand, by King James.'

The minister thrust a hostile glare at Neil but chose to pursue Wishart, if somewhat obliquely.

'Calum,' said he, 'there's but one king in Scotland, the Lord Jesus Christ, and this laddie, James, is but Christ's silly vassal.' He snedded the heads of a clump of seeding goosegrass with his staff. ''Twas not Jamie but that auld Episcopalian harridan, Bess, that vested the likes o' Kenneth Echlin with magisterial authority.'

'For all that,' said Wishart firmly, 'now that the laird's put his hand to it he intends to exercise his authority –'

'Authority? God gave authority of public instruction and correction but to two sorts of men: to his ecclesiastical ministers and to temporal magistrates. Note the order o' sequence, Calum man.'

'Mr Turnooth,' said Wishart, who was evidently enjoying himself, 'I'm only the bearer of a message. Do you share the examination with the laird?'

The minister nodded gravely as one bestowing a boon. 'Aye, ye can say that. When and where?'

'On Thursday night in the schoolhouse. It would be well to have witnesses o' the proceedings.'

Mr Turnooth halted. 'For why?'

'So that a true account goes out. Stories spoil in the carrying o' them.'

'Aye, true. I'll summon the kirk elders. I understand you're speaking for Tam McBratney?'

'To the best of my ability,' answered Wishart.

'That puir man's heid is no better than a frosted turnip.'

'Undoubtedly his defence, hinging on the counter-charge, presents problems.'

'Let me supplement your arguments –'

'Mr Turnooth,' said Neil, 'do ye consider it proper, at this stage, that an arbiter should express an opinion towards one side or the other? I speak for the Rushin Coatie.'

'Haud there, you'll hae my advice in a minute,' said Mr Turnooth, turning back to Wishart.

Neil had the most powerful inclination not to hold there. But his companions were pinned by the cleric and he could not leave.

'Calum,' said Mr Turnooth, 'that puir hav'rel is by nature a melancholious man, and the Lord God made him so. But that he's aye soused in strong liquor is the Deil's handiwork. And the Deil's agents are the Miskimmin clan. That brood o' miscreants concoct a raw muddy ale purveyed to their neighbours, including Tam McBratney, without tax paid on any side. Now, if secular authority, meaning Kenneth Echlin, would turn his attention to that!'

129

'Minister,' said Wishart with a smile. 'I think if I were to raise that, the dominie, as president would rule *ab inconvenienti* –'

'Ha!' cried Mr Turnooth. 'No Latin and it please ye! I'll no have Latin spoke. Recall that the elders o' the kirk are present. The guid Scots tongue will suffice. And you, young man,' giving his attention to Neil, 'I would advise tae con the Good Book. Consider Exodus twenty-two and eighteen, "Thou shalt not suffer a witch tae live", and again Deuteronomy, eighteen and ten –'

'Sir,' said Neil who had recovered his good humour, 'permit me to remind you that I am assigned to refute the charge of witchcraft held against the Rushin Coatie. But, with the assistance of Angus, who is better read in it, I shall certainly consult the Bible. And I hope to look into the King's *Daemonologie* and gain some help thereby.'

The minister shook his head sorrowfully. 'A profane work by a profane hand.'

'You have read it?'

'I have not. The consension of sensible opinion values that opuscule as no better than a whuff of chaff. But dinna fash yourself, Master Gilchrist, Lucifer will have to outbid my Lady Echlin for the auld beldame's corpus. Her immortal soul is my concern,' concluded the minister darkly.

'I trust, minister, that such a divorce will not be called for.'

'Aye,' returned Mr Turnooth slowly, his gaze lingering on Neil. 'A glib tongue should serve the auld woman well.' He grasped his staff and called his dog. 'If ye feel in need of further guidance, gentlemen, ye ken where I'll be.'

On their road to the schoolhouse they turned occasionally to watch the minister as he strode homeward. They saw his staff rise and fall as he beat down briers and branches that would have ensnared him. When next they looked man and dog had gone.

'The reverend man should carry a crook on the head o' his staff,' said Wishart. 'For all his fulmination against episcopacy he's of a prelatic disposition – all things his way.'

Angus Ross spoke in a kinder tone. 'Ye underestimate the guid man's spiritual fervour, for he cherishes the kirk. Forbye, he gave way to what you proposed, if a shade gracelessly.'

'He did,' agreed Wishart in a grudging note. 'But one could love the kirk well enough, without aye riding in the rigging of it.'

'Peh!' cried Neil, 'that's his trade. What makes my hair creep is all this abuse of the King and secular authority. What if he's overheard by the laird or some government agent?'

'His reply,' said Ross with a chuckle, 'would be that of John Knox to Mary, ". . .both my vocation and conscience crave plainness of me". He has his exemplars, has Mungo Turnooth!'

Neil was not persuaded, 'Calum foresees the arrival of a government emissary. I hope he's as tolerant wi' the Reverend Turnooth as you, Angus.'

Later, as they sat at supper, Neil asked. 'Does it not strike ye that this gallimaufry could have been avoided if the laird had sent McBratney packing? For that matter why has he borne with the Miskimmin brood for so long? The holdings wouldn't lie idle. There's a willing family arriving near every month.'

'He did that once,' said Ross. 'The man and wife and their bairns raised such a scraich of lairdly injustice on Portpatrick quay it was heard as far away as Edinburgh. Mr Echlin swore never again.'

'And I must remind ye,' said Calum Wishart, 'of the Reverend Mr Turnooth's obligation to lost sheep.'

'Mark those texts he quoted for me, Angus,' said Neil rising from his stool and taking up the laird's volumes, 'I'm away to my eldritch studies.'

12

Neil had not got far into his Grace's dialogue on the detestable cult of enchantment when weariness overtook him. A dozen such works he decided would still leave him mute before the imperious query: 'Did he trulie understande why the Deil worked more sorcerie with anciente women than with others?' Then, just as he was about to give up, he came on a passage amenable to proof, a fixed stone in the grummly rush of words. Remembering Wishart's injunction he closed the volume gently and went to bed.

The clachan was only stirring next morning when he rode out to the manse. To his relief the barking of the dog brought Mistress Tabitha to the door. They had barely exchanged greetings when the minister appeared, his breeks dragged hastily over the tails of his nightshirt.

'You're early on the trot, young man. What's so urgent that ye get me from my bed?'

'It's your sister I came to see, sir. Would ye be so good as to step out with me, Mistress Tabitha?'

Whatever the Reverend Mr Turnooth had to say was cut short by his sister informing him that his breakfast was on the hob. She drew a shawl around herself and stepped out with the young man on the shorn space in front of the house.

Puzzled and somewhat offended, the minister watched them stroll backwards and forwards, the dew sparkling up from their steps. A smell of singeing forced a hurried retreat to the kitchen. When he returned, supping from his bowl, the two were still deep in conversation. They paused and the minister watched as Neil took money from his pocket.

Together they walked to Neil's tethered horse. 'Ye understand, Mr Gilchrist, that I should tell the minister of this?'

'I'm aware, Mistress Tabitha, that you will harken to what's right in conscience. But please to remember that Mr Turnooth is an arbiter still to be persuaded by my argument.'

Mistress Tabitha's thin face creased in a smile. 'Those years were not without profit, young sir, ye spent studying to split hairs.'

Neil felt somewhat aggrieved at this parting remark but concluded that anyone who had to live day in, day out, with Mungo Turnooth should be permitted a little flippancy now and then.

A dour Dan Drummond met him at the office. 'I thought ye were for the upper woods theday, Neil?'

'I was. Now there's all this stir about Tam McBratney. . .'

'You're speaking for the auld woman? You'll have to be good – for her sake.'

There was a slyness about Drummond's manner that made Neil pause. 'Dan, is there more to this than I have knowledge of?'

'Ye should have acquainted yourself afore ye started,' answered Drummond, a scatheful note in his voice. 'The auld kimmer *is* a witch!'

''Sfaith, man, what makes ye say that?'

'Ech, 'twas common knowledge to folk long afore Tam McBratney lost his cow. Long afore you came here,' added the factor pointedly. He gave his head a shake. 'If ye fail the neighbours'll run her out. I wouldn't be in your shoes with her Ladyship. . .'

At this Neil smiled slowly. 'And you'll see to it, Dan?' He considered the factor for a moment. 'Dan, I was here on the morn McBratney told ye Rushin Coatie had put a cantrip on his beast. But you'll remember ye were too busy. Ye turned him off on Calum Wishart.' Neil's smile broadened. 'I think ye would be well guided, Dan, not to get tangled in this affair.'

Late that afternoon one of the Neilson bairns, halted by Mistress Tabitha on his way home, carried her missive to the schoolhouse. Angus took it from the boy and handed it to Neil.

133

He glanced down at Mistress Tabitha's letter then slid it between the covers of *Daemonologie in Forme of a Dialogue*. He had gleaned little from Philomathes's pat queries and Epistemon's tortuous eruditions. Whether Mistress Tabitha's findings would serve him better had yet to be seen. At least it would save him from standing like a gowk before the laird and the minister.

Word came from Rathard House that Lady Echlin would not attend the inquiry. But her Ladyship left no one in doubt as to her lively interest by directing that there must be other women present besides Rushin Coatie. The minister thereupon sent out word that the wives of elders were expected to accompany their husbands to the kirk for prayer and then to the trial.

Tam McBratney, escorted by his advocate, was first to arrive at the schoolhouse. Neil noted askance that he had been brought from his sordid muddle of a home shaved, combed, and possibly sober. With no stomach for Rushin Coatie riding pillion behind him he had asked Dugal the smith to fetch her. When she arrived he led her to a stool across the room from McBratney.

'Sit here, Rushin Coatie.'

Obediently she sat down. 'Sir,' said she, 'I shouldn't be here. There's a family with bairns from Scotland at the lodging-house. . .'

He looked down and met the aged eyes behind the veil of locks. God's name, he thought, but this auld beldame has done as much for Kenneth Echlin's estate as any trig guidwife in Ravara. He hunkered down beside her. 'Rushin Coatie, I'll ask ye one or two questions. The answers will come to ye as clear as daylight. I'll see to it that you're not kept o'er long. Then ye can return to your charges.'

The thump of the minister's staff announced the arrival of the elders and their wives in their Sabbath homespun and solid shoes. The elders, including the disgruntled factor, took the stools set out by the dominie, the women standing behind them as was the way in the kirk.

The minister summoned Neil and Calum Wishart. 'How's your charge?' he demanded of Wishart. 'Drunk or sober?'

'Sober as a judge.'

'Aye.' The minister's eyes slid away from the other's bland expression. 'Put the halter on him if he starts any blethering. We don't want to be here till cockcrow. And you, young man, how's the Rushin Coatie?'

'Concerned that she has to leave a newly-arrived family and subject herself to this frivolous charge, Mr Turnooth.'

'Heh!' cried the minister, 'but the auld carline has grown unco loquacious of a sudden!' He snuffed his sardonic grin. 'Whether the charge be frivolous or not, waits on *our* finding.' The Reverend Mr Turnooth turned on his heel and ascended to one of the two chairs sitting forward on the shallow rostrum.

Echlin hurried in, brisk, impatient. He paused, gave a curt bow to the assembled folk. With a word to Mr Turnooth he sat down and looked around him. What he saw did not please him. He beckoned Ross to come close. The exchange between the two was muted and brief. Ross crossed the room and ushered Dan Drummond to a stool on the platform; a little withdrawn but above the assemblage.

Echlin turned to where the dominie had now taken up his station at the tall teaching desk. 'Begin, Mr Ross,' he said.

Face flushed, Ross shuffled some papers that lay before him. 'Gentlemen,' he began, '– Mr Echlin and the Reverend Mr Turnooth, ye are here to consider and give your judgment on divers complaints affecting two tenants of Ravara. One, Tam McBratney, cottar, the other, the lodge-keeper, commonly known as the Rushin Coatie. A most flagrant incident occurred in the month of May past, when McBratney sealed up the lodge-house in an attempt to smother the occupant, the Rushin Coatie. Many witnessed the assault, some of whom are present here.' Half his narrative over, the dominie pressed on with more assurance. 'Tam McBratney, for his part, alleges that the

135

lodge-keeper put a spell or cantrip on a milking cow of his with the result that the animal died and he suffered grievous loss thereby. In short, he accuses the woman of sorcery – that she practices the heinous art of witchcraft. . .' Ross shuffled his papers. 'I think that is as far as I can go, gentlemen.'

Mr Turnooth half-turned and raised his hand as much as to say that the dominie had done well enough. Then he and Echlin put their heads together. All present were witness to the degree of accord between the two leaders of their little world. The laird gave a final nod of agreement.

'We'll hear what's to be said on the charge of witchcraft against the lodge-keeper,' Echlin announced.

The elders and their womenfolk stirred in anticipation. The good wine was not to be kept to the last.

'Mr Wishart,' said Angus Ross.

'Haud a minute,' cried Mr Turnooth. 'Is it seemly that Tam McBratney and the Rushin Coatie should be seated during these pleadings?'

'Gentlemen,' said Neil with a hasty glance at Wishart, 'it was not our intention that either McBratney or the auld woman should speak –'

'We'll decide that, Mr Gilchrist.'

'Neither of them has been sworn, Mr Turnooth.'

The laird's ring clashed against his chair-arm. 'Mr Gilchrist, I can't think of a greater folly than that a bodie should lie, or be encouraged to do so, before this company. Proceed, Mr Wishart.'

Listening to the dominie outlining the purpose of the inquiry, it had become plain to Wishart that he was like a man who had taken on himself to plough a stony acre. He wished he had a book to flourish like Gilchrist. For once his lively fancy was as empty as his hands.

'Sirs, I make no attempt to exonerate McBratney. The assault on the lodging-house was an act of madness. It failed, by great good fortune –'

'By the will of the Almighty,' interjected the minister.

'Or some other power, minister,' said Wishart, gazing into the startled face of the reverend gentleman and conscious of the sudden rustle among the elders behind him.

'To a cottar in McBratney's circumstances, the death of the cow was a sore blow. He was fully persuaded in his own mind that the beast was destroyed by the malefic powers exercised by this woman. There is no other explanation,' and Wishart threw up his empty hands.

'Eh, Mr Wishart,' exclaimed the minister, 'we must search longer and deeper than that!'

Echlin nodded in emphatic agreement. 'Mr Wishart,' he said, 'this was not the first time that Tam McBratney had sickness in his stock?'

'That's true, laird. His feeding is not of the best —'

'Let's set that aside for the minute. Tell us of the previous complaint.'

'About two years ago an animal fell ill. He alleged to Mr Drummond that it had been bewitched by the Rushin Coatie.'

'To the factor, eh?' The laird glanced across to where Dan Drummond sat, fingering his knees.

Drummond looked up and interpreted his master's scrutiny as requiring an answer. 'I warned him to mind his tongue and sent him to Calum Wishart.'

'As one would expect, sound advice.'

The factor sat up straighter on his stool.

'The beast was down,' said Wishart. 'I administered a bolus. Next morning she was on her feet and feeding.'

'A nostrum against witchcraft?' murmured Mr Turnooth.

The sardonic note stung Wishart. 'Ye cannot but be aware, that I have succoured much of the stock that has fallen ill in Ravara.'

The laird made a placatory gesture but Mr Turnooth continued, 'Then why not in the case we are now considering?'

A mischievous desire took hold of Calum Wishart. Instead of

playing the role he had cast for himself he had been man-oeuvred into the situation of a rapidly drained witness. 'For two good reasons, Mr Turnooth. First, an animal may be too far gone for any medicine to revive it. Second,' he paused, 'an evil influence can in some mysterious and diabolical fashion be directed towards a persecuted individual or his possessions. For that, reverend sir, there is *no* nostrum.'

A stir ran through the assembled elders.

Echlin sat up. 'In plain language, Mr Wishart, are ye saying that this was a work o' sorcery – that the Deil was in this?'

Wishart shrugged. 'I have no answer to that, sir.'

'But as I understand it the cow went down with a complaint ye would readily recognise.'

'True,' replied Wishart, 'but there is testimony enough that the servants of Satan employ common maladies to deceive us.'

Echlin sat silent. This imbroglio was becoming more tangled and dangerous every minute. He wished to God he had fol-lowed his common sense and turned a deaf ear to his wife's blandishments. The eyes of the elders were intent upon him. He turned to Neil. 'Mr Gilchrist, have you anything to say to us?'

Neil stood up, the volume in his hand. He had listened to Wishart with growing unease. Now he had an overwhelming urge to demolish him.

'Yes, gentlemen, I have something to say. I came here with little relish – or knowledge – to defend, as best I might, the Rushin Coatie against this charge of destroying an animal, the property of the cottar McBratney. The clishmaclaver that you have listened to from Mr Wishart relieved me of that task. . .'

There was a murmuring among the elders and their women-folk. It was evident that they did not share the young man's sanguine conclusion. Unobtrusively but surely, as Neil ob-served, these authors of opinion and prejudice had taken upon themselves the function of a jury.

'Mr Wishart has referred to "a persecuted individual",' Neil continued. 'I want to ask McBratney a question. The laird has warned us of the folly of lying to this assembly. I want to ask McBratney did the Rushin Coatie by word or deed ever persecute or threaten him or any of his family?'

Every eye in the schoolhouse was turned on the cottar, miserable in his sobriety. There was a brief tussle of peremptory questioning by Wishart. He then straightened up. 'McBratney says that some time before his beast died Rushin Coatie, with her skirts kilted to her knees, ran past his door.' Wishart offered this disclosure with the air of one who would be surprised if any notice was taken of it.

'Maybe,' an ancient voice opined, 'she was afeard of being asked in.'

A cackle of merriment rose from the gathered kirk worthies. The laird frowned.

The minister slid forward on his chair, waving a finger. 'Elders and brethren you're here to listen and mark. You're not here to comment.'

Neil waited for the elders to settle. 'Now, can I have an answer to my question: does Tam McBratney still maintain that the Rushin Coatie persecuted him, or threatened him, or any member of his family?'

This time Wishart didn't trouble to confer with his client. He shook his head. 'No, he does not.'

Neil ran his eye along the row of elders. 'Mark that, guidfolk,' he said.

'Aye, all well and guid, Mr Gilchrist,' cried the minister with the air of one caught up in the excitement of disputation, 'but ye haven't explained how the cow came to die!'

'Nor need I, reverend sir,' answered Neil. 'If Mr Wishart, skilled in the use of bolus and drench, doesn't ken how an ill-nourished beast dies in a filthy cattle-house, it's not for me to make a guess.'

There was a murmur of agreement and a nodding of heads among the elders. Neil watched them; it's my criticism of a neighbour's husbandry that has them grinning, he thought. If

Mr Turnooth had a rejoinder he kept it to himself.

'Hae ye said all, Mr Gilchrist?' asked the laird.

'There is still the charge o' witchcraft to be disproved, sir.'

'Then proceed,' said Echlin settling back with the air of a man who had decided that the evening might not have been completely misspent.

'Gentlemen,' Neil began, 'I've discovered in the last twa-three days that there's a lang-held hearsay in Ravara that the Rushin Coatie is a witch.' He held up his hand to restrain the minister. 'Mr Turnooth, I quote from good authority,' and his gaze rested for a moment on the factor. 'And I'll tell ye why she's dubbed a witch. She's an auld woman, she lives alone, she's of independent mind, the strange duds she wears makes her a kenspeckle figure in this community. That's enough for mirk minds and malicious tongues. Is that no unco strange,' he turned a soft smile on the elders and their wives, 'when ye mind that it was the Rushin Coatie who cooked your meal and shook out your beds when ye first arrived cauldrife and spent from Scotland?' He won no answering smile from the cluster of dark figures.

'McBratney's drunken assault is the first violence shown to the woman. It rests wi' this tribunal to assure there's never another –'

'Nor will there be,' said the laird with a trace of impatience.

'But more's needed, Mr Echlin,' said Neil firmly. 'It is not enough that this woman should continue under ignorant suspicion restrained from worse only by her Ladyship's patronage.'

Echlin's face showed that he did not take kindly to this. It was the minister who asked, with a condescending smirk, 'And how do ye propose to go about that, Mr Gilchrist?'

'By showing that the Rushin Coatie never had any traffic with the Devil nor the Devil with her.'

'That may lie outside *your* eloquence, young sir,' said Mr Turnooth snappishly.

140

'Indeed that's so, sir. But I've had the good fortune to consult the greatest authority in Christendom on these matters, his Grace, King James, *Malleus Maleficanum* – the Hammer of Witches. I had thought to read at length from his work,' continued Neil flourishing the volume, 'but I will keep the extracts brief –'

'The Lord be thankit for that,' muttered Mr Turnooth.

'But, gentlemen, I would have ye understand that if ye fault my conclusions then his Grace is agley in his. For I stick close to the text.'

'We accept that,' said the laird.

'The Devil,' Neil began, 'stands closest to those tormented by worldly appetites. These he undertakes to satisfy if his victim will but defect from God and abjure his Christian baptism. On these he sets his secret mark, the Devil's Nip. The foul and unclean spirit of Satan uses every man and woman according to their complexion and nature. To the gambler, at the price of his immortal soul, he gives skill at cards and dice to deceive his neighbours thereby. What horse shall win at match-running –'

'Mr Gilchrist,' said the laird frowning, 'are ye making jest o' his Majesty's writings?'

Neil held up the book, tapping it with his forefinger. 'It's all here, laird.'

The minister grinned maliciously. Echlin sat back like a man found doubting his own testament.

'The mighty, who are for all that his bond-slaves, Satan makes privy to conspiracies and the most secret conclaves at home and abroad. On the wealthy he heaps wealth. Those frenzied by a curiosity after knowledge not necessary for their salvation he leads into the black hell o' necromancy –'

'Young sir,' interrupted the minister, 'I'm 'feard you're enjoying this over much. What o' the Rushin Coatie?'

'Mr Turnooth, I am but endeavouring to show that there are few who can call themselves safe when the whisper is witchcraft. None less than those of poor and base degree, from which,

141

according to his Grace, the greatest number of witches come. The Devil has a preference that they be young, sonsy and well-favoured. . .'

Neil, leafing through the book, let the words hang in the air. The elders and their wives all turned their stare on the Rushin Coatie.

'. . . and the manner they gain reward abases them all the more. If they but kiss the Devil's buttocks their tables are laden with dainty dishes. There are other gifts I will not recite before this grave assembly. Rushin Coatie, what was your supper on the day Tam McBratney's beast died?'

Startled, the old woman clawed back her hair. 'It's aye the same sir, kale. . . what's left in the pots.'

'Rushin Coatie, does wine ever run from your walls?' As he waited Neil held the book towards the arbiters, tapping it, silencing them. 'Rushin Coatie, does wine ever run from your walls?'

Suspicious, she peered at her interrogator. 'Rain water runs down my walls. . . there's a muckle great hole at the eaves. . . Wine!' Suddenly she raised her heels from the floor and threw back her head in such a shrill cackle of merriment that the elders and their wives, perforce, shook and gasped and wiped their eyes.

The laird held up his hand for silence. 'Mr Gilchrist, do ye consider that ye have cleared the auld woman from the charge of witchcraft?'

'It's no comfort that ye have to ask, sir. I have but one more statement. Earlier I spoke of the Devil's Nip whereby Satan marks his own. His Grace makes much of this stigma, for it's ineradicable. Today the Rushin Coatie was examined by Mistress Tabitha –'

There was a squeal of fury from Mr Turnooth. He was on his feet pointing a trembling finger at the young man. 'So that was. . . that was. . .'

Faith, and the good lady was able to keep her own counsel,

142

thought Neil as he drew the missive from the book and calmly unfolded it. 'This is what was discovered. D'ye wish to hear it, gentlemen?'

Face flushed in anger, Mr Turnooth was still on his feet, until he was forced down by the muscular grip of the laird.

'Read it, Gilchrist,' said the laird.

'Mistress Tabitha took with her two witnesses, Meg MacIlveen and Chrissy Maclennan.' Neil tipped the paper to the fading light of the September evening. '"We have searched the Rushin Coatie with great care from the crown of her head to the soles of her feet. We found naught but old scars, burn marks on her legs and arms, warts, brier tears and flea bites. There was no mark we did not recognise as common and natural to a woman of her age and duties."'

There was a sudden babble and nodding of heads among the elders and their women. Only Meg MacIlveen stood silent as if waiting for more.

Neil folded the paper. 'Mr President, you may wish to retain this document.' As he handed it up to Angus Ross he saw on the laird's face an expression of amusement and surprise.

But Mr Turnooth was still in an ill-temper. 'My sis – these women were instructed what to look for?'

'Mr Turnooth,' said Neil, 'I regret that you could not be informed. But as a judge in this case, that was not possible. Yes, Mistress Tabitha knew what to look for.'

'Then,' said the minister, 'one of your witnesses is in a right puckle at what you've just read to us,' and gleefully he indicated Meg MacIlveen who was gesticulating as boldly as she dared.

Neil smiled. 'She's not reneging, minister. I ken what's troubling her. Gentlemen, I've said all I have to say.'

Laird and minister put their heads together. Their parley was brief. The laird knocked on the arm of his chair. 'Guidfolk, it grows dark. There is little to be said about the charge of witchcraft. It has no body or substance whatsoever. As Mr

Gilchrist rightly said it was born of mirk minds and malignant tongues.'

With that the laird gave way to the Reverend Turnooth, who shuffled his backside forward on the chair the better to address the gathering.

'Let it be clearly understood, brethren,' began the minister, 'here and beyond, that the Rushin Coatie is, and always has been, as distant from Satan and his deceits, as any baptised soul under this roof. Are ye o' that opinion?' He cocked his hand to his ear to receive the consentient chorus.

Well, thought Neil, that's generous enough.

'Your laird and I have considered the charge against Tam McBratney. Tam's a puir drouthy bodie, but he attempted the life of the auld woman. For that he'll stand on the penitent stool through all the services for six Sabbaths.'

There was a murmur among the elders which could be interpreted as surprise at this leniency, for the dowf creature was as familiar perched in that situation as seated with his family in the body of the kirk.

Mr Turnooth held up his hand. 'Your laird's to speak.'

'From themorrow McBratney or one of his family will tend the garden at the lodging-house. It will be dug, manured and kept clean, and such plants as the lodge-keeper requires – to be supplied by McBratney – will be set at the proper times. That will continue in and out o' season till I advise the factor otherwise.'

The simplicity of the judgment and the labour it promised for their errant neighbour much appealed to the elders. Dan Drummond also nodded vigorously as one warmly approving the decision and indispensible in seeing it carried out.

The windows, high in the walls, were now no more than glimmering shapes, quickly fading. Meg MacIlveen rested her hands ever heavier on Alexander's shoulders. Angus Ross moved stiffly from his desk, bent his legs froglike and, lowering his head between the laird and the minister, asked should he have Chrissy Maclennan bring a lamp.

Echlin rose abruptly. 'Guidfolk, this examination is at an end. Mr Turnooth and I are agreed, a just and equitable end. We trust ye took tent to what passed here, and will no be blate,' the laird permitted himself a bleak smile, 'in informing your neighbours of the outcome. We wish to thank the elders for their presence and Mr Wishart and Mr Gilchrist for their help in our deliberations.'

The Reverend Turnooth appeared at the laird's elbow. 'Away home, frien's,' he said with a gesture of dismissal, 'while there's still light to see where you set your feet.'

The laird and the minister were the last to leave the schoolhouse. Mr Turnooth thumped past Neil with a curt goodnight. Echlin paused with a smile and a shake of the head.

'Ye should never have left your law books, Gilchrist. Goodnight tae ye.'

There was a silence as the three gathered at the hearth in the living-room. Ross, eager to speak, glanced anxiously from one companion to the other.

Wishart spurred the fire into life with his foot. 'Ye gave me some shrewd dunts, Neil,' he said with a grin.

'It was for the auld woman, Calum.'

'She had a good advocate.'

'Supper, my frien's!' cried the dominie, making a happy clatter with bowls and spoons.

Wishart paused in his supping. 'The auld hen, MacIlveen, what was troubling her?'

Neil laughed silently. 'The three good women added a rider. That the Rushin Coatie would be the better of soap and water and a clean new sark.'

13

No one submitted more readily to the yoke of daily labour than Alexander MacIlveen. The Langstane field had been tilled and sown in good time. On the morning he and Sorley bore their sickles and forks to harvest it he heard Moses's promise on the breath of wind running through the green bushes. The Lord thy God shall bless the fruit of the land, the corn, the increase of thy kine, in the land which he swore unto thy fathers to give thee. Sorley too, was preoccupied. He was wondering if, with the field cleared, he could plant two or three drills of winter kale.

For different reasons his parents were not in favour of this. Alexander, aye canny, felt that Mr Drummond would think they were taking too much, too early, out of the land. Sorley scoffed at this. Next year the richest part of the field would be where he had set the kale.

Meg was feared that Sorley's eye was bigger than his wame. Now that they had lost the braehead, more time, she said, could be spent in the cottage outfield. But the guidwife knew, as her son knew, that Rab Purdie, with the three spades of his father and brothers busy around his own home, was always willing, eager indeed, to step over and give Ellen a hand in cutting scraws or any task that could employ two people. So Sorley got his way with the kale-planting in the Langstane field. The crop demanded daily attention, for all Meg's muttering. No drills were ever kept so clean. No plants as assiduously earthed up. Neil Gilchrist, riding by the burn one day, noticed that young MacIlveen had now the assistance in his husbandry of that fey lass, Elphie Miskimmin.

Since losing Archie Gill to the mill, Neil worked alone. Archie had been a genial companion, a man of good sense and dry humour, a coaxer of seedlings, with a judicious eye and ear for the run of seepage in a wooded slope. No doubt another assistant would be found, but Neil felt put out that he should have to remind the laird or Drummond.

It was Archie and he who had thrown up the rackle of turves and boughs close to the edge of Lough Reagh. It was no more than a shelter in which to eat their midday meal before they pushed on to the farthest plot of saplings. Now, working alone, it was his turning point. He was about to dismount when he heard voices from the shelter. He sat motionless, listening. There was no cultivated land on the rushy loughside, no reason why anybody from Ravara should be here. A man came from the shelter, dragging the carcase of a young heifer at his heels. A second man appeared and a third, the belts of all three sagging under a miscellany of weapons. Peering through the foliage Neil observed the tangled locks and unkempt appearance of men who slept rough in the woodland.

A fourth man came out, stopped, and glanced carefully around him. He was a huge creature, made even bulkier by the plaid cast over his shoulder. Neil felt the skin of his face tighten as the scrutiny came slowly round to meet his motionless gaze and pass on without a flicker. With cautious fingers he drew his pistol from the saddle-holster. The ruffian's name came to him as he cautiously cocked the weapon. If God grants me one pistol shot before I'm downed, the ball is for the breast of Lachie Dubh.

But the monstrous reiver seemed satisfied by his scrutiny. He picked up a cudgel from where it had been lying at the entrance to the shelter like some drover's stick. Swinging it loosely he issued his commands. A trimmed pole was thrust between the bound legs of the carcase and hoisted on to the shoulders of two of the men. A cur came out of the undergrowth, belly to the ground, tail wagging, and having been greeted with a lick of the cudgel that sent it staggering, fell obediently in at the heel of its master.

The young man did not stir until sight and sound had faded far into the woodland. As he rode back he brooded on the creature, Lachie Dubh. He would have had little difficulty in finding a passage to Ireland. Perhaps he and his crew had seized a craft, leaving behind them a corpse or two at some fishing inlet. The watchful survey as Lachie came from the shelter marked him out from the rogues he commanded. Neil's scruff prickled as he remembered that slow gaze crossing his leaf-shrouded face and passing on. He clapped the docile animal under him. 'Long life to ye, auld lass, for ye preserved mine this day!' As for the shelter that Archie and he had built, he would have it pulled down and scattered. He had seen it fouled.

Echlin, Neil and Ronane were gathered in the laird's study. '. . . and I would warn ye that Lachie Dubh is as cunning as he is. . .' Neil hesitated, at a loss to convey to the two veterans the impression of evil that emanated from the monstrous creature '. . . as he is brutal. He's wanted in Scotland for murder. . .'

The laird glanced up at Ronane then back to Neil. 'He might be fit to tell who killed and stripped Watty Mackechnie.'

'They seem like the gillravagers Alfred Porson chased from the Cordwaine estate.'

'Aye, very likely.' Echlin rose briskly. 'We'll hunt 'em. You take one party, Ronane, and you, Neil, another. How many did ye say were with him?'

'Three others.'

'Porson thought there were six in the crew he pursued,' said Ronane.

'They could have another lair further back in the forest. With the crops in, you could muster about ten men apiece. See to it that at least two stay with the horses when ye search the brushwood on foot.'

'I've a feeling,' said Ronane, 'that Porson would want to be with us.'

'Very well. If he has Mr Cordwaine's permission, Porson and his Englishmen would be welcome.' Echlin gave a hard little grin. 'Tell 'em we're hunting Scots miscreants. That should make 'em all the warmer.'

'I think Ronane should take Archie Gill with him. He's as familiar wi' the country there as I am.'

'Then see to it, both of ye.'

Neil was at the door when Echlin called him back. 'Why were ye riding alone?'

'I've had nobody since I lost Archie Gill –'

'Damn it, that was four months ago!' The laird struck his desk. 'Let you and Dan Drummond find you an assistant. And tell Drummond that no man is to travel any distance alone till we've redd up this rat's-litter.'

Little time was lost by Ronane and Neil in mounting a search for the outlaws. There were more than enough young blades eager to pursue a two-legged quarry. Card-houses and dancing were unknown in Ravara; the reprobate fiddle-playing Miskimmins only proved the iron rule. Better for a birkie to be out in the forest aisles among the muskets and lanterns of his fellows than stranded at the hearth with blethering auld women.

Before the week was out Neil had completed his muster which included Rab Purdie, Sorley MacIlveen and one of the Miskimmins, Samuel, a gangling creature with a sly grin and there because he was the best musket shot in the countryside. Neil heard with satisfaction that Ronane had enlisted the help of Archie Gill. Alfred Porson rode to Rathard House to tell Echlin that he had twelve yeomen ready for the pursuit. And the laird sent a message to his neighbour, Mr Lowry of Ballymacashon, advising him to be on the watch for Lachie and his gang breaking from one demesne to the other.

The Sabbath intervening, the Ravara men assembled on the manse green on the Monday morning. Little was said between Neil and Ronane for they had heard that Porson and his men were already combing the boundary woods on Cordwaine's land.

As Ronane was about to mount, Neil asked with a smile, 'What of your bow?'

'I don't waste shafts on vermin, Mr Gilchrist.' The steward halted, staring over Neil's shoulder. 'What – who in hell comes here?'

About a dozen men, armed with knives or staves, had appeared on the far side of the green. At their head strode a young man in the garb Neil recognised as that of a chieftain among the Irish. With an oath Ronane seized his horse's bridle and retreated a dozen paces. There he turned, resting a hand on his pistol butt, and watched the newcomers with an inimical gaze. Uncertain, the men of his party drifted around him.

The young Irishman ran a haughty eye over Neil and the men with him. 'Mr Drummond?' he asked.

'He's not here,' said Neil.

'Who are you?' To Neil the manner of asking sounded too peremptory.

'Neil Gilchrist.'

'Have you any authority here?'

Neil did not hasten to answer. Leisurely he examined the combed locks, the handsome insolent face, the quilted jerkin drawn in by a belt accoutred with two fine pistols and a sword, until his eyes rested on the laced buskins. He raised his head slowly and nodded. 'And you – what d'ye want?'

'Give him,' whispered Samuel Miskimmin in Neil's ear, 'a kick up the arse.'

It was impossible that the young man could have heard, yet Neil saw his hand hover at his sword hilt.

'Your name, sir, and your business here?' Neil demanded again.

He touched himself on the breast, 'Cahir O'Hagan. I come from Turlough MacCartan to see that these thieves are taken.'

Neil's eyebrows went up. 'Why, Mr Echlin will be glad of your assistance.'

'We are not here to assist the Echlins. We have lost cattle. These Scotch dogs have taken them.'

150

'You seem curiously well-informed as to their origins,' responded Neil coldly, 'but, I grant ye, they may well be the miscreants.' He glanced at the men standing behind O'Hagan, strong-boned fellows, listening impassively while their leader conversed in a strange tongue. 'You have no horse?'

'We will wait for you,' said O'Hagan dismissively, 'at the thick of the woodlands. What way do we take?'

Neil, deciding to keep his own party between the Irish and Ronane, gestured to the left. 'I warn ye, they have firearms!'

There was no response from O'Hagan. With an abrupt signal to his followers he set off at a loping pace. Neil watched until they had disappeared behind the manse. He had been much relieved when Mistress Tabitha, unwilling to see her green beetled under the hooves of a score of horses, had taken her brother off to Newtownards for the day. If the speeding brogues were light on the manse garden, the minister need never know of O'Hagan and his *bodach*s. Neil had paid no attention when Ronane had ridden off with his party. Now his men waited for him. He cracked his fingers and signalled Samuel Miskimmin before him. 'Never again,' he hissed into the grinning face, 'open your gab to me wi'out ye first ask leave. Now, mount.'

The Irish were indeed ahead of the Ravara men. When Neil handed over his horse they were already beating to the west of the lough. Neil observed the thoroughness with which they combed each thicket and glade. He remembered Dan Drummond's words that to the Irish their cattle were their gold. Each man probed with a long dagger at the ready. If a musketeer in ambush brought down one of these fleeting figures he wouldn't live to load a second time. He saw that his men were of the same opinion and drawing his pistol moved forward between them and the Irish.

About mid-afternoon Dan Crockart came on the marks of a fire. Neil drew his foot through the still-warm ashes.

'How long would ye say, Dan?'

'No later than this morn, Mr Gilchrist. It's a trick to set us agley.'

O'Hagan had joined them. 'What does the man say, Mr Gilchrist?'

Neil didn't answer. 'How a trick, Dan?'

'There's no trampling around the fire, no holes in the ground for cooking-sticks. They want to send us agley. They've gone another road.'

'Ye could well be right,' said Neil, thinking that Crockart was a deal sharper in the wits than his ways suggested.

'Cattle, what of the cattle?'

Crockart looked at him. 'No cattle, mister. If cattle had been keppit here, there would be broken bushes, dung on the ground. Look for yoursel'.'

'He says, Mr O'Hagan, that neither reivers nor cattle were this way, other than those who lit this fire to fool us. God knows where they are. They could be deep in the hills.'

O'Hagan shrugged and was about to turn away when Archie Gill came briskly through the undergrowth and, pushing his way through his neighbours, stared down at the ashes of the fire.

'What's the meaning o't?' he asked.

'Nothing, Archie,' said Dan Crockart.

'I have a message for ye,' said the miller turning to Neil. 'Mr Porson sends word he's reached the bounds of the Cordwaine place. That's as far as he was authorised to go and he and his men are turning for home. Ronane would ken what ye have in mind.'

Neil looked around him. The lustre of the day was fading and threads of mist were moving across the glade.

'We'll turn. Tell him we'll turn.'

The cottars did little to hide their discontent. They had set out to lay hands on the murderers of their neighbour, Watty Mackechnie. Now, when they should have been at their farm-work, they had wasted a day tramping through country most of them would never have put a foot in.

O'Hagan, a few paces away, watched the Ravara men turn back. As Neil passed he said, 'You are giving up the pursuit of the cattle-thieves?'

Neil stopped. 'Mr O'Hagan,' he said, 'we were pursuing rogues of which one at least is sought for murder. If we had come up with them and you found your beasts – all to the good. But we had graver business in hand.'

'Do your men,' the Irishman asked, 'lack the stomach to go on through the night?'

'They didn't come furnished to do so. They have families and farms to tend. But if you have a mind to go on, Mr Echlin isn't likely to object.'

O'Hagan glanced back at the darkling woodland. 'I do not think MacCartan would take kindly asking permission to travel in country that was his.'

'Mr O'Hagan,' said Neil with a hard smile. 'I think ye are trying to anger me. Let us bid each other good e'en, and go on our ways.'

Neil hastened to catch up with his men. As he trudged through swathes of fallen leaves he was filled with bitterness that they had failed to snare Lachie Dubh. He had a foreboding that a grievous price could yet be paid for that failure. But he had one small satisfaction in directing Samuel Miskimmin and another cottar to throw down and scatter the shelter where he had seen Lachie and his crew.

A small boy stationed at the gate of Rathard House told Neil and Ronane that the laird was waiting for them in Dan Drummond's office. There was a brief exchange between the two as they rode on.

'Crockart was right,' said Neil. 'That fire was a hoax.'

'Ye believe the Irishman had cattle stolen?'

'I do. I saw Lachie's gang with a dead animal.'

After that they rode the short journey in silence. At the factor's office Dugal of the smiddy took the bridles. 'They're baith in there,' he said.

Their entrance halted Echlin in full flow to an attentive Dan Drummond. The eyes that the laird turned on the two were live with excitement. Faith, thought Neil, he's put more weight on our pursuit than I thought likely.

'Well,' asked the laird, 'what speed did ye come?'

Neil, drawing off his gauntlets, sat down wearily. 'No trace of them. Only the embers of a fire.'

Ronane had taken up his usual stance against the wall at the door. 'There were Irish claiming to look for stolen cattle.'

'Ech, in Ravara, without the laird's permission?' demanded the factor.

'Their captain,' said Neil turning to the factor, 'a bold callan named O'Hagan, inquired after ye, Dan –'

'What!' cried the factor springing up. 'I never gave permission – I knew nothing –'

'Sit down, man,' said Echlin. 'O'Hagan? He's kin to the MacCartans. He was abroad and he's returned. Ye believe he was seeking stolen cattle, Gilchrist?'

'I can think of no other reason why he should be there, laird.'

'Nor can I.'

'He wasn't over-civil in asking permission to search beyond Lough Reagh. But I think he would be willing to join us if we set out again.'

'There never was a time when I wanted less truck with the MacCartans than now. Ye won't be setting out again.'

'Then what of Lachie Dubh and the rogues that are haunting the upper forest?'

The laird brushed the question away with an impatient gesture. 'Winter and the wolves will give them over to us, Gilchrist. Something of great import has come on us.' The laird stood up, resting his knuckles on the table. 'The Lord Deputy is to honour me with a visit at the New Year.' His eager glance darted from face to face, his eyes alight again.

Drummond brought his hands together softly as if in

applause. Neil, in answer to Echlin's scrutiny, grinned and nodded in approbation. Ronane, in the corner, refolded his arms.

That evening, after supper, Neil stood at the schoolhouse doorway. Wishart had been right. The skirmish with the Irish had reached the ear of government. To the west, a blade of light, startling against the night sky, ran beyond oak forest and hill. In that darkness lurked Lachie Dubh and his fellows. Neil turned to go in. Let wolf eat wolf, O Lord.

14

The Lord Deputy's letter had been delivered at Rathard House by a young equerry with two troopers in his wake. Accepting a glass of wine, he informed Echlin that he was on his way from Carrickfergus to Dublin in haste, that he had left the rest of his escort in Newtownards, that he hoped to be in Newry by nightfall and that he had made a detour to deliver Echlin's letter and three other missives in what he had been informed was the same neighbourhood.

'So,' said Echlin, alert, 'perhaps I could relieve you of that errand?'

'Not in having them delivered, for I've been instructed to put them into the hands of the gentlemen named. They are,' and he drew the packets from his wallet, 'Mr James Lowry of Ballymacashon, Mr Luke Cordwaine and Mr Fiach MacCartan. When I tell you that the last two bear the King's seal you will understand my anxiety. But it would be of assistance, sir, if you could point me the way.'

'The three gentlemen you name live in different airts. I'll send someone with you that knows the road.'

Having sent a servant with the officer, the laird went indoors to savour again Chichester's letter.

'It would be useful if our sons met the Lord Deputy,' he said to his wife. 'I'll have Hamilton and Francis here.'

'Anne should be here,' said Lady Echlin.

'Anne should be here,' agreed her husband. 'We have two months till the New Year. That should see my letters safe to London and Cambridge and yours to Dunblane.'

The laird set afoot preparations in house, gardens and estate. No one, from Mungo Turnooth to Tam McBratney, was left unaware of Lord Deputy Chichester's impending visitation. But even as he busied himself Echlin could not rid his mind of an ever-increasing curiosity as to what was in James Lowry's letter and above all, why His Majesty, in remote Whitehall, should have to write to persons like Cordwaine and the Irishman, MacCartan.

His wife eased his disquiet a little. 'The Lord Deputy, being in the neighbourhood, might want to meet James Lowry.'

'Aye, good, Seraphina. But what of the King's communication with Cordwaine and MacCartan?' To that Lady Echlin had no reply.

A man of habitual good sense, Echlin reproached himself for this avid inquisitiveness, out of all reason. He realised that if he were not so hungry for royal commendation (as measured by his wife, a knighthood), he would have cracked his fingers, a little enviously perhaps, at Cordwaine and his letter. Now mere curiosity was giving way to phantoms of suspicion and fear, distracting in the busiest hours of day, tormenting the sleepless hours of night.

Seeking relief, he summoned the only two men to whom he could talk, Calum Wishart and Neil. In his study he filled three glasses with wine.

'The messenger who brought my letter from the Lord Deputy brought letters from the King to Luke Cordwaine and Fiach MacCartan. What had his Grace to say?'

Wishart looked at Neil then back to Echlin and shrugged.

'Think, man!' To Neil's startled gaze the laird had the look of a man close to desperation. He wanted to ask what threat, in God's name, could there be to the industrious well-respected landlord in two letters addressed to neighbours.

'I'm of the opinion that Jamie and Fiach MacCartan have met. In May 1603 the Irishman passed through London on his way home from Spain,' said Wishart.

'I didn't know that.'

'You've forgot. There was words about it in Dublin at the time. But Fiach settled down here quietly and nothing more was said. That was the year when Jamie the Saxt of Scotland was transmogrified into James the First of England. In those days he had a tender regard for Irish chieftains, great or little. Here was one in London, a well-read one forbye, for MacCartan was returning from a sojourn in Salamanca. What more likely than the bookish Jamie had discourse with him?'

'Why should the King resume a correspondence with MacCartan after all this time?' demanded the laird.

'I said nothing about resuming a correspondence. Indeed I would wager there is little pedantry in the letter. Nothing more than formal courtesies. It's the *timing* o't that's significant.'

'The Lord Deputy'll be aware that the King has written to MacCartan,' agreed Echlin. 'But –'

'It's protection handed down from the throne. When they hear that Chichester's in the offing, the Irish, that is the Irish with anything to lose, look to their treasure. Frown as ye like, laird, but ye know that's the way o't – and so does Jamie. Chichester will hardly summon before him a man with a letter in his pocket on which the royal wax has barely cooled.'

Echlin smiled. The evening's talk, the wine, had for the moment, freed his wits. Then his face darkened. 'But what of Luke Cordwaine?'

Wishart smiled. 'If the report o' Jamie's way with his English servitors is true, I think it more likely he's seeking something from Mr Cordwaine.'

As he refilled the glasses Echlin shook his head. 'That may be so at court – but here? I can't think of anything or any service that Luke Cordwaine commands that would interest his Grace.' He studied Wishart for a moment. 'And I think you're prejudiced against Chichester, Calum.'

'Feggs, who am I to have prejudices? It was in London I heard it said that Bess sent her eagles against Spain, her vultures to Ireland. One or other, the Lord Deputy flies high above my head.'

'For all that,' said the laird severely, 'keep branks on your tongue while he's here. And the same,' he continued as if

sensing a snag downstream, 'for the Reverend Mungo Turnooth. I want no rant from him on the matter o' episcopacy.
During this visitation I expect all to behave with civility and
compliance.'

'Whether above or below the salt I'll be the quintessence o'
decorum,' said Wishart.

'You'll meet him.' The laird examined the figure sprawled in
the chair opposite with mingled amusement and irritation.
'Wishart, you'll disgrace us all. As soon as ye may, Neil, take
him to Crawfurd and fit him with decent garb. Mark it to me, if
need be. Now, finish up your glasses and away with ye.'

Cold moonlight threw their shadows before them between
the files of rowans. Their steps rang on the hard earth.

'He'll be recounting your vagaries to her Ladyship,' said
Neil.

'Heh,' returned his companion, 'let her Ladyship make what
she can of them. She's not fool enough to believe that Cordwaine's lifting his eyes to an advancement. But she's eaten up
with the notion her husband's fit for it.'

'The arrival o' the Lord Deputy must be the answer to a
prayer.'

Wishart chuckled drily. 'We would need Mungo Turnooth's
check on that.' He stopped at a fork in the path. 'I tell ye what
Ross and you should do. Blow the dust off Echlin's genealogy
and set it out in a fair hand as far as you've got. Ye can show
you were willing. I'm leaving ye here. There'll be a hard frost
afore morn.'

'What colour o' cloth d'ye fancy, ye disreputable dog?' Neil
bawled after him. But Wishart had disappeared into the moonlight.

Dan Drummond, meeting Mr Cordwaine on Rathard House
avenue ushered him to where the laird sat alone at breakfast,
again very much his own master. 'Mr Cordwaine, laird,' announced Drummond and went about his business.

'You're early abroad, man,' said Echlin, surprised as much

by the concern on his neighbour's face as by his appearance at this hour.

With a groan Cordwaine dropped into a chair. His elbows on the table, he framed a flushed distressful countenance in his hands. 'Tell me, Echlin, what do you know of hawks and hawking?'

Echlin stared at the younger man. 'Hawks. . . hawking? What are ye talking about?'

The Englishman drew a folded document from his pocket and laid it on the table. 'Read it, Kenneth.'

Echlin looked down at the broken but still impressive seal. 'But it's yours – it's from his Grace –'

'Read it, for God's sake!'

Echlin opened the letter with care and lifted it to the morning light.

'"To my much-esteemed and loving subject, Luke Cains Cordwaine, Esquire,"' read the laird. '"Hearing that ye have a gyre-falcon, much thought of in your place, we take occasion effectuously to request and desire you, seeing that hawks are gifting gear, that of courtesy you will bestow on us that gos-hawk. Gin it arrives with us well and tenderly cared for, so shall ye find us ready to requite your courtesy and goodwill with no less pleasure in any way as occasion shall present. . ."' Echlin raised his head in a guffaw of laughter. 'It's a jape, Luke. God knows why, a prank –'

''Ods, but it's no prank!' cried Cordwaine furiously. 'Look, the name and the body of the letter are in the same hand. And the seal, in God's name!'

The laird, in soberer mood, ran his eye down the missive again. 'Aye, true.' This time he took in the significance of the last few lines.

'But who could have filled the King's lug with such a fantastical request?'

'My father.'

'Your father?'

160

'My father is an uncommon commoner. He helped to fill the King's private purse. He is accepted in the King's apartments. He has overheard his Grace say that he wants a hawk. My father has a son who owns forestland in Ireland. He tells his Grace that his son Luke owns,' Cordwaine studied his letter, '"a gyre-falcon much thought of".' Cordwaine threw up his hands.

The laird looked askance at his neighbour. 'You think that was the way o't?'

'It's likely.'

'But what would your father hope to gain by this?'

'Nothing. He needs nothing. He's extremely rich. Sound reasons why the King encourages his company. True, he's wed my sister to a title and my elder brother's mounting to a diocese. But for himself nothing, and my mother being dead there are no womenfolk to goad him to a title.'

Echlin's gaze shifted for a moment. Cordwaine jerked his thumb over his shoulder. 'He bought me Edenmore to keep my hands busy.'

'Good God,' said the laird under his breath. He tapped the letter. 'But what of this? No matter what your respected parent thinks, trained hawks don't grow on trees.'

'He could have bought a bushel of the damned fowl, somewhere,' said Cordwaine bitterly.

'Aye, so,' said the laird stifling a smile. 'But it's with ye now. And a reply will be sought.'

Disquiet, like a cloud, descended again on Cordwaine. 'What's to say, Kenneth? That's why I rode over this morn.'

Unlike his wife and the supercilious Lowry, Echlin had a liking for the Englishman. In their transactions he had found him a straightforward good-natured fellow. Now that he had heard his tale the laird understood better his neighbour's indifferent handling of his property.

'You'll take a glass, Luke. That is,' added Echlin tactfully, 'if Porson isn't waiting your directions for the day?'

Mr Cordwaine admitted that that was unlikely and the laird poured the wine.

'You'll acknowledge his Grace's letter. If ye wish I'll make out a draft for ye to transcribe in your own hand? Good. Happily acceding to the request, you'll hint, discreetly, that the problem is to convey the hawk safe and unhurt to London. And that, my friend,' said the laird stroking his chin, 'is nothing less than the truth. This ye are pursuing with all dispatch.'

'But where's the damned hawk?'

'If you're your father's son,' responded Echlin drily, 'you'll know what's sought with money can be found. And when the Lord Deputy's here drop the word that his Grace's letter has been answered, for assuredly Chichester will know of its contents. Now, is there aught else?'

Cordwaine drained his glass. ''Ods, Kenneth, I'm much obliged to ye. I'll leave the letter and await the answer.'

As they walked to the door Echlin laid his hand on the other's shoulder. 'See to it that your bawn is complete and everything trig against the Lord Deputy's arrival. He, too, will be writing to Whitehall.'

Returning to the table Echlin picked up the letter and studied those closing words. For a time he pondered on the significance and value of his Majesty's gracious *quid pro quo*.

'Mother,' said Ellen from her vantage in the doorway, 'there's folk coming up the brae. It's them Miskimmins.'

Meg left the baking board to peer over her daughter's shoulder. There were three of them: the father, Sawney, Samuel and the lass, Elphie.

Sawney, a musket cradled in his oxter, halted some thirty paces from the cottage and raised his voice in a bellow. 'MacIlveens, come out till I see ye!' He had relished bawling out that challenge all the way up and although he saw Meg and her daughter in the doorway, he would not deny himself.

'Will I go for father and Sorley? They're working at the outfield.'

'They would be deaf,' said Meg, 'if they didn't hear that.' She inspected the three: the father, musket dangling under his arm, the son with the leering grin, the girl hanging back, irresolute. She picked up a herding-stick from the door-cheek and beckoned. 'Come fo'rrard, Sawney man, come fo'rrard and state your errand.'

Miskimmin cast a swift glance to right and left as if mustering his forces and stepped forward. 'I'll tell ye what my business is here, guidwife,' he said loudly. 'Your loon of a son has lifted my wee lassie's kilts and is like tae make her the shame of the countryside. We're here tae make him marry her!'

Meg steadied herself with a great effort. She didn't need to glance at the girl a second time. But at that moment she was consumed with rage that Miskimmin had dared to come armed.

'And what hae ye the gun for, Sawney man?' she demanded in a hiss. 'For murthering your new son-in-law and his family?' She raised her stick and struck the musket barrel a ringing blow. 'Lay it doon, ye hen brain!'

This was not at all as Sawney had envisaged the encounter. He glanced at his son. Faced by the angry matron, Samuel was bereft of words or motion.

'Doon with it – against the wall!'

As the cottar, with shrugs and grins, shuffled over to lean the musket against the cottage wall, Meg glimpsed a figure at a Purdie window.

'Now, into the house with ye. We're no for gabbing o'er this in a field.'

She was shepherding them in when her husband and son came round the gable; Alexander all startled concern at the loud voices, Sorley, having glimpsed the Miskimmins, pale and defiant under his red thatch. He braved his mother's grim stare as he followed the others.

163

Meg closed the door. 'Seat yoursel's,' she said. Then as Miskimmin opened his mouth she continued, 'Alexander, Sawney's here to say that his lass is big with bairn by our son.'

'Planting more than kale with my puir wee Elphie,' said the injured father with a catch in his voice. 'What have ye to say, Alex MacIlveen?'

If Alexander had a pinch of pride in his being it was that of his reputation as a dutiful parent, an industrious tenant, a respected elder of the kirk. This was now suddenly and brutally assaulted. He was aware of Sawney Miskimmin's gloating scrutiny, of Samuel Miskimmin's leer. He was aware also of his wife's steadfast demeanour as she waited for him, as parent and neighbour, to deal with the charge against a member of their family. He turned to Sorley.

'Is there truth in what he says?'

'Jaysus God,' cried Sawney, 'will ye look at the lassie's belly!'

'Aye, it's true, Father.'

Meg leaned over Miskimmin. 'Put branks to your tongue, Sawney man. Under this roof we don't use the Lord's name lightly. And you,' she turned in sudden anger on his son, 'take that donnert grin aff your face!'

'He can't help it, Mother,' said Sorley from the hearthside. 'It's the way his face is.'

As Meg stepped back Ellen touched her elbow. 'Mother, what of Rab and me? The crying shame of this —'

Meg turned on her daughter. 'If the two o' ye can't weather this you'll weather nothing in life. Get the lass a sup of milk.'

His hands spread on the arms of his chair, Alexander waited until he had silence.

'We'll do what's right, Sawney. Our son will wed the lass.'

Meg thought she saw the ghost of a smile pass between the two young people. 'Aye, I'll wed her,' said Sorley.

Sawney Miskimmin's expansive nods and grins of triumph to his son were interrupted by Alexander.

'What tocher comes with your lass, Sawney?'

164

Open-mouthed, Sawney stared at the questioner. He threw back his head in an outraged howl. 'Tocher? Tocher, did ye say? By Jay –' He caught Meg's eye. His voice dropped to a curmurring of protest. He turned to his son. 'The guidman did say "tocher"?'

Samuel agreed with an emphatic nod that that was indeed so.

Sawney gave his attention to Meg. 'Ye ken we have three younger after Elphie.' He allowed himself a survey of the simple comforts of the room. 'Will ye – can ye no take the wee lass wi'out a tocher?'

Sorley had crossed to sit beside the girl. He watched in silence. This was a business to be settled between parents. Meg saw her husband waver at the plea. She also had a vision of Miskimmin tumbling in a ditch with laughter once he was out of sight and earshot.

'Ye didn't bring your wife with ye, Sawney,' she said regretfully, 'and more's the pity. I was thinking she would be ill-pleased tae see her eldest daughter go out into the world wi'out a fritter to her name.' Her voice sharpened: 'Am I right, my manny?'

This time Sawney didn't take counsel with his son. Both knew that when they got home Mrs Miskimmin would hold a totally opposite opinion and express it at length.

'Aye. . . weel.' Then with a muttered: 'Aw, t'hell with it,' he turned on Alexander. 'What are ye looking, MacIlveen – beasts or money?'

'Neither,' said Alexander, his resolve steadied by his wife's words. 'This'll be the way o't. You and your sons'll raise a cottage for the two of them at the Langstane field. Sorley will show ye where and how he wants it. It'll be soundly built and well thatchit. When it's finished we'll furnish it.'

'Weel. . . aye. . . aye, that's agreed,' responded Miskimmin uncertain whether or not he had been foxed.

'Sound and well thatchit,' repeated Alexander.

'I'll see to that, Father,' said Sorley.

'I think that's all, neighbour, for the time being,' said Alexander.

'That's all,' agreed Miskimmin. He and his son sprachled to their feet from the creepy stools.

Meg had gone over to the lass Elphie. Drawing back a midnight lock from the girl's brow she considered the perfection of the small face. 'Aye, you're a bonny thing – gin ye had your face washed. Now, drink up that milk, lass, afore ye go.'

The girl raised her eyes to the older woman. 'Yes, 'm,' she said.

Alexander remained seated as the Miskimmin men began to clump out through the doorway.

Something told Meg that this was not a time when the young should part as abruptly as their parents. 'Sorley, get the cuddy and leave the lass home.' Then. 'You're no 'feard to go among the Miskimmins?'

'Heth!' laughed Sorley and released himself from her hand.

Meg followed Miskimmin and his son outside. 'Don't forget your gun, Sawney,' she called sweetly into the gloaming.

The receding Sawney spoke to his son but the words were meant for the household they had left. 'Feggs, never asked had we a mouth on us. . .'

Alexander sat in his chair, shoulders drooped. All the pith seemed to have gone out of him. He raised his head as Meg came back.

'They're away?'

'Aye, they're away.' Meg too, felt her spirits droop now that the excitement of the encounter died.

'The world will say we should have kept a closer eye on the chiel.'

'What more could we have done, Alex man?' But recalling long absences of her son she felt a stab of guilt.

'How can we sit in the kirk, me an elder, and see Sorley raised on the penance stool? For that's what the minister will surely enjoin –'

166

'Come, man,' said Meg briskly. 'What's done's done. Ye bore yoursel' well.' She laughed in spite of herself. 'Where did ye get the notion o' them building a cottage?'

Alexander raised his head. 'I wasn't sure,' he said to the rafters, 'how it would be taken by Sawney Miskimmin.'

'Ye knocked the wind out of him. Now, enough talk. Ellen, push the parritch pot to the heat. And take that waeful look off your face, lass.'

'I was thinking of me and Rab –'

'Now, that's another matter,' began Alexander. 'Rab Purdie'll not –'

'Enough!' cried Meg angrily. 'If this makes any differs to Rab Purdie then he's not worth a boddle. Shame on ye baith. When we're on our knees we'll ask the Lord's guidance. Get the spoons and platters out, girl.'

What Meg, after a restless night, proposed at breakfast seemed less of heavenly guidance than shrewd expediency. But there was a saving element of uncertainty in it which, if things went agley, could be interpreted as a divine affirmation that the transgressor should not escape censure.

'Since the time Rushin Coatie was afore the minister and Mr Echlin,' said Meg to the anxious faces round the table, 'Mr Gilchrist has been gey thick wi' Mistress Tabitha. Now I'll ask Mr Gilchrist to ask Mistress Tabitha to tell her brother that our Sorley and Elphie Miskimmin are tae be wed as soon as their names can be called in the kirk.'

'But what if the minister holds that the two should be punished?' cried Ellen.

Her mother's face lengthened. 'Then the Almighty has got tae the guid man's ear afore us. Redd up the table, lass. I'm away to catch Mr Gilchrist.'

The young man wasn't greatly surprised at the burden of Meg's tale. On occasions as he rode past the Langstane Burn had he not observed their heads together, heard the accord of their voices? In those moments the woodland he was riding towards seemed to him a tongueless gloom. Yes, he agreed he might command Mistress Tabitha's ear. But whether she would intercede was a matter for her. With that Meg had to be satisfied.

If ye want anything done, ask a busy man, thought Neil as Meg left the schoolhouse. Following Wishart's advice Ross and he had charted Echlin's family as far as they were able. When they had delivered the laboriously penned document at Rathard House the laird had thanked them, put it aside, poured wine, and when the glasses were emptied bade Neil stay behind.

'D'ye know aught of hawks and hawking, Gilchrist?'

There came to Neil's mind his uncle Nicol's glove and jesses hanging on the wall at home. But by the time he had come of age to employ these contrivances the starling and the corbie crow had taken over the roof ridges, cotes and courtyard at Balwhanny. He shook he head.

'Would ye recognise,' the laird consulted a letter bearing an impressive seal, 'a gyre-falcon? Ye might have seen such a bird stooping on the herons at Lough Reagh or some other water?'

'I can't tell one hawk from another. Why not ask Alfred Porson? He's an experienced –'

'No.' said Echlin decisively. 'Cordwaine,' he glanced away, 'doesn't pursue – Think of somebody else.'

'What o' John Bell of the tavern? He's likely tae know the gentlemen in the neighbourhood who follow that sport.'

'Indeed aye, Neil,' said the laird eagerly. 'When you're next in Newtownards mention it to Bell. Cannily, if ye please, as if it was of no great consequence. The main brunt o' your message could be that we would welcome Mrs Bell and one of the tavern's cooks to help Rusk, the housekeeper, while the Lord Deputy's at Rathard House. Then the matter of the hawk in passing.' He saw Neil's puzzlement. 'Just discover where the bird is. I'll go for it myself. I don't want it brought to my doorstep.'

For all that, Neil left Rathard House wondering why Echlin should seek a bird of prey in such a furtive manner and at this time, with Chichester and his retinue on the horizon.

The young man had barely departed when the laird drew paper and ink before him. 'Your Grace,' he began, 'I consider myself honoured and willingly bound by your request. I shall be careful to provide the falcon and to be answerable to your Majesty for the same.' Echlin paused and chewed the end of the pen. Writing the letter in his head he had thought to introduce his name as the helpful neighbour. Now that sounded all too artful. Anyway, only God knew what Cordwaine's father had said or promised. 'I will be answerable likewise that he has been in no way stressed but as well treated as any hawk could be. Neither shall your Majesty suspect that I would further retain him for my own pleasure. Therefore, if there be delay, your Majesty will readily understand that search is being made for a trustworthy messenger to convey the hawk from Ireland to London; for your Majesty's meanest contentment is the devoted intent of your respectful and obedient. . .' Echlin laid down the pen. Let Cordwaine sign as he wished. Let him add or take away as he wished. A little blunting of the original would do no harm.

Next morning, riding softly by the manse garden, Neil saw Mistress Tabitha spreading bed linen on the rimed grass. Standing in his stirrups he succeeded, by coughs and gestures, to catch the good woman's attention and summon her to join him on the woodland path. As briefly as possible he communicated Meg MacIlveen's dire news and her plea that clemency be exercised towards the erring couple. 'I need hardly add, ma'am, that I promised only to lay the matter before ye. Though I must confess to a liking and respect for Alexander MacIlveen and his wife.'

Mistress Tabitha shook her head as if in dismay. 'You must know, Mr Gilchrist, that such falling away among his people deeply saddens the minister. And he is the more likely to be greatly censorious with those parties from whom more is expected. That it should be one o' an elder's family that has strayed will cause him despair.'

'Understandably so, Mistress Tabitha, understandably so,' said Neil with answering gravity.

'But,' continued the minister's sister speaking rapidly and passionately, 'he's sick to the wame with one or other culprit aloft on the penitent's stool every time he wants to do no more than speak to the heart o' his flock!'

Neil was surprised at this vulnerability of the formidable Mr Turnooth. But he had the grace to put it down to his own ignorance and said nothing.

Mistress Tabitha felt she had said too much. 'My brother will ask for guidance and act thereto. The girl is near her time?'

'The guidwife MacIlveen sounded urgent.'

'Very well, Mr Gilchrist. I'll speak to the minister. Do you arrange that MacIlveen and Miskimmin present themselves here with the young couple early after breakfast tomorrow. My brother will know what is seemly to say and do.' She watched Neil mount. 'Your concern shows kindness of heart, Mr Gilchrist.'

Neil looked down on the woman's face on which the lines of autumn were encroaching. 'I was irked that I should be asked to bear this message. You never fail to teach me better, ma'am.' Carrying Mistress Tabitha's smile with him he rode away.

The laird also was early in the saddle. The draft of the letter for King Jamie in his pouch, he was announced at Edenmore where Mr Luke Cordwaine was breakfasting in the bosom of his family.

15

The laird returned from Edenmore with Cordwaine's ready agreement to billet a number of Chichester's escort. Earlier he had consulted with Ronane the likely strength of the Lord Deputy's force. As the country through which he would make his progress had been cleared of the Irish they calculated about forty troopers, no more than fifty. Assured of Cordwaine's support Echlin rode over to Ballymacashon to inform James Lowry that he would be expected to supply quarters, food and fodder for about a dozen men and their horses for the duration of the Lord Deputy's stay.

Lowry looked down his long nose at the laird, 'I ken that this visitation has been brought on us because o' your skirmish with the MacCartans –'

'*Not* the MacCartans, Lowry,' broke in the laird irritably. 'I explained all this to ye before. I'm confident the MacCartans gave the wood-kernes no encouragement to attack my property.'

'I hope ye can persuade Chichester of that. We'll do better here letting sleeping dogs lie.'

The laird thought of the royal missive in Fiach MacCartan's possession. 'I think ye can rest easy on that. Now what of these quarters for Chichester's troops?'

'I agree.'

'One more thing. I'm giving a banquet at Rathard House for the Lord Deputy and his staff. Lady Echlin and I will be pleased to see you and Mrs Lowry there.'

'Thank ye, Echlin. It will be expected of us.'

Echlin hoped that, apart from filial obligation, his children viewed the summons to Rathard House in the same manner as did James Lowry. Anne, as a dutiful daughter, would happily accede to his will. It would be unreasonable to expect the same pliancy in Francis at his studies, or, above all, Hamilton engaged in military service. But he wanted them home on this occasion; their presence, he felt, would enhance his consequence before the Lord Deputy.

Kenneth Echlin, to his tenants' thinking, was a fair master. What was good for them, industrious husbandry, was good for his estate. In hard weather he allowed the gathering of fallen timber for kindling. Dan Drummond knew to turn a blind eye to a hare or rabbit hanging behind a cottage door. There were few cottars who had not, at one time or other, received a free sowing of grain. An honest man could hope for a bateing of his rent until a crop or a beast was sold. The laird had become a ward between them and the caprice of powerful men in distant places.

But now the laird was demanding labour from them outside duty days. From each man not much was asked and most had finished their ploughing. Yet they did not fully understand why the factor should put them to widening the road where it entered Ravara, cut back the encroaching undergrowth, break stones to fill pot-holes. All this for the arrival of a personage before whom, it was said, Echlin would take off his bonnet. Shadows that had not vanished stirred in the memories of men who had fled the lowlands before such authority. Their disquiet spread to the womenfolk. When Dan Drummond, at her Ladyship's urging, instructed them to redd-up their dwellings, inside and out, he got dark looks from guidwives who had been brought up from childhood to scrub, sweep and scour with religious fervour.

The Echlins themselves were not sparing in money and effort. Gilfillan and his two apprentices, squeezing the last glimmer of light from the brief December days, built furnishings for the hall and the bedchambers. There was little colour in the garden beds but under Lady Echlin's hand they were as trim as new-minted coins. Dan Drummond was instructed to see to the fencing at the coney-warren, Archie Gill told to hold back some milling for the interest of the visitors. Nudged by Lady Echlin, the laird borrowed one of Cordwaine's coaches. (It had long been her complaint that while the Lowrys had a coach and the Cordwaines two, her husband had never thought to put a carriage at her disposal.)

For once Echlin listened carefully to his factor when Drummond advised him against billeting the visiting troopers in the cottages.

'For why, Dan?' asked the laird.

'Will these sojers be Englishmen?'

'Aye, that's likely.'

'D'ye see our people clearing a place at the hearth on a lang night for a bodie they can't understand?'

'You're right, Dan,' said the laird. 'Clear out the granary behind the big house. I'll get Gilfillan to fit it with cots, tables and benches.'

One afternoon in the middle of the month, Echlin summoned Neil. The young man found the laird in ill-humour.

'My daughter Anne has arrived at Bell's tavern from Donaghadee in a fish cart. Why she travelled in a stinking cadger's cart is a mystery. I want ye to take the coach and fetch her.'

'Drive the coach?' inquired Neil, bridling.

'No, Sim the stableman will drive. We're sending my wife's maid, Rose. I want ye to escort the coach and see my daughter safe here.'

'How am I to know –' began Neil.

'For God's sake, Gilchrist, how many laird's daughters are waiting at Bell's?' cried Echlin. 'Now, will ye start? Cordwaine and his wife are due, a visit we could well do wi'out. . .'

The laird was still muttering angrily as Neil left for the schoolhouse and his horse.

'Echlin's daughter's in Newtownards,' he informed Ross. 'I'm to fetch her.'

'Have ye ever seen her?'

'Once, I think, when I came here first. A fat doleful bairn.

Keep my supper warm.'

Riding briskly, he overtook the coach about a mile from Rathard House. Inside, Rose, Lady Echlin's maid, sat with her skirts flounced on the wide seat.

'Will ye no tether your horse to the back of the coach, Mr Gilchrist,' she cried, 'and sit with me?'

'You're a bold blade, Rose,' said Neil with a grin. He tapped the saddle-pistol. 'I'm here to protect ye from all manner of rogues and ravagers.' For all that, he thought, as he took up station behind the coach, it's an orra world where a man has more chance of laying hands on a willing lass in a lumbering carriage than in all the broad acres of Ravara.

There was no market that day and few passers-by to stare as the coach rolled to a halt at the tavern. Neil dismounted and tossed the reins to Sim Watt.

'Will I unyoke, Mr Gilchrist?'

'No, we'll be leaving right away,' said Neil, and entered the tavern, followed by Rose. No errand boy, he would be polite but aloof. There were few people in the dining-room. None bore any resemblance to the young person he sought. John Bell came hurrying forward.

'Looking Miss Echlin?'

'I am, John.'

The tavern-keeper set off among the tables, Neil at his heels. Reaching a corner of the chamber, Bell stopped and, with the gesture of a conjurer, announced: 'Miss Echlin.'

A pale-faced girl, ensconced in a heap of bundles and trunks, looked up at Neil. He introduced himself with a brief and formal bow.

'Neil Gilchrist. Your father has sent me to conduct ye to Rathard House.'

The girl made an effort to extricate herself. Neil put out a hand to steady her. When she stood up he saw that under her cloak she was slender. And tallish; up to his brow at least, Neil reckoned.

'Thank ye, Mr Gilchrist.' Her voice was high and clear. 'We

174

had a rough crossing. I lost my breakfast over the ship's side.'

'Not all of it,' said Neil, his eyes on traces of vomit crusted on her cloak.

'Oh,' she put a hand to her bosom. 'My clothes stink of fish.'

'No more than a breath, I assure ye, Miss Echlin.'

She studied Neil. Was this sober-faced fellow exercising his wit on her? She withdrew her hand from his. 'I'm quite steady now.'

She has none of her Ladyship's looks, thought Neil, more her father's daughter. Younger, his hair was likely of the same tawny hue. And the nose, smaller and finer; same chin, but rounder. No, she lacks her mother's dark handsomeness. He wondered sardonically what young gallant was languishing for her return to Dunblane.

'I have a coach waiting, Miss Echlin.'

'That,' she pointed to a long bundle leaning drunkenly against the wall, 'contains tapestries. Deal gently with them. They're mouldering.' And Miss Echlin, followed by Rose, set off for the street and the waiting coach.

Having seen the two young women seated, the servant with her back to the horses, Neil proceeded, with as much delicacy as possible, to build the diverse baggage around them.

'They still smell,' said Miss Echlin.

'It's a pervasive odour,' Neil agreed. 'But it should blow away.'

When Watt and he had carefully roped the tapestries on the coach roof, Neil sent an interested stablehand to fetch his horse. Mounted, he signalled Watt forward. To a hurroo from the spectators the burdened coach and its escort moved off down the village street.

As his horse plodded behind the coach, Neil, against his will, fell to wondering what sort of figure he had cut before Miss Anne Echlin. He felt gey confident that he had fulfilled the laird's charge. But could he not have been more attentive? He should have sympathised at greater length with the puir lass on the rough sea crossing, commiserated with her on having to travel on a fish-cadger's cart. How could he have forgotten to offer her a glass of wine before they quit the tavern? Sim Watt could have done as well and with a deal more sense.

They cleared the outskirts of the village and entered the softer track that ran through the woodlands. Neil watched the carriage pitch and lurch and imagined the buffeting of its occupants. As he swithered if he should ride up, a hand appeared. His startled horse carried him forward in a flurry of pebbles. Miss Echlin balanced a fallen bundle on her knee.

'The tapestries, Mr Gilchrist?'

He glanced up. 'They are quite secure, Miss Echlin. I trust the journey's not too wearisome?'

'Rose tells me we haven't much farther to go. I'd forgotten.'

'True. We'll soon be entering Ravara.'

Thinking of nothing more to say, he would have let the coach draw ahead but she detained him with a slight movement of her hand.

'My mother asked for the tapestries. But these,' she indicated the baggage pressing on herself and the serving-lass, 'my grandmother wanted rid of.' She smiled on him.

The path, narrowing here, put an end to their talk. Neil fell back to his station at the rear. But he sat straighter in his saddle, sensing the hues and odours of the darkling woods with a new awareness.

A cold night wind was rising among the trees when the carriage turned laboriously into Rathard House avenue. A hand appeared for a moment at the coach window.

'Thank you, Mr Gilchrist,' came a clear voice. 'Thank you, and goodnight.'

The gates of the bawn stood open and he saw a gleam of light at the house doorway. He sat until sight then sound died in the darkness. When he heard the great gates close he turned his horse's head.

16

Mistress Tabitha was successful in her advocacy. From the manse went out word that Sorley MacIlveen and Elphie Miskimmin were to wed in a few days' time. Mrs Miskimmin, an eye on her daughter's condition, goaded her menfolk to finish the building of the cottage for the young couple. Sorley was aye present to keep sharp watch on the soundness of the work. On an evening, while it was still light, his parents went with him to the Langstane Burn to survey the new cottage. His father examined roof and thatching, knocked the heel of his hand against couplings and doorposts and declared himself satisfied.

'Had ye any trouble with the Miskimmins?' he asked.

Sorley shook his head. 'None. Aiken set a rafter agley. I gave him a couple of dunts in the ribs and brought him back to what he was about.'

'Is Aiken the one that makes the profane songs the family sings?' asked Meg with marked distaste.

'The same. If he was let he would drift away, making rhymes in his head.'

Troubled, she watched as son and father trod down the earthen floor. What was this tribe of rif-randies her son was marrying into? Alexander, assured that Sorley was to escape the penitent's stool, had shrugged off that question. His talk was now of practical things: the need for more tools, the sharing of the horse and plough between the two bits of land. The Miskimmin lass was bonny, Meg allowed. But a cottar's wife needed more than good looks at the hearthstone and the cradle. Rab Purdie and her Ellen were as an open book to her. Obedient to God's word and their elders, leal, thrifty, prudent, they would be a staff to Alexander and herself. Sorley trampled to and fro, to and fro, tramping down the broken clay. In time, as it bore the daily traffic of himself, his wife and children, it would become firm, knotty, polished as wood.

'I pray that all things will bear up as secure in your life and Elphie's,' said Meg.

He looked up with a grin. 'Aye, Mother.'

Alexander steadied himself, breathless, against the wall. 'We'll give it the flat of the back of the spade in the morn, Sorley.'

'Aye, Father.'

To Neil, at the back of the kirk with the factor, the Reverend Mr Turnooth did little to temper the chill of his manner to the strayed sheep. His final words fell more like an admonition than a blessing on the two young people before him.

As Neil and the factor stepped into the kirkyard a dozen heads jouked down behind bare-twigged bushes. Two or three muskets lay half-concealed at the base of the kirkyard wall. Drummond seated himself close to them.

'We're surrounded by a cloud of witnesses,' said Neil, settling beside the factor.

'Aye,' said Drummond, eyeing the sky. 'They're here to see the Miskimmins anticking about and blarging off with their guns to let the world ken their daughter's married.' The factor pursed his lips. 'They're in for a sair gunk. The minister's ruled there should be no firing near the kirk. I'm here to see he's obeyed.'

Neil ran his eye disconsolately along the drumlin ridge to the north-east. 'I thought somebody from the Big House would have come to see a cottar wedding.'

The factor emitted a dry chuckle. 'Better they should see one where the parties said grace afore supping. Here they come.'

Mr Turnooth appeared in the kirk doorway. Behind him the newly-weds paused irresolutely on the threshold. The two men rose to their feet as the minister strode towards them, hat clapped sternly on his brow, gown fluttering in the cold thin air. He stopped abruptly.

'I see they brought firearms, Dan.'

'Aye, minister, but –'

'They would have been better employed in bringing a hurdle to carry the bride home.' He fumbled in his gown. 'I understand, Mr Gilchrist, ye gave Rab Purdie money to pay for the service?'

'I did, minister.'

Mr Turnooth pressed a piece of silver into Neil's hand. 'I would not expect or accept money in such circumstances. Dan, there'll be no unseemly clamour round God's house.'

'I'll see to it, minister.'

'As for you, young sir – 'twas a kind thought.' A curt nod and Mr Turnooth had gone without as much as a backward glance at the straggle of figures coming from the kirk. With his departure men and women slipped out from behind bushes and walls. Sorley, supporting his bride, acknowledged the greetings of his neighbours with a jaunty air. There was, nevertheless, a restraint in their manner, perhaps in deference to Meg and her husband, or fearful of putting a match to Sawney Miskimmin, already circling in jig step, arms upraised, at the tail of the procession.

Neil watched this fooling with mingled amusement and annoyance. 'What about his guns?' he asked.

'Dinna fash yourself,' said the factor knowingly. 'He has an eye on them and us. Here comes the loon.'

As Miskimmin approached, Neil saw that he had shaved and decked himself in a neckcloth, more or less clean. 'Ye look gey trig, Sawney,' he said.

'Aye, Mr Gilchrist,' returned the cottar, but his eyes were on Drummond, reproachfully. 'Ye moved the guns from the kirk door, factor.'

'Ye were told not to bring them, Sawney.'

'And throwed them down in the wet grass. They could get rusted.'

'I knew ye would lift them in good time, Sawney,' said the factor. 'And Sawney, for fear ye would be tempted to impud-

179

ently pull a trigger afore I lose sight of ye, I've shook out the charges. Now, take the guns and away with ye.'

Miskimmin scrabbled the firearms together and tucked them under his oxter. He grinned maliciously at the two men, then turned and in goatlike skips set off in pursuit of the wedding party now out of sight on the path to the Langstane.

Dan Drummond let himself down from the wall and pummelled his chilled buttocks. 'I'm not over-fond of young MacIlveen,' he said, 'but I wouldn't wish such a father-in-law on any man.'

Around midnight the factor at his fireside and the Reverend Mungo Turnooth turning angrily in his bedclothes heard the distant and faint musket fire as Sawney and his sons, on their own doorstep, let fly a defiant salvo into the icy starlight.

Neil suspected rightly, that the MacIlveens were too shy or timorous to approach Mistress Tabitha on her kindly intervention. It was therefore with the smug satisfaction of taking up another's burden that he approached the manse. He arrived unannounced, the prudent hound having left with its master. Seated in the manse kitchen, he stretched his legs to the fire. 'I felt obligated,' he said, 'to convey thanks for your help, ma'am. I'm sure the MacIlveens would wish me to do so. For Alexander or Meg to have spoken might wrongly suggest a conspiracy in that you condone their son's, ah – transgression.'

'That reveals an admirable delicacy on all sides,' said the good lady with a smile. 'I understand the young couple were shortly left in peace after their arrival home.'

'It would seem,' said Neil drawing in his legs and picking up his bonnet, 'that Rab Purdie persuaded the Miskimmins to gang their gait after a cup or two.'

'Persuasion is aye the better way,' said Mistress Tabitha. 'Miss Anne Echlin walked over from Rathard House to call on the minister and me. My brother allows she is a modest and becoming young woman.'

Neil's bonnet stayed on his knee. 'I escorted Miss Echlin on her arrival.'

'She told us at some length of the journey. Nor did your care go unmentioned.'

'I'm afraid it was a rough one. I trust she suffered no more than some discomfort?'

'Had ye come to kirk on the Sabbath ye would have seen her in the laird's pew.'

'Aye, so,' said Neil, a man stricken at the abysmal depth of his stupidity.

'In her face she favours the laird rather more than her mother.'

'Would ye say so, Mistress Tabitha?'

'My brother is of the same opinion, Mr Gilchrist.'

Her companion being silent Mistress Tabitha continued. 'But like Lady Echlin she is a horsewoman. She expressed to us her desire to go riding in the forest –'

'No – no –' Neil was on his feet. 'She mustn't do that Mistress Tabitha. Wolves were at Donach two nights ago. And there are others. . . she doesn't know the woodland rides. She could put her horse into a morass. . .' He drew his bonnet on slowly. 'But there, it's none of my concern.'

'Nor should I have mentioned it,' said Mistress Tabitha, accompanying him to the door. 'But maybe ye should warn the laird.'

'Ye think so?' queried Neil anxiously.

'It would be no more than your duty to Mr Echlin. And,' continued the lady graciously when Neil was in the saddle, 'if ye come on the MacIlveens tell them I'll call on their son and daughter-in-law as soon as I find time.' Mistress Tabitha stood at the door as Neil rode off and saw him turn his mount in the direction of Rathard House.

Echlin was standing over his study desk, fingers splayed on a plan. He looked up in surprise as the young man entered. 'By God, Neil, ye wasted no time.'

Neil looked at him, questioningly, hopefully.

'I sent Neilson for ye but five minutes ago.' Echlin tapped the

181

plan spread on the desk. 'I was swithering on how many of the Lord Deputy's officers will expect to be lodged here.'

'Aye, the Lord Deputy. . .'

'But,' continued the laird, pushing the sheet aside, 'I have to tell ye that my daughter Anne has arrived –'

'I accompanied Miss Echlin from Newtownards.'

'Ye did, Neil. I forgot. She came in smelling of fish. Well now, she wants to go riding. She won't be content ambling round the farms. She wants to see the demesne – the hills and the woodlands, as she puts it.'

'Alone, that is too perilous,' said Neil firmly.

'I've said as much to her. So?'

'You wish me to accompany your daughter?'

'I would be obliged, Neil. I ken it's groom's work –'

'I'm at your and Miss Echlin's service,' said Neil.

'Guid, I'll summon her.' He called into the great hall, 'Have Miss Anne attend me.'

There was the movement of someone aroused. A door opened and closed. 'Now,' said the laird rubbing his hands with an expression of pleasure and relief, 'the Lord Deputy. I invited Fiach MacCartan to the banquet. He's declined, courteously enough, I must say. In his place comes Turlough, the nephew, and *his* son. I hadn't thought of bairns being present, but with the Irish one has to ca' canny in these matters.'

Neil nodded absently.

'And I've trysted an Irish harper to play for us –' he consulted a list on the desk, '– one Lochlainn O'Daly.'

Neil stared at him. 'A harper?'

'To entertain the company. I'm told this O'Daly is made welcome at some o' the great houses in Dublin and Drogheda. . .'

Neil heard her footsteps as she came across the hall. He glimpsed the reynard brown of her hair, the green dress, the shallow white ruff at her throat. Then she was in the doorway.

'Now to this jaunt o' yours, Anne. Gilchrist agrees ye can't

182

go alone. He knows the ways better than any other. He'll ride with ye.'

'Thank you, Mr Gilchrist.' There was no doubt of the warmth of her expression. 'Tomorrow?'

'Tomorrow at ten. And,' said Neil in a sudden flush of inspiration, 'ye might bring some refreshment, Miss Echlin. Then there'll be no need to turn back so early.'

Miss Echlin expressing her full approval of this, Neil took his leave of Rathard House. Ross Campbell, clearing a wayside ditch, was surprised to see Mr Gilchrist, as he rode past, take off his bonnet and birl it round two or three times before replacing it. He stared after the rider wondering what stinging creature could be bizzing round the young man's head this cauld weather.

The rowan boughs, though leafless, had broken the fall of the night's frost. Beneath them the avenue from the Big House ran dark and unsmirched between the hoar-white meadows. Neil followed Miss Echlin, drawn on by the brisk pace she set. There had been no delay in the stableyard. Sim Watt helped her into the saddle as soon as Neil rode in. Just as promptly Mrs Rusk, the housekeeper, had appeared with a basket of food for the young mistress. Neil placed it in front of him, taken aback by its weight and seeming variety against the scrimpy parcel of barley bread and cold bacon that Chrissy Maclennan left for him as was her custom. The two set out from the stableyard with no halt at the front of the house. Those in Rathard House seemed to set little store by their daughter's excursion.

Riding behind her, Neil observed that she answered each mute stare of curiosity from man, woman or child with a greeting. In that also, he thought, she doesn't take after her mother. Beyond the clachan she drew rein.

'They've tongues?' and she indicated a man and woman she had passed, the woman stealing backward glances at the figure on horseback. Under the blue velvet cap with its curled feather her face was slightly flushed, her expression lively as she questioned him.

'They're not folk much given to touching the forelock,' answered Neil.

The girl's face clouded suddenly and she turned away. 'That's not what I meant, Mr Gilchrist,' she said, urging her horse forward.

Neil, contrite, caught the rein. 'Yes, they've tongues, Miss Echlin. Tonight, they'll talk of you at their hearths. Tomorrow they'll greet you kindly.'

Miss Echlin, partly mollified, changed the subject. ''Twas you talked of bringing provisions,' she said over her shoulder. 'At this pace we'll eat them at supper.'

'You're right,' responded Neil with the feeling of one reprieved. 'Pray let me lead. I know a path that shows the woodlands to advantage.'

Sometimes the two rode in file, sometimes, where clearances had widened the track, side by side. Neil was the conscientious guide. He pointed out to Miss Echlin where timber had been cut towards the building of her parents' pride, the cornmill; drew her attention to a row of saplings that stood in unnatural orderliness amid the profusion of the forest floor; explained how a patch of land, succumbing again to bracken and bramble, marked the defeat of a wouldbe settler. The young lady, not much to his surprise, showed only a minimal interest in these signs of industry. She much preferred to set her mount at a long glade, scattering those small creatures abroad on a winter morning and sending forth a cascade of fallen leaves from her horse's heels. The first time Neil had set out in pursuit, dire warnings of rabbit holes and cracked bones on his tongue, and ended gazing at her joyous face and sharing her laughter.

The undergrowth rising taller and grown more dense, forced them to dismount and lead their horses. Here the trees of the virgin forest stood close. Through the bare branches light fell on the sombre green of holly, yew and juniper. Miss Echlin spied a clump of hazel. She called to Neil and stretched to pluck nuts still clinging to the bushes. Reaching for a higher spray she stumbled and would have fallen had not Neil caught her. His fingers brushed the firm roundness of her breast. The girl disengaged herself promptly.

'Mr Gilchrist,' she said, busying herself with the hazel twigs, 'bring the food and find a place where we can eat.'

They spread the provisions on a stone beneath a lichened ash tree. Miss Echlin's share took up most of its surface.

'I brought my usual midday meal,' said Neil, gloomily viewing the cold bacon, barley bread and flask of buttermilk.

'As you've given up your time to entertain me, *I* should supply the refreshments,' said Miss Echlin graciously. 'As you see, that was my intention. Taste this cheese, if you will. I brought it from Dunblane.'

Neil pronounced the cheese excellent. He also tasted the chicken, the ox-tongue, the brined trout, the freshly-baked white bread and Mrs Rusk had put in figs and two apples so the buttermilk lay untouched.

Miss Echlin insisted on sampling his barley bread and bacon and said that he must find it sustaining in his work. 'What is your work, Mr Gilchrist?'

Neil smiled. 'I knew you weren't paying heed when I told you I planted the saplings. When I arrived here your father dubbed me his arborist.'

'Arborist – and what did you do before that?'

Since the coach journey from Newtownards on the day of her arrival he had wanted to establish himself in her eyes. But this was not the question that opened to such an explanation. And yet, he might never have such an opportunity.

She was aware of his silence. 'I shouldn't have asked you –'

'No, I've nothing to hide. I'll start at the beginning. . .'

He told her of his return from college to the ruinous house and estate, of his ailing elder brother, of the angry exchange with his father, of setting out for London and how he had been diverted by meeting a peasant family fleeing to Ireland. 'And so I found my way to Ravara,' he concluded, 'and the laird, your father, gave me work.'

She looked at him gravely as if weighing what she had heard. 'You'll have to return to Balwhanny some day, Neil.'

Only for a fleeting moment did he consider what she said. The solicitous use of his Christian name drove all else out. Then he gave thought to her words.

'But not penniless. Not without money to rescue my house.'

'How does one get money like that?'

Neil laughed. 'My dear lady, cleverer heads than mine swither o'er that!' He rose, gathering the remnants of the meal into the linen piece she had spread. 'I'll take this and see the horses are safe tethered.'

On his return they started for the little lough. Neil, used to trampling and wading his way through undergrowth, ooze, grassy tussocks and fallen boughs, saw that such progress was not to be so speedy for Miss Echlin no matter how nimble. The hand he offered her was accepted. So with some laughter and much stumbling they reached the clearer verge of the lough. Beyond a minute half-moon of white sand and through a tunnel in the reeds the water lay calm and silent.

'Pooh!' cried the girl, 'you said there would be birds here!'

'We made too much noise.'

She saw a brightly-coloured water weed and, drawing off a glove, gave him her other hand as she knelt to pluck it. As he steadied her he looked down on the nimbus of bright hair under the feathered cap, and told himself that this morning, without doubt, was the most wonderful of his life. The plant out of water was drab and limp. She tossed it back and looked across the grey-blue stretch of the lough.

'If I were to live at Rathard I would have a boat here.'

A sudden constriction of fear kept him silent.

'Is there fish in it?'

'Aye, there's fish. Come, I think it's time we were turning.'

This time she held out her hand, her ungloved hand, for him to take. As he guided her footsteps through the debris of time and weather the fear that had seized him by the loughside

186

waned but he still did not dare to question her. Fingers intertwined, they paused at the venerable ash under which they had feasted.

'There should be a merle singing in that tree,' said Neil.

She looked into the thin naked twigs and smiled. 'Yes,' she said.

Riding back Miss Echlin showed no eagerness to gallop down the long glades. She jogged along with the thoughtful air of one to whom knowledge had suddenly been imparted.

They had reached the avenue of the Big House when Neil, troubled by her silence, said, 'The day – are ye disappointed?'

She looked at him gravely, aware and wary that their relationship had changed since they set out together. 'No.' She shook her head, 'I'm not disappointed. Indeed, I have to thank you.'

Neil, afraid of saying too much, said nothing other than a grunt accompanied by a dismissive wave of the hand.

As they approached the house Miss Echlin changed tack. 'I can tell my father that you found time to go with me to Lough Reagh –'

'Found time!' cried Neil heatedly. 'Found time? That was not the way o't, Anne!'

'No – well. What of tomorrow?'

As calmly as he might he replied. 'Tomorrow. I'm at your service tomorrow as well ye know.'

'Can you come with me to the village. I've some purchases to make.'

'Yes. I'll be here at ten o'clock.'

'And can we have dinner at that tav –' Her eager voice ceased abruptly. Neil saw two elegantly-dressed men come from the house.

'Hamilton,' said the girl above her breath. 'My brother Hamilton. . .'

The taller of the two approached, smiling, arms outstretched. 'Sister Anne!' As she tried to dismount he caught her and set her lightly on the ground. 'It gladdens my heart to see you, dear sister,' he continued, his red-lipped smile widening. He didn't acknowledge Neil's presence, but raised a finger. 'See to Miss Echlin's horse,' he said.

Neil, stiff in the saddle, saw Captain Hamilton Echlin take his sister by the elbow and urge her towards the door at a pace too quick in a grip too harsh. He watched as the other fine gentleman was presented to her. Then the door closed on all three.

17

Brightness, piercing the window-covering, brought him out of his bed in a bound. Tiptoeing across the floor, he peered into the schoolroom. Angus Ross was still seated at breakfast. At the hearth Chrissy Maclennan was scraping the porridge pot. He pulled back his curtain and light flooded the bedchamber. A dazzling whiteness of snow lay across the countryside. Had it drifted on the road to Newtownards? For all his anxiety he dressed with some care.

He wished Ross a good morning and drew a stool to the table. Mrs Maclennan set a full porridge bowl before him.

He helped himself to milk. 'How are the roads, Chrissy?'

'No mair than a skimp of snow in some places. Thick in others where the wind's blowed it against dykes and trees,' and the guidwife went back to the hearth.

'Have ye to travel today, Neil?' asked the dominie.

Neil scanned the guileless face of his companion. 'Only if the weather allows it. Tell me,' he went on before Ross could question him further, 'did ye take Wishart to Crawfurd's for the suit of clothes?'

'I did. He chose what's close to hodden grey.'

'Against Crawfurd's advice?'

'And mine. I told him the laird would expect something more lively.'

Neil ran his spoon around the bowl. 'He'll look like an assistant to Turnooth.'

Ross smiled. 'That also was brought to his attention but he wouldn't budge.'

'He'd be all the better of that guidman's company!' cried Chrissy Maclennan.

Neil lifted his bonnet, expressed the hope that Una Drummond and the scholars would arrive safely and escaped into the chill brilliant morning. The air was cold enough to hold a thaw in check but, the day before being dry, there was no black ice under the snow. For all that, he rode carefully away from the schoolhouse. Where the path joined the road to the clachan he met Una shepherding three or four children ahead of her. Her flushed face, the traces of snow clinging to her clothing and that of the pupils spoke of an ambush or that they had been sporting themselves on the way. The young man rode on, wondering mildly how a sensible well-spoken lass had contrived to steer her young life between such a paltering father and a malicious chattering mother. But then, thought Neil, she spends much of her waking hours in the company of the dominie. Why they didn't marry was a question that had crossed his mind. But as so often with those of a sweet-tempered disposition, Ross's nature checked impertinent questions.

As he paused to buckle on his rapier, flakes circled down on him and the horse. He looked up and read a sky heavy with snow. If we push briskly for the village, he decided, and Miss Echlin can be persuaded not to linger over her purchases while I order dinner, we could be on the road back in afternoon light.

There were few souls about on the tracks or in the clachan. A woman came with brimming milk pails from a cowhouse. Two boys, whom Neil felt should be at Angus Ross's feet, were dragging a broken bough to their cottage. By the time he had reached the approach to Rathard House the flurry of snow had ceased. To his mild surprise a pattern of wheel tracks and hooves ran the avenue's length.

Rose was clearing snow at the house entrance. He had a strange feeling, as he approached, that she was doling out the task so that she would be there when he arrived.

'She's awa, Mr Gilchrist!' she cried before he could speak. 'Miss Echlin's awa!'

In as cool a manner as he could summon, Neil asked: 'Has the laird or Miss Echlin any message for me, Rose?'

But she was not to be fobbed off. Leaning on her broom, eyes sparkling with malice, she repeated: 'She's awa. Awa to Ballymacashon. There's no word left for ye, sir.'

Neil rode round to the stableyard. The coach was in its house. Leaning against the doorpost, his legs crossed, was a man clad in red doublet, tight red and green hose and buckled shoes. Drawing a straw backwards and forwards across his lips, the stranger surveyed rider and horse in a cool appraisal that darkened Neil's face. Sim Watt came across the yard from the kitchen.

'Ye were early on the road this morn, Sim.'

Watt came close, resting his hand on the peak of the young man's saddle. 'I drove Miss Anne to the Lowrys after breakfast – on the laird's orders.'

'When do ye set out for her again?'

'I can't tell ye that, Mr Gilchrist. The laird packed her off in the coach with a valise. It looked to me that the young lady's away for a while.'

Neil was about to ask Watt why he spoke in little above a whisper but thought better than to be drawn into a confidence with a servant. All the time he was aware of the unwavering inspection of the gaudy figure under the eaves of the coach-house. 'Who's the pied fellow?' he inquired, not troubling much to lower his voice.

Watt didn't need to look behind him. 'Kyte, sir. Mr Kyte, Captain Hamilton's man.'

Neil gestured the ostler's hold away, and turning, rode slowly to the front of the manor. Rose had gone, the great doors were closed. Not a sound, not a flicker of movement came from Rathard House. It stood in the white sheen of the snow like a place deserted. He was half-way down the avenue when from the upper reaches of the house came the high gleeful laughter of a young man.

Setting his bonnet against the rising wind, Neil rode on in no sweet temper. It was *she* who had proposed the excursion to the village, had talked of sharing dinner at the tavern. It was impossible that she should forget. What entertainment was likely at Ballymacashon House? He recalled the Lowry family: the son at school in Scotland, three daughters at home, little more than children. No matter what the reason, she could have left a message for him. Then, under the hurt of his anger crept a darker surmise: the laird or her Ladyship had abruptly put an end to any footing between their daughter and him. He recalled the coachman's words of how the laird 'had packed her off' to the Lowrys. No matter how bereft his life had been before he met Anne Echlin he wished to God he had his peace of mind again. But for today, he decided morosely, I'll put it out of mind. I'll ride to Bell's for a skinful of food and liquor.

As if waiting on the thought, the snow fell again, thick and blinding. Spinning columns, driven by the wind, raced towards him on the road to Newtownards. With an oath he turned back towards the clachan. As he rode past the cottages children were disappearing indoors, too tossed by the laden gale to threaten a solitary rider with snowballs. Reaching the schoolhouse he stabled the horse, rubbed the beast down, shook out fodder, then stamped indoors. The dominie, meticulous as ever, had drawn a seat to the fire to note in his log that this day he had closed school early because of inclement weather. He drew back as Neil shook his snow-laden jacket over the fire.

'Ye didn't get far.'

The fall of snow dwindled, then ceased, as the evening darkened. A dundering blow on the door roused Angus at the fireside. Calum Wishart came in stamping his feet on the schoolroom floor. He laid a parcel on the table. 'Dugal the blacksmith left that with me. It's from Una Drummond.' He removed his outer garment and seated himself. 'To tell ye the truth, men, I wouldn't have left my shelter if my dowsing fingers hadn't spelled foodstuffs.'

'Bless her,' said Angus Ross.

'Amen,' said Neil.

The girl had packed a fair lump of bacon, two loaves and a flagon of ale. Neil seized the bacon, drew his knife, and headed hungrily for the kitchen when Wishart, with the air of a conjurer, brought a small bottle from his pocket. He held it up. 'Usquebaugh!' he exclaimed.

'Ha!' cried Neil. 'Thy name is Jupiter. Where did ye get it?'

Wishart turned the crystal liquid before the firelight. 'From the laird's own hand.'

Neil handed the bacon and knife to Angus. 'You've been to Rathard House?'

'I set out to thank the laird for the suit of clothes.' Wishart made a gesture: 'Long overdue, I'll grant ye. He met me with a face of slate. "What's your errand, man?" I began to thank him when he cut me short with "Aye, aye, aye, some other time!" Then he fumbles in a cupboard for this, comes round the desk, claps me on the shoulder, claps the bottle in my hand. "Some other time, Calum," he says, and I'm out.' Wishart considered the vapour rising from his ragged leg-coverings. 'There's something sadly agley in that family.'

'Ye – saw no one else?' asked Neil.

Wishart shook his head. 'Even the fellow who showed me out avoided my eye. Gentlemen, I'm famished.'

For three days the snow lay unbroken, the noises of the countryside muted under the soft undulations stretched across worked land and deep into the forest. On the fourth morning Neil awoke to flauchts of lightning and the mutter of thunder in the hills. Outside, herbage was breaking in narrow blades across the meadows, trees creaked as they shed their burden of snow, the path that he had helped Angus clear to the schoolhouse was a running stream, wagons were rumbling on the roads again.

He ached for a thaw to his own anxiety and foreboding. At supper that evening Wishart had voiced his usual bland indifference to the laird and his family. But Neil felt that this shrewd man, who knew so much more about the darker corners

193

of humankind than his younger companions, guessed at something in Rathard House that he was not disposed to talk about. Neil had an overwhelming desire to ask questions of someone less artless than Angus Ross. Not the Reverend Mungo Turnooth. But he could talk to the minister's sister. His only fear was that she would have nothing to tell him.

The manse door was opened at the second knock by the Reverend Turnooth. Wrapped in a baggy dusty gown, quill in hand, he peered up at the visitor.

'Guid morning, reverend sir. I trust I haven't disturbed ye?'

'Ye have. Doubtless ye want to see my sister. If she didn't hear ye chappin' like thunder on my door she must be in the back garden. Here,' the little man halted Neil's move toward the kitchen. He brought down a great iron key from the wall. 'If your onerous duties permit, look in at the kirk. If there are any signs of snow damage tell Dan Drummond. Ye may leave the key with him.'

Neil dutifully expressed his compliance to the back of Mr Turnooth's gown as the minister returned to his study. In the kitchen he met Mistress Tabitha, her hands full of wintergreens. The lady's face lit up in pleasure.

'Mr Gilchrist, I've news for ye. Do pull up to the fire.'

As calmly as he could he brought forward a chair. Mistress Tabitha seated herself.

'You'll be glad to learn that young Elphie MacIlveen has been delivered of a bonny man child.'

For a moment Neil was unable to speak. He had fooled himself into thinking that he expected little news of Anne Echlin at the manse. But now that this was evidently so, he felt a surge of fury against Mistress Tabitha. 'That – that may signify to those concerned,' he stuttered.

'A minute, if ye please.' Mistress Tabitha held up her hand, more than a shade puzzled at how her innocent news had been taken. 'The burden of my news is that the parents want to call the child Neil, after you –'

'Let them call the brat what they please!' cried the young man, springing to his feet. 'Mistress Tabitha, have ye any word on the people at Rathard!'

'Rathard?' Mistress Tabitha sounded hesitant, evasive.

'Yes, Rathard, ma'am. Four days ago I was to accompany Miss Echlin to the village. When I went to meet her —'

'She had gone to Ballymacashon House.'

'How did ye learn that?'

'Miss Anne was to call with me the day before yesterday. When she didn't arrive I put it down to the snow, although the distance between the two dwellings is small. Then I thought the lass was ill and it was my part to inquire —'

'Aye, and what have ye found, ma'am?'

'The eldest son, Captain Hamilton, had arrived from London with a companion, Mr Dudley Tickell. . .' Mistress Tabitha's voice had slowed.

'I'm aware of that,' said Neil impatiently. 'At least, that the son was there.'

'Do ye ken why Miss Anne was sent off to the Lowrys?'

'No, but I would be interested to learn.'

'Captain Hamilton does not conduct himself in a seemly manner before his sister —'

'A bully-boy, Mistress Tabitha.'

'Yes. . . I. . . I. . . yes. . .' She studied her folded hands for a moment. 'If that were all. . .'

'What can ye mean by that, ma'am?' Neil stooped to look into her face. The distress he saw there struck him into silence. Sitting down again he laid his hand gently on her folded hands. Mistress Tabitha took courage.

'When I entered that house the laird was barely civil to me. Lady Echlin was keeping to her chamber. My informant was the housekeeper. Miss Anne had been sent off for fear of what she might see and hear. What I learnt from Mrs Rusk forced me to my knees when I reached home. I prayed for the strength and guile to keep my brother from visiting the laird's family till

195

Captain Hamilton Echlin and his. . . his. . . friend depart.'

'I will not embarrass ye,' said Neil in a low voice, 'by pretending ignorance. Calum Wishart guessed at. . . something hurtful.'

Mistress Tabitha grasped his hand fiercely. 'Neil,' she cried, 'it's a house of abomination!'

'All the greater call that Anne Echlin should be out o't.'

Mistress Tabitha smiled wanly as she released his hand. 'Miss Anne's your first concern, and rightly so. She's a sweet lass.'

'She is.' Neil stood up. 'Where the Deil does it end? Hamilton Echlin will be at Rathard till the Lord Deputy arrives.'

'In my prayers I await the word of the Lord God. Do you as much, Neil.'

Neil gave his promise. 'I've a couple of errands, ma'am; to look in at the kirk for the minister. Then to put a piece of silver in the fist of the new-born Neil MacIlveen. I understand that to be the custom.'

Kyte, Captain Hamilton's man-servant, was the instrument chosen by Providence to resolve the crisis at Rathard House. A scape-gallows, soft living in the captain's service had not impaired his malignant nature. On the day of his arrival he began to question aloud why his master had brought him to this bleak abode where he had to spend his time among peasants of dour looks and unintelligible speech. The only person who gratified his eye was Katie, a young kitchen-maid. He discovered that it was her task to bring breakfast eggs from the barn. Following her in one morning, he threw her on the straw and settled himself on her, his hands busy. The attempt to rape the lass was ill-timed. Her screams brought Sim Watt running from the coach-house and Neilson and Ronane from the kitchen. Elbowing the others aside, Ronane plucked the Englishman up by his hair and belt and flung him with stunning force against a wooden bin. For a moment Kyte seemed as shocked by the strength of his assailant as by the crunching impact. Ronane

196

saw the hand steal to the waistband. As he dodged away from the descending dagger the long blade opened the sleeve of his leather jerkin from shoulder to wrist.

Kyte retreated across the yard, flourishing his knife. It was plain to the onlookers that he was still half-stunned. Blood flowed from a gash in his head and was lost in his red doublet. Foul-mouthed, he called on his assailant to come at him.

Watt grasped Ronane's shoulder. 'For Christ's sake, let him be. He's Captain Hamilton's man!' He brought Ronane to halt. 'Away and tell the laird all that's happened. Get your word in first, man!'

Ronane shook off the coachman, then thought better of it. 'Aye,' he said, and turning his back went into the house followed by those who had witnessed the brief affray.

Echlin was scrutinising the tenant rent-ledgers when Ronane presented himself. When the steward had finished his story the laird remarked on the split sleeve.

'Nothing,' said Ronane, 'no more than a scratch on the arm.'

'What of my son's man-servant?'

'On his feet and cursing when I left.'

Ronane gone, Echlin returned to the ledgers. He had difficulty in giving attention to names and sums. What he saw there did nothing to ease the dark and bitter anger that possessed him. He bent his mind again to the pages. Perhaps Dan Drummond was mistaken in his figures? As he pushed the books aside with an oath, Captain Hamilton came into the study. His usually elegant figure spoke of one hurriedly summoned from his bed.

Father and son regarded each other unsmilingly. 'My man-servant has been assaulted, sir,' said the captain.

'Aye, I've heard. He tried to ravish one of the kitchen-maids. I have the power to hang him for that.'

'He tells me she led him on.'

'I'd as lief believe Ananias.' Thwarted pride and anger welled up in Echlin. He broadened his tongue the more to distance

197

himself from the smooth insolent face before him. 'I'll say this, if the lass had a maidenhead, the man was mair likely tae take it than his master.'

The two regarded each other in cold virulent hostility.

'You're pleased to speak in riddles, sir.'

The laird stood up. 'Then let me make myself all the clearer. You're a pederast, sir.' There was no way back now for Kenneth Echlin. 'And I want none of ye.'

'I wish to Christ,' and Hamilton stamped his foot, 'I had disobeyed your summons!'

The childishness of the protest almost disarmed the laird. 'On that we're agreed,' he said in a harsh voice. 'Now rouse that scented jessie, Tickell, out of his bed – or yours, as maybe. I want ye both out of this house within the hour.'

'My mother –' began the young man.

The laird strode round the table in such a fury that his son shrank as from a blow. 'Don't lip your mother's name to me! Now, pack and go!'

The young man paused in the doorway. 'You've nothing here I lack. As for your Lord Deputy,' he waved his hand, 'I dine with his masters,' and Captain Hamilton was gone.

If that was meant to wound me he has failed, thought the laird. I need now have no conscience about him. He listened to the fall of his son's footsteps across the great hall, the rapid ascent of the stairs, the opening and closing of a distant door. He reached for his bonnet. No, that would be craven. He sat down and dragged the ledgers in front of him. He had barely thrown open the cover when he heard what he waited for. Light, swifter footsteps descended the stairs and sped towards him across the hall. He heard the sibilant whisper of her garments as she swept into the study. Lady Echlin's face was white with passion and she grasped the table to steady herself as she faced her husband.

'Good God,' she whispered, 'what can you mean? Ordering my son from the house. . .'

The laird rose slowly, walked to the door and thrust it closed with his foot. Then he turned to his wife. 'Madam, if ye must ask me that, then your son has lacked the stomach to tell ye why. Let it suffice that he protested not at all at my reason for asking him and his friend to leave Rathard –'

'It does not suffice!' cried Lady Echlin. She brushed back a lock of black hair from her pale face. 'You bring my son from London and then reject him. . . reject him. . .' The last words choked on a sob.

'Wife,' said the laird, his voice low, 'you're no fool. Nor are ye blind or deaf. Well ye ken that all is not right with Hamilton. He's not the braw lad we saw off to London. He's. . . he's tainted. . .'

Lady Echlin's head sank. For the past week she had turned her whole being away from a dread that she refused to name even in the secrecy of her thoughts. If Hamilton had but come alone. 'What does it reck,' she muttered, 'until the Lord Deputy's gone. . .'

'No!' cried her husband. 'You'll not toy with our good name!' He grasped her by the arms so fiercely that she winced. 'God in Heaven, give a thought, will ye, to what *I* have lost. Our son – my heir – is a pander – a sodomite!' She staggered as he released her. He turned his back. 'I don't want to see him again.'

But Echlin, suffering in his eyes, was at a window, covertly, to watch as his son rode away. First went Hamilton, unabashed and aloof, a fine figure in the saddle; then the bemused Mr Tickell, peering about in search of a friendly glance; Kyte, his head patched by the charitable Mrs Rusk, wearing a sneer like a vizor against anyone fool enough to wish Godspeed. But yard, stables and gardens were deserted. Echlin stayed at his window until he could no longer make out his son's figure in the morning mist drifting across the avenue.

Together, he and his wife ate their midday meal in silence. He finished his wine and set down the glass. 'Ye could write to

Marion Lowry and thank her for entertaining our daughter,' he said.

'If we fetch her back now it will seem that she was sent away only because. . .' Lady Echlin fell silent.

'True, then let her bide a while longer.' Echlin rose from the table, called his dogs and left the house.

Archie Gill clapped the reins of the horse between his knees while he pulled up his jacket collar against the evening frost and dragged his bonnet over his ears. Behind him, James Mackechnie, his musket across his belly, lay curled on the score of sacks purchased from Bothwell and Leslie's. The strong mulled ale of the tavern was dying in the two. Archie was about to shake up the reins when the trembling of a bush caught his eye.

'James,' he said over his shoulder,' stir yoursel'. There's a chiel on the roadside ahead of us.' Archie let the horse plod on, while he groped for a bar of mill iron under his feet.

When they drew abreast of the wayfarer he was revealed as nothing more formidable than a young fellow resting on a grassy bank, his staff and a strapful of books beside him.

'Good evening to ye,' the stranger called cheerfully.

''Even,' responded the miller and drew horse and wagon to a halt.

The young man stood up and shook himself. 'Are ye for Ravara?'

'Aye.'

'Then ye might find room for me?'

Archie Gill considered this for a moment then slid his backside along the seat. Lifting staff and books the young man clambered nimbly into the wagon.

Having settled himself, the stranger didn't seem disposed to converse. Instead he began to hum a tune in a manner that Gill and James Mackechnie found pleasant enough to the ear.

Mackechnie, from his vantage on the floor of the vehicle, had been taking a skelly at the young man's well-worn shoes.

'You've travelled far?'

'Far indeed,' said the stranger over his shoulder. 'But on this island only from Belfast.'

'Aye – so?' said James. 'I've never been to Belfast.'

'You've missed little, my friend,' said the young man, and again picked up his tune.

As they trundled on it became evident to the sagacious miller that the wayfarer, by his bearing and speech, was no pedlar or vagrant of the roads, whatever his errand to Ravara. But as one who did not conduct his own concerns in the marketplace, Gill respected the privacy of others. If this young fellow chose not to explain what brought him here, that was his affair.

'You're in Ravara now,' Archie announced as they descended the road to the clachan.

The young man looked around with lively interest. 'The houses of the tenants?' he asked.

'Aye, some of them. Where d'ye want set down?'

'At Mr Echlin's house.'

Archie drew up at the avenue to Rathard House. His passenger climbed down. He slung the books on his shoulder and grasped his staff.

'Thank, ye.'

But Archie Gill had some misgivings at landing a stranger unannounced at the laird's house. 'Are ye expected, sir?'

'I hope so,' replied the young man smiling. 'My father has sent for me.'

18

Word went out from Rathard House that Captain Hamilton Echlin had been hastily summoned to London. The laird was not simple enough to believe that all or many would swallow the story; there had been too many clacking tongues. But it would, at least, ward off inquisitive neighbours. Now he intended to make a little more of Frank, the second son, than Lady Echlin and he had purposed.

Although they were well into the first week of January Echlin called his staff together to drink a glass to the New Year. When Neil arrived at the Big House the laird, Lady Echlin and their son were surrounded by the people from the estate. As Neil made his way through the throng he looked in vain for the head of bright hair he sought. He bowed to her Ladyship, shook hands with the young man and took a glass of wine with the laird. Standing there he felt Lady Echlin's close scrutiny – her glance following his glance where it strayed. Then she was called on to seem affable to Mrs Drummond and her daughter. Neil took the opportunity to move away. To his surprise he was followed by Frank Echlin.

'Mr Gilchrist, I'd be obliged if you could favour me with a little of your time – and knowledge.'

Neil eyed the young man. His manner of asking seemed sincere enough. 'In what way can I be of service to ye, Mr Echlin?'

'I would like to know more about the workings of the estate.'

'That's the concern o' the laird – and his factor,' said Neil politely.

'No, not about lettings and rents. What I mean is *farming* – cultivation, pasturage, the crops sown –'

'They come in their seasons, Mr Echlin.' said Neil in a chaffing note.

'That of course, I know. But I understand from my sister that you're well-informed on these activities. I don't want to discuss such matters with my father — as yet.'

'Your sister?' Neil looked around the chamber.

'She's not here. She's still with the Lowrys. I rode over to see her —'

'Mr Echlin,' cried Neil, 'I'll be happy to give ye what information I can! We'll set off from the schoolhouse after breakfast.' And Neil, having taken leave of the laird and his wife and paid his respects to the minister and Mistress Tabitha, left Rathard House with a lighter step and heart.

To learn that he had been in Anne Echlin's thoughts rejoiced Neil's heart. But the why and wherefore of the matter was not so happy and became less so as he turned it over in his mind. Whatever young Echlin had been set to study at Cambridge it was unlikely to have been rural economy. That he should wish to conceal his interest from his father filled Neil with suspicion as much as puzzlement. What Frank Echlin was up to Neil could not guess; but he would not allow the youth to raise a thicket between himself and the laird.

Neil's reception of the young man on the following morning was polite but cool. Keeping a prudent distance from Dan Drummond's office he led him up the long rise to the holdings of the MacIlveens and the Purdies. His attitude was no more than that of introducing a son of the landlord to his father's tenants. Yet, as he watched from the saddle he could not help but observe the eagerness with which young Echlin questioned Alexander and Tam and the attention he gave to their replies. He felt his scepticism diminish but not his bafflement as to what the young fellow was up to.

At the cornmill Frank Echlin greeted Archie Gill warmly and followed the amiable miller with the closest attention as they scrambled through the building and across its water-courses. With such an appreciative audience at his beck Neil could do no less than ride round by the coney-warren and explain its origin and its seasonal contribution to the laird's purse. Then drawing rein on a height above the substantial Neilson farm he pointed out the advantages enjoyed by a family of four or five hard-working folk dwelling under the same roof. They were now close to the Newtownards road. Urged by hunger and curiosity Neil proposed that they should eat at the village tavern.

As was customary at this hour, the dining-room was abuzz with voices, the clatter of crockery, the rapid flight of Mrs Bell and her handmaidens among the tables. The innkeeper found them a table. Neil caught his inquisitive glance at the new-comer.

'John,' he said, 'this is Mr Frank Echlin.'

Bell ducked his head. 'You're right welcome, Mr Echlin. I'll send a lass tae ye, gentlemen.' Off he went through the thronged room, pausing at a well-clad back now and then to whisper that laird Echlin's second son was with them.

From the corner of his eye Neil saw rubicund faces raised, jaw movements suspended, to stare at his companion.

Healthy appetites kept the two silent until their plates were cleared. Neil called for the tankards to be refilled.

'Tell me, young sir,' he said, 'what was your design in this morning's jaunt?'

'To discover something about the place where I intend to live and work.'

Neil laughed. 'Ye may think otherwise when you've finished your studies.'

'I have finished with my studies. I'm not returning to college.'

Neil set down his cup. 'Have ye told the laird?'

'No.'

'Ye mean,' demanded Neil, 'you're telling me this before you've talked with your parents?'

'I don't think my parents will be greatly concerned,' said the other with a slight smile. 'I doubt if they could tell you what I was doing at college. Maybe preparing for the Church –'

'My concern,' said Neil interrupting him, 'is that your father doesn't think I'm party to this ram-stam decision of yours. What in the Deil's name has persuaded ye. . .?' He stopped, fearful that he sounded like somebody hectoring a younger brother. 'You'll tell them when ye get back?' He waited for young Echlin's nod. 'Drink up. It's time we were on our road.'

Frank Echlin handed his horse over to Neilson and, intent, went in search of his father. The laird, they told him, was in his study but could not be disturbed. A messenger had arrived from Carrickfergus. The Lord Deputy and his company were on the road. He would be at Ravara within three days.

For Kenneth Echlin the news was a key opening a lock. He was now at liberty to put to use all the furnishment on which he had spent so much time and considerable money. Even the disappearance of his elder son seemed now of little importance. It re-established the faith of his servants that the laird was a man of consequence after all. For Neil it raised the eager hope that Anne Echlin would be seen again at Rathard House.

Not that Echlin had found any need to summon him to the manor house. Through Dan Drummond he was instructed to ride into the village and request the innkeeper's wife to present herself and one or two of her lasses to Mrs Rusk as soon as they might. Neil bridled at the menial nature of the errand and at the factor's manner. But he made use of his journey by purchasing linen shirts for Ross and himself from Crawfurd and picking from a pile of second-hand finery an ornamented rapier-belt.

To avoid similar errands Neil spent the next two days close to the manse. Better to suffer the Reverend Mr Turnooth's wonderment at his presence there than Dan Drummond's borrowed authority. From Mistress Tabitha, who had established herself as his confidante, he learned that Anne had been summoned back to Rathard House but that there was little chance of their meeting. Lady Echlin had pressed the girl into service upstairs and downstairs.

205

Seated at table Neil told the minister and his sister that the laird had bought Calum Wishart a suit of clothes but was likely to be aggrieved that the cloth was of such a dark hue.

Mr Turnooth sopped his oatcake in milk. 'I'm glad to learn,' he said, 'that Wishart had such guid sense in his pow.'

Neil stole a glance at the minister's faded garb. 'I should tell ye, sir, that when in Crawfurd's I saw a cloak of fine dark material most fitting for a clergyman. . .'

Mistress Tabitha made an encouraging gesture.

'Young man,' said her brother forcibly, 'Lord Deputy or laird, they take me as they find me.' His stern eye took in Mistress Tabitha. 'We dress in a sober and seemly manner here. No need to play the episcopalian grandee.' The good man drained his milk and stumped off to his chamber.

His sister listened until she heard the door close behind him. 'Would Mr Crawfurd still have the garment?'

Considering her brother's stature, Neil thought that very likely.

'Then bring it to me Neil, and I'll pay ye.'

Very early on the third morning the avenue to Rathard House sounded to the clatter of hooves. At the head of the cavalcade rode Sir Arthur Chichester. At his shoulder Kenneth Echlin. Following close came three gentlemen in feathered caps and a score of troopers, their steel morions winking dully in the chill January light. On the road from Newtownards Sir Arthur had brought the party to a halt so that Echlin could point out in which airt MacCartan's land lay. It had been a summary reminder to the laird as to why the Lord Deputy was riding towards Ravara.

19

The Echlins had set a table with refreshments near the great
fireplace. The heavy tread of the Lord Deputy as he approached it was more that of a victor than a visitor to Rathard.
He and his officers accepted food and drink from their hosts
but Chichester with an air of impatience declined to sit at table.
He dismissed the two younger men, retaining his aide, Herbert
St John.

'Now, Mr Echlin,' said he, 'let us talk.'

'Bid Ronane attend me,' said the laird to his wife and led the
way towards his study. Chichester with a curt bow to Lady
Echlin, and St John with a more elaborate salute, followed him.

Echlin had barely seated his guests when Ronane entered the
study. 'My seneschal,' said the laird.

Mr St John granted Ronane a brief glance of curiosity. The
Lord Deputy didn't trouble to turn his head. He didn't welcome
the fellow's arrival. With a member of his household present the
Scotsman would expect to be dealt with more formally than his
Excellency had intended. He waited with studied patience until
Ronane had taken his stance behind the laird's chair.

'As you're aware, Mr Echlin,' the Lord Deputy began, 'my
main purpose in travelling here is better to inform myself on the
attack by the Irish on your estate and the lives of your family and
your tenants.'

'Perpetrated by one, MacCartan,' interjected Mr St John. 'A
felonious act which should have been reported to his Excellency,' he added with an admonitory smile.

The laird's expression hardened at the rebuke. 'You're in
possession o' knowledge denied to me –' he began.

'It's our understanding,' persisted Mr St John, 'that the
MacCartans inflicted a bloody onslaught on you and your
people.'

'There was no such aggression here –'

'God's bread, sir,' cried Chichester, a scowl on his bearded face, 'the story was heard in Dublin!'

The Lord Deputy's brusqueness sounded a warning in the laird's ear. Suddenly and clearly he saw that he could indeed be drawn into a conflict with the MacCartans that threatened a waste of substance and possibly life. 'I much regret that your Excellency has been misinformed. We had no more than a brush with wood-kernes. I have no reason to suspect the MacCartans had a hand in it.' He threw the query over his shoulder. 'We suffered no loss of life, Ronane?'

'None, Mr Echlin.'

'Or aught,' and Echlin's gaze rested on Mr St John, 'that would merit the name of a bloody onslaught?'

'No, laird.'

Mr St John was conscious of being twitted. With some effort he contained his anger – but not the sneer in voice and face as he addressed Ronane. 'Bloody or not, you consider yourself an authority on such matters, steward?'

'I have seen service, sir,' answered Ronane evenly.

'Where?'

Ronane paused. He could have been recalling some bitter affray from a roll of campaigns.

'Virginia.'

The Lord Deputy, who had been betraying some impatience with the talk, now examined Ronane for the first time. 'You have been in the Americas?'

'I have, your Excellency.'

'You served under?'

'Captain Francis West – and others.'

'Aye,' grunted the Lord Deputy. Some of this fellow Ronane's story was coming to mind; the shrouded deed on the Appomattox, the nameless protector who had plucked him up like a chess piece to set him down in obscurity in Ireland. Wily and subtle in his dealings with the planting landlords,

208

Chichester had informed himself on Echlin's military service. But he had not expected that his host employed this hardbitten mercenary in his household. He should have been kept better informed and he scowled sidelong at Herbert St John. As for the two before him, they were neither hungry Edinburgh lawyers avid to grasp a quick fortune from expropriated acres, nor the downy second sons of wealthy English merchants, willing to play at lord of the manor. It would be impossible to persuade London that such men as these had failed to protect their holding against the Irish – or for that matter would let it slip into the grasp of rapacious officers, like St John, in his establishment.

Ronane bent to his master. 'I've work, laird.'

'See to it, Ronane.'

'And see to our horses,' said the Lord Deputy. With a creaking of leather and clank of metal he eased himself from his chair. 'There are works you wanted us to see, Mr Echlin.'

Together the two, Herbert St John in their wake, rode from Rathard. The laird drew his visitor's attention to the manner in which he had raised and strengthened the earthen arms of the ancient rath until they stood a formidable bawn encircling the house. The Lord Deputy acknowledged the improvement with a nod.

As they approached the clachan women and a few men were to be seen in the doorways. More in mistrust than deference the cottars stared at the two strange gentlemen riding by with their laird.

'Do not these hobbes breed?' cried Mr St John.

Echlin was not well pleased. 'The children are at school, sir,' he replied with a snap.

Mr St John seemed ready to question the advisability of such concern when he was interrupted by the Lord Deputy. 'Whither are we bound, Mr Echlin?'

'I thought to show ye the cornmill her Ladyship was so active in having built.'

'Aye, to be sure,' responded his Excellency, sounding a shade less interested than Echlin would have wished.

Down by the rushing waters of the Langstane Burn Sorley MacIlveen saw the three riders approach. He seated his wife, Elphie, infant Neil on her knee, on a cutty stool outside the cottage. The two English gentles rode past without as much as a glance, never to say a coin for a young mother's lap. Nor did his Excellency, having reined up on the slope above the mill, manifest any desire to go farther in that direction.

'To my eye it looks sound, Mr Echlin – and much to your lady's credit. Now,' continued the Lord Deputy cocking his beard interrogatively, 'where, from here, lie the Irishman's lands?'

The laird's immediate response to the query was one of umbrage. But he was canny enough to see that the Lord Deputy had no errand here other than to seek breaches, legal or material, in an undertaking. A half-finished bawn was of greater moment to the sharp eyes of Chichester and his henchman than cornmills or coney-warrens. From further down the stream came the ponderous mutter of wheels and shafts as Archie Gill set the mill in motion. Echlin turned away his horse's head.

'If ye care to accompany me to my factor's office, your Excellency, I can show ye how our properties abut. Or perhaps,' he continued with a glance at Mr St John, 'ye would prefer to ride along the lough shore and view the Irishman's holding?'

'No, no,' said Chichester with a wave of his hand. 'The estate plan will suffice.'

They found the factor's office empty; Dan Drummond, fraught with her Ladyship's instructions, was bustling around the back offices of Rathard House. The laird drew out the map and spread it on the table. Sir Arthur was content to trace the boundary line with his finger.

'These MacCartans – they are father and son?'

'Uncle and nephew. Fiach, the old man, and Turlough. I

understand there's a child – Turlough's son.'

'And their womenfolk?'

'I know nothing of them, Sir Arthur.'

'How much land does this tribe occupy?'

Echlin pointed to the map. 'There, it lies between Ravara and Cordwaine's estate.'

Chichester studied the legend under the portion indicated by the laird: *MacCartan their territory five billaboes*. 'Now, what does that signify between civil men?'

'About six hundred Irish acres.'

'How long have they been in possession of this?'

'Since the time of Adam and Eve, if they stick to the usual cant,' opined Mr St John.

Echlin's response was in a more sober key. 'In Edinburgh I was told that all this land from Strangford Lough to the Kilwarlin woodland was once MacCartan country. Then, in the late Queen's time, the greater part was lost to Fiach MacCartan's father by Act of Attainder –'

'– for his treasonable support of O'Neill,' added the Lord Deputy.

'I've heard as much, your Excellency.'

'Their present holding skirts Strangford Lough?'

'Yes.'

'A convenient landing-place for popish priests, eh, Mr Echlin?'

'I know nothing o' that, Mr St John.' The laird spoke as one not wishing to be misunderstood. 'I know nothing of the MacCartan household and I've never been to their dwelling. Turlough I've met but only at fair or market.'

'What of your tenants and the Irish?' continued the Deputy's aide.

'The odd time they may trade in cattle and my people have been known to sell them oats. But there's little traffic between them.'

Mr St John gazed at the hut rafters. His tongue ran over his lower lip. 'A modest scope, Sir Arthur, six hundred Irish acres. The lake is open to sea fish, Mr Echlin? I thought so. Modest, and yet there are those who would say the King is not well served here, that so much should be left in the hands of Irish cattle-herds and cockle-gatherers.' Mr St John lowered his gaze and there was a predatory gleam in his eyes. 'You agree it could be put to more profitable use, Mr Echlin?' St John indicated the chart on the table. 'I see it as an appendage to a greater estate. Put into the care of a lesser gentleman it could be a profitable undertaking for a new owner and still pay all regal duties on fish taken from its waters.'

The laird, uncertain as to a trap, glanced from one Englishman to the other. 'Gentlemen, ye are best informed on these matters. But the property is occupied by an Irishman in enough good regard to be honoured in corresponding with the King.'

'Ye know of the letter to Fiach MacCartan.' There was no note of interrogation in Chichester's voice.

'One of my servants directed the bearer.'

'Did ye learn aught of its contents?' asked Mr St John sharply.

'Why no,' answered the laird with an expression of mild surprise. 'But I've heard that his Grace and the elder MacCartan have a common interest in ancient manuscripts and things of that nature. That could well have been the burden of the letter. What is of import to *your* plan, sir,' he continued with a harder note to his voice, 'is that the King must have addressed MacCartan amiably enough for it caused no stir in the Irishman's camp.'

'It was a well-timed letter,' said Chichester broodingly, running his finger over the map before him.

'But in his Grace's interest,' said Mr St John, 'ill-judged.'

The Lord Deputy stood up abruptly. 'The King's pleasure is not to be reasoned against nor his intention disputed. We're at your pleasure, Mr Echlin.'

The laird paused at the door. 'Among those who will pay their respects at Rathard this evening will be Turlough MacCartan.'

212

Chichester stared at the laird then he shrugged. 'You are his host, sir.'

'It occurred to me,' continued Echlin, 'that the Irishman having received such a signal token of his Grace's goodwill, your Excellency might wish to say that ye had spoken with one of his family when ye were here.' With that he opened the door and the two Englishmen filed past him in silence.

Neil, arriving on foot at the manse late that morning, discovered the Reverend Amos Dalgetty with the minister and Mistress Tabitha. The reverend gentleman was not unknown to Neil. On several Sabbaths he and Mungo Turnooth had exchanged kirk services. Tall, thin, with sloping shoulders, he had always reminded Neil of a worn scythe blade gapped with rust when he raised himself in the pulpit. He had arrived at Ravara this morning with his landlord's family, the Finlays of Ringtoye. Mr Finlay had not seen fit to include Mrs Dalgetty in his train. How, asked the bereft man, could he comport himself before the Lord Deputy as keeper of his flock and his guid lady left behind in Ringtoye.

Mr Turnooth was about to give his opinion that the Lord Deputy was not much concerned over flocks of Scots Presbyterians or their ministers' wives, when his sister inquired if Mr Dalgetty had purchased his wife a new gown against the occasion.

'Four pounds, Tabitha,' affirmed Mr Dalgetty with bitterness, 'and still in its folds.'

'Lairds,' declared Mr Turnooth oracularly, 'are a law unto themselves.'

'Aye, true, Mungo,' agreed Mr Dalgetty, 'and can't be gainsaid.'

Mr Turnooth's face reflected a different opinion but he held his peace.

'Robert Finlay is a man baith leal and sagacious, as his neighbours and his tenants would bear witness.'

'His name's a byword for it, Amos.'

213

'No wonder then,' continued Mr Dalgetty ignoring the minister's sardonic grin, 'that he should be dumb-struck to learn that your Mr Echlin has invited the Irishman to meet Sir Arthur Chichester.' Mr Dalgetty paused to look at the others with a smug superiority. '"Ye cannot," says Mr Finlay, "mingle two swarms of bees under one hive. It leads to nothing but confusion and trouble." That,' concluded Mr Dalgetty with a smack of the lips, 'is Mr Finlay's opinion.'

Mungo Turnooth glanced at his sister and Neil, then turned to his visitor. 'Amos,' he said, 'it would seem that Mr Finlay and your guid self are privy to knowledge withheld from us. We've heard naught of mingling with the Irish on this or any occasion. And it is not a remissness a laird is likely to be guilty of towards a minister of the Gospel,' continued Mr Turnooth fixing the other cleric in a hard stare. 'No, as I understand it, it's more an act of homage. MacCartan has been summoned to present himself before Chichester. Isn't that the way o't Mr Gilchrist?'

'Eh?' cried that startled young man.

Mr Turnooth patiently expanded his query. 'That Mac-Cartan is to bow the knee now that the Lord Deputy had deigned to visit this corner of King Jamie's possessions?'

'That well could be,' responded Neil, obligingly. 'Since the old queen's time the MacCartans have held their land direct from the Crown. If there is an intermediary it would be the Lord Deputy. It is understandable that he should meet the Irishman.'

Mr Turnooth, folding his hands across his belly, nodded to his fellow-cleric.

But Mr Dalgetty was not so easily put down. 'Aye, verra fine, young man,' he said with a dismissive wave of the hand. 'But what hasn't been said is that MacCartan has been asked to sit at table – *verra likely above you and me, Mungo –*'

'That's at the laird's dispensation, Amos,' objected Mistress Tabitha.

'Oh, weel may ye say so, Tabitha, weel may ye say so,' agreed Mr Dalgetty with heavy irony. 'And more – he's employed an Irish harper to entertain the company!'

'There are those who are diverted by such whim-whams, Amos,' said the minister, but in a voice of unwonted mildness. 'For us,' and he indicated his sister, 'the chaunt of our people's voices raised in kirk is sufficient melody.'

'Then tonight ye may stop your ears against one of the tribe of harpers.' Mr Dalgetty emitted a cackle in keeping with his rusty-scythe visage. ''Tis said their jangling comes frae the fairyfolk. And weel it might be, for such eldritch bodies are lice frae Baal's locks.' Clasping the arms of his chair Mr Dalgetty thrust head and neck forward adder-like. 'And the players themsel's are infidels – all papists are infidels!'

The minister sat gazing at his folded hands. He was silenced, Neil felt, less by the observance of hospitality than that he shared his visitor's opinions. 'There are exigencies of temporal government, Amos,' he said at last, 'that we have to thole at times. . .'

Mr Dalgetty shook his head. 'Mungo,' he said, 'ye canna whistle and chaw meal at one and the same time. Ye canna suffer your laird tae entertain the Irish, a barbarian people, afore his household and your congregation.' The cleric drew his shoulders around his ears. 'Stand up, brother, like Moses at Rephidim, and declare that the Lord's anointed must oppose the Amalekites from generation to generation.'

'Mr Dalgetty,' said Neil, 'I take it that ye never have had call to counsel Mr Finlay in like manner?'

'No,' cried Dalgetty fervently, 'there's no an Irish bodie living within five miles of Ringtoye!'

'Then, Amos,' said Mistress Tabitha not without a certain air of satisfaction, 'you'll be under the same roof as an Irishman by three o'clock this day. That's the hour set by Mr Echlin for us to attend at Rathard House.'

Mistress Tabitha's disclosure hurried Neil from the manse.

Had he left earlier he would have seen Echlin and the Englishmen ride by on their way to Rathard House. There, Lady Echlin at her most gracious, served wine to the three. The laird felt her questioning eye.

'Sir Arthur,' said he, 'I have campaign memoirs that may interest ye. Be pleased to bring your glass.'

If Mr St John felt like following the two to the laird's study, a honeyed query from her Ladyship pinned him where he stood.

Chichester allowed that the martial documents displayed by his host were indeed of peculiar interest. The laird watched as his guest with his blunt heavy fingers turned the leaves and undid the scrolls, now and again emitting in his perusal a grunt of appreciation or surprise. In his active career Echlin had never asked favour nor sought clandestine advantage. He was not a vain or presumptuous man. But he had accepted his wife's promptings as his own resolve. He had reached the years when he could expect some honour among his fellows for a life valiant in war and now active in settling this barbarous land. That he should have to beg for such recognition. . . his gorge rose at the thought. . . at this moment he needed Seraphina's cool assurance. . .

Chichester pushed the last of the documents from him. 'You've seen service, Mr Echlin,' he said. His appraisal of the laird was shrewd and calculating.

'I should like to call my wife, your Excellency –'

'No need, man, no need,' said Sir Arthur rising. 'We are about to join her Ladyship.'

Echlin held up his hand but the Lord Deputy did not take his seat again. 'We – I would know your mind. . .'

'You want something?' Chichester glowered at the man opposite him. 'Body o' me, Echlin, d'you think you're the first? What is it you ask?'

'That I should have the honour of knighthood bestowed on me.'

Chichester looked at the drawn face of the laird. 'A lesser

216

man would have found it easier to ask,' he said gruffly. 'Sit down,' and he took his own seat. 'Echlin, you would have to take your place among –' he sought for words '– the pick-thanks and toadies. They're always before me – Dublin, Car-rickfergus, wherever I go. Some, such as you, sue for titles, some seek land, some surveyorships of taxes not yet collected, some hold out their hands for loans. Is this the company for you?'

Echlin was not to be dissuaded so easily. 'I don't rely solely on these, your Excellency,' said he, pointing to the documents on the desk. 'I hope I'll be given credit for what you saw this morning –'

'I saw no more than I expected to see,' answered Chichester curtly. 'D'you think his Grace dubs a citizen for fulfilling an undertaking? It may not,' and he pointed a heavy forefinger, 'go so well with some of your neighbours. It's my intention to punish those who are faulty and thus quicken all to finish that which they are bound to do.' He sat back, fingers splayed on the desk and gave a hoarse chuckle. 'I play Momus among ye, Echlin. I find fault where fault lies. I do not laud a man for keeping a promise.'

'My wife's family –' began the laird with the air of a man playing his last card.

'I'm aware of your wife's family. I've met the Earl of Finnart, a worthy gentleman. Echlin, it's of no avail.' The Lord Deputy eyed the man opposite. Clearly he had dealt his aspiration a grievous blow. Chichester realised that he had to step caut-iously now. He might wave the earl's name aside, but he did not know how Finnart stood with the King or for that matter, how the laird stood with his father-in-law. Then there was said to be a younger Echlin at present much in favour at Whitehall. It would not at all be to his convenience to make an enemy of the Scotsman. In the depths of the woods and marshlands there were always the Irish. . . a serious upsurge and Chichester knew that half of his landlords would be off to England and

217

Scotland as fast as they could scamper. This fellow would not be one of them. . . The Lord Deputy leant forward, his expression grave, questioning. 'Regardless of what has passed between us, I can always call on your support as soldier and loyal subject?'

Echlin gazed steadily at the other man as if, for a moment, he was fool enough to think he had been offered a bargaining counter. Then he shrugged. 'I'm sure you're aware, Sir Arthur, that in the event of trouble I'm committed to two horsemen and six footmen, well-appointed –'

'And your own valuable service?'

'And my own service.'

To impress his host, Sir Arthur was about to inform him that he had lately seized Sir Cormac O'Neill, Sir Donnell O'Cahan and Sir Neil O'Donnell and shipped them to London on suspicion of conspiracy. Second thought gave him pause. This was not the time to remind Kenneth Echlin that three treasonable miscreants now lying in the Tower had been thought worthy of the accolade. He stood up and gave the laird a buffet, almost fraternal, on the shoulder. 'Come, man, give a thought to your good fortune. You have a flourishing property in a condition which I shall not forget to commend in my report to his Grace. You have a most elegant lady to manage your household. I understand your elder son is well-placed in his Grace's establishment' . . .the laird winced at this. . . 'and your second son tells me that he is wishful to help you make your estate profitable. You have a daughter, a quick, pretty lass, sure to make a good match.'

Echlin listened to this catalogue of his assets in silence. Chichester eyed him as if waiting a response.

Getting none he continued in a colder voice: 'I remarked this morning that much of your arable has been won back from woodland.'

'Many of my early tenants took holdings on the understanding they cleared them, your Excellency.'

'Don't wait for that,' said the other in a heartier manner. 'Study the timber market. Take yourself to Newry and Belfast. You have oak? It's gold above ground, Echlin.' The laird's expression was impassive and respectful, it was hard to tell what mood the Scots dog was in. 'I've talked overmuch,' said the Lord Deputy. 'I'm thirsty. We'll join the others.'

20

Brands flared at the entrance to Rathard House. In twos and threes dark figures, summoned to be present at this hour, made their way past the prying torchlight and into the house. The principal guests, those from beyond Ravara, were already within. Half-a-dozen carriages overflowed from the coach-yard and Neil heard the clatter of hooves and the voices of men in the crowded stables.

Sky and air had foretold frost so Ross and he decided to walk. They had made a detour to call for Wishart and found him waiting. From some cranny he had brought out a silver chain and it now hung around his neck. Neil bent to examine its massy medallion bearing quartered arms.

'A handsome piece if I may say so.'

A smile, a wistful smile in so far as his features could encompass it, passed over the other's face. 'My last piece, Gilchrist.'

Wishart's locks and beard had been trimmed. His shoes and hose were clean and sound. Mrs Drummond had found a lace cravat to embellish his new shirt. The dark-hued jacket set off the silver on his breast. There was altogether an air of dignity and seemliness about the fellow that discouraged any banter from the younger men.

'Your heaviest cloak, Calum,' said Ross at the door. 'It's a chill night.'

At Rathard House the three gave up their outer garments to Hamish Neilson. A little withdrawn from Neilson stood one of Chichester's troopers, a sober reminder to each guest of what lay behind the hospitable gathering. Neil and his companions, accustomed to two or three at most clacking their way across the main chamber, were taken aback by the noisy concourse that filled it now. Light from the fire that snored in the great hearth and from torches and lamps on walls and sills fell on lairds and their ladies, officers of the Lord Deputy, clerics, factors and their womenfolk.

''Sfaith,' said Wishart, 'here are gallants in all sizes of cobbler's last!'

Until the house fell in flame and smoke thirty-odd years later, Francis Echlin and his family in refuge, it was the greatest assemblage ever brought together under the roof of Rathard. Among all these men and women, talking or listening, laughing or grave-faced, Neil sought for Anne Echlin. A shallow ruff rising from her blue figured-velvet gown framed her face and gleaming hair. It seemed no more than chance that she should glance up as Neil entered. He saw the swift colouring of her face, the faintest gesture of a hand. Then she turned back to an officer.

Neil was at a loss. He was unsure whether or not he should first present himself to Echlin. But the laird and his wife were clustered with the Lord Deputy, Mr St John, Mr Cordwaine and others of the Echlins' chief neighbours. It was not a moment when the laird could be expected to concern himself with the civility of an estate employee. Wishart, who didn't give a bodle for such niceties, was already deep in talk with two clerics at the fireplace, his tails hitched up to warm his backside. Ross had threaded his rapid way to Una Drummond's side.

He heard his name. Coming towards him, a roll of paper fluttering in his fingers, was Francis Echlin.

'Gilchrist, I'm glad to see ye!'

'And I you,' said Neil taking the proferred hand.

'I've a task for ye.' Young Echlin flourished the paper.

'If I can be of assistance,' said Neil politely.

'To be nearer the mark, it's at my father's bidding. We're to shepherd the guests to where they sit at table.'

The tables had been set out in the upper part of the hall. They were arranged in a T, the upper and shorter table raised on a

221

dais. Above them, between the windows, hung the tapestries Anne Echlin had brought from Dunblane. The depicted huntsmen, horses and hounds had lost much of their colour, the weight of the fabrics had opened rents, the edges were frayed. Yet under the torchlight they shed an air of rich antiquity that softened the atmosphere of aged stone walls and new timber in the chamber.

Neil was about to reach for the list when Echlin drew back with a smile. 'My sister,' he said.

She came rapidly across the thronged floor like one released from a tedious duty. A murmur, a bow and they both fell silent. Young Echlin's presence put a bridle on their tongues. But the smiling, yet anxious, regard with which each studied the other seemed at that moment, sufficient.

Ronane, attired in his seneschal's authority, appeared and spoke in Francis Echlin's ear. The young man turned to Neil. 'The laird will present his people to the Lord Deputy.' Softly Anne touched his hand and was gone. Neil was shuffled into a straggling line. In front of him was Dan Drummond who clearly would have dispensed with the honour awaiting him. Behind Neil stood Wishart and Ross. He heard Wishart's voice. 'Men, when the vice-regal shoulder is turned in your face, the audience is ended.'

'Look to yourself, Wishart,' said Neil, but marked the hint.

Echlin approached them. Gone was the lively expectancy with which he had carried himself that morning. He ran a dour eye over the four men. 'Speak only if his Excellency questions ye,' he said curtly. 'Now, Drummond,' and Dan Drummond stepped forward.

The factor's audience was brief; his name, function and bow received a brusque jerk of the vice-regal head and nothing more. Dan, put out, glanced distractedly at the impassive laird, bowed again, and with a muttered incoherence (against all instructions) backed away in the direction of his spouse and daughter.

'Gilchrist.'

The great man did not respond to Neil's bow.

'You tend Mr Echlin's woodlands?'

'I do, your Excellency.'

'How so?'

'I divide the saplings into coppices. I observe the seasons and instruct my foresters –'

'What of oak?'

'Ravara is well-furnished with oakwoods, your Excellency.'

At this Chichester turned his heavy bearded face in a knowing manner to the laird. Reckoning that the vice-regal shoulder was now in line with his breast bone, Neil took three backward steps, bowed with the hint of a flourish, and sought out Francis Echlin. To his disappointment the youth was alone.

'Your sister. . .?' queried Neil.

'My mother called her away. We must wait till this is over.' And young Echlin indicated the cluster of people around the Lord Deputy. Calum Wishart, hands softly clasped behind him, was conversing in the most amiable manner with Chichester and the laird. The dog, thought Neil enviously, he could chaffer with the Deil.

Wishart, released from the vice-regal presence, joined Francis Echlin and Neil. As he did so there was a stir at the entrance to the chamber. Heads turned and a hush, like a spell, spread through the chattering throng. Mr Turlough Mac-Cartan, with his formidable attendant, had arrived. Behind them were the shadowy figures of an elderly man and a boy laden with a harp.

Those who knew of MacCartan's likely appearance at Rathard viewed his arrival according to their knowledge or their ignorance of the circumstances. The Reverend Amos Dalgetty and his kind awaited the encounter with malicious expectancy. Those better informed knew that the Irishman's arrival had nothing to do with Kenneth Echlin. As James Lowry said drily to Cleland of Ringdufferin, the Irishman's

223

presence saves Chichester's face.

Echlin stepped forward, beckoning MacCartan to approach. The Irishman was clad in a crimson and black cloak, clasped at the breast with three gold aiglettes. He was a colourful figure among the soberly-dressed lairds and rivalled only by Chichester's officers. As the two men passed Neil and his companions, the laird said to his son, 'Attend to Mr MacCartan's people.' The guests shuffled back, leaving a passage to where the Lord Deputy stood with Lady Echlin and Herbert St John. The Irishman did not wear a wig and Neil wondered what passed in that neatly combed head as he approached this most inimical adversary of his people.

Only those close to him heard in what manner the laird introduced Turlough MacCartan to the Lord Deputy. The bows they exchanged were such that the eyes of neither man left the face of the other. The exchange of courtesies was even briefer. Then MacCartan turned with a deep bow to Lady Echlin. The hum of voices rose again as from a stirred hive. So much, thought Neil, for the act of obeisance, and he sought for the Reverend Amos Dalgetty's face in the throng.

'That's a handsome cloak on the Irishman,' said Francis Echlin, watching his mother – in answer to some query from MacCartan – raise her hand with smiling grace towards the wall tapestries.

'A braw garment, indeed,' said Wishart. 'I warrant ye a goodly number of his *bodach*s go naked on backside and empty in belly to hang that cloak on the gentleman's shoulders.'

An angry glare from his father recalled Francis Echlin to his duties. 'Gilchrist, help me with these people.'

Sim Watt and Hamish Neilson, porters for the night, were hard put to it. Sullen-faced, MacCartan's retainer was peering over the heads of the throng, seeking his master. The old man, arms folded under his cloak, was staring into the rafters, nor did he lower his gaze with the arrival of the two young men. The youthful harp-bearer shifted from one wearied leg to the other.

224

'What's wrong here, Watt?' demanded Echlin.

''Tis this carle, Master Francis,' said Watt indicating the gigantic henchman. 'He claims it's his duty to stand ahint his master's chair and he's for going to him whether we let him or no.'

'And so he shall stand behind his master's chair,' declared young Echlin, 'once we have his master seated. Body o' me,' he suddenly cried, flourishing the list of names, 'I'd forgotten! Gilchrist, see to the others,' and the laird's son darted back into the hall.

Neil was not over-pleased to be left so abruptly with such a task. He turned on Sim Watt. 'What's the hindrance with this gentleman?' he demanded, indicating the venerable figure still in contemplation of the roof.

Sim leant his chin on Neil's shoulder. By his breath, he had been fortifying himself against the exigency of office. 'He's a musicianer, Mr Gilchrist.'

'That's evident.'

'Mr Drummond said all such entered the Big House by the rear door.'

At this, the boy spoke. 'It is the peculiar right of Lochlainn O'Daly that he enters in and is received at all great houses in a manner as befits his lineage and his standing in the world.'

Even as the lad spoke Neil observed that his master had lowered his eyes and was now waiting for the response in some anxiety. In spite of himself Neil chuckled. 'Well spoken, my bold callan, e'en if by rote.' He turned to the harper. 'Mr O'Daly, I take it upon myself to speak for the laird of Ravara, who invited ye here, to say that Rathard House will be no exception. Tell me what ye require.'

The harper freed an arm from his cloak and pointed with a long-nailed finger across the chamber. His voice sounded as if the evening frost was still in his throat. 'I would take my place there, to the left of the chieftain. A chair on which to sit and a stool for my bearer. And God o'mercy, gentle sir, but I would

225

not frown on a glass of wine.'

Neil beckoned to Hamish Neilson. 'Fetch a chair and a stool and follow me. Now, Mr O'Daly,' he continued, 'let us find a likely place for you and your harp.'

When Lochlainn O'Daly stepped into the torchlight Neil saw that the russet cloak he wore reached to his heels. A fit covering, thought Neil, for an old man in winter. The harper's ample locks fell over the cloak's fringe, and strands among the white hair spoke of a more fiery head in his young manhood. Neil paused to take a full beaker from the long table. As he did so one of Chichester's officers stepped in front of him. The Englishman nodded towards the aged musician.

'This Irishman – his mantle. Are you aware, sir, that he's in breach of the law?'

Neil glanced at the harper then back to his interrogator, with a puzzled frown. 'In what manner, sir?'

'The outer garment he wears – the Irish mantle – is proscribed and has been for years.'

The information was imparted civilly enough and for a moment Neil thought to direct the officer to the laird, then decided that that might have unforeseen results. He shook his head. 'No, I knew nothing of this.'

'*He* knows, I wager. He's travelled. Will you see to it that he removes the garment? My friends may not take so easily to it,' and he indicated his fellow officers now drifting with their partners to the dinner table.

'Aye,' said Neil. 'I'll see to it.'

The delay had allowed Neilson, laden with chair and stool, to overtake them. Neil watched impatiently until the old man was seated.

'Now that ye are indoors, Mr O'Daly, ye can shed your cloak.'

The harper blinked upwards as if in some confusion. Neil lightly drew back the pot of wine. O'Daly shrugged out of his garment, letting it fall over the chair-back. Neil handed him the brimming beaker and watched with widening eyes as the venerable bard downed it in one great gulp.

Lochlainn O'Daly handed the vessel back with a sigh. 'What is your name, gentle sir?'

'Gilchrist.'

'"Servant of our Redeemer". You're well-named –'

'Aye, so.' Neil said abruptly. He turned to the youthful assistant. 'Meat will be on the table soon. See to it that your master's served.' He left the two with the feeling that the sharp-eyed callan would need no second bidding. Savoury odours, drifting into the chamber, were hastening the company to their places.

At the upper table, facing across the chamber, the Lord Deputy was seated between the laird and Lady Echlin with the principal guests flanked to left and right. Opposite them the clergy with their womenfolk, stretched down the board like some ecclesiastical bawn.

Neil found himself seated at the lower table between Mrs Porson and a thin lady apparelled in a voluminous grey material. In response to his polite address, he learnt from her that she occupied a post of no small consequence in Mr Cleland's household. With peering anxiety she hurried on to inquire as to the identity and rank of those she found herself seated among. Having learnt her name, Neil presented her to Mrs Porson and Mrs Drummond across the table. He turned to look for Anne Echlin. To his chagrin she had been seated at the far end of the upper table. He could glimpse her only when two of the reverend gentlemen leaned together in brotherly discourse. The lady in grey bocasin was becoming uneasy at his silent scrutiny over her shoulder. Downcast, he sat back and poured himself a glass of wine. As he did so he saw Mr Lochlainn O'Daly watch with relish as his acolyte topped him up a bumper.

21

Lochlainn O'Daly emptied his glass, drew the harp towards him, struck three ringing chords that silenced the hall and bowed to the upper table. Kenneth Echlin rose to his feet. What he had to say in welcoming the Lord Deputy and his party was but half-heard at the lower table.

But even to those with dull lugs the laird's demeanour spoke more of acknowledging, with every mark of respect, the vice-regal presence, than showing any joy in it. He made no mention of the affray that had brought Sir Arthur to Ravara; rather he thought it fortunate that peaceful times allowed friends and neighbours this occasion to offer their humble vow of fealty to his Grace through his august Deputy. And with a deep bow to his chief guest, the laird of Ravara sat down again.

Chichester did not rise. He leant forward in his chair, thrusting his clasped hands on the table. Beyond him, at the entrance to the kitchen quarters, Neil saw, through a mist of vapours, the faces of servants, listening.

His visit, said the Lord Deputy, had been brought about by a report of insurrection. But he had been persuaded by Mr Echlin that there was no truth in it. 'Did I need further evidence – which I do not – your presence here would convince me that Mr Echlin and you, gentlemen, enjoy a condition of tranquility which will much gratify his Grace, the King. His Majesty has spoken of his subjects so mixing through alliance and daily conversation, such as here today, that the inhabitants of this kingdom may with time grow and weld into one. . .'

MacCartan, Neil observed, had found some detail of interest in the tapestry above him.

'. . . That is as it should be. That, and the affirmance of your loving allegiance, I shall convey to his Grace.' The Lord Deputy sat back, leaden-eyed.

There was a scatter of applause from the upper table. To the canny Scots seated there, the trite words had carried no threat of meddling in their affairs. A nod from the laird and Mr Turnooth arose. On his pillow the good man had given thought to a tilt at the episcopacy. What he had not thought of was the effect of insidious and appetising odours stealing round a famished audience. His grace-before-meat was brief and, to the laird at least, seemly.

A gesture from her Ladyship, and a flock of laden domestics, headed by Mrs Rusk, poured into the hall. The centre-dish set before the laird and his guests bore a fine joint of beef. On either side of this great platter appeared roast geese, and venison pies. The abundance flowed to the lower table. A collar of brawn was set down, flanked by mutton, and veal pies in divers shapes. Pie crusts were delved, meat was carved prodigally, glasses were filled to the brim.

Dan Drummond paused to lick his fingers and lean across to Neil. 'This'll cost,' he nodded to the upper table, 'a muckle pile of siller.'

'Then make the most of it, Dan,' said the young man. He glanced up at Echlin. The laird had the look of a man watching corbie crows in his orchard.

Lochlainn O'Daly had pushed his harp away to make room for a laden plate. He ate fastidiously with one hand, the other encircling his glass. The harp silent, voices were heard calling only for wine or for attendance. Back and forth hurried the servants, marshalled by the shadowy figure of John Bell in the doorway.

Appetites sated, men and women found time to talk to each other. Lady Echlin accepted the compliments of those around her. Her daughter, from what Neil could glimpse of her, had entered into a flirtatious dispute with a young English officer. Turning away, he observed with jaundiced eye the lady high in Mr Cleland's household adroitly flick a thick slice of meat into a napkin and hide it in her skirts. John Bell in the kitchen

229

doorway beckoned Ronane and whispered in his ear. A grimace of extreme annoyance appeared on Echlin's face when Ronane passed on Bell's information. Then he nodded a reluctant agreement.

'The wine's run out,' said Neil across the table to the factor.

'D'ye say that?' And Dan shook his head with the air of one who had foreseen this or some similar calamity.

But there was wine galore for the occupants of the upper table. Among the English officers there was an air of bending and unbuckling, their voices and laughter a little louder. It was time, Lady Echlin decided, to withdraw. Gracious as ever, she took her leave of the Lord Deputy, summoned her daughter and led the females and clerics from the hall. Neil craned to glimpse Anne Echlin. He was rewarded with a smile, a small gesture of the hand. He sat down again and watched in blissful unconcern Bell and his tapster set out pots of ale on the table where before there had been muscatel wine.

With a baleful glare, Lochlainn O'Daly, master harper, watched the women depart. The lady of the house had gone without a word. The master of the house had not stepped down to greet him. And now, by the Blessed Hand, Englishmen and Scots drank wine while he was offered a pot of ale. He thrust it from him so that it japped the table with froth.

The tapster replaced it firmly. 'Slocken your thirst with that, auld billie,' said he, 'or go dry.'

In a fury O'Daly struck the stoup with the back of his hand and sent it slopping across the board. His glare was fixed on the tipsy conviviality at the upper table. Drawing the harp towards him he raised his still-resonant voice in a lament for departed friends and kin that was more scatheful than sorrowful:

> *Atá againn 'na ionad*
> *dírim uaibhreach eisiodhan. . .*

Enough of the meaning pieced together in Neil's consciousness and his scalp crept as he followed the defiant voice:

> . . . in their place we have a conceited
> and impure swarm
> of foreigners' blood – of an excommunicated
> rabble – Saxons are there and Scotsmen
> This is the land of noble Niall's posterity
> They portion out among themselves. . .

Neil looked up at MacCartan. The Irishman, expressionless, was nodding gravely as he listened to an exploit of the hunting English officer. St John, his glass resting on his belly, had cocked a foot on the table. Cleland ventured a joke with Lowry. The Lord Deputy leant almost cordially towards Luke Cordwaine. Echlin had called Porson up and was deep in conversation. The fleering words fell on them all like feathery ash:

Coimhthionól tuatha i dtoigh naomh

A boorish congregation is in the house of saints. . .

Neil stumbled to his feet, waving away the dominie's restraining hand. Stepping across the hall to the entrance, he took his cloak and rapier from Hamish Neilson and left Rathard House.

Coming from the glare of torches and lamps, he was surprised by the calm still light of the early evening sky. A crimson inlay beyond the oakwoods promised a night of frost. The high notes of the harp still came to his ear. As he thought of those fine fellows prattling on unwittingly, he began to laugh. He leant against the bawn wall, so shaken with drunken merriment he could scarce make his water. He shivered, suddenly sober. In no mood to go back to the dull confinement of the schoolhouse, he climbed a hillock, stumbling occasionally on its rough flank. Reaching the summit he looked back at the solidity of Rathard as if expecting a sudden conflagration to lift its roof. But there was only the distant luminosity of the

231

windows of the great hall.

Suddenly, from somewhere below him he became aware of voices. Crossing to the other side he looked down. The noise came from a rabble of men, English troopers by their garb. They stood in a circle round a watery hollow. In the middle of this slough was a small islet. On the islet stood a child. Neil recognised him as MacCartan's son. The troopers were sporting themselves poking the boy from side to side of the grassy patch with the butt-ends of their weapons. Tiring of this, one of them reversed his halberd and slowly advanced the blade towards the boy. Neil emptied his lungs in a great shout of fury.

The tormentors were suddenly still. They looked up to see against the light the figure in cocked bonnet, cloak, hand on sword hilt.

'He's from the damned Scottishman's house,' said the fellow with the ready blade.

He went lumbering away, followed in twos and threes by his comrades until all were gone. The boy stared up at Neil, marking him. Then he sprang from his refuge to the bank. Sinuous as an otter, he vanished among the reeds and was gone.

Neil, truly sobered, turned back. 'Who sent me up here?' was the question he bore down the track between whinstone and whinbush.

22

'It has been a costly affair, Seraphina.' Echlin carefully smoothed John Bell's tally on the heap of bills.

'For nothing,' said Lady Echlin.

'Faith no, madam, not for nothing. Chichester's gone with what he came for – the assurance that I'm a leal subject and one who fulfils his undertaking. What's missing,' he spoke with bitterness, 'is what *I* asked for – but we'll say no more on that.'

If this was warning or reproof, her Ladyship let it go by. She touched the pile of bills. 'Perhaps Lowry or Cordwaine might offer to foot some of these?'

'If they offer, yes. They'll not be asked by me.'

'If that purse-proud woman, Helen Cordwaine, carried home her praises she may persuade her husband –'

The laird shifted impatiently. 'I have other designs – and they go far beyond this,' he indicated the pile of statements. 'Will ye send Neilson for Gilchrist. I want him here.' She lingered and he looked up. 'I'll tell ye all – when I ken more myself.'

But he was to have an earlier caller than Neil Gilchrist. Word came that Mr Cordwaine was on the avenue. A shrewd lady, my wife, thought the laird. If he offers to help I'll accept. After all, he can breathe easier now that he has talked with the Lord Deputy – and 'twas at my table. But pride made the laird slip the bills into a drawer before Luke Cordwaine was ushered in.

Whatever hope Echlin had had of his neighbour opening his purse was quickly snuffed. Having congratulated the laird again on the success of the reception, Mr Cordwaine announced that his wife and he could do no less than respond with a similar entertainment.

'But I warn ye, no twanging harper!' concluded Mr Cordwaine, laughing.

Echlin looked at him morosely. 'D'ye expect to see Chichester in these parts again?'

'No, no,' said Cordwaine waving such a likelihood aside. 'A gathering of neighbouring families, no more. I'll see Finlay and Lowry and perhaps the Clelands. . .' Fishing in the breast of his jacket as he spoke, it was evident that Luke Cordwaine had come on more urgent business than future conviviality. He drew out a letter and opened it. 'From my father,' he said.

The laird, in no mood for family correspondence, nodded silently.

'He's much concerned about the bird –'

'The bird? What the Deil are ye talking about?'

''Ods, Kenneth – the falcon the King asked for. You drafted a reply for me in which I accepted the charge. You remember?'

Echlin, recalling the duplicity of his offer, would gladly have forgotten. 'Aye, I remember,' he answered sullenly. 'Well, what have ye done?'

'I? Nothing. I thought you were to find for me –'

'God's faith, man! Ye ken well how my time was taken up preparing for Chichester's visit!'

'Then no search was made?' Cordwaine's voice was much cooler.

'By me? – none. I said, if I remember aright, that a falcon could be bought for ready money.'

Cordwaine tapped the letter. 'My father says that the King does not lightly forget a promise kept – or broken.'

'All the more reason for ye to bestir yourself, then.'

Cordwaine picked up his hat and whip. 'I bid you good morning, Echlin.' He turned at the door. 'I'll be obliged to you for my coach.'

'I'll have your horse yoked now,' the laird snapped, 'and ye can drive it away.'

Neil entered Rathard House in cheerful expectation of seeing Anne Echlin. He barely noticed that Mr Luke Cordwaine didn't answer his greeting as they passed each other. The laird, seated behind his desk, was only a little more cordial. 'If ye were to fell oak, where would ye start?'

'For convenience?'

'For convenience.'

Neil thought. 'Tullycarnet Wood.'

The laird located this on the map. He looked up. 'My bid for a knighthood came to nothing, Gilchrist. I tell ye this now, for I don't want it mentioned again.'

'I'm sorry the Lord Deputy. . .' murmured Neil.

'The Lord Deputy left me a consolation. He would have me a rich man,' continued Echlin with a smile that had little warmth. 'There's a thriving market in oak timber, he says. It's my intention to supply that market. It'll be your first consideration to see that the timber is forthcoming.'

'It's a trade I ken nothing of, sir,' said Neil with some anxiety.

'I've thought of that. I want you and Gilfillan to look into it. And,' added Echlin as if reading the other's mind, 'I'll tell Dan Drummond that the head carpenter is the man wanted here, for none of us kens as yet how the timber is set up – whether it be split or trimmed or no.'

'And where do we start?'

'Wherever timber's bought,' answered the laird briefly.

'I'll ask Robert Bothwell,' said Neil standing up.

'Aye, do that.'

'I wonder,' said Neil lingering, 'if Miss Anne would care to ride into the village with me?'

'That I cannot tell. Ask Mrs Rusk to send for my daughter,' and the laird dismissed Neil by opening a drawer and taking out the sheaf of bills.

On the young man's inquiry Mrs Rusk sent one of the girls upstairs. She returned with a message for Neil that Miss Echlin would be with him in a minute.

Part of the half-hour Neil spent at the stables readying Anne's mount. Then he sat down out of sight of the servants, checked the money in his pouch and wished he was wearing his better coat.

235

From her olive-green cap with its single pearl to her sensible riding boots she was a delight to his eye. His gaze said so as he lifted her lightly into the saddle.

'To the village.'

'I have business there for your father.'

'We were to eat at the inn, if you recall.'

'We were, we were,' cried Neil, pleased that she had remembered. He looked up at the clear sky, warming a little as the day grew. 'Let us make amends for that,' he said, wheeling his mount to follow her.

As they rode down between the rowan trees Lady Echlin watched from an upper window.

Restrained from meeting, each had lived vividly – if perhaps not quite accurately – in the other's thoughts. Yet even when the road to the village allowed them to ride side by side they had little to say. The girl felt that some awareness was spying on her. Shyness and pride forbade her to speak of it to Neil. And Neil, for his part, could not rid himself of the feeling that he was still escort to his employer's daughter. But he felt no need to chatter. It was enough for him that they were together again.

As they entered the market square the usual flock of urchins that hived when gentry rode in gathered round them offering to tend their horses or run errands. But Neil, taking his companion's bridle, pressed on to the tavern. John Bell was informed that the two would expect a meal to be ready for them about noon, away from the bustle of the public dining-room. Then the two crossed the square to Mrs Calder's shop.

'If ye tire,' said Neil, 'join me if ye wish. I'll make my business with Mr Leslie and Mr Bothwell as brief as possible,' and with that they parted.

The meal was set out in the family parlour. The guidwife Bell herself served the fish, the meat, the apples in honey, and her coming and going was in such a manner as not to disturb the felicity of the young couple. The plates removed, John Bell came in for the pleasure of sharing a glass of wine with his guests. He told Neil that now the country was more settled and ladies more of a mind to travel he would add a dining-room for the convenience of the gentry. Neil, with an eye to the future, gave his opinion that no addition to the inn could be more welcome and indeed, more pressing.

There being nothing more to hold them in the village, Anne and Neil set off homeward. Their pace along the woodland road was leisurely for neither felt any urge to reach Rathard and separation once again. They talked of matters of no great consequence, finding pleasure in each other's company.

The girl brought her mount to a halt. 'Look!' she cried.

A glade led to a mere, on its dark water a solitary swan. The sun was still high and a beam illuminated the bird so that it shone at the end of the narrow clearing. Where the rays were broken by the overhanging boughs they fell on the forest floor in splintered silver. Neil's gaze followed her pointing finger and he wondered what should stir him in response. He could think of a score of such glades in Ravara woods. Useless. Too over-hung for planting, too cramped to even store cut timber. Anne was looking at him, beseeching him to share her delight. Well, yes, he thought. Yes, if ye looked at it that way. . . He slid from his horse.

'Let's explore,' said he.

The moss was soft under their feet. Without thought they took each other's hand, as they had months ago. They paused at the pool's verge. The swan bent its neck in a curtsy.

Neil slapped his pocket. 'I wish,' said he, 'that I had brought some of Mrs Bell's bread with us.'

Anne, laughing, turned to him. The swan dipped its head a second time. As she turned, Neil took the girl in his arms.

'I love ye, sweet Anne,' he whispered. He cradled her close, his cheek against the bright strand of hair beneath her riding-cap.

Then he held her off. 'Ye haven't said. . .'

237

'Yes, yes, my dearest, I love you.' She slipped her arms around his neck and drew him down to her kiss.

The flight of the swan as it toiled upward in glittering sparks of water startled them. Anne shivered and he drew her close.

'My dear lass, what ails ye?'

'Nothing, nothing.' She glanced upward to where the bird had vanished in the eye of the sun. 'I wish the swan had not flown away. . .'

'Ha,' cried Neil as if resisting a spell, 'we've said what's in our hearts. Let all the swans in Ireland take to the air!' Then in soberer tone, 'It's time we were away. They'll be watching for our return.'

They were lovers unable to speak of the future, for neither knew where it lay; but for the girl it held a sense of foreboding. Where the track permitted they stretched smilingly to touch hands as if to reassure themselves of each other's presence.

At Rathard's gates Anne said: 'When we have a garden, I'll have a pool and a swan on it.'

She urged her horse forward and they rode up to Rathard House, the laird's daughter followed by her squire.

With a hound's head on his knee Neil sat waiting on Echlin's return. When the laird appeared he summoned the young man as he crossed to his study.

'So, what speed did ye come, Gilchrist?'

Neil, prickly at being left to stand, answered curtly. 'There's a market for your timber.'

'Bothwell is a shrewd chiel. What did he think of my intention?

'Leslie's the best informed on the timber trade. He said oak today was next to gold.'

The laird looked down but Neil caught the gleam in his eye. 'He said that?'

'He said that.'

'Aye,' The laird's voice was a murmur. 'That was Chichester's opinion. . . Pull yourself in a chair, Neil.'

'Provided,' continued Neil when he was seated, 'ye get it to the market.'

'Well,' the question was sharp. 'ye gave some thought to that?'

'Leslie gave the name of Carmichael, a dealer in Belfast. Bothwell and he think highly of this Sam Carmichael.'

'And how is the timber got to Belfast?'

'That, and the way the trees are made ready is a matter for the buyer. Leslie was very strong on that.' He was about to add Mr Bothwell's advice that the more the seller did for himself, the better, but decided that for the time being he would hold on to that knowledge.

'I want ye to take Addy Gilfillan with ye to Belfast and talk to this dealer Carmichael. See to it that ye get away tomorrow morn.' From a leather bag in his drawer Echlin took half-a-dozen crown pieces and pushed them across to Neil. 'What about fire-boot on the estate?' he asked.

Puzzled, Neil looked at the laird. 'Isn't that the factor's –'

Echlin gestured abruptly. 'Ye see more than Dan. Do the cottars take much wood?'

'Not more, I think, than serves them for fencing and kindling. They think they've that right –'

'They have, they have. But nothing's to be felled without permission. Above all, oak.'

'There's but few single oaks standing on their holdings, Mr Echlin,' said Neil in some surprise.

'What there is I want marked and the tenants warned against cutting. Nothing's to be purloined.'

Neil glanced in curiosity at Echlin. It was the first time he had heard him hint at theft by his tenants. 'I'll see to it,' said Neil as he rose from his chair. 'I should tell ye that John Bell is adding a private dining-room at the tavern.'

'Good,' said Echlin, 'a convenient place to do business without the chatter of the market crowd. Ye took Miss Echlin to Bell's at midday?'

239

'I did.'

'I'm glad to hear that. She gets few outings.' Again the laird dipped his hand into the leather bag. He laid a few coins on the table. 'Will that suffice?'

For a moment Neil thought of refusing the money. Then prudence intervened. 'Thank ye, Mr Echlin, that will suffice.' He picked up the coins, put them in his pocket and left the house.

The laird was about to send for her Ladyship when she came into the study.

'Something passed between those two today.'

Echlin sat up. 'And what, in God's name, does that mean, madam?'

'Anne is not an artful concealing puss. When she came in I knew by her face that something had been taken – and given between the two –'

'Are ye telling me they've fallen in love? Is that what you're saying?'

'That's what I fear. Neil Gilchrist is more than an ostler, Kenneth –'

'Not much more, by God, for all his gentle birth! You'll recall what James Lowry learnt in Edinburgh about the family. The laird Balwhanny is a braggart and a sot, his estate gone to rack and ruin, his elder son and heir a puir wandering ninny. . .' The laird hesitated and muttered, 'But that's nothing to do with it. No,' he declared roundly. ''Sfaith, that's a burden we refuse,' and he gave a decided cock of the head.

Lady Echlin eyed her husband in a manner close to scorn. 'D'ye think all that will deter the maid? Gilchrist is a braw enough fellow in face and figure and when he puts himself to it, he can charm.'

'Then what the Deil d'ye propose? Anne is not going back to Dunblane. Since she came home she's been as a light in the house.'

'That was not in my mind, Kenneth,' replied her Ladyship

240

curtly. 'To admit we can't look after our own daughter!'

'Aye, well – then the two must be kept from each other's company –'

'But cannily, my dear, cannily.'

The laird struck the table in exasperation. 'Deal with your daughter how ye think best, madam!' Then in a calmer voice, 'I warrant ye from now on the birkie Gilchrist will have little time for jaunts. As to Anne, ye might see to it that she gets out more. The Lowrys, their sons are due back soon from college, there's the Finlays even,' he added with a grunt. 'The people at Edenmore. Stir Francis to squire his sister oftener. There was talk of Dan Drummond's daughter keeping Anne company – I ken the lass, well-read, pleasing in her manner. And,' the laird searched, 'there's the cottar MacIlveen's daughter, word has it that she's a skilled needlewoman. Tell her to attend Miss Anne when ye think fit. See to this, madam, and you'll leave the girl little time for mooning over any penniless carle. And m'lady,' the laird leaned forward with a grin, 'if my venture goes well, as I'm confident it will, ye can visit in a manner befitting ye. I'll tell Gilfillan to find me a coach in Belfast, a coach fit for the Echlins of Ravara!'

Lady Echlin bent gracefully to kiss her husband on the brow. 'Ye have much eased my concern for our daughter.' As she closed the study door there was a small complacent smile on her face.

23

'Calum,' said Angus Ross holding up a scrap of paper, 'hoped ye might find these articles in Belfast.'

Neil, shaving his chin with care, grunted.

'And these – for the school.' The dominie held up a second list.

Neil laid down the razor. 'Angus, I ken nothing about Belfast, whether it boasts a stationer or an apothecary.' He looked at the other's doleful face. 'Aye, I'll look if I've the time. No,' he added irritably, 'give me no money.' There was a pause as he stiffened his chin to the razor. 'My mind's not at ease about what I've undertaken, Angus. I may come back empty-handed –'

'All the more regard for ye if ye succeed,' said the generous Ross.

There was a clatter of hooves on the schoolhouse path. Neil opened the door to see Neilson dismount.

'Your nag for Belfast,' said the stableman, offering the reins.

Neil looked at the low broad-chested animal. 'What would I want with this cuddy, Hamish? I have my own mount.'

'Aye, but it's no accustomed to pull on the shaft. Addy Gilfillan has the mate o' this beast. The two o' ye are to bring back a coach. Isn't that the laird's orders?' Reluctantly Neil took the reins. 'Will I stable your own horse when you're away?'

Neil shrugged. 'Thank ye, Hamish. And fetch my saddle as ye come. There's my travelling bag and pistols on the bench.'

'I'll tend to them, Mr Gilchrist. Gilfillan's waiting for ye at the end o' the avenue.'

The laird was with Gilfillan when Neil arrived. Greetings were exchanged cordially enough.

'G'speed to ye both.' Turning to Neil, the laird said with

urgency in his voice: 'You'll no be all the time with Carmichael. Buy some lass a drink, Neil. Get yourself a pretty quean for the night.' This was accompanied by a wink and a leer that sat ill on a face whose habitual expression was reserved and seemly.

Neil shifted in his saddle. 'Aye, as ye say, Mr Echlin. But my first concern is the timber.' He touched his bonnet and rode after Gilfillan.

A solid well-made fellow of middle years, Gilfillan looked matched to the beast under him. As well as his horse-pistols he bore a short sword and a musket across his back. Neil knew little of the master-carpenter and had no wish to start the journey in silence. Riding alongside he said, 'Ye seem well-armed, Mr Gilfillan.'

The carpenter smiled and scratched his beard. 'It's usage, Mr Gilchrist. When you've ridden back and forth 'twixt Dumfries and Berwick for a wheen of years you're used to setting out with more than a herding stick.'

'Ha, you've worked in the Borders?'

'For nigh on ten years, sir. Then the feuds and the tulzies grew so thick around me, my wife feared for my life and we moved with our bairns to Edinburgh. 'Twas there I met Mr Echlin.'

'So he brought ye across with him?'

Neil barely heard the carpenter's response. The laird's parting words slithered into his mind like a rat. As he thought over them his face coloured in anger and humiliation. He had been encouraged, like some stableboy free for an evening, to take a drab to bed. He felt that behind that grotesque exhortation of Kenneth Echlin's lay a sinister intent. Anne and he had parted without any hint of secrecy or subterfuge. Yet, in her innocence, the girl may have spoken too freely. Sunk in gloom he plodded behind Gilfillan. Fortunately the animal he rode was not given to skittishness nor the carpenter to idle chatter.

The early morning mist was lifting before them as they rode out of Ravara on to the Newtownards road. There was no call, said Gilfillan, to go through the village and he turned off at a track leading north-west towards the valley of the river Lagan. They met few travellers on their way and those they questioned answered the two buirdly horsemen readily enough. The carpenter's sense of direction proved trustworthy and they made steady progress through O'Neill territory until, about noon, they came to the clear beaten track leading down the Castlereagh Hills to Belfast.

To Neil, as he descended the gentle if lengthy slope, there seemed little more to Belfast than the castle. Closer, he saw a scattering of squat drab dwellings and stores built on the banks of a stream running to where the river Lagan emptied into Knockfergus Lough and the sea. Gilfillan, keeping to the left bank of the stream, pressed on to the inn, Sir Moses Cellars, a three-storey building that sat somewhat askew to the main track as if ashamed of its neighbours.

The landlord led them into a substantial room where a dozen or so of the inn's patrons were busy with knife and spoon. At a centre table five or six of the castle guard, their empty plates pushed back, called noisily for wine.

The innkeeper came to a halt. 'Mr Carmichael – Mr Gilchrist and – aw – Mr Gilfillan.'

Mr Carmichael sat at a corner table as one occupying an established position. He wore a black patch over one eye which gave him a somewhat raffish look. But Neil had the impression that the good eye had already appraised them as they made their way across the room.

'Ye have my name?' he queried in the tone of one who considers that something has been filched.

'It was given me by Mr Charles Leslie of Newtownards,' said Neil.

Mr Carmichael's mouth lifted in a smile. The one eye opened wide. 'Ha, ha! Charlie Leslie! Tell me, what o' Rab Bothwell? A canty chiel!'

'He speaks with equal warmth of you,' said Neil politely.

'Now, your business, sirs?' Then he banished such thought-lessness with a wave of the hand. 'No, no, no, you've travelled a brave distance. You'll join me, sirs. Sit down, sit down – Job?'

The innkeeper hurried to set two chairs. Having assured himself that the braised ribs before Mr Carmichael would be to the liking of the guests, Job departed for the kitchen. The timber merchant looked expectantly at the two.

'I am Neil Gilchrist, employed by Mr Echlin of Ravara, beyond Strangford Lough. With me,' Neil indicated his companion, 'Addy Gilfillan, master-carpenter at Ravara –'

'Ye want to buy timber?'

'No, Mr Carmichael, we want to sell it. 'Twas for that reason I went to Leslie and Bothwell, known to us through dealings in seed and grain.'

'And what have ye, Mr Gilchrist?'

'Oak. I can't tell ye how much but it runs to the estate border, untouched as yet.'

'Oak?' said Mr Carmichael. 'Guid. There's a ready market for that. When you two gentlemen have eaten your dinners we'll go to my yard and I'll show ye in what shape I need the timber.'

The innkeeper was persuading the troopers that at this hour they should be elsewhere. At last by command and cajolery he got them on their feet. When he had seen the last of them gone he came to inquire if there was aught else required by Mr Carmichael and his guests.

Neil had watched the departure of the soldiers with interest. 'Is the Lord Deputy in residence at the castle?' he inquired of the timber merchant.

'I'm no conversant with Sir Arthur's comings and goings. Sufficient for me he's rebuilding the castle, ithers are following him, and it all adds up to a muckle need for woodwork. But Job here,' and he indicated the innkeeper, 'loses custom when the men-at-arms are away.'

Job skilfully steered a pile of crumbs into his open palm.

'Vagabonds and knavish rogues creep back when the Deputy's men are not here. As a magistrate ye know that well, Mr Carmichael.'

'Aye, true.'

'What of the town watch?' asked Gilfillan.

'Little more than a staff and a lantern,' said Job with a glance at Mr Carmichael.

'The Castle has promised them halberds,' said the timber merchant.

Neil recalled the uninviting huddle of drab buildings. 'What draws these blaggards here – to find a vessel bound for Scotland?'

'No, no, young man,' answered Carmichael. 'That's where maist o' them fled from. A rope's waiting them there. No, it's women, shelter, cards, liquor –'

'Throats and purse-strings to cut,' added the innkeeper.

'Aye, true,' said Mr Carmichael. 'If it's your intention, sirs, to take a dander after supper-time tonight, go armed. And now,' bending his good eye to their plates, 'that you've redd up your dinner, we'll head for Stave Lane.'

At a brisk pace Mr Carmichael led them along the left bank of the stream, acknowledging in his progress the salutes of his fellow-citizens. To Neil, the dwellings and outhouses were no more prepossessing seen close at hand. But across the stream, close to the castle walls, new timber houses with chimneys were rising that Gilfillan recognised as in the English style. It was as if the settlement was sloughing its dingy birth-skin. Mr Carmichael acknowledged complacently that much of the timber-work in these new dwellings had been shaped by his craftsmen.

The clatter and bustle of the timber-yard filled Stave Lane. Carmichael's yard *was* Stave Lane for across from the workshop the carriageway was bounded by a long shed where the timber was stored, dried and seasoned. In the workshop itself a dozen men and apprentices laboured with adze, mallet, wedge and saw. The two men from Ravara gazed with some surprise

246

on the stacks of beams, cask-staves and lathes reaching to the roof.

'Run your eye, Mr Gilfillan, o'er what the men are at,' said Carmichael.

'I have, sir. I doubt,' said the carpenter with a glance at Neil, 'if we could even bring our wood down to beams.'

'I wouldn't want as much. But let us get out o' this stour and din.' Mr Carmichael lifted his eye patch to reveal a hollow socket. 'I do little measuring-off since I lost an eye to a knot o' wood that came at me like a pistol ball. We'll talk over here,' and he led them across to the quiet and pungent atmosphere of the wood-store.

The timber-merchant waved to the others to settle themselves. 'Now,' said he, 'gin ye have the trunks snedded clean, how far can ye get them from Ravara – to the coast?'

Neil shook his head. 'We've no wagons as yet. We could have them to the estate entrance on the Newtownards road.'

'Aye, well I could lift from there and draw to a schooner off Donaghadee or Groomsport. Ye understand that would come off the buying price?'

Neil understood well. 'That's agreed, Mr Carmichael – with the proviso that in time we would look to the haulage ourselves.'

Mr Carmichael was heard to say that that matter could be settled as between two honest parties.

'How often would ye want to lift at Ravara?'

The timber-merchant stood upright and dusted the seat of his breeches. 'Young man,' said he, 'dinna fash yourself on that. Let the timber pile up near where's handy. If it's what ye say it is then the trees are betwixt eighty and a hundred-and-fifty years auld. They're no likely to turn to butter in a month or two.'

Neil accepted the probability of this conjecture. 'Can ye give me a figure for Mr Echlin?'

'No, sir, I can not. But ye can be assured that for hale sound wood I'll offer a price better than ye could command at Carrickfergus or Newry – and that holds for any straight hazel or ash ye cut. Here's my hand on't.'

Neil, mightily relieved that on his return he wouldn't stand dumbstruck before Echlin, took the other's hand readily.

'You'll inform me,' said Carmichael as they left the wood-store, 'if Mr Echlin agrees my offer and if you've timber to lift?'

'At the earliest opportunity, sir.'

'Mr Carmichael,' said Gilfillan, delaying the timber-merchant, 'Mr Echlin is looking a coach for his family. Is there a coach-builder in the town – or better still, a coach for sale?'

Mr Carmichael's eye opened wide. His face was suffused with the pleasure of a dealer who, unexpectedly, can satisfy a demand.

'Ech, man, I ken the very yoke for ye! The choice o' two fine vehicles lying under cover in Job Pluckrose's yard –'

'Tavern conveyances?' Gilfillan pulled a long face.

'Not so, sir, not so, or I wouldn't have lipped a word on them,' said Mr Carmichael, vexed. 'They were left there by two of the castle officers who were hurried back to London. Job was given orders to raise money on them as quick as he was able. The cordovan leather and the paintwork and the metal furnishings are as fresh as the day they were put thegither. I can't say better than that,' cried Mr Carmichael.

'Very good, sir. I don't doubt ye. If I think one or t'other is what Mr Echlin seeks and I can come to a price with Mr Pluckrose, I'll take it back with me. I'm obliged to ye, Mr Carmichael.'

Mollified, Mr Carmichael took leave of his visitors with a final word to Neil that if he had any more queries he should call at Stave Lane before starting homeward.

Neil and the carpenter parted for Gilfillan was impatient to inspect the coaches at the inn. Neil set out to make what purchases he could for Ross and Wishart. None of the booths he peered into offered other than clothes, food or tools. The one that could have passed as an apothecary's shop was closed.

A girl, passing, told him that the owner was off to a fair in the country. She was a pretty lass and lingered as if willing to come to the help of the braw young stranger in any other perplexity. If Neil's thanks and bow in parting from her had been thrice as courteous it would not have pleased her.

He thought again of the laird's parting advice as how he should employ his evening in this place. Echlin, with his sense of propriety, must have known that the grossness of what he said would be evident to his retainer. And even if he did spend the night in the stews and Gilfillan the taciturn became a babbler, of what use would that be to Echlin? He could not believe that the laird would abase himself further by using it to wound his daughter. It had been nothing more than a clumsy trap set for his feet. What it revealed to Neil was how deeply Echlin and his wife feared an attachment between himself and Anne.

He must act warily if he was not to endanger sweet Anne's liberty or spur her mother to send her out of the country. As he rode to Belfast he had suffered anger and hurt pride as he recalled how he had listened to the laird: the puzzled stare, the knuckle to his bonnet. Now he felt that he had played the dull coof in a manner that would have done credit to any of Wishart's playactors.

Cheered by this thought he mounted the stairs of the inn to his chamber. Voices were rising from the courtyard. Looking from his window he saw Gilfillan, the landlord and the inn's stableman, gathered round a coach, a solid handsome carriage in dark green and silver. The deal, it appeared, was concluded. Gilfillan gave the vehicle a proprietary slap, then drew a coin from his pocket. The ostler pocketed the tip, touched his forelock, took a couple of parting swipes at the coachwork with a cloth and retired to the coach-house. The master-carpenter and Pluckrose disappeared to Neil's eye as they entered the rear of the inn.

Gilfillan was already at table when Neil went down for supper. 'I saw ye close the deal, Addy,' said the young man as he drew in a chair. 'Are ye satisfied with it?'

'Mr Carmichael was right about the quality of the workmanship, Mr Gilchrist. Both coaches run true. I understand they were built for dashing young blades of officers. I've bought the least showy of them. Better suited to a country laird and his family.'

The dining-room was busy but that evening Neil and Gilfillan had the undivided attention of their host. As he circled the table, Pluckrose would pause, shake his head and let loose a great sigh of relief. Demands by the late owner of the coach, he told them, had turned to threats as he grew more impatient to see the colour of his money.

'But is he not in London?' asked Neil.

'He has friends at the castle,' said the innkeeper, nodding to a group of officers seated at a table. 'I've handed them the money. Let them post it to London as pleases them. Ah, gentlemen. . .' and again Mr Pluckrose shook his head as a man greatly eased in mind. 'Now, sirs, a fine wine. . .'

The soldiers raised a cry for candles and cards. Neil glanced at them and recognised the officer who had objected to the harper's cloak at Rathard House. He averted his face. 'Addy,' he said, 'when you're finished, let us take a turn in the open air before bed.'

Neither mentioned it but both recalled Carmichael's advice and armed themselves. The innkeeper was in the hall as they left. He nodded approvingly as the carpenter slung his musket on his shoulder.

'I'll have mulled ale ready on your return. Step warily, gentlemen.'

There was a scattering of lights along each bank of the Farset. The feeble glow escaped from windows and doorways and did nothing more than throw quivering reflections here and there on the running water. The farthest pinpoint seemed to stretch the night over the dark waters of the lough.

'We ken what's on this side of the burn,' said Gilfillan. 'Let's cross over and see what's to be seen by the castle.'

Neil followed the other across a low bridge that spanned the
stream. He had not gone far before he wished that he had
stayed in the comfort of the inn. The ground under their feet
was rough and broken. The few lights that struggled from a
cluster of hovels close to the castle wall seemed only to deepen
the mirk. A violent stumble wrung an oath from Neil.

'I've had enough. Ye could break a leg here!'

'We're likely on the military exercise ground,' said the carpenter. 'We'll turn –'

Suddenly there was a woman's anguished scream. The door
of the largest shanty was thrown violently open. Against the
light stood the massive figure of a man, a cudgel clasped under
his arm. With a swing of his free hand he dragged a woman
from behind him and cast her bodily into the darkness. Neil
shuddered as if he heard her body break on the cobbles.

The light from the open door was broken as the denizens of
the grog-house wriggled out past the monstrous creature on the
threshold. Five or six men and a couple of females, they came to
a halt at the inert body of the girl. One woman stooped to touch
her. The others looked down, whispering, tittering drunkenly.
The man in the doorway stepped out, elbowing them aside. He
drew back his foot and before Neil or Gilfillan could move,
kicked the body so that it rose and fell again like a half-empty
sack.

'Thou foul gangrel. . .' said Neil unbelievingly.

It was no more than a whisper but it brought the boozers
alert, like beasts of prey. For a moment they eyed the two
strangers in the dusk. Then stepping across the woman's body
they began to edge forward.

Gilfillan unshipped his musket. 'Hold,' he said, 'no farther.'

There was a silence. Then a voice, jeeringly: 'They've but one
shot between them!' and the fellow stepped away as if to
outflank the two.

Gilfillan raised the musket breast-high. There was a click as

251

he cocked the firearm. 'Then which of yous is for Hell?' At his query the stealthy advance died. None of them carried arms but Gilfillan and Neil had no doubt that dirks nestled in their tatters.

The baleful creature behind them let the cudgel slither from under his arm until it lay in his grasp. Neil gaped. He had seen the motion and the weapon before.

'It's the gallowsbird —' he cried half to himself, '— Lachie Dubh!'

In the play of torchlight and mirk the two stared at each other.

'My soul in Hell,' said Lachie, 'it's the cockrel frae. . . frae Pinwherry!' There was a squeal of triumph in his voice, recognition accomplished.

Neil pulled aside the skirt of his coat to reveal a pistol butt. Without taking his eyes from Lachie Dubh, he freed the weapon and give it over to Gilfillan. 'Here's business for me, Addy,' he said, and drew his rapier.

Lachie Dubh flourished the murderous stave in his hand. 'I maun scatter this wee lairdie,' he announced.

As Gilchrist was not small and not, as far as Gilfillan knew, a laird, the carpenter inferred that these two were known to each other and that this was a grim jest. So he held his peace and waved the rabble to make room. Willingly they drew back. Either this braw young gentleman would go down crushed under Lachie's club and his purse-strings cut before the town watch arrived or they would be rid of the bully who had been among them too long.

'With a rapier in your hand,' Kenneth Echlin had once said, 'you are a cat.' Neil danced a step as he took guard. Lachie Dubh shuffled round to face him, club swinging loosely, from his other hand the glint of a dirk. Club raised to strike, he came to Neil in a sudden rush. Then, with a dexterity that totally foxed the young man, levelled the weapon and thrust it at Neil's head. A desperate backward stumble in which he almost lost his footing on the greasy cobbles saved Neil's face. The head of the club struck his shoulder with numbing force and he heard his sleeve rip. The shadowy vagrants around the two screeched and jigged. Gilfillan raised the pistol warningly. Neil sensed the danger. At the full stretch of Lachie's arm the iron-hard club outreached his rapier, and the ruffian handled it like a broadsword fighter.

Neil circled warily but could find no way to reach his opponent. His strokes either broke on the other's club or were thrown off by the dirk. He was slow in avoiding a venomous thrust that tore at his cheek and ear. Again there was a howl of glee. Neil licked the sweat and blood that ran to his lips. I'll tire before this hellhound does, he thought, and for a space held off.

'Come fo'rrard, wee mannie,' Lachie began in a soothering voice. 'Come fo'rrard, ye whelp, till I finish ye,' and he levelled his weapon again.

Neil shortened his stroke and stabbed at the hand that held the club. He was rewarded with a bellow of fury. For a second Lachie fumbled with club and dirk as he sought to free the gashed and bloodied hand. In that moment Neil leapt forward like a cat. The thrust of his rapier into his enemy's breast almost took him into the other's arms. The stricken giant's mouth and eyes flared in agony and astonishment. The cudgel dropped from his grasp. He raised the dirk again. His whole body went back with the gesture and he crashed to the ground, the dagger tinkling across the cobbles. The onlookers gabbled like driven geese. One fled to secure the dirk. The others followed him swiftly into the darkness.

Gilfillan came forward with Neil's pistol. ''Twas well fought, Mr Gilchrist. But I was 'feard for ye.'

Neil wiped his blade clean on the fallen man's clothes. 'He used to wear a plaid that would have turned a pistol ball. . .'

'Ye knew him lang syne?'

'Aye.' Neil stumbled uncertainly.

'Ye need tending, Mr Gilchrist.'

253

'Let us look first to the female.'

An old woman, stooped over the crumpled figure, made to move away as the two men approached.

'She's dead, sirs.'

'Who was she, mother?' asked the carpenter.

'Bess – poor Bess – Lachie's quean.' The crone was sidling away as she answered.

A fine rain was falling. Neil looked around him in a darkness totally deserted, for even the ale-house was shut, its light extinguished.

'She can't be left here,' he called. 'Isn't there a physician – the church – had she a cleric –'

The old woman, gathering her skirts, glanced over her shoulder. 'Bess – let into a church? Ah, God mend your wits, sir!' she screeched and scuttled away into the gloom.

At that moment, from the opposite direction, came the swinging ray of a lantern and the sound of footsteps. Out of the darkness appeared a stout fellow bearing a staff and carefully lighting the way for Mr Sam Carmichael armed with a pistol.

The timber-merchant swivelled round to turn his eye on the corpses before he spoke. He shook his head. 'A sorry night's work, gentlemen. But I'm relieved to see ye on your feet.'

'Thank ye,' said Neil.

But Gilfillan turned on the stout man bearing the lantern. 'Ye were over-long in coming, watchman –'

'Hoots, toots, man,' said Mr Carmichael severely. 'The watch was about his business. Job Pluckrose grew gey concerned at your absence and sent him for me. What's that?' and he nodded to the body of the dead woman that seemed, under the rain, to sink and merge into the wet earth.

'A poor drab – Bess by name.' Neil spoke with an effort for his jaw was stiffening painfully.

'Pish! They're all called Bess or Meg. And this?' Carmichael turned to the other body. 'Your light, Alec.' He took the lantern from the town watch and shone it into the dead face, then straightened abruptly. 'God Almighty, it's Lachie Dubh!' He stared open-mouthed at the two men. 'Whose work is this?'

'Mr Gilchrist,' said Gilfillan, 'was forced to run him through.'

The timber-merchant trotted forward, hand outstretched. 'Mr Gilchrist, your hand in mine. The town's beholden to ye. As a magistrate *I'm* beholden to ye. Lachie was a monster of iniquity.' He raised the lantern higher. 'Damn me, sir, but you're hurt. And you're drookit. We'll all be drookit in this rain. Alec, your arm to Mr Gilchrist. Mr Gilfillan, the lantern, and light us fo'rrard to the inn. And Alec, when we're there, away for Joe Pollok and his cart and see them two bodies lifted afore the town's dogs get at them.'

Job Pluckrose shepherded them into a back parlour. Towels and blankets were brought. Mr Carmichael requested the inn-keeper to send for Mr Quill, the apothecary.

'Oliver Quill,' said Pluckrose, 'is just returned from Kells fair. He's in the taproom.'

'Then ask him to step in here with his lotions and potions. And Job, ye could set up the mulled ale.'

Job gone, Mr Carmichael confided: 'There's them that would dub Quill a quack. But,' he closed his eye, 'he has the touch. Ye can throw yourself on his skill with confidence, Mr Gilchrist.'

Neil, who would much rather have thrown himself on his bed, found it hard, with a stiffening face, to show his appreciation of this assurance.

A tall thin fellow paused inquiringly in the doorway. Mr Carmichael leaned back, caught his eye, and pointed to Neil. The apothecary came in and set a tattered valise on the table. It was plain that he had ridden straight to the inn from his rural transactions, for chaff and straw dust clung to his shoulders and wig.

'An accident, sir?' he asked stooping to where Neil sat.

'No accident, Oliver,' declared Mr Carmichael roundly. 'But

an hour ago this rare young gentleman rid us of Lachie Dubh!' and the timber-merchant mimicked a sword thrust.

'The scoundrel! You'll have my best attention, sir. A noisome scoundrel, Lachie Dubh.' He bent to study Neil's face, saying: 'May he grill eternally on the hobs of Hell.' The malediction came oddly from the prim mouth. He clicked his fingers behind him. 'Fetch warm water and a clean clout. But I've treated those that fared worse. Have ye lost teeth? Try about, sir,' and Mr Quill ran his tongue over his gums.

Neil gingerly did likewise and shook his head with great care.

The apothecary expressed his satisfaction. When a serving-lass brought him basin and cloth he proceeded to cleanse the injured face with a remarkably light and sure touch. A dip into the valise produced a reddish lotion which he applied to the bruised jaw, then topped it off with a linen strip from temple to chin. He stepped back to an appreciative murmur from his audience. Neil fumbled for his purse. Mr Quill raised a restraining hand.

'Sir, you've rid us of a beast of prey. *We* are beholden to *you*. Would ye not say so, magistrate?'

'I've already said so,' declared Mr Carmichael, 'and I say so again. Now, Job, the ale.'

The innkeeper brought the flagons of fragrant steaming liquor. Neil was about to reach for his when the apothecary drew it away.

'No, no, sir,' said he gently but firmly. 'Mr Pluckrose hasn't his equal in mulling ale. But it would fire the blood and I want ye to sleep. Better this,' and he took from the valise a bottle and a not-over-clean glass. He filled the glass and placed it before Neil. 'Down it, sir. Down it.'

Neil downed it and grimaced in a lopsided way.

'Now,' said Mr Quill, taking a swig from Neil's flagon, 'if the injured party could be put to bed as expeditiously as is possible.'

256

Gilfillan and the innkeeper oxtered the young man up the staircase and his feet were trailing by the time they had mounted to the top steps. They laid him on the bed, removed his boots and threw a coverlet over him. He was deeply asleep before they creaked out of the room.

24

Able driver though Gilfillan proved to be, the progress of their return to Ravara was much slower than their going out. Several times he had to cast back to find a track that would take the ponderous vehicle. Even where the land had been cleared he drove with watchful caution, fearing to shatter a wheel on a hidden boulder or tree stump.

Suffering by being thrown about in the body of the coach, Neil clambered up beside Gilfillan and forgot his aches and bruises when the carpenter trusted him with the reins. The sky was darkening towards evening as they drove into Newtownards. Men and women, lighting lamp or candle, peered out in unease at the strange coach clattering across the market square and lurching on into the gloom. Once on the well-kenned road to Ravara Gilfillan smartened up the pace and did not draw rein until he brought the coach to a halt at the avenue to Rathard. A light gleamed in a lower chamber of the house.

'I'll no trouble the laird at this late hour,' said Gilfillan.

'No, Addy?' Neil was aware of an immense feeling of relief. There would be no call for him to present himself to Echlin before the morrow. He had returned with the information his employer sought. He sickened at the thought of what would lie between them unspoken if he chapped now on the door of Rathard seeking his master. There was no light for men to sit under more treacherous than candlelight, when they said one thing and their thoughts were busy with another. 'Ye think the morrow would be better?'

The carpenter turned in his seat to glance down at the body and wheels of the coach. 'She's gutters to the waist. I'll take her home with me and send for Neilson in the morn to wash her. 'Twould be fitting for the laird and his lady to see her in the state I bought her.' He picked the reins up. 'If ye come with me my wife would set up a supper dish.'

Neil thought of the long road across the estate, even on horseback, to the schoolhouse. 'That would be kindly of her, Addy, but I long for my bed.' He stepped down with his bag.

A moment's pause and Gilfillan held out his hand. 'Goodnight to ye.'

Neil returned the firm grip. 'Goodnight, Addy, and thank ye.'

He stepped back to watch the willing animals take the strain on the shaft. A spark of light, from some invisible source, played on the metalwork of the coach. Then the vehicle plunged into the night-dark foliage. Neil tossed the bag on his shoulder and tucked the sword behind him. Now, thought he, for my sup of gruel with Ross, my mattress and blankets. I'm no more rooted in this place than on the day I left Balwhanny. He trudged gloomily on, stirring only a dog in the sleeping clachan. Then, like a spark of light, a shining head and a sweet face came to mind. Long before he reached the schoolhouse Anne Echlin had his whole concern.

'Sim Watt was here early,' said Ross as Neil sat down to breakfast.

'With my nag?'

'And a message for ye. The laird will be at Dan's office.'

When he entered the office the laird and Drummond were at the daily business of the estate. Echlin forestalled any greeting. 'Sit down, Gilchrist,' he said pushing away his papers. The peremptory words, the gesture, told Neil what the mood of this exchange would be. The factor rose from his chair with the shuffle of one dismissed. 'Don't go, Dan,' said the laird and pointed to a seat in the corner. Twice Echlin glanced at the young man's bruised and discoloured face and looked away irritably. Then: 'Gilfillan tells me ye had a set-to in Belfast.'

'We were challenged by a drunken rabble, Mr Echlin.'

'Ye killed a man.'

'I had no choice.'

'Did ye stir up ill-will against any future business there?'

Drummond, in the corner, drew in his stomach with a breath. He could think of no reason for this ill-natured spiering of Gilchrist. But no doubt the laird had his reasons and Dan eased himself back discreetly in his chair.

'The timber-merchant Carmichael is also a magistrate,' replied Neil stiffly. 'He held that I had rid the town of a monster of iniquity – his words.'

'Carmichael. . .' Relieved, the laird pounced on the name. 'What of Carmichael? What speed did ye come there?'

'He's a ready purchaser of oak timber. He showed an interest, forbye, in straight ash and hazel –'

'Aye, aye – but did he give ye a price for the oak?'

'No, he did not.'

''Steeth, man! Isn't that what I sent ye for!'

Dan, in his corner, made a gesture of indignation and sympathy for his master.

'Mr Echlin, ye sought a market for your timber. I found one. As to price, all Carmichael said was that he could offer ye more money than ye would get if ye had to take it farther – to Carrickfergus or Newry.' The young man made little effort to keep the sneer from his voice. 'How was he to put a value on timber when he knew nothing of its condition, of its girth, or where it had to be drawn from? Carmichael has never heard of Ravara or what airt it lies in.'

To Echlin the practical sense of what Gilchrist said outweighed the insolence of his manner in saying it. He stared at his knotted hands. 'Well, what now?'

Neil lifted his bonnet. 'We continue felling. Then ye advise Carmichael.'

'Gilchrist, if ye have any news for me send it by my son. And if ye must see me, let it be here, not at Rathard.'

Neil paused as if to observe the laird's bidding. The voice he heard behind the words was Lady Echlin's. 'As ye say, laird.' He drew on his bonnet and left the office as Dan Drummond emerged from the corner.

Neil climbed slowly into the saddle and turned his mount to the schoolhouse path. I would have told him, he thought in a sudden stab of self-pity, that he was in my mind when I faced Lachie Dubh. For the first time he was aware of how much his daily existence in this place rested upon Kenneth Echlin, not only for bread-and-butter employment but more for the presence of an equitable and generous fellow-creature. What filled him now was a poignant regret for his loss and resentment at the manner in which it had been inflicted.

Without dismounting, he called Chrissy Maclennan to the schoolhouse door. 'Tell the dominie,' he said, 'that I'm for Tullycarnet Wood and then for the village. I'll be back to supper.'

At Tullycarnet half-a-dozen woodsmen were clearing scrub. Neil summoned Iain Mackechnie the gaffer, a sensible industrious fellow.

'Ye can set them to the oak. Remember, the stumps as low as ye can make them.'

'You've found a buyer, Mr Gilchrist?'

'The laird has found a market. And cut a score of rollers. The timber'll have to be moved to the main gates.'

With Mackechnie he marked the trees that were to come down. The fell beat of axe and saw was sounding through the woodland before he mounted again.

At the mouth of the avenue to Rathard he glanced up at the house. The deep-eyed windows looked down impassively. Did Anne sit at one of them? Did she see or hear him as he rode past? The lines came to his head:

> Fair Margaret sat in her bower sewing,
>   Sewing at her silken seam;
> She heard a note in Elmond's Wood,
>   And wished she there had been.

261

> She loot the seam fa' frae her side,
> And the needle to her toe. . .

The conceit passed swiftly. The only woman's face that he had ever seen at a window of Rathard was that of Lady Echlin, watching with cold curiosity his departure from the house.

His thoughts went back to the factor's office. No man of spirit could thole the affront Kenneth Echlin had put on him that morning. He should have mounted there and then and left Ravara for ever. But what of Anne in that house, its doors locked against him? He had no answer to that and he doubted if a more nimble mind could offer one. Swallow the slight, thole on and watch. That he was now determined to do. And that would be his bearing for longer than Echlin and his wife might reckon on. For all his resolve he kept his eyes steadily ahead as he passed the glade where Anne and he had spoken of their love. He could not bear to learn if the swan gleamed on the tarn. He had no one to tell.

At Bothwell and Leslie's store an old woman sweeping up spilt grain was laying the dust. She wiped her nose with the wet clout as she considered his query.

'They're away for their dinner,' she replied with a gesture across the market square.

The corn-chandlers greeted him affably. A chair was drawn in, the innkeeper called upon to bring another plate.

'You've been to Belfast?'

'I have, and I'm the bearer of Mr Carmichael's compliments to ye both.'

'Aye, Sam. Ye would find him in good heart. Well now, what about the oak timber?'

'He would be a ready purchaser. There's still the rub of how we get the felled trees out of Ravara.'

Mr Bothwell glanced at Mr Leslie. 'Mr Gilchrist,' he said, 'when you've redd up your plate there's something we would like to show ye.'

262

Together the three crossed the square to the premises of Messrs Bothwell and Leslie. Mr Leslie led the way to the rear of the cavernous store. Daylight flooded in as he opened a door. 'There, Mr Gilchrist,' he said.

Neil looked out. In the yard, half under a tarpaulin, was a long skeletal four-wheeled vehicle.

'Charlie put it thegither when we were in the timber business. There's only one yoke like that anywhere. Mr Echlin should take it. He'd be free to move his timber on his land or out o't.'

'I'll tell him. He'll certainly be eager to ken what price you're asking.'

'Three pounds,' said Mr Leslie promptly. 'That wouldn't cover the wheelwright's work the day.'

'I'll inform Mr Echlin. And now,' continued Neil, 'what of Carmichael?'

'In about s'en-days time me and Charlie are for Belfast to get some paperwork done by a notary there. We'll tell Sam that Mr Echlin's timber can be moved to Donaghadee or a suchlike place on the coast. That'll please him for I think when he's in this airt he'll be nebbing around to learn if any of Mr Echlin's neighbours is in mind to sell timber.'

Mr Leslie had closed the yard door. The three were moving to the street entrance. 'Did I understand ye to say,' queried Neil, 'that ye lack a notary here?'

'We do that. And a bad lack it is, for trade is thriving in Newtownards. It's a sad waste of time and money when a merchant has to set off for Newry or Belfast to get a wheen of business papers put to rights.'

Leaving the village he spied a small outbuilding with a good glazed window that overlooked the market square. A fitting place, he thought, for a young notary to lay out his papers and pens and keep an eye on the tide of buying and selling foreseen by Mr Bothwell, particularly on its litigious froth.

On the Ravara road he began to think on how he could get word to Kenneth Echlin of the grain-chandler's offer. If the laird or his son were not to be readily found then he would leave the news with Dan Drummond. It would puff up Dan's self-importance like a dried pig's-bladder. But better that than hanging about, bonnet in hand, hoping to gain the laird's ear.

He now urged his horse to a brisker pace. As he did so he heard the approaching rumble of wheels. It was a sound only too familiar. He drew his horse into the secrecy of a roadside thicket.

Peering through the foliage he saw the Echlin coach, with a clatter of hooves and a drumming of wheels, come lurching round a bend of the track. Sim Watt was at the reins with Neilson the ostler up beside him. The ground quivered as horses and carriage rushed past the hidden watcher. In that instant he thought he glimpsed a shrouded figure drawn back into a corner of the coach.

What he saw with startling clarity was the aloof handsome face of Lady Echlin. He shrank back as if she had sensed his presence. At that moment, in that cold face, he read his total rejection. When he stepped out the coach was disappearing in an eddy of dust. With the dust his daft dream of the notary fell to the ground. The Echlins would never suffer his existence in the neighbourhood near Ravara. A notary would come to Newtownards but it would not be him. If need be the laird and his powerful neighbours would see to it that a change of mind was wrought in Bothwell and his fellow-merchants. In dull impotent anger Neil Gilchrist resumed his journey.

To his relief Francis Echlin was at Tullycarnet Wood. With young Echlin he was always at ease and the two greeted each other in friendly manner. Neil looked at the felled trees.

'You and Mackechnie have done well, Francis. I've a message for your father. Bothwell and Leslie of Newtownards have a wagon built to carry timber. The price they're asking is three pounds.' Neil paused for the other's nod. 'Bothwell recommends it. With it the laird can move trunks to wherever he thinks fit.'

'I'll tell him, Neil.' As Neil moved away young Echlin followed him. 'There's two cottar families arrived from Kintyre. Would this bit of land,' he indicated the denuded stretch behind them, 'be suitable for tenants?'

Neil looked at him. The young fellow was eager enough to learn. Neil hardened his heart. 'The letting of land is for your father and his factor to decide on,' he said as he regained his saddle. 'The timber cart should be foremost in your mind, Francis,' and he rode off.

The laird and his wife sat at supper. There was a silence when Lady Echlin finished speaking. Her husband leant forward to refill the glasses.

'Perhaps,' said he, 'given time, the girl will forget. . .'

Her Ladyship responded in angry impatience. 'Time! Tell me, husband, why should she forget when she knows we are keeping her and Gilchrist apart? He'll aye be in her mind as long as he haunts Ravara!'

'Ye have the coach —'

'It makes no difference. I took her out today. She sat at the Cordwaines' table mute as a stone. In the end I had to tell her go seek the Cordwaine children. Ye know how she loved sporting with them.' Her husband remaining silent, she continued: 'Ye say Gilchrist brought back from Belfast what ye sent him for?'

'He did.'

'Does Francis know what's to be done with the timber?'

'Aye, with Mackechnie's help.'

'Then of what further use is Gilchrist to ye? Stir yourself, Kenneth. Get rid of the fellow!'

25

Kenneth Echlin awoke with a load on his mind. In his day he had rid himself of not a few subordinates, the cowardly, the deceitful, the slothful, some of them summarily enough. Gilchrist was none of these. Clinging like a burr was the realisation that this fellow was what he would have wished his elder son to be. He cursed Neil Gilchrist for his poverty, that he hadn't made himself more a suppliant to her Ladyship, that he and his daughter Anne should have been drawn to each other.

As he breakfasted alone he swithered whether he should face Gilchrist in the factor's office or summon him to Rathard House for the last time, and dismiss him over a glass of wine. Still undecided, he took himself to his study. There he got through some business by sending for Francis, giving him three pounds and instructing him to ride with Sim Watt to the village and bring back the timber wagon from the corn-merchants' store.

In her bedchamber Anne Echlin tapped with the toe of her riding boot as if telling off the minutes. She arose, picked up her gloves and left the room. Her mother was approaching along the gallery. 'You are bound whither, dear Anne?'

'To speak with my father.' The expression on the girl's face, the manner in which she brushed past, drew her Ladyship's gaze after the figure descending the stairs. A moment's pause and Lady Echlin followed with light footfall.

The laird's morning greeting clouded as he observed his daughter's costume.

'Father, why is Gilchrist not here to take me riding?'

'He's working in the forest for me, Anne.'

'Every day, sir? This is now the third morning –'

'It's an urgent task. When Francis returns ye can go with him if ye so wish.'

'He's an indifferent horseman and the tracks are still strange to him. Gilchrist knows his way.'

The laird looked up as Lady Echlin sidled in to stand beside him, one hand resting lightly on the table. 'I warrant ye he does, my dear,' said she smiling sweetly on the girl.

'Anne,' said the laird, 'Gilchrist is first of all an employee on my estate – a woodsman –'

'Neil Gilchrist is as well-born as I am, sir.'

The laird straightened abruptly in his chair. 'So, he has told ye his tale, has he? What else passed between ye?'

'Nothing that I would not wish to hear from him, Father.'

'And what the Deil does that mean, pert miss?'

Anne's voice was firm, her words deliberate. 'We spoke to each other of our love.'

'And where did this baring of hearts take place?' asked her Ladyship with a cold smile. 'Not under your father's roof?'

'On – on our way to the village.'

'On the roadside – like any ploughman's wench.' Her Ladyship spoke with a measured and cold contempt.

The girl's eyes filled. The laird looked up at his wife in angry rebuke.

'Anne,' he said in softer tones, 'in all honour Gilchrist should have come to me –'

'Would he have been better received, sir?'

'He would not,' declared Echlin forcibly. 'Neil Gilchrist is but a penniless carle –'

'I'm aware of Mr Gilchrist's condition. It makes no difference to me –'

'Well, by God, buird,' cried the laird, 'it's of consequence to your family! Now hark ye, daughter,' he leaned across the table, 'Neil Gilchrist has already been forbidden this house. Under no circumstances whatsoever are ye to meet or communicate with him inside or outside these walls. Ye understands that, Anne?'

Getting no response he repeated the question. The girl raised

267

her pale face, bowed slightly, and turning, left the room.

Lady Echlin looked on her husband with silent approval. Wit warned her that this was no time to offer commendation. Echlin brooded on the wary defiance he had glimpsed in the eyes of one he had thought of as little more than a child. He looked up at his wife.

'I'll give him two days to leave Ravara,' he said in answer to the unspoken question.

There was no school that day for on the morrow the minister and two of his elders were to catechise the scholars on their knowledge of the Holy Word. Neil shared a late breakfast with Angus Ross then set off for Tullycarnet Wood. For the last two mornings he had ridden at a leisurely pace to the woodlands with the intent that Francis Echlin should be there before him. It irked him to do so but he would give the laird no cause to think he was pushing his neb in where it was no longer welcome. When he arrived at the oak clearances, Mackechnie informed him that Archie Gill would speak with him.

'Aye.' Neil looked around. 'Where's Francis Echlin?'

'He's away with Sim Watt to bring back a wagon from the village. You've seen the yoke, Mr Gilchrist?'

'I have.'

'They tell me that when it's loaded it'll take four horses to draw it.'

'Who told ye?'

'Mr Francis. But he had Watt at his lug.'

'A knowledgable birkie, Sim Watt,' said Neil drily.

'He was making it plain that *he* wasn't going to drive the timber cart. He's the grand family coachman now, ye ken –'

Neil was not to be drawn into a stour over the issue. 'We'll find somebody to handle it. Now, where's Archie?'

'He'll be at the cornmill, Mr Gilchrist.'

'The mill? What does he want with me?'

'That I dinna ken. But when I met him on the road this morn, he had a face as dreich as a rain cloud.'

Gill was a man respected by Neil for his probity and intelligence; one of the few tenants for whom he would ride the length of the Langstane Burn. He mounted. 'Iain,' he said from the saddle, 'if Mr Francis is here with the wagon before I'm back, start the men loading it.'

Archie Gill, a disconsolate figure, was seated on a heap of grain sacks. He stood up as Neil entered.

'It's guid o' ye to come, Mr Gilchrist.'

'Aye – what is it, Archie?'

'Yesterday her Ladyship dismissed me from the mill.'

For a moment Neil thought the other man was about to ask him to intercede with the laird's wife. But Gill seemed to feel that his dire news was as much as was needed. He sat down again on the grain sacks. Neil beside him.

'Why so, Archie?'

'Her Ladyship told me from now on I was to increase the multure taxed on the meal.'

'What was your answer?'

'That that was the factor's business. It wasn't for me to tell my neighbours to give up more of their meal. Her Ladyship knew well she should have gone to Dan Drummond. But I had disobeyed her – and that's the end of me here.'

'Ye may go back to the farm, Archie.'

Gill was slow to answer. 'I gave over my scope of land to my brother when I started here. He's loath to give it back. Can ye get me a start at the wood-cutting Mr Gilchrist?'

Neil sprang up with an angry laugh. 'Certes, Archie, that would be the end of both of us! Ye disobey her Ladyship and I start ye working for her husband! No, go home and bide your time. You're too guid a man for the laird to let lie idle. Wait,' Neil paused in his departure, 'ye can handle a team of horses. I've seen ye drawing in big loads from the back-end of the estate. Go to Francis Echlin and Mackechnie and tell them you're fit to drive the timber wagon to the coast. They'll be gey glad of the offer.'

'What o' her Ladyship?'

'She doesn't meddle in that.'

'It's not much.'

'It's all there is,' said Neil impatiently.

'I'll do it, Mr Gilchrist.'

Rarely had the plans and writing tools on Dan Drummond's desk been so neatly disposed. For all that, Kenneth Echlin's fingers still smoothed a document, straightened a quill. The door opened and the factor came in.

'Well, where is he?'

'I seen neither hilt nor hair of him, laird.'

'Damn ye, man, where did ye look?'

'I rode to Tullycarnet,' replied Drummond in an aggrieved voice. 'Mackechnie says he was there this morn but left for either the mill or the village –'

'What would take him to the mill? Did he ken that my son had gone for the timber wagon?'

'I would think so, sir.'

'Maybe he rode after Francis and Watt. . .' In mounting frustration Echlin glared at the man across the table. 'Dan, I want Gilchrist brought to me. I'm sending him away from Ravara.' The laird took his eyes from the factor for a moment. 'Now that my son is settling here I need that young man no more.'

'Aye, 'deed, laird,' said Dan Drummond softly. 'Mr Francis can count on me –'

'When he first came to us he was for London, wasn't he? – Something like that. I'll let him go at once.' The laird moved to the door. 'Don't come back without him.'

Never did Dan Drummond depart from his office with greater alacrity.

Neil returned to Tullycarnet Wood. There was still no trace of young Echlin and Watt with the timber wagon.

'Maybe,' said Mackechnie, 'the grand coachman has cowped it in a ditch.'

'It'll go ill with your job if he has,' said Neil. 'The morning it's loaded Archie Gill will take it out for the coast.' Whatever the surprised gaffer had to say was cut short by Neil announcing he would ride out along the village road to meet Francis Echlin. He was away before Mackechnie remembered to call after him that the laird was demanding his presence at the factor's office.

As he approached the clachan, Neil heard the shouts and laughter of children. A stranger, a packman by his looks, mounted on a sorry nag, had ridden into the clearing in front of the cottages. He rode dejectedly, without stirrups, his thin legs thrust forward, his progress slowed by the flock of bairns dancing before his horse's nose, the bolder plucking at his dusty cloak. Neil wondered why he did not, like all his tribe, clear the way with maledictions and staff. A guidwife, standing arms akimbo, let fly with a shout at the noisy throng. The rebuke, and the sight of Neil watching them, scattered the children. The rider threw back the cloak from his arm and summoned a boy to his side. Cautiously, ready for flight, the child drew near and listened to the stranger.

'Aye, aye,' he shrilled, 'there he is.' He turned, pointing to Neil. 'Mr Gilchrist, this auld man wants ye!'

Neil dismounted slowly. There was something familiar about the stranger, but the presence he conjured up was so unlikely here in flesh and blood that the young man approached with a feeling of disquiet. He looked up into the face of the man on horseback. Then he fumbled for the rider's hand. 'Hunter Murray – Master Murray! In God's name, what brings ye here!'

The aged man smiled down on him. The thin hand tightened its clasp. 'I thought never to see ye.'

Neil put his arm around Murray's waist. 'Let me help ye down. But if ye would rather ride. . .'

'No, no, no, by all that's sacred let me off this beast.'

He stumbled as he touched the ground. Then for a moment the two looked into each other's eyes. 'Ye ken, Neil, what brought me?'

271

'Aye. . . my brother Gilmor.'

Master Murray nodded. 'He slipped away at the New Year. Your father wants ye back, Neil.'

'I lodge at the schoolhouse, we can talk there.' He beckoned one of the older lads. 'Fetch the horses after us.'

On the way to the schoolhouse Murray told the young man how, with the help of the Portpatrick notary and the master of the coble and a word in the village of Newtownards, he had traced him to Ravara. But his story held only part of Neil's attention. Behind the news of his brother's death, of his father's plea, a growing fear invaded Neil's mind: *What of Anne, locked in that great house?*

'. . . I made what haste I might, Neil, for Balwhanny's a spent man, aye asking for ye.'

Silently Neil pressed the other's arm. Although it was the plaint of a selfish silly old man, the words stirred a response, even if closer to pity than affection.

A sense of urgency possessed him. Pride demanded that he alone should tell Kenneth Echlin the news brought from Scotland. He left Hunter Murray in the dominie's care and set off for the factor's office. At a bend in the track he almost ran full tilt into Dan Drummond.

'Feggs, Gilchrist, ye nearly had me off!' cried the factor reining back.

'More speed than caution, Dan. You're on an errand yourself?'

'Ye may say. I've ridden myself sore hunting ye. You're wanted by the laird. He has,' there was a watchful pause, 'unco grave news for ye.'

Neil knew he was being tempted to ask a further question. And the answer was plain to see across the factor's broad face. Echlin was casting him out from Ravara.

'Dan,' he said with a hard smile, 'I've some unco news for the laird.' As he urged his mount away he heard the sprachle of hooves as Drummond wheeled to follow him.

272

The office door was opened abruptly. Neil stood on the threshold. Echlin straightened himself.

'They found ye, Gilchrist.'

'I wasn't lost, sir.'

'Come in. Sit down. I have to tell ye –'

A large hand thrust forward, palm outwards, cut Echlin short. 'I'll stand, thank ye. I've news for ye. I'm quitting Ravara.'

The words were curt as blows and had a similar effect on the man seated at the table. His mouth still gaped as Drummond came stumbling in and for once Echlin welcomed the sight of his factor.

'Eh, leaving Ravara? This is sudden –'

Neil smiled drily. 'I think not, Mr Echlin. A messenger has come from Scotland to say my brother is dead. My father, an ill man, commands my return to take over the management of Balwhanny.'

The weight of all this was not lost on Echlin. He recalled James Lowry's words: 'a derelict property'. Nevertheless his equal, in birth if not estate, was standing across from him. 'For God's sake, sit down, Gilchrist.'

Obligingly, Neil slid his backside on to a seat.

'Your elder brother, eh? I'm sorry to hear o't. . . I may tell ye,' continued Echlin glancing at Dan Drummond as if to exonerate himself, 'that it was my intent to ask ye to go. Now that my son Francis –'

'How long were ye to give me, Mr Echlin?'

'You're a man of few chattels and no ties here. Two days.'

Neil rose. 'That'll suffice. I'm owed a month's wages.'

'See to it, Dan.'

The factor brought out a purse of money with a promptness that told Neil nothing would have been allowed to stand in the way of his departure.

Echlin was chary of making any further claims on the young man. But he was equally eager that his money-making project

273

should not falter. 'No doubt but you'll leave all clear at Tully-carnet?'

'There's trunks lying trimmed and Mackechnie kens what's next to come down. The only thing missing is the wagon your son was to fetch.'

'He fetched it all right,' declared the factor.

Neil acknowledged this information. 'I found ye a driver in Archie Gill.'

The two stared at him.

'Ye mean the miller?' asked the laird.

'Miller no more. He was dismissed by her Ladyship. But,' continued Neil airily, 'no doubt you're aware of that.'

In the way the laird's face darkened it was evident that he was not aware of it.

'If ye want my advice,' continued Neil, 'I wouldn't meddle with Gill for the present. He's one of the few men fit to handle such a load to the coast.'

The use of the word 'meddle' was not much to Echlin's liking either. But he could do no other than agree. 'Very well. Now how is the timber-merchant to learn that the load's delivered?'

'Carmichael will be in this airt within a week. He'll call on Robert Bothwell. Your son can keep ye informed.'

All this had gone forward in the driest and most curt of tones and Dan Drummond wondered again what was the enmity that lay hidden between the two.

Neil lifted the purse and pocketed it. 'Good day to ye, gentlemen,' he said and left the factor's office.

His thoughts were in turmoil as he rode off. Two days Echlin had given him. He might as well have turned him away that evening. *A man of few chattels.* Aye, true enough. *And no ties.* The stab had got home. Now was the time to order his thoughts and actions in the way he would set out a row of saplings. Pride in what order he had brought to Ravara woodlands urged him first to Tullycarnet. He found Mackechnie and one of his men tidying up at the loaded wagon. He dismounted and walked round the burdened vehicle testing a tie here and there. All the time Mackechnie eyed him in silence, questioning his presence there. The laird's word had travelled fast from Rathard. He came round the rear of the wagon, his inspection completed.

'She should hold well.'

'Aye.'

'I'm leaving Ravara, Iain.'

'So I hear tell.'

'Iain, I killed a man in Belfast.'

Mackechnie paused at this abrupt shift. 'Aye, I heard Gilfillan say as much, Mr Gilchrist.'

'I want to tell ye, Iain, he was likely your brother Watty's murderer.' Then from the saddle he added. 'Thank ye for your labour at the oak-felling, Iain. I wish ye guid fortune.'

It matters not a boddle, thought Neil as he rode away, whether Mackechnie and his ilk think that I'm leaving of my own will or being thrust out. But the manner in which Lady Echlin would tell her daughter of his leaving Ravara would do little for his fidelity and good name. Some way must be found to get word to Anne. His message-bearers were few. He thought of Una Drummond, of Ellen MacIlveen, and as quickly put them out of mind. Discovered by Lady Echlin carrying his letter, neither would last long at Rathard House, or beyond it. Mistress Tabitha would be allowed to call on the girl. To-morrow morning the minister would be at the schoolhouse presiding over the scripture examinations. 'Twas then, he decided, he would call on the good lady of the manse and ask for her help.

Master Murray and the dominie had found much to talk about. Ross looked up as Neil entered with the air of a man who had taken part in an exchange as stimulating to his intelligence and spirit as it had been wholly unexpected.

'I hope,' said Neil, 'I haven't been too long absent?'

'We could have spared ye for another hour,' said Ross. 'Now that you're here I'll step across and ask the Drummonds to give

Master Murray a bed for the night. But,' he turned with a smile to the elderly man, 'he's engaged to have supper with us.'

The dominie gone, Neil drew his chair to the hearth. For a time Murray and he talked of Balwhanny and its occupant. It was a subject soon exhausted. Neil came to a matter that had bothered him since Ross's departure.

'You'll find Mistress Drummond hospitable. But inquisitive – aye spiering as to people's condition in the world. I would take it kindly, Master –' he hesitated, 'if ye said nothing of the condition Balwhanny's in.'

There was no response from Murray. Neil looked up to meet his puzzled scrutiny.

'Balwhanny – d'ye mean by that the man or the manor?'

'Why, the manor – the estate.'

'Even in the short time ye spent there, ye lacked the seeing eye. Balwhanny's in no poor condition, Neil. Balwhanny's as well-fau'red a property as you'll find in the west of Scotland –'

'But great God, Master, the crumbling house, the whingeing servants, my father's purse aye empty –'

'Let me tell ye about your father, Neil. When that sweet lady, your mother, died, in the handling of his affairs Balwhanny became no better than a coof. He quarrelled with his factor and dismissed him. It was done against my advice and that of your mother's family, the Skenes. The Skenes, as stiff-necked as they are rich, never set foot in Balwhanny again after the funeral. Your father's pockets aren't aye empty, that ye ken well. They're full enough when he sets off on one of his jaunts to Edinburgh. He borrows that money from some of his stronger tenants, men like Selkirk or McPhee. 'Tis no more than a moiety of the rents that would – or should come to him anyway. For a time James Selkirk brought his rents to me and I paid the servants unbeknown to your father.'

'I can understand why some of Mr Echlin's neighbours have a different picture of Balwhanny.'

'Have any of them ever been there – ever seen beyond the manor house?'

276

'Not to my knowledge.'

'If ye met your father in an Edinburgh drinking-house what picture of him and his property would ye carry away?'

Neil winced at this. 'Aye,' he said, 'I suppose you've the right to ask that. Can the management of the estate be put to rights?'

'With a good factor – a strong man at your elbow, Balwhanny could be itself again in the span of two, maybe three harvests. It'll take that time,' Murray added drily, 'to make the house fit to live in.'

'Thank ye, Master, for telling me of this. Although,' he said with a wry smile, 'I could have done with the knowledge earlier.'

'What could ye have done?'

Neil was relieved from answering by the return of Angus Ross. A bed would be made ready in the factor's house. The dominie, determined however not to be robbed of the visitor's company until that time, had brought back supper prepared by Una Drummond. With the contents of the basket spread before the three, Neil remarked that all they needed was Wishart to appear with a drop of usquebaugh. But for once Ross did not seem concerned at that worthy's absence.

Supper over, Murray and the dominie resumed the discussion that had so engaged Ross earlier in the evening. Neil sat back and pondered over what he had learnt from Hunter Murray. What indeed could he have done possessed with such knowledge? Would the Echlins – or anyone – have trusted the son (and heir) of a moidered old fool seemingly intent on scattering his patrimony? The dominie claimed his attention. Master Murray had borrowed Bacon's *The Advancement of Learning*. Before returning it he could copy extracts for Ross. Would Neil see them safely despatched?

Neil realised with a sudden sense of melancholy that to his friend it seemed he had already departed from Ravara. 'Aye, I'll see to it.'

The tutor rose from his chair, a weary old man who had endured a long day. Ross brought him his cloak and staff. Together the two young men aided his steps to the factor's house. There Neil stepped in to thank Mistress Drummond and an uncommonly benevolent Dan for their kindness in giving shelter to his friend. Ross brought Una forward to meet the visitor, and Neil, not wishing to hurry such a moment, promised to call on the morrow and took his leave.

He was on the path above the lodging-house when he heard the singing of women. The gloaming was still clear enough for him to make out the figures of four or five girls at the entrance to Rushin Coatie's abode. The voice of a lass, seated in the doorway, came to him with such thrilling sweetness that it brought him to a halt. This must be one of the cottar families Francis Echlin spoke of. He wondered if there were men among them fit to move rocks and tear up roots. No doubt Dan would find them a clear and level holding. He began to call on his memory for such places, until, with an oath, he drew back from his hiding place and strode towards the schoolhouse. The singing, drifting through the half-light, was with him as he closed the door.

26

'Ye could leave Master Murray at the factor's house this morn,' suggested Ross. 'Because of the scripture examination, Una'll not be here. He'll have her company.'

'That would be kindly of the Drummonds. When do ye expect the minister?' The question was as casual as Neil could make it.

'Soon, soon I hope,' and the dominie glanced at the three rows of scrubbed apprehensive faces. 'And you, Neil?'

'Hunter Murray needs a mount for tomorrow morn. I'm to see to that.'

Iain Mackechnie appeared at the schoolhouse door. He removed his bonnet and stood turning it in his hands. 'Mr Gilchrist, could I have a word with ye?'

Neil stepped to the door. 'Aye, what is it?' He had not forgotten how readily the gaffer had accepted his departure from Ravara.

'I –' Mackechnie glanced at the dominie. 'My brothers and me want to thank ye for finishing Watty's murderer. . .'

'Lachie Dubh had many debts to pay. Your brother's death was certainly one of them.'

'Is there aught we can do for ye, Mr Gilchrist?'

'There is. I need a horse for a friend that's riding with me to the coast tomorrow.' Neil fumbled in his pocket.

'Money!' cried Mackechnie warding off any suggestion of payment. 'We wouldn't hear o't. Let your friend leave the nag at Donaghadee and one o' us will lift it sometime. Oh,' the gaffer paused. 'Ye should ken that Archie Gill is taking out the first load o' timber at seven in the morn.'

Neil nodded at news that was no longer his concern. 'I want nothing spirited, Iain. My friend's an auld man.'

'I'll mind that. I'll get ye a quiet beast. You'll have it within the hour.' Leaving, Mackechnie passed the Reverend Mr Turnooth on the schoolhouse path. The minister came forward with his customary firm tread, his eyes fixed on Neil.

'I'm sorry to learn of the death of your elder brother, Mr Gilchrist.'

'Thank ye, Mr Turnooth.'

'You've come into property, I understand.'

'My father,' replied Neil warily, 'has summoned me to return.'

'I'll miss ye, Gilchrist. I enjoyed stropping my tongue on ye.' The stubby figure marched into the schoolhouse. Neil heard him exchange morning greetings with the dominie.

There was, Neil felt, something furtive in what he was about to request from Mistress Tabitha. Her brother's ungracious parting allayed his conscience only a little. He tethered his horse some distance away and approached the manse on foot. The barking of the dog brought Mistress Tabitha to the window, then to the door.

'Mr Gilchrist,' she cried, 'I knew ye could call! I hear, to my sorrow, that you're leaving Ravara. Is that true?'

'Yes, ma'am. My father wants me home.'

'Aye, that's as I heard it. But, come in.'

As Neil followed the good lady into the little living-room, he knew which version of his departure had been conveyed to the minister and his sister. The people at Rathard would have no wish to leave his name linked with their daughter.

'Sit down, Mr Gilchrist. You've come to say goodbye?'

'I could never leave Ravara without bidding you farewell, that ye know. But there is more to it. Mistress Tabitha, I want a message carried to Miss Echlin.'

'Aye, Miss Anne. . .' for a moment the woman's voice and looks were guarded. 'Then why not carry it to Rathard House yourself? I'm sure you'd be welcome –'

'No, ma'am. As far as her parents are concerned I would not be welcome.'

280

The minister's sister looked away. 'I thought as much. But I didn't want to learn why. I thought you'd be gone – quietly, peaceably –' She turned on him abruptly. 'Everybody in the Big House knows you're leaving. Then what more's there to say to Anne –'

'That I love her.'

Mistress Tabitha would not have been true to herself had she not wanted to know more. 'What of the girl?'

'I wouldn't be here if she had turned me away.' He held Tabitha in his gaze. 'Ma'am, you can see her – will ye carry my letter?'

She sprang to her feet. 'No, Mr Gilchrist, I will not carry your letter. Your guid sense should tell ye that you'll find no one to carry a letter into Mr Echlin's house behind-backs. I'm pained,' she gave her skirts an angry flounce, 'that ye should think the minister's sister could be privy to such a deceit.'

Neil rose slowly. 'Mistress Tabitha, I can only plead despair. I leave tomorrow morn.'

'Neil, sit down, sit down,' and the good lady resumed her own chair. 'Of what avail is a letter to the lass? To tell her you're leaving? – She kens that already. To tell her ye love her? Well, well. . . of that she's aware, if ye say true. I'm for Rathard and it's likely I'll see her. I'll tell her it was your intent to leave her a message. That's the truth, and I need not be ashamed of it,' concluded Mistress Tabitha firmly.

Neil looked at her in dull politeness. 'Aye, ma'am. . .'

'Neil,' Mistress Tabitha leant forward, speaking slowly. 'I'll tell Anne it was your *wish* to send her a message.' She searched the downcast face.

Neil rose. 'Mistress Tabitha, it's little – but in our quandary it's much.' He lifted her knuckled hand to his lips. 'I thank ye, dear lady, and bid ye goodbye.'

She watched until he disappeared from her sight. It had not been her intention to visit Rathard House so early but now she made ready to go.

281

Once in the saddle Neil could see the upper windows of Rathard House. One of them lighted Anne's chamber. He had no means of telling which for all stared over the countryside with a grey indifference that chilled him. As he rode dejectedly away he wondered at the folly of hoping that Mistress Tabitha would bear his words to the girl. His mother had been much given to tales of impoverished young suitors wooing fair maids locked up in great houses. To their aid came always an ageless crone invested with magical powers. But his aged women had been no witch gifted with Circean enchantments. Only a kindly soul with a deep-seated regard for what was honourable and honest — and for commonsense. For what doors could a letter unlock? This time tomorrow he would have left Ravara without Anne. He turned away from that and gave his mind to the practical and drear tasks ahead.

Mackechnie had kept his word. A stalwart cob munched and snorted in the school horse-stall. Taking the animal with him, Neil rode for the factor's house. He informed Mrs Drummond that as an errand would take him to the village he and Master Murray would eat their midday meal at the tavern. The factor's wife accepted this with secret relief, for the tutor's discourse, if of interest to her daughter, sadly lacked the spicy tittle-tattle that she felt she had a right to expect from someone arrived from the outside world. So Hunter Murray was released on the understanding that he returned to the shelter of the Drummond house that night.

Having assured Neil that the new mount suited him, the tutor and his former pupil journeyed towards the village with few words between them. We could, thought Neil gloomily, press on to the coast and a ship for Scotland. He had no worldly goods, the laird had said, no ties to bind him. For the first time there crept into his mind the thought that Anne might have succumbed to her parents' blandishments, and as quickly he accused himself of treachery. Not until the last moment would he leave Ravara, admitting defeat.

As they ate he ordered a basket of provisions and wine to be made up. 'For four people, John. My last supper. I leave for Scotland tomorrow.'

'Heh, sir, for guid and all?' asked Bell in surprise.

'For guid and all.'

'We'll miss ye, Mr Gilchrist.'

'Thank ye, John.'

The meal finished and the tally paid, the horses were brought up from the inn yard.

'Set out on your road early, Mr Gilchrist. I hear high water's at noon.'

Even the tide is hurrying me off, thought Neil. 'My compliments to your guid wife, John,' he said.

Within Ravara again, Neil gave Murray the basket of provisions. 'I've a cottar family to call on. They crossed with me from Portpatrick. Tell the dominie I expect him to invite Calum Wishart to supper.'

He had barely parted from the tutor when he saw Echlin and Ronane turn to bear down on him, and on the laird's face was the look of a man who had run a hated quarry to earth. Neil reined up sharply as Echlin pulled across his path.

'Gilchrist,' and the words were ground out, 'where is my daughter?'

Neil's heart gave a great leap. He looked at Echlin, then at Ronane, then again at Echlin, his eyes on the strange pulsation of the livid scar on the laird's cheek. What he read in their faces was murder.

'Your daughter? What of your daughter?'

Ronane bent to the laird's ear.

'Shut your mouth, Ronane,' said Neil, his scrutiny never leaving Echlin's face. 'I'm waiting on your master's answer.'

The laird's expression now was one of sullen rancour. 'Tell me where you've been today, Gilchrist.'

'It's no longer your concern where I've been,' replied Neil. 'But I'll tell ye. I've bid goodbye to Mistress Tabitha. I've secured a horse for my friend to ride out tomorrow. I've been to the village to eat at the tavern.' He picked up his reins. 'Now I'm on my way to the MacIlveens.'

Baffled, Echlin drew back his horse and let him pass. Again Ronane spoke in his ear.

The laird turned on his henchman. 'You're losing your wits, Ronane. I want my daughter alive, not Gilchrist dead.' As he watched Neil's receding figure he murmured: 'I think the fellow knows no more of this than I do.' He wheeled abruptly. 'Search on, Ronane, search on. . .'

Neil Gilchrist rode on, more confused than the laird suspected. If Anne had *escaped* from Rathard, and there could be no other reason behind her father's fury, what had become of her? She must have got beyond the environs of the house. The laird would not be riding through the demesne before every room and stable-corner had been searched. And what did she expect of him? Did she think they shared knowledge of some place of assignation – the boat-slip at Lough Reagh or the swan-haunted tarn on the village road? He put these imaginings away as too fanciful – such places were difficult to reach on foot, too open to discovery. She needed him and he was powerless to find her.

Neil was pleased enough to find Sorley and his family with the older MacIlveens. It saved a trip to the Langstane cottage. Alexander and Meg assured him that they were as thriving as they deserved at the hands of the Lord. Sorley too, it appeared, stood in much the same accord with the Almighty. Neil noted that Elphie MacIlveen, her beauty unimpaired, would soon give young Neil a brother or a sister. He felt their silent questioning.

'I'm here to bid ye goodbye. My father wants me at home.'

'A son's aye a comfort,' said Meg turning her eyes where Sorley held the child between his knees.

Neil caught the boy's eye. 'How's wee Neil?' he asked fumbling in his pocket.

284

Wee Neil, watched by Sorley with fatherly approval, came forward, hand outstretched. When he returned to his father's knee Sorley relieved him of Neil's gift.

'You'll no be leaving a scope of worked land that a bodie could take over, Mr Gilchrist?'

Alexander caught the sly grin on his son's face. 'Mr Gilchrist has left his mark on the woodlands, Sorley.'

'Aye, true. . . true. . . till it grows over.'

Neil lifted his bonnet. He turned to the family calling for their attention. 'Do any of ye remember a scoundrel called Lachie Dubh? I want ye to ken he's dead.'

Alexander and Meg stared at each other. 'Lachie. . .' said the elderly man with a polite but puzzled smile.

'Feggs, aye!' cried Sorley of a sudden. 'Lachie Dubh – I remember the gomeril! Ye remember him, father,' he pressed the older man impatiently. 'Whether we wanted or no he was coming with us as our ploughman.'

'Och, I remember him now. A blaggard. We were well shot of him. We didn't need him.' Alexander glanced round as if he could see through the walls of the dwelling to the fields beyond. 'No, we didn't need him. We did very well in ourselves, eh, Sorley? Me here, you at the Langstane.'

'There was mair than the two of ye,' cried Meg, turning sharply on her husband. 'Rab Purdie never stinted in the work! Our Ellen,' continued the guidwife in a calmer voice to Neil, 'is marrying Rab Purdie. Did ye no see the building work at the gable as ye passed? They'll live there.'

'I'm pleased to hear that,' said Neil. Lachie Dubh's death had gone up the chimney with the peat smoke. 'When's the wedding to be?'

'When the Purdies and us have our seed sown,' said Alexander. 'There's aye a breathing time after that.'

'My regret is that I'll not be here for it.'

'Ye would have been welcome,' said Meg as she and Alexander followed him to the door. 'The Lord tend ye on your road to Scotland, Mr Gilchrist.'

Aware that they were watching him he drew rein to look at the dwelling rising to shelter Ellen and Rab Purdie. He raised his hand as if in approval. As he rode on he could not but compare the cottar family to his own puny history since he came to Ravara. Delving, sowing, reaping, generation following generation, the MacIlveens and their humble like promised to put down roots in the soil that would outlast Cordwaine's elegant mansion, Echlin's patchwork castle. The whirlwind uproots the cedar tree but passeth over the seeded land and disturbeth it not.

The minister, elders and children had left when Neil reached the schoolhouse. To his surprise Dan Drummond was there. He could see the factor eyeing him, swithering if he was still worthy to be given news of the laird and his family.

It was too much for Dan. 'Have ye heard, young sir, that Miss Echlin's away?'

'I have. The laird told me of it.'

'Heh, is that so? Well, did ye hear her horse came back to the stables?'

'No, I hadn't heard that.' Then, with what he considered sufficient interest: 'So she had gone riding?'

'"Gone riding?" Aye, ye could say that.' Dan eyed his audience. 'The young lady was out for a dander with Mistress Tabitha and when the guid lady left, Miss Anne, instead of returning to the house, goes to the stables, takes out her horse and rides off. And now the beast's back wi'out her –'

'Maybe,' said Ross, 'her mount slipped away from Lowrys –'

'Lowrys? They've been to Lowrys and to Edenmore and to the Finlays and two men's been to the village. Ne'er a whisper of the young lady.'

As calmly as he might, Neil seated himself beside Hunter Murray. 'Do they think she's been thrown?'

'The laird says her horse hasn't had a fall. And the reins was looped up so the animal wouldn't trip.'

'Miss Echlin is a horsewoman,' said Ross.

'Aye, but it's all gey strange.' The factor picked up stick and bonnet. 'Ye understand, Angus, I was doing what I was bid? Anywhere the girl could take cover, her Ladyship said.'

'I understand, Dan.'

Drummond opened and closed the door on the gloaming that seemed to Neil to advance too swiftly on the world outside. Nothing had seemed more hopeless than freeing Anne from her parents' house. Now that she had fled Rathard she was even farther away, wandering, perhaps hurt, under a darkling sky. He turned to see Ross light a lamp.

'Do we need that yet?' he demanded irritably. Then he smiled like a man caught in an act of folly. 'Aye, light it, Angus. But ye seem to be hurrying my last evening here to an end.'

'Then make the best of it. Let you and Master Murray set out what ye brought us for supper.'

Chicken drumsticks came from the basket and roast ham and crisp bread and butter and two flagons of wine. They were spreading this fare on the dominie's table when Calum Wishart arrived. He brought with him four fair-sized trout that he claimed he had tickled from the upper Langstane, although he admitted that one of the Crockart women had dressed and broiled them for him.

'Out with it, Wishart,' said the dominie.

Wishart drew from his coat a bottle of crystal-clear liquid which he set down in the middle of the supper-table.

'Usquebaugh, Master,' said Ross. 'Third run, I warrant. . .'

Murray smiled and said that he would take a thimbleful of Irish usquebaugh all in good time. Then he stretched out his hand as if stilling the others and nodded to the dominie.

In his grace over the food the dominie said that they were on the eve of the departure of a dear friend and that the school hearth and table would never be as companionable again. He wished Neil and the tutor Godspeed and a safe arrival.

'Anne Echlin picked an ill night,' said Wishart.

'Why should ye say that?' asked Neil, raising his head.

'I smell a mist coming up.'

'That might be welcome to a fugitive,' said the tutor.

'I don't see Miss Echlin,' said Ross mildly, 'a fugitive from her own parents.'

'Angus,' said Neil, 'tell us how your young charges fared at the hands of the minister today.'

'Taking them as a sheaf I would say as well as ye could expect. Taking them stalk by stalk, I would say that there's some bent heads among them tonight.'

Between mouthfuls the talk drifted among the four in lively fashion and Anne Echlin's name was not mentioned again. Platters were emptied, glasses filled and refilled. The tutor was persuaded to take another 'thimbleful' of usquebaugh.

'I'll let it settle,' said he, 'then I'll be grateful for an arm to the kindly Drummonds.'

'When you're ready, Master,' said Neil, then sought the tutor's cloak and staff as the elderly man took leave of Wishart and the dominie.

Neil stepped out under a starless sky. Where now was Anne? He thought of her wandering from darkness to darkness or lying hurt as the night and its creatures closed around her. He would rather she be found and carried back to Rathard even if it put an end to all his hopes. Hunter Murray stumbled on a stone. The tutor had enjoyed more liquor and food at supper than he had seen for many a day. Now Neil's whole care was given to guiding the elderly man's wayward steps until he handed him over to the care of Una Drummond and her mother.

As Neil turned from the factor's house he saw that Wishart was right. Mist was uncoiling from the Langstane torrent and creeping upwards through the woods. He shivered, but not from any chill in the air. When he was over the lodging-house he glanced down. Four or five of the cottar lasses were standing or sitting around the doorway. Tonight they were as silent as the grey wraiths rising from the burn. Neil was glad of it for this sad night was no time for singing.

Ahead of him he saw a stirring as if some creature had gained the bushes at the top of the slope that ran down to the lodge. He stepped warily, sidling out on the track to give himself room. Then low and urgent he heard his name: *'Neil, Neil.'* He halted, to peer agape into the heart of the foliage. It was a girl dressed in the grey duds of those clustered below. She freed herself and straightened before him, her face raised to his.

'God in Heaven!' he said in a whisper. 'My sweet, how come ye here?'

Anne did not speak but sought his arms. Her bright hair was hidden under a ragged cap. There was a smear of soot on her cheek.

'Anne, my love, how come ye here?'

'Did ye search for me, Neil?'

'Anne!. . .'

'I heard my brother talk of the two cottar families and their daughters. . .' She spoke hurriedly with a glance back at the lodging-house. 'I let my horse run and came here and busied myself among the pots and pans. Rushin Coatie thinks I'm a cottar lass, *they* think I'm the old woman's drudge. I keep my mouth shut and play the part –'

'Sweet mouth,' said Neil and kissed her again. 'And the duds?'

For the first time she smiled. 'I add to my wardrobe, piece by piece, Neil.' She grasped his arms fiercely, 'Ye leave Ravara tomorrow?'

'Aye, at seven by the clock. . . But,' he spoke slowly his mind conjuring what lay before them, 'not alone. . . At that hour a timber wagon leaves Ravara for the coast. I want you seated on that wagon beside Gill, the driver. Leave here early enough to be near the clachan at the hour of seven. I'll be close to the wagon. Come forward to me and ask for a lift on the wagon. You're,' he thought, 'you're for Donaghadee to meet kin of yours due from Scotland. I can think of no other way. Is it too much, dear Anne?'

She shook her head. 'It is not too much.'

'Remember, ye don't know me. You're acquainted with no one.'

'I must go. Help me with the kindling.'

He saw then that she had been gathering firewood. He helped load it into her arms and they kissed across the bundle. For a moment he felt wracked to cry out that he couldn't let her go again. Her steadfastness and trust in him shamed him to silence. He watched her shadowy descent of the slope. For a fleeting moment she paused with the girls at the lodging-house door. Then, still carrying her burden of kindling, she went in. With a firmer step Neil resumed his path.

He opened and closed the schoolhouse door with a clash, skipped to the table and thrust his glass forward with a cry: 'Gentlemen, a drink, there's fog in my thrapple!'

The dominie, obliging with the flagon, wondered at this sudden change in spirit. During the meal there had been an air of inadvertence about Gilchrist as if he were elsewhere and only to be called back by some direct question. The seeming indifference had pained Ross. He was losing a friend who had brought an active companionship into a life in which to-morrow mimicked yesterday. It was different he knew for Wishart. The older man had known many meetings and partings. By tomorrow Neil Gilchrist would have joined that half-remembered throng.

Neil rose from the table. 'Bring your glasses, men. Let us draw our chairs to the fire like olden times!'

At first Ross's curiosity pursued not the past but what lay before Gilchrist when he returned to Scotland. Neil skirted round the question adroitly enough. 'I'll allow that Hunter Murray paints a fairer picture of Balwhanny than I recall. It may be that I didn't ken where to look.' So the talk between the three became slower, musing, discontinuous, the small coinage

290

of reminiscence, until bottles and flagons lay on their sides, exhausted.

Calum Wishart stood up, picked out his bottle from the debris on the table. 'I'm glad to have known ye, Gilchrist. I wish ye and Murray a safe journey.' He paused at the open door. 'The mist's hanging in the trees. I hope the lass Echlin's under a roof.' Then he was gone.

It had been a guid parting after all, the dominie thought as he undressed for bed. It was only when his head was on the pillow that it dawned on him that Gilchrist had never hinted or hoped that some day the paths of the three might cross again.

Feet and hooves disturbed the low-lying mist as Neil led the two horses along the path to the factor's door. Hunter Murray, already breakfasted, waited beside his bundle. Neil joined the tutor in thanking the Drummond women, then took his leave of them. The factor, nightshirt tucked into breeks, followed the two travellers out.

He sniffed the raw morning air. 'They say mist means calm water.'

'I've heard as much, Dan,' said Neil, mounting.

'We had our unco strange times, Neil, eh?' said the factor with a smile and a shake of the head as if recalling momentous decisions affecting the lives and property of all at Ravara.

'Unco strange times, Dan,' said Neil taking the proferred hand.

Mist shrouded the lodging-house. Neil, riding past, detected a pinpoint of light from the dwelling. He thought of Anne stealing away undetected, of her weary passage through the dripping scrubland. Murray wished to halt and bid the dominie goodbye. Neil led him firmly past the schoolhouse.

'I've made our farewells. We have a tide to catch, Master. Better too early than sorry.'

As they rode towards the clachan he was dismayed to see

291

cottars, some on horseback, some on foot, making ready to leave for the village market. Then, as he watched them, havering and gossiping, accepting money and orders from their neighbours, he took comfort. The departing mist gave their figures a strange hallucinatory appearance. Anne might walk in among them unobserved.

The moment he came round the last cottage gable Neil looked towards the avenue to Rathard. Echlin sat mounted, whip in hand. Beside him on foot was Mackechnie. With a rumble of wheels and a clatter of hooves the timber wagon came up from the woodland. Gill drew his team to a halt on the broad beaten track leading from the estate.

Neil dismounted and busied himself with the girth on the tutor's mount. Now was their fortune's testing-time. His fingers were on the girth buckle, his gaze on the boscage beyond the clachan. Perhaps she had never won free of the lodging-house. . . Then he saw her. She came steadily towards him, through the straggle of folk bound for market. A ragged shawl bound her head, in her hands a basket like any other village wench and she dragged a foot as she walked.

Whether she spoke to him or not he could not tell but he bent his head as if listening. With an abrupt gesture to follow he strode towards the wagon and Anne went hirpling after him. On every step he took he felt the weight of the laird's scrutiny.

'This lass,' he said to Gill, 'begs a lift to the coast. If I understand her, she's kin to meet at Donaghadee.'

Gill stared at her smudged face. 'What way had she meant to get there?'

'God knows,' said Neil and strode past her without a glance. He climbed into his saddle.

'Are we ready now?' Murray asked in sorely-tried patience.

Neil peered across the clearing. Anne sat beside Archie Gill. 'Aye, Master, we're ready now.'

As Neil rode round the rear of the wagon he turned and touched his bonnet to the laird. Echlin, with cold unsmiling

292

face, raised his whip in response. Thus the two parted without a word spoken between them.

Once clear of the market-folk on the road, Neil was concerned that he might draw too far ahead of the wagon. But Hunter Murray (and his cob) dictated the pace by settling down to little above a steady plod. Neil could look back and see Archie Gill, with firm hand and keen eye, bring the ponderous vehicle safely round each bend of the road. The two horsemen arrived in the village only a little ahead of the wagon.

Neil led Hunter Murray into the tavern. John Bell hurried forward to serve them.

'I hear Miss Echlin's lost. A bonny lass.'

'Aye. Wine if ye please, John. How did ye hear?'

'It's the talk o' the market-place. And two o' Mr Echlin's men are on watch over there.' Bell pointed, Neil refused to look. The tavern-keeper craned his neck and corrected himself. 'They're no there. They're away back to that shebeen round the corner. I refused them. One o' them's that loon McBratney –'

'John,' said Neil. 'Mr Echlin's timber wagon will be here. Send out a pot of ale to the driver and a cup of milk for the lass that's with him –'

'Milk?'

'If she's dry, whatever she'll have.' Neil put down some money. 'If you're ready, Master.'

Bell put out a hand to detain him. 'Mr Gilchrist, a gentleman seeks a word with ye.' He jerked his thumb. 'He's in the back parlour.'

Neil had feared such an interruption. 'John, ye ken well we've a tide to meet at Donaghadee. 'If it's Robert Bothwell –'

'It's no Mr Bothwell. It's Mr MacCartan – Turlough Mac-Cartan.'

'MacCartan?' Neil frowned. Even if he was leaving the country he had no wish to be known as having had private parley with an Irishman. 'What does he want with me?'

There was, on the tavern-keeper's face what Neil could only

293

consider a sly grin. 'If ye would step this way, sir.'

'And stay with us, Mr Bell. Master Murray, if ye would follow me. . .'

MacCartan and his kinsman, O'Hagan, were seated at wine when Neil and the others entered. Politely Neil declined to join them.

'My friend and I are on our way to the coast. We sail for Scotland on the tide.'

'If you're leaving for Scotland, Mr Gilchrist, I won't detain ye,' said MacCartan.

Neil saw a smile flicker on O'Hagan's face. MacCartan stooped and lifted a woven basket that he placed on the table. Neil saw, between the plaited osier-strands, the gleam of a bright wicked eye.

'A gift for you, sir,' said the Irishman.

Neil leaned closer. 'But it's a hawk – a gift, sir?'

'As a token of my gratitude for a good deed ye did for a member of my family. If my son were here he would thank ye in person.'

'Ah – the lad in the hollow. But it was no more than anyone would have done –'

MacCartan smiled mirthlessly. 'That was not the opinion of Chichester's soldiery.'

The Irishman waited. Neil saw that he would have to tread cannily.

'Mr Gilchrist, did ye not tell Bell that ye sought a hawk?'

'True – true. But 'twas not for myself. Kenneth Echlin wanted such a bird. But,' continued Neil rapidly as he eyed the expressionless faces of the Irishmen, 'I am indeed grateful that ye should have gone to the trouble. . .' A moment's deliberation and he went on. 'I trust ye would not take it ill if I completed my errand. Would ye agree to Mr Bell seeing that the bird is delivered to Rathard House? That would give me great satisfaction, sir.'

There was a pause then MacCartan bowed. 'If that is your

wish, Mr Gilchrist. I'll detain ye no longer. *Slán is beannacht.*'

Neil bowed in response as the two Irishmen left the chamber. 'John,' and Neil smiled slowly, 'will ye see that this bluidy bird reaches its quarry?'

'I'll make sure, sir,' said the innkeeper primly, 'that it's delivered safe to Mr Echlin. Your wagon's left for Donaghadee lang syne.'

My wagon indeed, thought Neil, as he and Murray left the inn, for it bears all that's precious to me. He didn't trouble to look for McBratney. Echlin or Ronane would have set a more able spy than that glackit fool to con the market crowd. Perhaps Sim Watt was watching him now from some corner, or perhaps the fox-faced ostler had guessed enough to set him galloping for Ravara. Time in their favour was running out. Echlin would have weighed the significance of the peasant girl lifted to a seat in the wagon. In the lodging-house the cottar families or Rushin Coatie must be swithering over the strange disappearance of the hearth-wench and telling their story to Dan Drummond.

He drew alongside Hunter Murray. 'We lost time with those Irishmen. More speed, Master, more speed,' Obligingly, the tutor touched the cob's flank with his staff and soon the wagon, rumbling onward, came in sight.

Neil galloped ahead as if to reassure Anne of his presence on the road; but with never a glance between them. Then he fell in beside Gill. 'If Carmichael wants this timber afloat today,' he shouted above the roar of wheels and hooves, 'we'll have to catch the tide, Archie.'

''Twas me was out of the village first, Mr Gilchrist.'

'Aye, true, Archie. But keep up, keep up.'

And Archie, bidding the silent girl beside him take a firm grip, urged his team to greater effort until stones flew from the drumming wheels like musket balls.

Always Neil kept glancing back. He trusted more to his ears than his eyes. The drumlin country through which they travelled afforded only short vistas of the road, and mist still hung treacherously in coppice and above the wayside burn. He drew the two horse-pistols, glanced at the primings, set them back in their holsters. It would be his endeavour to kill Echlin and Ronane before he was taken for he could expect no mercy at their hands. Only the slim straight figure, now thrown about so cruelly in the wagon, would live to be punished.

The road slid down between two drumlin sides. From Neil came a muted cry of relief. Before them a straggle of cottages, folk busy at their doors. Beyond that a shining blade of water. Three vessels lay offshore and one of them, even to his inexperienced eye, was trimmed to sail. The wagon rumbled and swayed down the last slope to the clachan. Men and women scattered as Gill stood to drag horses and wagon to a halt. Neil flung himself from his horse and ran to help Anne alight, a courtesy watched by Gill with some surprise. As she touched the ground she gave a small cry of pain. 'My ankle. I fell in the woods.'

'Certes,' cried Neil between laughter and tenderness, 'and I thought ye were playacting! Perhaps,' he turned to a woman nearby, 'this guidwife would bind your ankle?'

'Readily,' said the woman and offered Anne her arm.

'Make haste,' cried Neil after them as they set out for the clachan.

'What's the hurry on ye?' a villager asked Neil with a note of derision. 'Your load was near cowped on that last brae.'

'Where's the master of that ship?' inquired Neil, pointing to the vessel that now, more than ever, looked on the point of departure.

'That's no a timber boat. That's for Portpatrick –'

'*Where's its master?*'

'He's at the water's-edge,' replied the man, stepping back in some alarm. 'Hannah – Captain Hannah –'

Neil had taken a stride or two across the beach when there was a hoarse cry from Archie Gill. From his vantage place on the wagon he was pointing to the girl limping off with the village woman. Anne had taken the shawl from her head. Even the vaporous sunlight could not dim the beauty of her hair.

Gill leapt to the ground. He came close to face Neil. 'In the name of God, Mr Gilchrist, what have ye done!' His voice was low but there was a charge of anger and fear in the words. 'It's the Echlin lass!'

'Aye, we're to be wed, Archie –'

'Where – here?' Gill made a scathing gesture over stones and sand.

'In Scotland – on board if the captain –'

'And what o' me? This is a hanging matter – for baith o' us. I can never go back to Ravara –'

'Archie.' Neil would have laid his hand on the other's shoulder but it was violently thrown off. 'Archie, I don't want ye to go back. I want ye to come with me –'

'With no more than the shoon I stand in?' Gill demanded bitterly.

'What waits ye in Ravara? Ye can't go back. Ye ken that. I need a man like you to help me –' Neil turned to call the tutor forward. 'Master Murray, ye said I needed a strong and honest steward if I was to set things right at Balwhanny. This is such a man – Archie Gill.'

'Mr Gill,' and the tutor's gentle voice could not but arrest the attention of the bewildered and angry man. 'There was a time when Neil Gilchrist would not have known what was best to do. Now, I believe, he does. If he says you are the man for him, I would take his word. Come with him to Balwhanny. You'll never rue it.'

For a long moment Gill looked from one to the other and found honest assurance in their faces. 'Although I left Scotland a guiltless man I never thought to return. I'll go with ye, Mr Gilchrist.' He turned abruptly to the wagon. 'What o' this?'

'Attend to it, Archie.' Neil drew money from his pocket and dropped the coins into Gill's hand. 'Find somebody here to

297

unload the timber against Carmichael's arrival and then drive the wagon to Bothwell's in Newtownards.'

'And what of your two nags?'

'The Mackechnies are to come for them. But fetch my pistols.' As Neil turned to hasten to where Hannah stood, he saw Anne come from the cottages and her step was lighter.

The master of the coble watched the young man plough through the shallow water to lean breathlessly against the rowboat's bow.

'You're in haste, young sir. What can I do for ye?'

'Have ye room for four of us?'

Hannah shaded his eyes. 'I've seen ye afore.'

'And in honourable circumstances. Can ye take us?'

Hannah glanced towards his ship swinging in the tide. 'I can. Have ye any baggage?'

'Little – none. And, Captain,' Neil leant forward, 'can ye wed a young lady and me?'

'Gin we're in deep water 'twixt the two shores I can tryst ye. But I'll see ye proper wed in Portpatrick. The minister's my brother-in-law.'

'Captain Hannah,' said Neil, 'you're a prince among mariners.'

Hannah watched Neil wade back to the beach. 'I think,' he said to his crewman, 'he's sober enough to get aboard.'

Anne, the tutor and Archie Gill stood at the water's-edge. Behind them, in the village, only the motionless wagon marked that they had ever passed through it. Neil reached out to take her hand. 'Your ankle?'

'Easier.' The girl smiled. 'She was a spae-wife. She promised us a safe crossing.'

'From Portpatrick we'll write to your parents,' said Neil and Anne gave him her hand again.

A mild altercation arose between Master Murray and Gill. Gill had offered to carry the elderly man pickaback to the rowboat.

298

'Thank ye, Mr Gill,' said the tutor indignantly. 'I can wade with the best of ye!'

The captain's halloo came over the water: *'Are ye for sailing or no?'*

'Gentlemen,' said Neil, 'our bark swings at anchor. Fo'r-rard!' He took Anne up in his arms and, without a backward glance, kneed his way into the surf.